glas

Cover art by Peter Kozeikin

http://twelvestories.narod.ru

Glas publishing: 119517 Moscow, P.O. Box 40, Russia
E-mail: perova@glas.msk.su

ISBN 5-7172-0055-2

A.J. Perry

TWELVE STORIES OF RUSSIA:

A NOVEL, I GUESS

glas

For all my friends

Moscow
January 1, 1998

Book 1. Eleven Yellow Words

(1)

At last I can say that Russia is neither here nor there, but less hopeless than inevitable.

Her people are never high, sometimes tall, often white, but *always* concerned about blacks in America. Seventy-eight percent of them are intelligent and beautiful; the other seventy-eight percent are unconditional and polite.

Kharms was Russian. So is Vadim. The novelist Lev Tolstoy was Russian on his mother's side. And although Alexander Pushkin's grandfather was not Russian *per se*, he did not sing in restaurants. Vladimir Vysotsky, despite being Russian, may very well have sung in restaurants though it is unlikely that he sang very well. Either way, students of history are best not to attempt these songs but should remember that Ivan Susanin, who is more amusing than Mikhail Gorbachev, achieved his glory in the middle of a forest. Then died. Unfortunately, cars of the past century had not yet become accustomed to Russia's roads and would not have been very useful in a forest anyway.

(Gorbachev himself has two cars but when traveling through wooded areas he prefers his cherry-red bicycle because it goes faster than the black one.)

(2)

Six and a half years ago, before I understood all this, before Russia even was Russia, I arrived into Moscow's second

Sheremetevo Airport with two suitcases, an empty backpack, and a German-English dictionary that my Aunt Helen had insisted I take.

The first suitcase, though small, was filled with those bare necessities that I knew would be scarce: toilet paper and peanut butter. The larger suitcase held gifts for people I did not yet know: nylon pantyhose, Marlboro cigarettes, and six solar calculators the size of credit cards. The backpack — also a present from Aunt Helen — was empty and therefore did not contain lubricated condoms.

(3)

I had not been surprised when my mother did not see me off at the airport.

It's strange, said Aunt Helen as we waited for the boarding call, She said she'd be here...

Yeah well she says a lot of things, I said.

It's probably the traffic...

I rolled my eyes but Aunt Helen continued:

...Or maybe something with the car.

You don't have to defend her, you know.

Nobody's defending anybody.

Yes you are. You're always trying to justify things for her. You're just as bad as she is.

Aunt Helen threw my name at me in shocked reproach. And as always I retreated:

Look I'm sorry — I didn't mean it. But can we please stop talking about her for once. For now can we just change the subject?

Aunt Helen became quiet, conciliatory. From her purse she pulled out a small wrapped present:

This is for you, she said.

The present was thick but hard, approximately the size of a Russian dictionary. I began to unwrap it.

In front of us a man had stopped suddenly and was worriedly patting the pockets of his coat one by one.

Thanks, I said and looked at the unwrapped present, ...But it isn't...

It has an inscription..., Aunt Helen added and pointed at the inside cover.

I read aloud: 'Use this dictionary in good health. May you have the patience to find meaning in every word.'

But it's not...!

Take it, she said, After all: words are the key to any language — you can't speak without them.

I know that... but the dictionary — it's not... I mean I can't...

Aunt Helen was looking at me. Her eyes were wider than a child's and it was more than I could do to tell her.

You're right, I said, Thanks.

Aunt Helen smiled and I put the dictionary away.

The man in front of us was now holding out one breast of his coat and with the other hand checking its inside pocket. Whatever he was looking for was not there. He tried the other pocket.

I glanced at my watch causing Aunt Helen to again speak up:

She really did want to come...

Who? I pretended to ask.

Your mother. The last time I talked to her she told me how much she wanted to see you before you left.

Well, I said, she's not here, is she? Is she here? Maybe you see her?

Aunt Helen could say nothing and so I continued:

You know I've waited my entire life to have a mother. All twenty-six years. And instead here I am sitting in this airport. And you know what? I think I'm old enough to have outgrown it.

Aunt Helen moved to object, but I spoke over her:

And you can tell her that... you can tell her that as of today things are going to be different... much different...

Oh stop being melodramatic, said Aunt Helen.

But I did not hear her:

As of today, I said, I don't have a mother.

Right at that moment the man in front of us stopped looking. He became as still as a staircase and looked as if he would be sick. In a few seconds he would turn around and walk back to the place where he had been before.

But for now he just stood there, silent and pale, and not knowing what to do.

(4)

It all began with an announcement in my local paper:

NEEDED: NATIVE SPEAKERS TO TEACH ENGLISH IN MOSCOW (RUSSIA)
APPLICATIONS DUE MAY 1

My job at that time was stable and promised further stability; marriage was right around the corner; I had reliable friends who played poker on Tuesday nights. I cut out the announcement and tucked it into my wallet.

A week passed and then another week. My job became even more stable; my friends even more reliable. I remembered the ad. Hadn't I always dreamed of living in Europe? As an American didn't I use English without thinking? Yes, I had. Yes, I did.

I applied anyway.

(5)

My acceptance letter arrived with an unsigned contract for one year and an information pamphlet titled 'Life in Moscow: Getting By.' On the pamphlet's cover a circus bear stood upside down; it looked beautiful but disturbed. I began reading:

'1) If you are arrested and interrogated answer only in English, especially if you know Russian. Otherwise...'

For an instant I imagined myself handcuffed and seated in a windowless Russian prison: a man in uniform stands over me. He is pointing a bright lamp in my eyes, his accent is thick and hard like a German's: If you will sign now..., he says — here he holds up a document in Russian and pulls the lamp closer to my eyes, repeating himself for emphasis: If you will sign now you can to avoid the unwanted problems! *Is the document a confession? A waiver of my rights? False testimony?* I shift uncomfortably in my seat. His words smell of danger and I correct them without thinking: If I sign now, I say, I can avoid unwanted problems. A smile pushes its way onto my face, my sweating hand grabs a pen, and slowly, so as not to smear the ink...

I signed the one-year contract.

(6)

I read on:

'2) American dollars can be exchanged for Russian rubles at the approximate official rate of one dollar to six rubles (1USD=6RUR). In addition it is often more convenient to purchase rubles from men in black leather jackets who offer unofficial rates that are much more attractive; however, this can be illegal and therefore should never be attempted at night.

3) Some Americans have had problems with local conmen and petty thieves; when speaking to strangers say you are from Canada.

4) Remember not to attract unnecessary attention to yourself. When possible look and act as a Russian would. Do not talk loudly. Do not gesticulate beyond reason. And most importantly:

(7)

Do not smile.'

(8)

The pamphlet went on to say that although life in the capital was changing, Moscow's streets, compared to those of any American city, were clean and safe.

I gasped. *Clean and safe?!*

On the last page was a list of items that were in short supply thereby making good gifts for Russian friends. Highly recommended were nylon pantyhose for women, Marlboro cigarettes for men and women. Lubricated condoms could also be given as gifts, especially to female friends, and if no such friends were available they could always be set aside for personal use. The logic was sound. But then it is not for logic that one moves to Moscow; and besides, as I learned later, Russian men rarely use condoms and Russian women tend to prefer solar calculators.

(9)

On the flight over I sat next to a mysterious German man. He was blond but short; his forearms were thick and hard. The man spoke excellent English and to each of my questions he gave cryptic answers which I later wrote down on yellow legal paper.

Asked where he was from, he answered: a country undivided.

Asked where he was going, he said: to the place where *here meets there*.

Asked if he had any use for a German-English dictionary he said that he had written it.

I complimented the man on his English. To which he simply shrugged his shoulders and paused without speaking. It was a significant pause, the kind that tremble with meaning. The man looked somewhere in the distance; his eyes became moister than I had ever seen them. And then slowly, word by word, he gave me eleven reasons to read attentively to the end of every story.

(10)

Six and a half years ago, between the baggage claim and Customs, in this no-man's-land that was not yet Russia which itself was not yet Russia, in a windowless corner of the second Sheremetevo Airport, something unremarkable happened: I found a two-kopeck coin.

It had been lying along a wall, but the other passengers had not noticed it. Or had not cared. The coin was thin and light, approximately the size of a lucky button. By then inflation was looming and the two kopecks were already worth slightly less than two kopecks. The metal was dirty and sticky. I tucked it into my wallet and headed on.

(11)

At Customs the uniformed officer pointed at my empty backpack. He did not smile. He asked something in Russian, which startled me. When I did not answer, the officer asked again. This time I was less startled and told him so in English. Hearing this he looked at me suspiciously and began rummaging through my things. His fingers were fat but deft. I sensed trouble. He rummaged anyway. I looked at his fingers again: now they seemed deft but fat. This did not help either. He held up a pair of pantyhose. Yours? he asked. I nodded but did not smile. It fooled no one. You are American, he said. It was not a question so I neither nodded nor smiled. I just stood there.

Like an unborn baby I waited helplessly, dumb and not smiling.

The man stared at me but I could not speak. I would not nod. And I most certainly did not smile.

And that was it: with an annoyed sweep of his arm he waved me through. To the windowless airport. To Moscow. To Russia which in all fairness had yet to become Russia.

(12)

Alone in my new apartment, I took out a sheet of yellow legal paper and wrote down what the German man had told me. I folded the words onto themselves until they were thick and hard, then stuffed them into my wallet.

When this was done, I stacked all the gifts in an old cabinet: pantyhose and Marlboro cigarettes on the bottom self; Aunt Helen's German-English dictionary — the inscription could be scratched out and it could be given away as well — on the top shelf next to the five solar calculators the size of credit cards.

I was *here*. Which yesterday had been *there*. And which for six and a half years has been *here* but will soon be *there*.

Eventually this grammar would make me tired.

But that would be then. And this was now. And now more than anything I was elated to finally be in Europe. More than ever I was ecstatic at being in Russia and elated that I was ecstatic. For me Europe was elation and Russia was ecstasy and it was not clear whether I was more ecstatic at my elation, or whether I was more elated at my elation.

And then I walked into the dark kitchen.

The floor felt cold on my naked feet. Water dripped from a leaky faucet. *Was I really in Europe?* In the darkness I ran my hand along an unfamiliar wall looking for the light switch. *Was I even in Russia?* My hand coursed over crispy peeling wallpaper until it finally grazed the light switch. *And if I wasn't in Europe and Russia hadn't become Russia yet, then where exactly was I?*

I flicked the switch. The room flared.

In the new light I could see a million cockroaches scurrying over the floor, the counter, my opened jar of peanutbutter. I froze. In a state of panic I stood shocked, my wallet in hand, trying frantically to chase away — there were so many of them! — trying to frantically chase away the doubts that were surrounding me.

Stay calm, I told myself, Don't panic now. After all, even if this wasn't Europe it was still Russia. *But it* wasn't *Russia!* And even if it wasn't Russia, well then it had to be something, didn't it?

Didn't it?

And besides, what was there to worry about? I had planned my journey so carefully and now, finally, everything was set: my gifts were ready to become gifts. *But when? And for whom?* I had eleven yellow reasons to stay. *But why had I come in the first place? What was I expecting to find?* My wallet contained... it contained... *Had I checked the bills to make sure they were small...?* My wallet contained exactly four hundred twenty-four dollars and two kopecks....

Kopecks?

The coin from the airport!

I lifted it to the light. I had expected it to sparkle, but in the dim kitchen light the coin itself reflected nothing — it was too old and too dirty. It was filthy. And gummy. And would soon be worthless.

Smiling to myself I tucked the coin back into my wallet. It stuck to the yellow sheet of paper.

(13)

'To master a language you must understand the people that created it, the culture that provoked it. To understand a people and its culture you must master the language that shapes them both. You must find inspiration in the eleven words that are not just words:

1) the word that regardless of context will surely bring laughter;
2) the single word that causes the ear to bleed with shame, and
3) the heart to burn with indifference, and
4) the eyes of men to moisten;
5) the word that is whispered in moments of passion, and
6) that is used to soothe the deepest despair;

7) the one spoken without reverence, and

8) the word that means absolutely nothing;

9) the utterance that at once expresses the soul of both speaker and listener, and

10) the word that is not and cannot be in any other language.

(14)

But it is the eleventh word that is most elusive because you already know it. Unlike the others, it will change and be changed until it will seem to be hopelessly beyond your grasp.

Live for all of these words, but do not seek them; in time they will come themselves. And when they have come, when you have understood that you understand, when all of the words are yours — only then will you know that their story has been told.'

(15)

My earliest memory of Aunt Helen is also one of my most vivid: I am four or five, my mother, who at that time is still my mother, has people over. There is loud music and everyone is laughing and I laugh too because it's funny to see Mother smoking. At first I like all the new people and run between their legs and squeal when they chase after me with drinks in their hands. Everyone is smiling and one man even gives me a cigarette and shows me how to hold it between my lips. Crossing my eyes to see the tip of the cigarette, I hear a woman say, It's just like a straw just like you're drinking a milkshake. Go on, adds the man, Try it! But when I do the smoke burns my throat. I cough it back out. Everybody laughs and I am jubilant. I put the cigarette to my lips again; this time the smoke does not burn but I cough anyway because I have learned that the people will laugh at this. Eventually the adults stop paying attention to me and return to their own conversations and I squeal and jump and run between their words.

But then my mother says that I am being bad, that I am bothering everyone and to go to my room and not to come out until she says so. I stomp off, slamming my door behind me. Through the thin walls of the room I can hear shouts and screams of laughter. But they are muffled, and although I put my ear against the cold wall I cannot make Mother's voice any closer. *Still, she's out there, I can feel her.*

Even at this age the toys in my room mean little to me. I want to go *there* to where the voices are. But I am here and Mother is even angrier than she was last week and it was last week that she...

I shudder and turn away from the door. The voices rise and fall. Slowly, my breathing slows. My eyes close. And while they are closed, the scene around me changes.

By the time I open my eyes, everything has changed entirely.

The room is dark. The house is quiet. Everyone has left and I am alone. Of course, it is not the first time, but I begin to cry. I am hungry and scared and cannot stop crying. *What if she doesn't come back? What if Daddy comes to kill me again?* He'll come when the lights are out, that's what Mother says, and now she's gone too. I bury myself under the blankets on my bed and sob in the warmed darkness.

Mother says that crying is for girls, but the tears do not stop. The sheets are wet under my cheek and it seems that this time I will cry forever, that not even the darkness can stop it. *She loves me. She'll be back soon. She won't leave me. She'll be back soon....*

Sleep comes first.

A restless absence of shape and sound takes me from dark to darkness...

When I awake I am already in Aunt Helen's arms. The room is black and then with a click it is a blinding red. I squint my eyes against the light until slowly, feature by feature, her face comes into focus. I smile; I must have known her even then. It's okay, she is saying, We're going home.

At her house cookies and hot tea are spread out on a table before me. The kitchen is light and warm. In the next room Aunt Helen is speaking to someone, her voice almost a whisper. I hear my name and smile; I like how Aunt Helen says my name.

* * * * * * * * * *

Book 2. Razvesistaya Klyukva

(1)

In August 1991 (1USD=50RUR) while President Mikhail Gorbachev was resting peacefully at his summer cottage, Soviet tanks rolled through the clean streets of Moscow to the city center. Confusion reigned. Gunfire could be heard to have been heard. At stake was the future of Russia which might never have become Russia.

Residents of Moscow, leaving the safety of their crowded homes, gathered together to form crowds on the safe streets. Some realized this irony and returned home. Others, not realizing the irony, also returned home. A third contingent of brave Muscovites (those who understood that democracy is much more important than irony) were even more heroic: *these* people returned to their homes as well, though somewhat later.

What a magical and carefree time for visitors with return tickets back home! What a perfect moment not to have Russian friends!

a. I stood on my balcony baring my chest to the events outside.

b. In the glare of the midday sun I closed my eyes and savored the strange smell of danger.

c. Grinning smugly I tried to imagine tanks in downtown U.S.A.

(2)

On the one hand, tanks and weddings are two very different things and should not be confused. Tanks, for example, have large guns that can shoot through white buildings, whereas weddings are already white and far less dangerous. Of course there are other differences but this is without a doubt the most important...

(3)

In the beginning Aunt Helen sent bulky care packages that could not have made it through Customs or the dilapidated postal system; and, as a result, they did not. I don't understand what the deal is, she would say, and: What's the matter with those people over there anyway? At least twice a week she would call to ask naive questions about the political situation in the country.

Once, right after the putsch when the telephone lines were hopelessly busy, Aunt Helen dialed nonstop for five hours before being connected. When she heard my voice she burst into tears; and even when she had stopped crying her voice continued to waver until with some effort she was able to compose herself enough to express her real concern:

Are you... are you eating your green vegetables? she asked.

Her timing could not have been worse. I was twenty-six years old. Summer was ending. I had no Russian friends. To each of her questions I answered tersely: 'No'.... 'When I can'.... 'If she wants it then give it to her'.... and then: 'Oh, just standing on the balcony.'

(4)

So here I was with a cabinetful of gifts for people who love democracy but do not use condoms. In America it's much simpler: first, there already exists a two-hundred year tradition of democracy; second, condoms have always been more accessible than abortions; third, there are people you dislike and there are people who dislike the people you dislike, the latter being referred to as 'friends' or 'good friends' or 'best friends' or even 'very best friends' depending on the degree of coincidence. It is all very American, that is to say, safe and artificial and, of course, convenient.

But this was not America. Nor was it Russia. In actuality, this was pre-Russia Russia and so the Marlboro cigarettes went first.

(5)

Luckily, it was raining when I bought potatoes for the first time.

I had arrived to the store at 12:55, exactly five minutes *after* the store's employees — all of them at once — had broken for their one-o'clock lunch break. Now I could either return home without potatoes or wait under the rain. My choice was as difficult as a dilemma and dubious to boot: potatoes versus peanutbutter, love versus warmth.

Months later I would realize that this had been the most important decision of my life: But for now I simply opened my backpack and took out a fat book that I was not reading.

(6)

I hunched over to shield my book from the rain, my hand traced lightly over the pages as if they were the contours of a married lover.

Was Love always this wet? And could It have anything to do with potatoes? And was there any difference between 'high' and 'tall'? Here and There? Heart and the Soul...? And why didn't anybody in Russia smile? Was it that they were waiting for Russia to finally become Russia?

By now my jeans were completely soaked.

But what did wet jeans have to do with anything? Did they necessarily mean that I would ever find love in this strange place? — what if the rain were to bleach my passport? What would I do then? Yet despite my doubts here I was standing faithfully under a downpour. Here I was buying potatoes...!

The fallen water had collected at the top of a nearby hill and was sweeping down the street in swirling currents. On the other side of traffic a trolleybus splashed through a large pool of rain; bystanders on the sidewalk scurried to get out of its way.

...Although, to be honest, I had always preferred peanut butter to potatoes. And besides, warmth was a physical necessity whereas love was not — Just ask my mother and all her boyfriends. Just ask anyone with the same last name as me, my father for example. People say he seemed to love his second wife, but who knows if that was just because she was helping him die. And then there's Aunt Helen. She once said that she had never fallen in love — never even married. And she is the happiest person on the face of the earth....

The water was now dripping from the end of my nose onto the book. The printed words ran together like a stream of consciousness.

...That's right. But why didn't Aunt Helen ever marry? She hadn't been unattractive. Her last name was different from mine. Was she afraid? Or uninterested? Or then maybe it was because she didn't want anything to come between us...

But what could possibly come between us?

When I looked up a man was standing in front of me, slightly to the west. His hair was redder than his umbrella. *How long had he been standing there?* The man looked at me curiously and then said in broken English:

I'm sorry please...

How did he know to address me in English?

...Where do you from?

Amer..., I started to answer and then remembered myself:... Canada. I'm from Canada.

The man did not smile. He looked at me and motioned to join him under the umbrella.

No thanks, I said.

He motioned again.

I'm okay, I said.

Again he motioned.

Really, I'm fine.

But your book..., and the man moved closer to me so that the dripping water would not fall on its pages.

I tried to smile awkwardly, but failed. Without thanking him I looked away.

The street was flooding. In the intersection across from us a car had stalled and a man was trying to push it out of traffic. The car, though small, was stuck in a low part of the street and each time the man pushed it forward the car would move a little, stop for an instant, and then roll back to where it had been before. The man tried again and again; and again and again it rolled back.

The redhead held the umbrella above me, his shoulders wet from the rain. But when I gestured for him to move the umbrella closer to himself he just shrugged off my suggestion, his politeness sliding from his shoulders and trickling onto the wet ground. We stood silently. He did not start a conversation and I was helplessly grateful to him for this.

Meanwhile, across from us in the intersection the man had completely given up on his car, leaving it to waterlog in the middle of the road.

I followed his retreating figure until it had disappeared over the hill. As I watched him the rain rapped on the fabric above me. Black clouds banged loudly against each other. And I wondered, *Is Love always this cold?*

(7)

Man (calmly):	Did you know Pushkin was one-quarter African?
Me (wet):	Who?
Man:	Our great poet Alexander Sergeevich Pushkin.
Me:	I'm sorry. I don't read poetry.
Man:	You don't! Why not?
Me:	In America nobody reads poetry.
Man:	America?! But you said you were from Canada.
Me:	Oh, yeah... but that was before I knew you.
Man:	I don't understand?
Me:	Now I know you and trust you...
Man:	So?
Me:	...So that means that I am not from Canada.
Man:	In other words you're not Canadian at all.
Me:	That's right.
Man:	But...?
Me:	Sorry.

(There is a pause as the man spreads a piece of bread with peanut butter):

Man (chewing):	Did you know that Daniil Kharms died in a mental hospital?
Me:	I'm sorry... Daniil Who?
Man:	Daniil Kharms, the popular children's author.
Me:	Hmm... That's a strange name. Is he Russian?
Man:	Yes.

Me:	Well, that would explain it.
Man:	What?
Me:	Americans aren't real big on foreign literature.
Man:	You're not?
Me:	No, unfortunately they're not.
Man:	Even *Russian* literature?
Me:	*Even* Russian literature.

(There is another pause as the man takes a sip of lukewarm coffee):

Man:	You have heard of Lev Tolstoy, haven't you?
Me:	Of course. But I've never actually read anything by him. In America...
Man:	Excuse me for asking but what *do* you read... I mean in America, that is?
Me:	I'm sorry?
Man:	Do you read Theodore Dreiser?
Me:	No.
Man:	What about Jack London?
Me:	No.
Man:	O. Henry?!
Me:	Never heard of him.
Man:	!!!
Me:	You see, the thing is that in America nobody reads...
Man:	...American literature?
Me:	Right.

(The man takes out a filtered cigarette but does not light it. He seems lost in an important thought):

Man:	Still, it's a damn shame....
Me:	What is? About American literature?
Man:	About the blacks. You really shouldn't have made them slaves.

(8)

At about twenty minutes to two, other people began showing

up outside the store, jostling for position in line. A large woman with a newspaper on her head tried to step in front of me, but at the last moment the redhead said something to her and she fell in behind us.

While I had been standing there, the rain had turned even colder and my hands began to shake. My lips trembled as they silently repeated the most important Russian words I knew: *give me please four kilograms potatoes; give me please four kilograms potatoes; give me please four kilograms potatoes.*

At exactly two-fifteen the store's employees returned from their one-hour lunch break and the throng moved inside. Despite the redhead's umbrella, I was the wettest person in line and so I stepped toward the cashier, who had not invited me to do so.

Give me please four kilograms potatoes, I thought, *Give me please four kilograms potatoes.* When this was done I thought it once more and then repeated it a final time: *Give me please four kilograms potatoes. Give me please four kilograms potatoes.* Then I stepped forward:

Give me please...!

A heavy hand on my shoulder stopped me. I shuddered, but it was too late: the first list had appeared.

(9)

As it turned out, some people had been waiting in line when the store closed for lunch and before leaving they had drawn up a list with their names on it. These names would have to be first; in this country it was something between etiquette and law. Unable to understand this, I quickly stepped back...

...and bumped right into the woman holding the second list. These people had received some sort of special permission from some sort of special person to receive some sort of special privileges; this too eluded me. Yet I knew enough to again step back...

...only to feel my neck snap as I was shoved from behind by the large woman with a newspaper on her head. She was holding a third list which was long and wet; the name at the very top was *Inostranets-Kanadets.*

Standing toe-to-toe-to-toe, the three listholders argued amongst themselves, spurred on by the people whose names they fingered. Some were shouting. Others were yelling. The woman with a newspaper on her head shook her list angrily and pointed at me. In response the second listholder pointed angrily at the woman and shook his fist at me. The third woman, with her list in hand, shook one fist at the woman, the other fist at the man, and finding herself with no more fists to shake glared angrily at me. The people in line — the names in the lists — followed the argument with self-interest. Some pointed loudly at me. Others shook their fists. Everyone was either yelling or shouting but each of them was doing something angrily — and most of them were doing it at me.

The one exception had bright red hair and a faded red umbrella and somehow managed to stay composed, even as the tension rose. I myself was far less composed than confused, my mind struggling to focus on a single thought and that single thought was: *give me please four kilograms potatoes, give me please four kilograms potatoes.*

Then slowly and ominously the sound began to die down. One by one we all looked up from the lists to see that the cashier had settled into her seat behind the counter; she was straightening her hair and brushing off the front of her smock. Thick viscous veins burrowed in the skin of her neck like purple worms. We waited quietly. The room seemed to be suspended on the tips of her plump fingers. Sensing this, the cashier slowed her movements even more. Lazily she motioned for the first person to step forward.

The first person?

The line exploded. I was pushed into the man ahead of me, my face smashed against his shoulder blades. Order was lost. All three lists were now on the ground, muddied and torn by our trampling feet. People were pushing from all sides and I could barely breathe.

Instead, I wrenched my neck around and looked behind: the redhead was working to free his arm which had been pinned to his ribs by the crowd. Twisting and prying the man could not wrest it loose. His muscles strained. His face was flushed. He groaned but nothing gave. He strained but nothing moved.

My God would this place ever become Russia?

First came the arm. In one instant it just seemed to free itself.

And when it was freed the man raised it to his face and wiped away a bead of sweat that had been trickling down his temple for many many years.

What am I doing here? I don't even like potatoes. And I hate cigarette smoke!

These are the thoughts that might have crossed my mind if it hadn't been for the crowd which at that very moment swelled larger and larger and then dropped violently; I was thrown forward to the front of the line and like a wedding bouquet I sailed right at the scowling cashier, who upon seeing me held out her arms expectantly.

Potatoes. Love. Marlboro cigarettes. New Year's.

At that moment how far away it all seemed!

(10)

Let's say — stay with me here — let's say you have three children. They could be any age, but let's say they're six eight and eleven. Your children are curious and devoted and have their father's eyes, the blue eyes that you built a home around. The eyes that promised a family.

Home for you is a small apartment that you will never own: four people in two rooms that in the beginning seemed empty; then small; now cramped. Three times a year the apartment shrinks still further.

You had a husband once but he left. Or died. Or maybe both. Now he's gone and all that's left of him are the children, who are seven nine and twelve. The children and the ugly scars on the inside of your belly.

Remember how your future husband held you after the first operation? Remember how he sighed forgivingly and pressed his lips to your hand? Of course you do. It was so long ago but you remember everything.

You cried when he left. Or when he died.

But not for both.

At work the other employees talk quietly about you. *Poor thing!* they say, *No husband and three children ages eight ten and thirteen. Three children and no husband. And just when it seemed that she'd finally stopped crying... just when it looked like she'd finally forgotten him... this happens. As if these things weren't random at all. As if, like blood, they could coagulate in some but not in others... Poor, poor thing...!*

They say all this behind your back, of course. But on Tuesdays they let you hear.

At some point you stop caring. About the gossip. About the scars. About the years which have drowned your hopes and thickened your neck. And besides, who has the time to care when there's a birthday to get ready for — your eldest child is turning fourteen and you are having guests at your small apartment, the small apartment which, regrettably, has just grown larger.

In the corner of your bedroom is an old picture. The photo is black and white and shows two unsmiling people, a young man and a younger woman, also in black and white. One of them has since left, or has died; the other one is you holding a bouquet of gray flowers. Everything was so much clearer *there* which for you means *anywhere but here*. Things were so much better *then*, which for you means *any day but this one*.

And still, sometimes when you least expect it you see his eyes, the blue that is neither black nor white. The blue that has been forgotten a thousand times only to appear again in the strange hue of summer water and smuggled denim. It's as virtuous as virginity; as inevitable as an escalator; and, in the end, as hopeless as the blue gaze of your children who are curious and devoted and who have already turned ten and fifteen.

(11)

The cashier extended her arms as if I were a wedding bouquet.

(12)

I offered the woman my money and asked her to give me please four kilograms potatoes. She was not impressed. Four kilograms potatoes, I repeated. Again she was not impressed. The woman looked at me blankly, the purple worms rising to the surface. Four kilograms. Give me please four kilograms potatoes... The woman glared at my words, her worms pressing against themselves. Potatoes four give me kilograms! I said again. Still no response. *Do something! Quick! Do something before she starts...!* Okay! Okay! I said to the worms, Give me *three* kilograms! But it was too late. They had blossomed like overfed capillaries; the woman began to shake the money in my face like a threat. She was shaking the money and yelling and pointing at an old wooden toy with beads on it. *But she wasn't yelling, she was screaming! And the toy wasn't a toy at all — it was an abacus!*

An abacus...?!

The woman yelled and screamed and when she could yell and scream no more, she began to shout. I stood shaking my head in confusion, trying to understand: *Was she yelling or was she screaming? Could it be that she was shouting?* I don't understand! I pleaded but by now the line was growling and surging behind me, around me; throbbing like a wound it was overtaking me.

I would lose my place in line. I was losing my place in line.

I had lost my place in line.

Was love worth all this grammar? At this point in my life the answer seemed to be no.

But then she stopped.

The redhead had made his way to the front of the line and was saying something to her. His voice was clear and confident. He spoke deliberately and when the cashier tried to interrupt, the man held up his hand calmly continuing his explanation until every last worm had retreated into the fleshy folds of her neck.

Standing there I watched the man speaking and heard the cashier listening. The crowd continued to move restlessly behind me.

But by now the worms had been buried.

The man held out his hand expectantly and the cashier, upon seeing this, set a piece of paper on the counter; the paper was approximately the length and width of a book of wet matches; it was lighter than potatoes. Expertly, the man picked up the piece of paper.

Why had she yelled at me? Why had she shouted?

I looked at the redhead for an explanation but he just shrugged his wet shoulders and with a sigh pronounced the first Russian words that I would ever understand with both heart and soul. As he spoke, clouds could be heard colliding in the distance, a piece of thunder snapped against itself like a red flag:

This isn't Canada! he said.

(13)

Pulling me aside, the man handed me the piece of paper and extended three freckled fingers so close to my nose that I could see the circles of wrinkled skin at the joints. As he spoke I stared at his spotted skin. *What did the fingers mean... three what?* Perhaps it was the time? Or his luckiest number? It could have been the amount of rubles that he had paid for my potatoes; or the amount of times I would have to stand in line each time I bought something green. It might have been the number of children that can fit in a small apartment; or adults in a small bed; or women named Tanya in a conversation that I cannot understand.

Really, it could have been any of these things — or every single one of them. All I knew was that the man was saying something very important, that his fingers were very freckled, and that in my hands I held a little piece of paper that weighed less but meant much more than just potatoes.

(14)

I was so grateful to the redhead I invited him to my apartment for coffee.

The man was my age. Old enough, he said, to have learned and forgotten English, respectively; and so we spoke in a mixture of both languages. Our conversation was awkward — more pauses than words, less grammar than desirable — but somehow we managed.

When it was time for him to leave I gave him the cigarettes. *All* of them.

The man thanked me but seemed embarrassed that the cartons would not fit in his arms. So I lent him my backpack to carry them in. On second thought, I told him, *Keep* the backpack — after all, what good is it if it's empty? At this the man shook his head and waved his arms in front of him. He did this so convincingly that I gave him a jar of peanut butter and stuffed a can of coffee into the backpack. The man seemed flustered. He began looking in his bag and after some time pulled out a head of cabbage that he had bought at the store. For you! he said. I accepted it with both hands. It's green, I said. The man seemed puzzled but agreed. I smiled and thanked him. He thanked me back. I thanked him a second time. He thanked me a third. Thank you, I said. Thank *you*! he said.

This continued for several minutes.

Then it occurred to me: the German-English dictionary! The inscription had already been scratched out. Its pages were as thick and hard as ever. But to this the redhead was adamant: no, no, no, he said and I reluctantly put the dictionary back on the shelf next to the four solar calculators the size of credit cards.

I thanked him for remembering his umbrella. He thanked me for not giving him the German dictionary. I thanked him for knowing Russian. He thanked me for thanking him....

It was getting late.

Taking out a deck of cards that I had been using for solitaire, I wrote my phone number on the King of Clubs; he chose the Three of Diamonds.

We exchanged phone numbers. Logically, I put his card in my wallet. Inexplicably, he did the same. Then he thanked me one final time, raised his umbrella over his head, and left.

I had gotten rid of the Marlboro cigarettes!!! I had made my first Russian friend!! Perhaps this meant that Russia might actually become Russia! Perhaps I really would find love after all. And maybe... Just maybe...?

That night my heart raced. My soul flew.

But later, when I opened my wallet, it became clear as a clover that love and logic are equally inexplicable: Instead of the man's phone number I saw my own handwriting and, underneath it, the King of Clubs.

The man had tucked the Three of Diamonds into his wallet, and with it, his own phone number.

* * * * * * * * * *

Book 3. Book 2 (cont.)

(1)

Ask any Russian and they'll tell you: six and a half years ago the winter came harsher and larger than it does nowadays. In *those* days the dry air would freeze; the ground would crunch like bones beneath your feet; and everything that mattered would lie covered in layers of white, like a virgin on her wedding night. It is all very Russian, that is to say, beautiful and unconditional and, at times, hopelessly inevitable.

But that was an eternity ago and a lot has changed since then. Even the seemingly inevitable. Many Russians still blame Mikhail Gorbachev for this even though, in truth, global warming preceded *perestroika* and by that time the country had already lost all remnants of her virginity anyway. Of course some changes are for the worst, but some are for the better. Or maybe: some for the better but some for the worst.

Is vodka forty percent alcohol or sixty percent water?

I have a friend now who drinks without asking. He says that in life there are only three things that never change. And that the last of them is White.

(2)

In the early morning of December 26th, Aunt Helen called: Merry Christmas! and then: Gorbachev's out you know and Get the hell out of that country while you still can!

I listened impatiently and then said: Hold on, someone's at the door...!

(3)

I opened the door: it was the redhead. He was holding a Three of Diamonds and laughing. Remember me? he asked and handed me a bag of potatoes. I had been taking a shower when the doorbell rang and so I accepted them with one hand:

Of course, I said.

What are your plans for New Year's? he asked.

I don't have any, I said, None at all.

If you want, you can celebrate with us.

I thanked him.

And feel free to bring someone...

No, I said, I'll be alone.

I apologized for my appearance and invited him to my dinner which was already on the table: peanut butter toast and lukewarm coffee.

(4)

From the very beginning I found my job to be — Isn't it the way with most jobs? — a job.

In the morning I taught the beginners to distinguish *a* from *the*. In the afternoon my intermediate class reviewed the difference between *a* and *the*. Evening classes with the adult students were devoted to discussion of more advanced themes: for example, *another* versus *the other*.

(5)

When I had remembered to take the phone I told Aunt Helen: Hey, I gotta go, I'll call you later. No, no, everything's fine... I'll call you later. Merry Christmas!

And after hanging it up I went back to my lukewarm coffee and our unfinished discussion of American slavery.

(6)

Time passed. Like an Indian Summer. Like peanut butter in winter. At work, the semester ended just as my English was beginning to improve. Snow began to fall around mid-October and just kept falling. My kitchen sink continued to leak. My supply of toilet paper ran out. And despite *all this*, the German dictionary remained on the shelf, thick but hardly touched, next to the three solar calculators the size of credit cards.

And the weeks passed. And the snow fell. And in time it became a wonder that I had ever used articles at all.

Then a few days before New Year's, a horrible panic gripped me: never before had I been to my first Russian New Year's party. *How should I dress? What about a gift? Would the other guests speak to me? Would I understand them? If so, would I understand them correctly?*

Worriedly I drew up special flash-cards with key phrases. Staring deep into my mirror I congratulated myself repeatedly; repeatedly I praised my knowledge of English. On the mirror's surface, the words condensed and then dissolved.

Outside, the snow was continuing to fall. I tucked up the collar of my coat and set off unsurely for the redhead's apartment.

(7)

My first year here (in order of importance):

1991
1. Democracy
2. Danger
3. Irony
4. Love
5. Marriage
6. Logic

(8)

By the time I arrived at the New Year's dinner, the other guests were already seated tightly around the table in the cramped living room. An empty chair stood at the far end of the room and as I picked a path toward it, squeezing awkwardly between rows of knees and the table, the seated guests tucked their legs into themselves to let me pass. In all, there were six people — three couples — and on my way to the empty seat I scraped against most of them. Embarrassed at this inconvenience, I tried to be profusely apologetic. But these words were too much for me. Instead I smiled stupidly:

Congratulations! I said.

KHELLO! they said.

Your English is very good, I told them.

KHELLO! they said.

At this point, my host, who had been watching this scene silently, laughed loudly but without smiling and introduced me by name:

This is '*our American visitor*,' he added proudly.

Everyone nodded enthusiastically: the year was old and they were still very impressed.

Once in my seat, I could not believe my eyes. The table was decorated with small plates of neatly overlapping coldcuts and beautifully arranged salads of red, orange, and kilograms of green. In the middle of the table stood a single bottle of semi-sweet Sovietskoye Champagne, its label partially unglued; three bottles of Georgian wine surrounded it; and, somewhere in the near future, six liters of the purest Russian vodka. To all this I added a bottle of French cognac which I had purchased at a hard-currency store, but it was quickly snatched from the table by the host.

As it turned out, each of the men had worn black to the party; that is to say, black slacks with black buttoned-up shirts. The women, in contrast, wore dark gray. Surprisingly, the men felt no qualms about this coincidence. Not surprisingly, the women were all named Tanya.

Sitting festively in my white pants and yellow polka-dotted shirt, I remembered all the black clothes that I had left at home. In my apartment. In America. All the black turtlenecks that I had wanted but never thought to buy....

It was exactly nine-thirty. The new year was only hours away.

(9)

After introducing me my host began a captivating story about potatoes. When I heard my name I realized that he must be recalling our first meeting. As the story unfolded his eyes sparkled more like vodka than champagne and the other guests laughed in unison, even when he held up three fingers.

I sat silently.

Then my friend pulled out a Marlboro cigarette. The others looked at him enviously and Tanya, who was sitting on my left, even asked me if I was married. At that particular moment I was more embarrassed than married and when I shook my head, Tanya, who was sitting to my right, asked me why not. I responded by shrugging my shoulders and experimenting foolheartedly with their language:

Irony, I told them, is more important.

It didn't pass. The other guests looked at me blankly. There was an awkward silence. A throat cleared. Then the sound of a Sovietskoye label peeling. In sympathy, Tanya, who was sitting across from me, offered a plate of pickles and I accepted; the vegetable crunched timidly in my mouth.

Seeing all this, my friend filled my glass. Russian vodka! he said.

I nodded.

This was at nine thirty-seven. The New Year was fast approaching.

But ever so slowly.

(10)

In my family there were two informal traditions connected with New Year's Eve.

The first was that each year Aunt Helen and I would count down the New Year starting with my age. We would look at the clock's second hand until the time was right and then scream: Ten! Nine! Eight...! and then the next year: Eleven! Ten! Nine...! In truth it meant only that another year had passed, no more no less. But Aunt Helen understood. She knew that for *me*, it was tangible and true, something to guide me when I had nothing else to count on.

The second tradition was also the only one that I had ever shared with my mother: each New Year's Eve, on that one night only, I could expect to hear from her. For months at a time she would disappear without a trace, missing my birthday, Christmas, other holidays. But on New Year's Eve she always called; for some reason she had made it our holiday.

Once when Aunt Helen and I were waiting for midnight — tonight we would count down from twelve — the doorbell rang. We had not been expecting anyone.

When Aunt Helen opened the door I saw an unfamiliar man and then, next to him, my mother. Her face was covered with makeup and she was stamping out a cigarette. Happy New Year, she said.

When they came in I was sitting on the floor in front of the television. The man stayed by the door in his coat. He looked around without interest and checked his watch. My mother handed him a plastic sack; her face was flushed.

Hi Honey, she said and held out her arms to me.

I did not move.

The man smirked: Looks like he doesn't remember you...!

Shut up! she snapped and turned to me: Well, don't just sit there... Come give your mother a hug!

The room was silent and then Aunt Helen said: Go on, It's New Year's.

Slowly I got up from the floor and walked to the woman who should have been my mother. When I was close enough she pulled me to her so that my limp body sagged against hers. Her clothes smelled strongly of perfume and when she spoke her words reeked of alcohol. She kissed my cheek and then with a handkerchief wiped away the lipstick:

This is my son, she announced to the man.

No shit, he said and looked at me blandly.

How's school?

Okay, I answered her.

Do you like your teachers?

They're okay.

My mother held me in front of her at arm's length.

You're so big! she said and then: What are you now, twelve?

He'll be thirteen next month, said Aunt Helen and quickly added: But then I guess you would know that, wouldn't you?

The man laughed and started to say something to my mother...

Shut up! she cut him off, Just shut the hell up!

The man yawned and checked his watch.

My mother turned to me: I think about you all the time, you know that, don't you? You know that I'm always thinking about you?

I nodded without listening.

Isn't he big for thirteen? she said to the man.

Huge, he answered.

My mother pressed me to her again and then asked:

Are you doing all right in school?

I'm doing okay, I said.

That's good: school's important, you know. I wish *I'd* done better....

The room became silent again.

Hey, I brought you something...! said my mother and motioned at the man who then swung the plastic sack at me.

I barely caught it. Inside was an unwrapped toy, the kind that Aunt Helen had given me the year before.

Thanks, I muttered.

Do you like it?

Uh-huh.

Really?

I said I liked it. Didn't I already say I liked it? How many times do you want me to say it?

Hey! said Aunt Helen but I had stopped listening to her too.

The room became as still as a stalled elevator. Then my mother spoke up:

You know honey, she said, No matter what happens I'm still your mother. And even though I may not be around that doesn't mean that I'm not with you. I am. Please remember that. And no matter where you are, I'm there too. Even when I'm not. Please remember that even when it seems like you're alone you still have a mother. You still have your mother. You still have me.

I said nothing.

Do you promise you'll do that for me? Do you promise you'll always remember?

I said nothing.

Honey?

I said nothing.

And at that Aunt Helen pronounced my name as she always did when I forced her to be my mother: severely, distinctly, articulating the whole name from beginning to middle to end:

Are you listening to what your mother's telling you? she added.

I'm listening.

And what do you have to say for yourself?

Whatever. Whatever she says is fine with me.

Once again the stillness of the room was all that could be heard.

The man shifted nervously. Then he cleared his throat. We gotta go, he said holding up his watch, We'll be late.

My mother looked angrily at the man and began to say something. Then she turned to me. She opened her mouth to speak but stopped. Inches away from her, I could see her lips move. I saw them trembling. There was so much to be said. It wasn't too late yet. There was still time. A few words. A few sounds could make it right. But when she spoke her words were transparent. She wanted to speak but couldn't.

Instead she kissed me again. Then, letting go, she whispered after me, her words as familiar as a dial tone:

'Tell Mommy you love her....' She said it every New Year's Eve.

But this time I stood silent.

Everyone was completely still. My mother waited for me to answer. Aunt Helen waited. The man looked at his watch and then down at me. I could hear him tapping his foot impatiently against our floor.

I closed my eyes. Without saying a word. I closed my eyes until the muscles in my cheeks hurt. So tight that no one would ever be able to open them.

I stood silent and alone, blinded by my own darkness. And when I opened my eyes to see nothing but light, she was gone.

(11)

Sitting silently at the table I tried to follow the conversation by studying the expressions of the faces surrounding me. Strange words swirled in front of me like fluttering snow. Because I could not understand, I smiled and smiled and smiled...

But my laughter rang false and slightly out of rhythm. Sometimes I would misread a cue and laugh alone, my voice cutting naked and weak into the unsuspecting conversation. And each time this happened I withdrew even further; my answers to questions became shorter, my laughter less certain, and my silence even more silent.

It was Tanya who first tried to involve me in the conversation; but each time she spoke her enunciation was poor. At first I did my best to make out her words:

What did you say? I asked in Russian.

Tanya looked at Tanya and then back at me. Then for my sake she repeated her words, but this time in English that was admirable though strangely inflected:

Excuse my English... It is very bad.

What? I asked in Russian.

My English is very bad. I am teaching English for two years but *with*out possibility for practice...

Your English is fine, I said in Russian.

Here she giggled shyly and thanked me in Russian, then continued in English:

Where do you live? she asked.

I answered her in Russian: In Moscow, I said.

But again she continued in English:

Yes, I know, but I want to say in America, Where do you live?

I told her in Russian.

Do you like Moscow?

Yes, of course.

It is my *dream* to go in America! It is very interesting country.

It's okay (I had reluctantly switched to English.)

Do you know, I very love America. I love the American movies. American music. Even the American languge. Yes, America is *very* good country.

Thank you.

Please.

Tanya moved her chair closer to mine:

But..., she said, ...In your country there has problems, too.

I'm sorry?

I want to say that America is good country, but you too have problems.

Well yes we do...

...America has very big problems because of neggers.

I choked on my slice of pickle. Excuse me? I said.

I know it is many neggers and that is why many problems.

At this Tanya interrupted her in rat-a-tat Russian; Tanya, for her part, responded just as quickly. The two began arguing back and forth and had seemingly forgotten about me. On the other side of our conversation, the three men were speaking Russian and laughing. Tanya, who until now had watched our conversation silently, also joined the fracas. The three spoke heatedly for some time. Finally Tanya waved her arm, first at Tanya, then at Tanya, and then turned to me:

Will you stay long in Moscow? she asked.

One year, I'm working as a teacher at the institute.

And *do* you like Russian women?

I... Yeah, sure.

To my mind American women are *not* so beautiful.

I... It's difficult to speak in general, really, but I guess...

And *do* you have the blue passport in America? I heard that in America your passports are dark blue!

Was she even listening to me?

Well, yes, as a matter of fact, our passports are blue...

Dark blue is my favorite color. Unfortunately, in our country all passports are *red*.

Again Tanya jumped in and again they began arguing. I shifted uncomfortably in my seat. My mouth was dry from the pickles and my head was beginning to ache from the warmth of the small room. When their argument had subsided, Tanya once again turned to me and said: Tanya tells that I must speak in Russian for your practice, She is very evil woman!

She glanced playfully at Tanya and laughed in Russian. Tanya also laughed, as did Tanya.

I tried to laugh but failed. Nevertheless, I felt relieved to have the spotlight out of my eyes.

The women fell silent and with this the two conversations were free to merge into one big conversation. But this larger conversation was in Russian and so I smiled and smiled and smiled...

At nine-forty the redhead stood up and wordlessly raised his glass until slowly and gradually it overwhelmed the other voices.

A toast...! he said and paused for emphasis. The room was breathless. I held my glass up to the light, the vodka sparkled like a fake tooth. And in its glow I strained to understand:

...To the ...... and absolute ...... that make ...... May they ...... in the ...... of the New Year!

It must have been profound.

Leaning forward the man held his glass out over the center of the table and all at once, from all possible angles, a collection of arms shot out and everyone began clinking their glasses to his and then to the glasses of their neighbors, first across and then to the side — left and right or right and left — leaning and twisting with hands stretching out farther and further until one by one the sound of glass touching glass had consummated the toast.

I offered my glass too and compared its light chiming to the sounds around me. Confident and clear, it was the perfect echo.

(12)

According to Russian tradition, drinking without toasting is just plain drunkenness:

9:44 (vodka): 'To the ...... of our two great countries ...... for years ...... and ...... cooperation ...... and ...... and ......!'

I had never been a drinker and as I drank, my head began to reel and I felt a dry bitterness backing up in my throat. I waited for it to settle but it did not. The conversation was becoming quicker just as my mind was becoming slower. But the sound of glass against glass bolstered my spirits:

9:53 (wine): 'To the future of ...... and Perestroika ...... Mikhail Gorbachev with ...... Ivan Сусанин ...... hopefully ...... because ...... at last ...... Russia!'

Everybody laughed. The ice had been broken. The party was gaining momentum. I also laughed.

By now there were only two hours until the New Year! Tonight

I would count silently from twenty-six and then loudly from ten — after all, Russians count down from ten, don't they? *Twenty-six years!* And on my twenty-sixth new year, I was *here*! What would all my childhood friends have said if they could have known? What would my father have said if he could have lived to see this? That I would someday teach others to speak. That I could possibly make it beyond the U.S. My own mother had never even left the country, except to buy tequila...

When I looked down, my glass was already full.

9:55 (vodka): 'When I was younger......'

...And now the New Year was coming and I would count down from twenty-six and what a glorious new year it would be! I did not understand anyone, but they could not understand me. I was different from everyone else; but in a good way. And if I did things right, maybe I could fit in. If I could learn to love the country, if I could find all eleven words, then maybe this new place would love me back. Oh, when would the New Year come? And what would it bring for me...?

10:15 (vodka): 'To love!......'

Somehow I noticed that my glass, which before had been filled before toasts, was now being filled *after* toasts.

...What would the new year bring me? *Something good, of course! I could have lived in the safety and convenience of America if I had wanted to.* But instead here I was in... I was here in... what was the name of this country? And what time was it? And why wasn't anyone celebrating? The glorious New Year was coming! And I needed to know when to count down... I needed to know twenty-six seconds before midnight so that I could welcome another year... *Could it be that I missed it? Could it be that I would miss it for the first time in my life?...*

? (wine): 'Whose turn......Sasha......toast!.......Goddamn!'

My head was spinning. The Tanyas had blurred into one. But she was three times normal size. And dressed in orange! My thoughts raged. I resolved to make at least five friends who could not understand my English. I resolved to call Aunt Helen at least once a week. And if I couldn't call, to write letters instead. I resolved to find all eleven yellow words. *But what could the eleventh one mean?*

I resolved to wait under every rain, to not quit on this country no matter what. I resolved to love vodka....

I held up my glass and heard it ring somewhere in the distance.

? (?): 'To all the beautiful people sitting around this table and to this glorious country with all its coldcuts and colored vegetables and to all six liters of the vodka that is backing up in our throats, and to the sound of glass touching glass and sticky filthy worthless coins and to the snow which, as we sit, is falling so beautifully outside our window and...'

Perhaps the speaker did not actually say this. But at that moment I knew that's what he meant; and sitting there I pondered his words. Of course, I would not make it to this new year; there could be no doubt about that. But it didn't matter. Everything was so beautiful: the toasts, the salads, each of the Tanyas — there were now six of them — the snow that was falling as softly as I would and the redhead with his cigarettes and the vodka that was already in my glass which was already in my hand and the heads that were now turning to look at me and the chair that was falling backwards to the floor behind me. God it was all so beautiful!

I stood up.

A toast! I said.

(13)

And then I fell down.

That is to say, I passed out.

(14)

(15)

When the dryness in my throat woke me, I was lying in the dark on my side, my cheek was pressed to a cold and unfamiliar kitchen floor. Somewhere a clock ticked. Next to me slept the redhead; his neck craned awkwardly against a stove.

As I lay there I felt the bitter dryness welling up in my throat. But I could not vomit. Nor would the dryness settle; it just lingered cruelly between two resolutions. Only the kitchen floor was cold solace against my cheek.

I turned over.

On the other side of me, lying face down in a puddle of food, was another man. A luminescent string extended from his mouth to the floor. *Lucky bastard!* I thought. Helplessly, I listened to the clock ticking away my chances one at a time. With all my strength I cursed its sound until at last it fell asleep.

(16)

Later that morning, with the dry taste still in my mouth but not in my throat, I thanked everyone for a wonderful time and set off for home.

It was a gloomy January day, too cold to be white, but too white to be black.

Once outside, the wind whipped my face. The ground crunched. I could hear shovels scraping the sidewalk behind me. Falling snow scattered across the tops of my boots like thrown rice.

At home I drew the curtains against the light and lay heavily onto my bed. On the streets people celebrated the long-awaited New Year. But in my condition I could not join them. Outside a new shade of snow was falling but I could not see it through the darkness of my room.

My friend says that Black is like White in that it can never change....

Or can it?

Lying there with my boots on my pillow I did not even notice. I could not vomit, let alone mourn the red and gold that would snap no more. I was too tired to celebrate and too sick to vomit. Instead I would sleep away the entire day; I could mourn later. But with your eyes closed you cannot see colors. And when you need it more than anything else, vomit can be as elusive as democracy. And that's precisely why I missed it. That's how I did not even realize that after years of uncertainty and disappointment, when it seemed as if change had forgotten its duty, that arms would never rise and bones would forever lie frozen, after all this, the moment had finally arrived: Russia had finally become

Russia had *finally* become...

(17)

The phone. The phone was ringing. *Who would call me at this hour?* I ignored it, but it did not stop. It would not stop. Meekly I lifted the receiver to my ear. There was a click then a pause then a voice:

Hello? it said. Despite the distance, the voice was as familiar as silence.

I held the phone to my ear.

Hello? the voice asked weakly.

I set the receiver in its cradle.

When the phone rang again I did not answer. It continued for some time and then, when it was no longer needed, the sound died away forever.

(18)

...As of the new year Russia had finally become the 'former Soviet Union.'

Or was it the 'Commonwealth of Independent States'?

Or the 'USSR and Successor Republics'?

In actuality, it wasn't clear what it had become; or where in the alphabetical listing we should look for it. All we knew was that the New Year had arrived and that we had deftly set aside a bottle of cognac to be enjoyed later.

Russia would never be the same.

Of course it would be years before all the signs in the country agreed. But by now no one gave a damn. We had waited too long to call it anything else!

* * * * * * * * * *

Book 4. The Russia Years

(1)

Ask any child in America and they'll tell you: the English alphabet is so well-organized it rhymes. In fact they will probably sing it:

A B C D E F G,
H I J K L M N O P,
Q R S T U V,
W X Y and Z.

But Russian words look oppressive when written with English letters and so an entirely separate alphabet was created. Like its English counterpart, this other alphabet starts out simply enough:

А Б В Г Д Е Ё ...

Then along the way it gets flustered:

...Ж З И Й...

Gathers its composure:

...К Л М Н О П Р С Т У Ф...

Only to lose it completely in the end:

...Х Ц Ч Ш Щ Ъ Ы Ь Э Ю Я.

The result of this is that even Russians are hard-pressed to remember the correct order of their own alphabet. In frustration some letters have been cast away; others remain, though they are seemingly irrelevant.

Fortunately, an alphabet is not about its parts, but about how it works as a whole. The important thing is that all the letters are there — in some order — and that if you start with *A* and progress slowly and patiently, letter by letter, and if you don't let the disorder discourage you, then you will eventually end up at *Я*.

(2)

A lot of important things can happen in six and a half years. For example:

#1. I find an old Russian coin which I tuck into my wallet. I decide that it will be my link to this new land and vow that as long as I am here the coin will stay with me. In less than a week I have lost my wallet, and with it, the coin.

#17. Although I do not smile or gesticulate, men in black leather jackets accost me with offers to buy rubles, fur hats and, sometimes, black leather jackets; instead, I buy a Russian-language edition of *Anna Karenina* which I carry conspicuously in public and which I conspicuously do not read.

#53. A man shows up at my apartment with my lost wallet. All the money is gone, but the coin is still there as are my passport and the yellow piece of paper. It is the last time I will part with the coin. I offer the man a reward, but he refuses. His nose is red, his breath smells of swallowed vodka. He is about my age and he is unmarried. His name is Vadim.

#78. Turning down a side street not far from the Kremlin I am surprised to meet a black bear lumbering along the sidewalk. Traffic has stopped; a policeman with a whistle is trying to maintain order by yelling and pointing. Suddenly, the bear rears up on his hind legs and roars angrily; bystanders on the sidewalk, in a fright, scurry to get out of its way. But I do not panic. Instead, I walk right up to the bear. I smile at him and toss him a jar of peanut butter which he paws clumsily before smashing open. Gratefully, he eats the contents, his jaws chomping loudly, his lips smacking. I pat his head. He licks my hand. I stroke his tongue. This continues for some time. Then as if nothing has even happened, he lumbers back through the traffic away from me toward the place where he was before.

#80. One day a female student from the adult group corners me in the hallway after class; she insists that I explain the difference between *high* and *tall*. Her question takes me by surprise — I have never thought about it! — still, I have the presence of mind to lie. There is no difference, I say. Are you sure? she asks. Absolutely! I say. I smile at her. She winks back. I invite her over for dinner. She accepts. I ask what her favorite food is. She tells me. We agree on a time and I am surprised that everything has happened so easily. She is intelligent and polite, though her English is not yet fluent. Later that night I set aside a solar calculator for her. Soon I will fall into deep love. With time her English will improve. Eventually we will break up. These months will fly by like a wounded eagle. But for the moment I have a more immediate problem: Tomorrow is Sunday, the stores will be closed, and by seven o'clock I need to find four kilograms of potatoes.

#91. I get drunk and pass out at a New Year's party.

(3)

In truth it was the redhead and his wife who taught me Russia. From them I learned how to buy potatoes. And how to eat them every single day. The redhead taught me to sneak onto a trolleybus, and that this, for some reason, was a good thing to do. Tanya, who worked for the government, was compelled to disapprove: You kids should live it up while you can, she would warn, because sooner or later your parents are going to come home!

(Tanya, it should be said, was a tax inspector.)

Between my morning and afternoon classes, while his wife was working, the redhead would show me the correct position of the elbow when drinking vodka, and how to sniff a pickle after swallowing to make it smoother. And how, the day after, to chase the bitter dryness of vodka from your throat by swallowing even more vodka.

If only he knew the word that changes and is changed! If only he could help me vomit!

Eventually I began to spend as much time at their small apartment as I did at my own. With time my Russian improved, and we began to speak less and less English, until finally we spoke none. And in return, I did my very best to explain the fundamentals of democracy; I fielded questions on America's race problem; at their whim I demonstrated my blue passport for inspection....

Time passed. The seasons came and went. Like passengers in the metro they blended together. In the spring we looked for mushrooms; in the fall we found them. In summer we took warm showers at each other's small apartments; and in the dead of winter we swam outdoors in what was then the pool that used to be a cathedral, and which is now the cathedral that used to be a pool.

Happily, we bought bread in stores named 'Bread.'

We played cards without a full deck.

We tossed kopecks into canals and made naive wishes for the future: the redhead for harmony between black and white Americans; I for democracy in Russia; Tanya for a blue passport.

Sitting in our crowded kitchens, my friends and I talked. And talked. And talked.... About Love. And marriage. About Kharms and Pushkin and the novelist Lev Tolstoy. About the country they had thought America to be. And the one that Russia was so inevitably becoming.

But most of all my friends taught me that I had not been taught. Things that I had known for years were suddenly called into question, and things that I had never known before now seemed worth knowing. Ideas that had once been so simple became impossible to explain. Things that I had never even thought about were forced before me for painful, scrupulous, tedious consideration. *Why did danger smell so good? Why had I so dreaded marriage? Was Gorbachev really as bad as everyone said he was? And was it my imagination or did Russians tie their shoes backwards?*

(4)

#136. I have Russian friends now who tell me that it is not my smile that makes it absolutely clear I am a foreigner; it is the well-thumbed *Anna Karenina*. I put the fat book back on the shelf next to the German-English dictionary and the three solar calculators the size of credit cards.

(5)

As it turned out, the redhead, despite his calm demeanor, was an artist; for months he had been working to finish a larger-than-life-size oil painting which — except for Tanya — nobody had been allowed to see. The painting had been guarded like a grave, its frame covered in a large sheet and propped up against a wall; it looked both imposing and heavy, and in the small room its size portended a masterpiece.

Tanya, unlike the redhead, was female and fiery, pretty but fiercely passionate. The painting, she told me, had been commissioned by a soon-to-be-opened bank that needed thematic portraits for its lobby. The bank would be called East-West Bank and had promised to pay the redhead a handsome sum upon completion.

My friends had been married for six years when I met them. They lived on the fourth floor of a twelve-story building and although their apartment was small, their marriage seemed to be steadier than most.

(6)

#170. My Russian is still weak and people speak faster than I can listen; with difficulty I can follow a conversation meant for me, but when Russians speak to Russians I understand nothing. To express my ideas, I convert English phrases word for word into Russian that is not really Russian. My friends listen patiently, and when I am finished they shake their heads and tell me that my problem is I know Russian from A to Z. For practice I begin reading Daniil Kharms in the original.

(7)

One day Tanya invited me to dinner. It would be a *special occasion*! she had hinted by telephone, and so I brought an extra bottle of vodka. When I entered the apartment I noticed immediately: the painting had been hung, still covered in the sheet, on the entire breadth of one wall.

It was finished!

Tanya had sent her husband out to buy something, and while we waited for him she addressed me seriously:

As you can see, she said, my husband finished his painting.

That's great.

He wants to show it to you.

Okay

Yeah, but there's a problem. You see he wants you to see his painting but he doesn't want you to know that he wants you to see his painting.

What?

You see, he's very modest and so he can't bring himself to offer to show it to you even though he really wants you to see it.

I see. Well, what if I ask to see it... you know if I'm the one who initiates it?

Oh no! If you ask he'll say no.

Why?

Because that would mean that he wants you to see it. And remember he's modest and doesn't want you to know that he wants you to see it.

It's complicated... he wants me to see his painting but doesn't want me to know that he wants me to see it and so he won't offer to show it to me, and if I ask he'll refuse?

That's right.

So what should we do?

You have to convince him that by showing you his painting he will be doing you a favor, some sort of good. In that case he'll feel that he *has* to show you the painting, that he doesn't have a choice. See what I mean?

Not really.

What you need to do is sort of drop a hint that you're a bit homesick for America...

Homesick! Why?

Just trust me... when you get the chance, try to mention that you are homesick... that you miss your country.

On the other side of the door a key could be heard turning in the lock. With a click the lock snapped open. In walked the redhead:

Hey! How are you! he said.

I'm homesick, I said.

What?

I miss my country.

The redhead stood for a few seconds trying to understand and then, assuming that I had made a mistake with my Russian and being too polite to dwell on it, he simply set his sack on the table:

That's nice, he said.

During dinner the redhead's tone was even more serious than usual. He did not even look toward the painting, let alone speak about it. Nor did I ask. As we ate, we did not talk about art, or work; carefully, we avoided speaking of things that could be considered heavy or imposing. For the most part, our discussion centered around how homesick I was, around how much I missed my country. But no matter how many times I subtly mentioned it, the redhead didn't react.

You know..., I would say, ...I sure am homesick!

Outside, the snow could be seen falling onto the ground. Gently it was covering itself in layers of white.

Well..., Tanya finally prompted.

Well what? the redhead pretended to ask.

Well...! she insisted.

The man crushed out his cigarette and looked at me: My painting's finished, he said.

Really?

Yes, I finished it yesterday.

Can I see it?

No.

Why not?

Because it's not very good. It's finished but it's not very good.

Well you have to show it to someone, don't you? I mean that's what paintings are for, right?

Maybe. Or maybe not. I paint for my personal satisfaction. For the sake of painting.

You're a liar! said Tanya.

I'd really like to see it, I said, Can I?

No.

Please?

No.

Pretty please?

No.

Tanya had been right... he really was modest!

Have I mentioned how homesick I am?

Homesick?

Yes, I miss my country terribly.

Well in that case....

Tanya clapped excitedly. The three of us moved into the living room and the redhead showed me where to stand in front of the picture — where the lighting was best, Tanya explained — and I dutifully stood in that exact spot. As I waited, the man watched my every motion, his silent stare broken only by Tanya's persistent questions:

Are you ready? she asked me.

I was.

Can you see all right? she said.

I could.

Should I get a camera? she asked.

For heaven's sake! the man answered and with a quick downward tug he removed the sheet from the canvas.

I gasped for a second time:

On the right side of the painting was a Russian flag and across from it an American flag. Both were red, white, and blue. But protruding through the Russian flag, as if it had torn its way through the cloth, was a pinkish hand; this pink hand extended out and clasped a black hand which had seemingly ripped through the American flag. The two hands clasped each other in friendship, a very evident display of harmony and reconciliation between us and them; here and there; black and pink. I stared respectfully but silently. Both the redhead and Tanya were looking at my reaction. At last, the man spoke up:

The flag on the left represents America, he told me.

It usually does, I agreed.

The black hand, he explained, stands for the ethnic diversity of your society.

I see, I said.

Tanya beamed.

Can I ask you a question? I said.

The man nodded.

It's about the black hand. I understand that it represents the ethnic diversity of our culture and all, but why... I mean... what's with the wrist shackles?

Obviously the man had thought this through:

The shackles, he said, are slavery and oppression. Slavery of the past and oppression of the modern day.

I see.

Do you like it?

Of course, I said.

Would you like to have it?

I smiled.

I want you to have it, he said.

Me?

Yes. A souvenir from my country to yours, from me to you.

Thank you, I mean I'm honored but I can't... I mean I couldn't...

No, really. I want you to have it.

Thanks, but ... what about the bank that was supposed to buy it?

The damn bank, said Tanya, decided to change its name to North-South Bank!

So they don't want the painting?

That's right.

...And that's why I want to give it to *you*.

It's thoughtful on your part, but where would I hang it?

On your wall.

I'd have to move the rug that's already there...

Well, then, on the other wall.

It won't fit.

How do you know?

Because it's way too big.

Look do you want it or not?

I smiled again.

The man looked at me and then suddenly became silent and I understood that my smile had slighted him. I started to say something to right the situation, but didn't know what to say. Awkwardly, neither of us said a word. He could not move, and I did not know how....

It was Tanya who broke the silence:

A toast! she said and handed each of us a shotglass of vodka: To friendship between nations and peoples of the world!

...Black and white! I offered.

The redhead and I touched glasses. For the first time since I had known him, he smiled. His teeth were sparse and misshapen. Hideously deformed. And despite everything, they meant more to me than any teeth that I had ever seen.

That night it took all three of us to carry the painting to my apartment, first by metro, then by bus, and then the last few feet by foot....

(8)

#205. A passerby with an unlit cigarette in his mouth stops me to ask for a match; I apologize for not smoking and continue on.

#236. Whenever I drink vodka a dry bitterness backs up in my throat. Each time this happens I would give anything to throw up; but I cannot and the poison gurgles precariously and sickeningly between my throat and stomach. I persevere, drinking insistently and with determination.

(9)

(10)

After we had hung the painting in my living room, the redhead went to buy more vodka; Tanya and I sat in my kitchen talking. Tanya began the conversation by asking me about my family, if I had anybody waiting for me back home.

Well, I told her, There's Aunt Helen — but aside from that I really don't have anyone.

No wife?

None.

No girlfriend?

No.

What about your parents?

My father died when I was small...

Oh, I'm sorry... And your mother?

I don't have a mother, I said.

Tanya looked at me strangely, started to say something, but then changed her mind. Grabbing a worn pack of Marlboros, she tapped out a final cigarette and lit up:

Do you miss your Aunt?

Of course.

Do you talk to her often?

Well, yes. Although not as much anymore. We mostly write letters. She calls once a month.

I'll bet she misses you a lot.

She does. She's just waiting for this year to end so that I'll come back home. To stability, green vegetables, things like that.

Tanya laughed:

Just imagine — most Russians are trying to get to America, and here you are doing the opposite!

And at that moment I felt extremely proud: Proud of my poor knowledge of Russian; proud that I had emigrated the wrong way; that I was getting by; proud that I was here, which meant that I had so distanced myself from *there*.

I'm not like most people, I lied.

Tanya was holding her cigarette in between her fingers and with her thumb lightly tapping away flakes of ash:

You know I've been wanting to ask you what ever made you decide to leave America for Russia?

I don't know.

How can you not know?

I'm not sure... I just like the idea of being here.

Yes but there has to be something that brought you...?

Irony... Danger... The Russian circus! She couldn't possibly understand... I myself didn't understand any of it!

...There has to be something that's keeping you?

It's hard to say, I told her, There're a lot of things...

Can you give me an example?

Sure. In fact, I can give you all eleven...

And here I pulled out the sheet of legal paper from my wallet. As I dictated the eleven yellow examples one by one Tanya listened with interest, then asked:

So you're trying to find these words?

No I'm not. The German man said that I shouldn't seek them, that they would come themselves. So I guess I'm just waiting for them to come.

How long do you think you'll wait?

I don't know — as long as it takes I suppose...

Have you found any of these words yet?

Only one.

Really — which one?

When I announced the word, Tanya laughed. Then she flicked another piece of ash from her cigarette:

You should be careful, though.

How do you mean?

You can't express the Russian Soul with words — you can't understand it using logic.

What's that?

Logic?

No, the *Russian Soul*. What is it?

You've never heard the term before?

No, I haven't.

It's difficult to explain...

Can you try, please?

Tanya propped her chin in her hand. She thought deeply and took a long drag of her cigarette. Then, without exhaling, she gave expression to her Russian Soul, the words wispy and white. For a second it swirled in the air, then disappeared.

It's beautiful, I said.

Yes, she said proudly, I guess it is...

Our conversation lulled. Finally, I broke the silence:

Hey Tanya, I said, You know Russian, right?

Of course, she said.

You see I heard a word today and I couldn't find it in the dictionary...

Which word is it?

I'm not sure if I heard it right... just a minute... I wrote it down...!

While I fished through my pockets for the paper, Tanya spoke up:

You know, she said, your Russian has improved noticeably.

Thanks.

No really it seems like you understand most of what we say.

I try, I said and with that I pulled out the paper from my pocket:

There it is! I said, That's the word that I couldn't understand. I'm not sure I spelled it adequately. In any case it wasn't in the dictionary...

And unfolding the crumpled piece of paper, I handed the word to Tanya:

ХУЁПТВОЮМАТЬЛЯЦ

For some time Tanya stared at the paper without reaction. When she looked up at me I noticed that her ears had turned redder than a balance sheet:

Where did you hear that word? she asked.

Standing in line for potatoes. Did I spell it right?

Almost...

Can you tell me what it means?

I can try, if you really want...

I'd appreciate it.

Tanya, after a few moments consideration, crushed out her cigarette in her ashtray:

Okay, she said, Answer me the following question — what do Americans say when something goes unexpectedly wrong?

You mean when something bad happens?

Well, yes. When something goes wrong unexpectedly. What do Americans say in these cases?

I told her.

Good, now what do they say when the exact opposite happens — in other words, what do Americans utter when things go *expectedly* wrong?

What?

What do you say when things go wrong *expectedly*?

I don't know.

Well, Russians do. And so we say x... x...

Хуёптвоюматбляц?

Well, yeah.

Right then the door opened, in walked the redhead with a new bottle of vodka. Brushing the snow off his coat, he set the bottle on the table along with a strange pack of cigarettes and a crumpled wad of rubles.

It's cold out there! he said happily.

We nodded.

The redhead looked at the table:

Has Tanya told you the 'terrible' news yet? he asked.

No, I said, she hasn't.

You haven't?

No, she said, I haven't.

Then, what *have* you been talking about here without me?

Nothing..., said Tanya.

...We've been discussing the Russian Soul, I agreed.

The Russian Soul?

But here Tanya waved off the suggestion:

Oh we were just saying that it's impossible for a foreigner to understand the Russian Soul. That is, without having things go expectedly wrong first.

The redhead nodded compassionately.

Tanya nodded in agreement.

I also nodded:

So what's this 'terrible news'? I asked.

News? What news? Oh yes, *news*...!

And without speaking the man pointed at the table.

(11)

#255. The ruble begins to lose all value versus other currencies (1USD=125RUR). My salary is only one hundred fifty dollars a month but it is paid in dollars; as inflation soars the population around me sinks into poverty. I buy tickets to the Bolshoi Ballet for five cents, to the circus for ten. I have more money than I can possibly spend and flush with shame when passing rows of old women pawning cheese in two-hundred-gram wedges.

(12)

The terrible news was that after many months the Marlboro cigarettes had run out.

The redhead returned to the cheap Prima cigarettes that he had smoked before he met me. He didn't seem to mind the change, but by then Tanya had become used to Marlboro and couldn't bring herself to smoke the filterless Soviet cigarettes. Unfortunately, Tanya's salary was barely enough to live on, so Marlboros were out of the question. The redhead continued to paint pictures but at that time the country didn't even collect taxes... let alone *art*.

I have an idea! I said and before anyone could object I had my scarf on and was out the door. When I came back I put three packs of Marlboros on the table:

How much do I owe you? said the redhead grimly.

Nothing, I answered, I just happened to find these on the street along with a two-hundred-gram wedge of cheese.

You *found* them? Tanya looked at me suspiciously.

That's right, I said, Right there in the middle of the street. And since I don't smoke you might as well take them off my hands.

What about the cheese? said Tanya.

You can keep that too. I'm lactose intolerant! I get violently ill from milk products.

Tanya laughed.

It's true! I reassured her.

Thanks anyway, said the redhead, But I'll smoke these....

And he took the Soviet cigarettes into his hands and looked at me with a look that I would understand only when it was too late.

As we sat around the table, our conversation rose and fell until it settled into a long drawn-out silence. Tanya was smoking a Marlboro. The redhead was smoking Prima. As I did not smoke, my hands were conspicuously free and so I smiled emptihandedly. The awkward stillness lasted a half-minute. Then Tanya's face lit up:

Do you know what we say about these types of silences?

I shook my head.

We say that when there's a long silence like that, you know like the one that we just had... when that happens we say that it means a policeman is being born.

The redhead didn't laugh:

I've heard the same thing about tax inspectors, he said.

Tanya didn't laugh.

Again the conversation died. And again a long drawn-out silence.

Another pause. Another awkward stillness. Maybe she was right? Maybe that's *why there were so many policemen here...?*

The silence lasted an entire precinct, until at last the redhead spoke up:

While I was gone did Tanya ask you the question?

No, I said, she didn't.

You didn't?

No, she said, I didn't.

Should we ask it now? he asked.

Don't ask me, she said turning to me, Ask him...

The man turned to me:

Can I ask you something? he said.

Sure.

Do you mind if we ask you a question? he said.

Of course not, I answered and smiled unsurely at the question.

If you don't want us to ask you the question, Tanya said, just say so.

No really — no problem.... Fire away.

The couple looked at each other cautiously and then back at me. I continued to smile as if to encourage their question. It was the redhead who expressed the words that they, apparently, were both eager to scrape off their chests. As he spoke his eyes sparkled tenderly, but the force of his words knocked the smile from my face:

(13)

#280. I am amazed as old women one after another fall from an apartment window. They fall and fall and when they have stopped falling I take the well-thumbed *Anna Karenina* from the upper shelf of my cabinet. A solar calculator comes with it hitting the floor with a thud. After checking to see that it is working properly, I put it back on the shelf next to the other two calculators.

#285. The ruble continues to fall (1USD=150RUR). By now the monthly salary of a tax inspector is less than the price of a carton of Marlboros. Circus tickets cost between two and three cents but are still considered a luxury. Fifteen-kopeck coins go for three rubles a piece and are sold by men in black leather jackets, leaving old women to pawn cheese in one-hundred-gram wedges. By day I am a rich foreigner frolicking self-consciously in the spoils of inflation. At night I buy cheese that I cannot eat; when my Russian friends talk about politics I try to change the subject.

(14)

Why is it that you smile so much? he said.

What? Me? That's your question?!

The redhead continued:

I think we've known you long enough to be honest with you, he said.

That's right, said Tanya, We wouldn't bring this up if we didn't know you and like you...

That's right, said the man, We were just wondering if you could explain why you smile all the time.

Why I smile? I don't smile all the time.

Actually you do.

No I don't!

Yes you do... you're smiling right now!

I am?

You are.

That's right. You see it's just that sometimes when you smile it makes us feel a bit uncomfortable because we can't understand why you're smiling. It seems false to us.

False?

Yes, as if you don't really mean it. As if that's just the natural condition of your face — a smile. We've been wanting to ask you for some time.

How long was a long time?! How many months had I been smiling in vain?

I don't know, I said, I never really thought about it, I mean I just do it when I think it's right to do it, I mean when I feel like it. I guess it just happens by itself, when I want it to happen.

Do you ever *not* want to smile?

Well, of course I don't smile then. I mean usually, although I guess sometimes I smile then too.

Okay let's take the metro for example. *Nobody* smiles in the metro! But for some reason you do. It's strange for us. Not to mention a bit embarrassing.

It's strange, well, yes it would be strange for people who have never ever smiled at anything in their lives...

Now, don't take this personally, we're just trying to understand your position. You see, if you smile all the time then how is it possible to express true happiness, that is if there's already a smile plastered on your face? How can you express your true emotions through that smile if it never goes away?

I had surprised myself with my own outburst and this made me even more awkward.

But this time I knew how to save the situation:

Where's that vodka? I said.

The man pulled the bottle from the table and filled my glass. Tanya went to the kitchen to get some pickles. When she came back the man raised his vodka, but before we could touch glasses, he stopped:

You know I'm always the one who says the toasts. I think it's about time that you try.

But I don't know how! I protested.

Just say whatever comes to your head.

Whatever comes to my head? Are you sure you want to hear whatever comes to my head?

Absolutely. Just say the first thing. If you think too long then it won't be sincere.

And so sitting there with the glass of vodka in my hand, I said the first sincere words that came into my head:

To vodka! I said.

We touched glasses. And as he knocked back the hundred grams I thought I saw tears form in the redhead's eyes:

To *водка*! he said.

(15)

#292. It is the single happiest day of my life: no one seems to notice that I am a foreigner; no one seems to care; in a store a salesgirl smiles at me for no reason; a friend compliments me on my poor knowledge of Russian; but he does not ask me about blacks; he does not pose any questions that begin with 'Have you read...?'; when I return home the sun is shining; the elevator has been fixed; the lady next door has conceded to take her jars out of the common area; and on my kitchen table there is an unopened bottle of bootleg vodka. And after they are finished — when I have swallowed and re-swallowed the happiest day of my life — I ask myself the question: *In America would I have appreciated such a day?*

(16)

By late winter Tanya had become tired of watching us drink day in and day out:

Why don't we do something different tonight, she said.

Like what? we asked.

Something unusual. Something that we haven't done before.

Like what? we asked.

I don't know. Something we've never even thought about doing.

We could drink *wine*, I said but at this suggestion the redhead looked at me disapprovingly.

We could look for mushrooms, said the redhead.

We've already done that, I countered.

Not at night!

I'm serious, said Tanya, All you guys do is drink.

That's not all, said the redhead, Sometimes we fall down.

But Tanya was not even listening to us: I have an idea..., she said

What's that?

The circus!

The what?

Remember how you once said you'd always wanted to see the Russian circus? Well let's go tonight!

Sounds fine with me, I said.

But the redhead objected:

It's too expensive, he said.

I know, Tanya persuaded, but then how often do we go to the circus?

We never go, he answered, because it's too expensive.

Hey let it be my treat, I offered.

No! said the redhead, We can pay for ourselves: under my bed is some money I've been saving to buy the color white...

Tanya jumped up and down and clapped her hands giddily—Tanya, it should be remembered, was a tax inspector—and excused herself to change clothes. Putting on my jacket I noticed that the redhead wasn't moving:

Aren't you coming? I asked him.

Take your time, he said, she'll be in there for at least a half-hour.

And he poured out another round of vodka.

(17)

#301. My first year in Russia is over: my contract ends. Aunt Helen eagerly makes my flight arrangements back home. She informs me that she has talked to my ex-boss about getting my old job back; he promises three-and-a-half percent more stability. Even my mother has mentioned wanting to see me. But as usual Aunt Helen has been unlucky with her timing. *After yesterday, how could I return?* And besides, I have only found three out of eleven words. My shelf is Marlboroless, but full of pantyhose and lubricated condoms. Not to mention the German-English dictionary! Aunt Helen cries when I try to explain all this. The institute extends my contract for another year on the condition that I will be more conscientious toward my work. That night I mark the milestone alone in my room with a bottle of vodka and a married woman who is finally beginning to speak to me.

(18)

An hour later Tanya came out; the redhead and I had already finished off half the bottle.

Let's go! she said.

Let's go, we said.

(19)

#306. Over coffee a friend asks if I am bothered by the smoke from his cigarette; I smile falsely and say, no.

#311. The ruble falls (1USD=250RUR)...

#335. A passerby with an unlit cigarette in between his fingers stops me to ask for a match; I apologize profusely for not smoking and continue on.

#340 ...and falls (1USD=480RUR) ...

(20)

By the time Tanya had changed clothes, it was early spring and the entire city was covered with wet. Rain rolled through the streets and into the underpass near the circus, filling it with water.

Tanya's mood had changed as well, and now she was obviously frustrated. Her makeup had been smudged by the rain. Her evening dress was sprinkled with brown mud. Standing in the ankle-deep water, she held up the sides of her dress above her high-heels and looked at the redhead angrily. She started to speak, but he knew her well enough to anticipate her words:

How was I supposed to know? he said and pointed at the flooded underpass.

You're always taking me the wrong way, she answered, Always...!

The redhead groaned:

In America do you have impossible women, too?

Yes, I said no longer smiling.

Tanya brushed off a slice of mud from her dress:

Oh so *I'm* the one who's impossible!

The redhead shrugged his shoulders but didn't smile.

You know I read an article, said Tanya, that in America seventy-eight percent of all women are feminists. Is that true?

I'm not so sure, I said, that figure seems awfully high...

But I *read* it!

When she spoke Tanya looked at me convincingly.

Well, if you read it then I guess...

In our country, she continued, we don't have feminists but women often make more money than their husbands. In America is that normal, that is, for a woman to earn more than her husband?

It's not unheard of, I said.

...And then for her to come home and take care of the children? Do American wives have to take care of the children after working all day?

We don't have children, said the redhead.

I shifted uncomfortably once again. Tanya shook off the muddy water from her shoes:

You are absolutely right, she answered, But that is no thanks to you. When's the last time you even *thought* about using...

She did not finish. A voice had interrupted her from behind:

What a nightmare! it said.

The voice belonged to an old woman who had approached the puddle and was looking at the collection of water in disbelief. Shaking her head, she sighed hopelessly:

What a nightmare! said the woman and looked at us, What a nightmare!

Just then, from behind, a man came up to study the puddle. He looked at the water deeply and seriously, stroking his beard, appraising the situation:

What a horror! he said.

The old woman agreed with him but objected anyway:

It's a nightmare! she said.

A horror, he answered.

A nightmare!

Horror!

Nightmare...!

I turned to my friends. In the background the woman and man could be heard sighing at each other:

Maybe we should leave, I suggested, You know we could go back up and try to find another way. I'm sure there has to be an underpass that's not so flooded.

But before they could answer, a second beardless man came up and getting a good look at the scene, sighed deeply at the redhead:

What an absolute lack of light!

The redhead shrugged his shoulders at the man. Tanya picked at the mud on her dress. I stood deciding whether to smile. Only the heated words of the arguing couple could be heard.

Standing there, each of us tried to cope with the situation as best we could. The second man was the first to give in, shrugging his shoulders sadly and setting off dejectedly for home. The old woman shook her head. The other man suggested laying rocks and boards across the water, and left to find some. But as soon as he returned, we recognized his attempt to be futile: the water was too deep, and although the man did his best, the boards floated away and the large rock simply sunk like a stone to the bottom of the puddle, slowly, until it was wet and out of sight.

Maybe we could just leave and find another way, I said but no one was listening to me. The old woman least of all; she was busy coping in her own way:

What a nightmare! she offered, What a nightmare! Things didn't used to be like this in *the old days*.

First of all, objected the man, it's not a nightmare it's a horror. And second of all, what 'old days' are you talking about?

3 — 1807

The good old days. Before ... before...

Disgustedly, the woman swept her arm around to indicate what, in her opinion, had come after *before*: the puddle, the mud, the dejected back of the man who had remained circusless, the foreigner in expensive blue jeans.

Before *what*? the man insisted.

Before ... before...

The woman seemed like she would burst, but then she drove her point home:

Before Gorbachev! said the woman, Before that bastard and all his ideas! He's the one that sold our country. He's the one that caused Russia to become Russia...

Tanya could stand it no more and again jumped in:

If you could be so kind, she said angrily, as to tell me exactly what it is that he ruined? What thriving country did he spoil? At your age, grandma, you should know better than anyone — Just remember how things used to be. At least now we can say that we have food in the stores. Now we can travel. Now our children have a future....

(21)

#359. I lose my visa.

(22)

Future? said the woman, What future? In the old days we knew better than to talk about the future — there was no future, but I always got my pension. And that was all I needed. And then next thing you know reforms here, reforms there. Gorbachev this, Gorbachev that. And what did it get us in the end? What does a poor pensioner like me get from it? Not my pension — that's for sure — I haven't received that for three months. And I'll be lucky to get it at all. And even if I do get my pension, what can it buy me? a few small wedges of cheese? a head of cabbage? If I weren't still healthy enough to plant my own potatoes outside my yard, if I didn't grow my own carrots in the vacant lot across from my apartment building, if it weren't for the jars of marinated cabbage under my bed... then what would I have? What other alternative would there be but to just lay myself down quietly and...

She did not finish because suddenly from the other side of the tunnel we heard a loud echoing voice shouting, Wait! Wait! and watched in amazement as a man came running at full stride through the water. In the dim light we could see his silhouette expanding. He was trailing something behind him and as he ran, raising his knees up to his chest, chunks of water splashed around him. When he got closer, he slowed to a walk and swung a small wagon into view:

The man was wearing waterproof boots and for a fee, he said, he would transport us in his wagon dry and happy to the other end of the underpass.

When the old woman heard the price she shook her head:

What a nightmare! she said.

The man next to her also shook his head, but took exception to her words:

What a horror, he said.

As the two argued, I reached into my pocket for my wallet, which at that moment contained approximately two hundred fifty dollars and two kopecks.

What are you doing? said the redhead.

I want to pay him.

Did you hear how much he's charging?

It's not a lot.

He's a swindler!

But he has water-proof boots.

He should be ashamed of himself asking for so much money.

Look It's no big deal. I can pay for it, It's really not a lot of money.

Maybe where you're from it's not a lot of money, but here...

...Let me pay, I said and opened my wallet....

Don't let him! Tanya told her husband, Don't let him pay!

But why?! I have dollars. It's not a lot of money for me. It's nothing....

Out of the question, said Tanya, Paying is a man's job.

I looked at her inquisitively.

He's not a man? the redhead protested.

Well no he's not.

I'm not?

No, she said, you're not — you're a foreigner.

I felt puzzled for my masculinity, and slighted that she had called me a foreigner. The redhead felt even worse; reluctantly he opened his wallet as if to pay.

But when he separated the wallet it became clear to everyone that he did not have even close to what the man was charging.

I'll get it, I said decisively and handed the man in boots a worn one-dollar bill.

The man's eyes lit up.

...And keep the change! I said to make my point.

The man thanked me profusely.

And with that Tanya climbed into the wagon. She did not thank me. The redhead thanked me weakly, but then became silent; he did not utter a single word the rest of the evening....

At the circus the three of us sat in silence. The performance was tense and seemed to last forever. Clowns ran after each other. Big men lifted big things. Black bears stood upside down.

(23)

#402... and falls (1USD=820RUR)...

(24)

Back at their apartment, Tanya went straight to bed — it was late and unlike the two of us she had a job that she could not be late for. In her absence the redhead grew sullen. Our conversation went from pink to gray, and then ultimately, to black. Sitting in the small kitchen, he lit cigarette after cigarette — always Prima — picking the stray pieces of tobacco from the tip of his tongue.

You know what I think sometimes? he asked and didn't wait for me to answer: Sometimes I think about getting out of this place.

Yeah me too, I said, that damn faucet...

No, he said, I don't mean *this* place, I mean this *place*.

What do you mean?

Leaving Russia.

What!

The man blew out a cloud of smoke.

But why? I asked.

There's no future here. Not for Tanya. Not for me. Who needs tax inspectors in this country? Who needs artists?

Don't be silly, I said trying to comfort him, There's not a country in the world that doesn't need tax inspectors.

The man winced.

Besides, where would you go?

Where would I go...

The redhead was squinting his eyes from the smoke. After a long pause he took a deep drag on the cigarette and answered in a soft voice, his words as gray as change:

I'd go *there*.

I looked over my shoulder but *there* was not there:

Where's that? Where *is* there?

What difference does it make? There is *not here*. There is... *there*!

And the man smiled again, this time hopelessly. As if to show how far this distance really was, he smiled in a way that I never could.

Hey don't think about it, I said.

But the redhead was inconsolable. Through the smoke forming between us, I looked at the man who had shown me so much:

Really, I said, It's not so bad. It's not as bad as it seems. Just remember everything that's right with the world, just be thankful for everything you have to be thankful for...

And I held up my glass of vodka.

Again it seemed that tears were welling up in his eyes, but this time of a different kind:

The bottle's empty, said the man and put it on the floor.

It is, isn't it. Not a problem... I'll go get some more.

If it's okay I'd like to be alone for a while.

No that's all right, I'll be fine. I have a bottle at home...

And with that I took my fat book, my sunglasses, and my overflowing wallet, and stepped outside into the warm summer night.

(25)

#410. For Russia 1993 was a turbulent year.

Inflation continued to ravage the savings of many Russians, turning pensioners into paupers and liberals into conservatives.

In the summer of this year (1USD=1050RUR) it was announced that currency reform would be implemented under the auspices of former president Mikhail Gorbachev's successor. In other words, the money now in circulation would soon be worthless. *This time* officially. Fearing the loss of their savings and desperate to obtain tangible goods before it was too late, people resorted to drastic measures. Some bought live chickens for ten times their real value. Others, meanwhile, were less fortunate and had to buy live chickens for fifteen times their real value. Still others — those high-ranking officials with political clout and reliable connections in banks — were able to reap huge profits by *selling* live chickens for ten to fifteen times their real value.

The city was in a panic. Chickens were everywhere. Thousands of people lost their life savings. Hundreds lost their savings *again.* Again the unrepeatable was being repeated.

A crisis was inevitable.

In October of that year, tanks were ordered into the center of Moscow. This time they were Russian tanks. But they were just as formidable. And this time they did not remain silent. Sadly, the country was divided. *And just when it seemed that Russia had finally become Russia...!*

By now I had Russian friends, most of whom did not have blue passports. Danger, I realized then, was not a game. It is as serious as slavery. As irreversible as emigration.

This time I did not grin. There was nothing to savor. I had lived in Russia too long to be smug.

And now I had something to lose.

(26)

...On the *other* hand, weddings and tanks have the same basic purpose: that is, to force change; or at least the prospect for change. For six and a half years it seemed that I might never have to attend a wedding. But now I understand that like everything it was only a matter of time.

(27)

#421. At a fancy hotel the Russian guard at the door assumes that I am Russian and stops me before I can enter; refusing to smile, I flash him the thumb-worn *Anna Karenina* and enter unimpeded.

#430. A passerby with an unlit cigarette dangling from his mouth stops me to ask for a match; I light his cigarette with a new disposable lighter.

(28)

Once outside, my thoughts rambled and I found myself wandering lost among *the* and *a*, somewhere between Primas and Marlboros, but still closer to the American Dream than to the Russian Soul.

But what was *the Russian Soul? And where could I find it? And why were Russians so convinced that they were the most spiritual people in the world... that they were the smartest? Didn't they realize that Americans were the smartest? Granted, Russia had invented vodka; but it was America that had invented peanut butter! Sure, they had a rich tradition of poetry; but we had an even richer tradition of toilet paper. And for raw ingenuity, could the Moscow metro — even though it was the world's finest — really be compared with the feat of engineering that produced American democracy...?*

The soles of my shoes burned as I walked on the blazing sidewalk. In the distance I saw a kiosk that looked to be open.

...But maybe I was wrong! Maybe Russians really were the smartest people on earth? After all, it had been proven statistically that all important inventions had been created either by Russians, or — in the few remaining cases — by Americans who had immigrated from Russia. And that despite what I had been told for years it wasn't America that had played the decisive role in all world wars; now I was learning that it was Russia who had suffered relentlessly, thereby forcing the enemy under its own weight to become soft and thin. In truth it was Russia, not America, that was responsible for western civilization...

I stopped before a kiosk:

Two bottles of vodka, I told the man behind the metal bars and he handed me a tall bottle whose label slipped off when I grabbed it.

(29)

#456. Between lessons a Russian student asks if she may smoke; I laugh without smiling and say, Go ahead I'm used to it! I light her cigarette with my disposable lighter.

(30)

I shoved one bottle in each pocket and started back.

But wait a minute..., I thought, *Russia isn't even* in *the West...!*

I stopped in my tracks. Something had occurred to me. I went back to the man who had given me the bottle of vodka:

Do you have any cigarettes? I asked.

The man pointed at the half of his display that was filled with cigarettes. In my haste I had only seen the half filled with alcohol.

Primas? he asked.

No no that's the whole point. I need Marlboros. Only Marlboros. He can buy Primas himself.

And counting out all the money in my wallet, I bought forty-eight packs of Marlboro cigarettes.

(31)

#460. I watch with horror as a married woman throws herself in front of a moving train. I have lived in Russia long enough to understand what it means, and the image stays in my mind for many months. Then I start *War and Peace*.

#463. At home my future ex-landlord asks me why, if I don't smoke, do I carry a lighter at all times; the question strikes me as logical and within a week I have begun smoking.

#533. But I still can't get used to vodka. The bitter dryness backs up and I do not fight it as much as encourage it. As if to spite me, it remains in my throat. I vow that I will learn to love vodka even if it injures me. I drink relentlessly. I disappear for days at a time. My teaching job is in jeopardy, and still I cannot make myself vomit. I drink anyway, stubbornly and persistently.

(32)

The redhead's apartment was a ways from the metro, and walking the distance I began to notice how short the days had grown. How cold it now was. How badly underdressed I had become: the end of my second end of summer. *Why had the redhead mentioned leaving? Was it a joke? Or was he serious? It did seem that his frame of mind had darkened lately. That during the last few months he had become as icy as a summer shower. For some reason his eyes had stopped sparkling altogether. He hadn't smiled since he'd smiled hopelessly. He hadn't smiled hopefully since we toasted his picture. But why? What had happened during the last year, aside from knowing me, to make him so discouraged...?*

(33)

#544... and falls (1USD=1510RUR)...

(34)

...It was as if he were bearing some sort of deep-seated grudge. Against me. Against everything. Hadn't he told me once that he resented America with it's blue passports, green money, and black problems? Hadn't he stopped painting? Hadn't he begun to grit his teeth when speaking about the number three? But most of all, it seemed, hadn't he grown to hate the country that Russia was becoming. Even more — it turned out — than the country it had once been! Could that be it? Could it be that some part of him had said farewell to the country that we had all naively believed it would become....?

(35)

#560. On the way home I am passed by a wedding procession — three ticker-taped Zhigulis filled with laughing teenagers in black and white. I remember the superstition that this will inevitably bring misfortune.

(36)

When I arrived back to the redhead's apartment it was a gray autumn morning. Tanya had already gone to work and I found the redhead sitting alone in his kitchen. When I put the pile of cigarettes on the table, the redhead did not thank me. He just picked through them distractedly and listlessly. He had lit a cigarette of his own but had seemingly forgotten about it; its ash crept toward his unfiltered fingers and I waited for it to fall. As he spoke he tapped the ash into an old coffee can:

Why do you always bring us cigarettes?

I know that you like them.

If you wanted, you could bring Primas.

But I know that Tanya...

Take them back! We don't need them, Take them back.

With a swipe of his arm he flung the cigarettes off the table onto the floor.

Then without warning the man's voice became calmer than I had ever seen it, his words slow and carefully chosen, as if he had spoken them many times before:

You think you're better than me because you have money, he said.

It was not a question, so I did not answer. Through the window a light rain could be seen settling over the city and I was thankful that I had brought my umbrella.

In truth, the man never actually pronounced these words; and the words he did pronounce were spoken over the course of several months. But the result was the same: the man never called me after that; Tanya never called. Suddenly and unjustly, I had lost my first Russian friend....

I had lost my first friends because of Marlboros.

(37)

#561. In the middle of winter I leave unexpectedly for America. Two weeks later I hang up the phone, still ringing, still unanswered.

#590... and falls (1USD=2040RUR) ...and falls (1USD=2810RUR)...

#613. Strangers compliment me on my Russian, saying that my accent is almost undetectable. Now I know Russian from *A* to *Я* *with the exception of X*. In other words, my speech is correct but dull, sickeningly proper, and unnecessarily cumbersome as if I were the novelist Lev Tolstoy struggling to carry an oversized mattress; for practice I buy Vladimir Vysotsky's cassettes and memorize the lyrics.

#636. ...and falls (1USD=3780RUR)...

#697. A letter arrives from America postmarked more than three years earlier. No one can believe it when I tell them. Some Russian students suggest that it is unprecedented, but I remind them that there have been cases when letters were received up to twenty and thirty years after they were mailed. They laugh and say, Those letters were probably mailed to Russia, too!

#732. The ruble falls and falls then holds steady then falls then holds steady then falls again before holding and then falling. (1USD=4850RUR). Prices climb so high versus the dollar that I have forgotten that they were once cheap. The price of a red rose rises to almost ten dollars. A taxi ride can cost up to fifty if it's from the airport. A cab *to* the airport is almost as expensive and so most people prefer to take the metro.

(38)

The calculators were my downfall.

(#80; #89; #661; #662)

I gave the first one to a student of mine from the adult class. She was intelligent, polite, and loved to talk in English about a wide range of subjects: everything from Russian literature to American literature. Sitting in my cold kitchen, she would confide to me in English the deepest darkest secrets of her Soul. In English that improved daily, she would pour out her heart and like a trolleybus driver I would offer my cup. We talked and talked and talked... our conversations sometimes carrying us through the night and into my morning classes. Of course we would do other things. But mostly we would talk, that is to say, she would talk in English and I would correct her mistakes without thinking. In return she would talk some more, and ignore my shortcomings in *the other things*. This continued for several weeks until one day when it felt just right she whispered, Okay!

The months passed, or more truthfully, they flew by like an eagle. It seemed that it would last forever. And in fact everything went smoothly until she became fluent and stopped making mistakes. I stopped correcting her. She stopped coming over. I stopped inviting her. She stopped accepting. Not long after that we realized something was wrong. Not long after *that* I realized we had broken up.

Alone in my room I became obsessed with the loss. Gone were the conversations in English — the forgotten article here; a dangling participle there; a 'Sit please, here...'; a 'go to there'.... Holding an inverted calculator in my hand, I typed 5507 and pondered the letters until the night erased them.

And in the morning, disgusted with myself, I threw the calculator against a wall that was still blank but would soon look heavy and imposing....

A long time passed before I could even think about solar calculators.

But then, just when everything seemed as hopeless as history, it happened: I fell in love again (1USD=4920RUR). This woman was also intelligent and polite and loved her solar calculator so much that I gave her another one which she loved even more. I loved her. And she loved me. She also loved restaurants. And taxis. Not to mention European clothes and red roses that were longer than my salary. By now prices were rising fast. But, thankfully, the dollar was keeping pace. Spring was just beginning. I was in love with someone who was in love with someone who was in love...

It seemed that it would last forever.

But then without warning the inevitable occurred: *the ruble stabilized*! Everyone was in shock. The dollar lost its value versus the ruble... It's complicated, something about a corridor, something about... I don't understand it myself! All I know is that right after this she left me for a man who had a thick wad of hard currency and whose accent was stronger than mine — in other words, a German.

I was despondent. Desolated. I waited anxiously and desperately for the ruble to drop. But to no avail. I was lost. I was newly poor. And now, once again, I was alone. My world — the one that I had known — had been turned upside-down like a cheap solar calculator....

It would be years before I smiled again.

(39)

#756. My life in Russia (in order of importance):

1991	1992	1993	1994	1995	1996	1997
1.Democracy	1.Love	1.Danger	1.(tie) Irony	1.Love	1.Democracy	1.Irony
2.Danger	2.Democracy	2.Irony	Love	2.Irony	2.Irony	2.Marriage
3.Irony	3.(tie) Irony	3.Love	3.Danger	3.Danger	3.(tie) Love	3.Democracy
4.Love	Logic	4.Democracy	4.Logic	4.Logic	Marriage	4.(tie) Danger
5.Marriage	5.Danger	5.Marriage	5.Democracy	5.Marriage	5.Danger	Love
6.Logic	6.Marriage	6.Logic	6.Marriage	6.Democracy	6.Logic	6.Logic

#831. During tea a Russian acquaintance, after crushing out her cigarette, looks at me blankly without saying a word; I grab the heavy glass ashtray and throw it crashing through my apartment window.

#850. I wander along Tverskaya ulitsa by myself. The street has been cleared so that a million people can surround me. Some are laughing. Others are laughing and kicking empty cans along the emptied street. I look at the faces of the people approaching. Now and then they look back. They are beautiful faces but I will never know them. They pass behind me and I do not look back. The faces, the people, the voices offering words that have kept me for six and a half years, they are all fading fast. And by the time I reach the Kremlin they are already gone.

(40)

It was early one winter morning when I stood outside my apartment door fumbling with my keys. Inside I could hear the phone ringing. My hands were trembling and I could feel my body swaying from the bitter dryness in my throat. The key was so small and at that moment my hands were so large. I forced the key into its hole but it would not turn. Inside the phone was still ringing.

Standing in the quietness of the empty hallway, I felt my head pound. I had been drinking all night and had stumbled home from somewhere. Somehow. It seemed like I hadn't slept for days, and at that moment my one wish in the world was to lie on my bed and to fall into a deep forgiving slumber.

The door would not open.

With absurd concentration, I focused my eyes on the key that was in my shaking hand. I took it out and tried it again. But again it would not open the lock. Once it fell to the concrete floor and it seemed the noise would wake every one of my neighbors. I looked around guiltily but no one came out. Still, the key would not go into its hole. And the more I tried to make it fit, the more it would not go in.

Disheartened and heavy, I slumped against the door. But the key was just as stubborn.

How long had I been standing here? How many times had I dropped the key?

How much longer would this scene continue?

Mercifully, the lock turned, the door clicked open and I walked into the lifeless apartment. I took off my hat and threw it on the floor. The phone was ringing loudly, almost pleadingly. I unwrapped my scarf and took off my jacket, dropping them where they fell. In the darkness I walked to the window and opened the curtains to let the moonlight in.

The apartment was just as it had been.

I fell onto the bed and only then took the phone's receiver in my hand. It was Aunt Helen; her voice was cracking:

Where the hell have you been?

Fine thank you. And you?

Don't get smart with me. I asked you where you've been?

Out, I said.

For three days? You've been *out* for three goddamn days?

Aunt Helen had never spoken to me like this. Ever. Her voice was hoarse. Something was wrong.

What do you mean three days? I asked.

I've been calling you every hour for three days, that's what. And all you can say is that you were *out*!

Had it been that long?!

So I was gone for a while. What's the big deal?

I'll tell you what the big deal is. The big deal is that you disappear for God knows how long and... and don't give a damn if someone has to... I mean... I called your landlord but no one there speaks English... I called the institute and they say you don't work there anymore... I even had the operator try to call you...

All right, all right, I'm here now. I'm listening.

Aunt Helen started to cry but all I could think about was my splitting headache and the dry bitterness in my throat.

I'm sorry, she said, It's not important, I'm sorry I yelled at you. It's just that...

It's okay

I didn't want to yell, but I've been calling for three days...

If you're calling to ask about vegetables you'll be happy to know...

She's gone.

What? Who?

Your mother, she died. Last week. I've been trying to call you for three days...

How? I asked, but could not have heard the answer over the deafening sound of my thoughts. *My mother died which means she is dead My mother is dead.*

On the phone the static rasped between us.

The funeral's on Monday, said Aunt Helen, You are coming aren't you?

I was as silent as sleep.

This Monday..., she repeated, ...As in: the day after your tomorrow.

Is it open casket? I asked.

Yes, said Aunt Helen.

Inside my apartment the stale air circled onto itself, lazy and forgotten. It was last week's air. I set the phone on the bed and walked over to the window. The metal latch felt cold on my fingers and gave with a loud click. The window groaned open, curtains flew up to the ceiling. I had forgotten to shut the front door and the wind blew right through the apartment, sending papers curling into the air. Light flakes of snow washed over my face like good news.

In the distance I heard the front door slam shut. Everything settled back into place.

When I picked up the phone Aunt Helen's voice was no longer hoarse. It was composed and tender like my mother's had once been:

The funeral, she said, is on Monday. Are you coming?

(41)

#976. Finally, after six and a half years, it takes a wedding for me to realize that I will never truly love vodka; not long after this I leave Russia forever.

* * * * * * * * * *

Book 5. Sleep

(1)

It could have been different.

Not the end of course. And not the beginning. But the middle, the part that is most important, could have been so much different if we had wanted it to be.

For my part I could have tried to understand her. I could have told her — I hadn't done it since my eleventh new year — how much she really meant to me. At any point I could have called — she didn't move around so much the last few years — and said, 'Hey Mom, you know what? You were a terrible mother,' — she knew this — 'In fact you still are a terrible mother. But you're *my* terrible mother. And that means more to me than danger; more, even, than irony.'

And when she attempted in her own way to do the same, I could have tried to see; I could have listened.

Now it was too late, the story's conclusion as much a given as gravity. *With one word, with one sound I could keep it all thousands of miles away; it was as easy as doing nothing. As easy as doing what I had done many times before. And all of it would stay* there, *which at that moment seemed so so far away from* here...

But something was troubling me. Something I had missed. Aunt Helen was waiting on the other end of the phone for my answer and as I listened to the distance rasping between us I tried to remember our conversation, something that had seemed so important but had been lost amid the words.

Was it something I had said? Was it something I had meant to say? Or was it something I had said but not meant... Or meant but never said?

And then I remembered. *The casket! Why had I asked about it? Could it possibly matter now that she was gone? Was it the vodka speaking? Or had I understood something in the question?*

My clock showed 3:15 a.m. It was Saturday.

The casket was still open. It would be open until Monday morning, and then it would close forever. It was my last chance...

Tuesday would be too late.

(2)

4:26 a.m.

Lying on my bed I fought the dry bitterness in my throat. My head was still pulsating to the sound of my heart and more than anything I needed to rest; it was the only thing that could help me now. But if my eyes were to close, they would not open in time: Aunt Helen had reserved a ticket on the very last Aeroflot flight and I needed to stay awake long enough to buy it.

You'll have other days to rest, I told myself, *other weeks, months, years... But for these next few hours — for the hours that separate now from there — for this short eternity you need to stay awake!*

But vodka can be as stubborn as a lock; and all my efforts could not keep my eyes from becoming heavier. *Maybe it wouldn't be such a bad idea to take a quick nap? Just for a few hours, just enough to get rid of the headache and the bitter dryness in my throat. I'd wake up, wouldn't I?*

Wouldn't I...?

Angry at these thoughts, I forced myself to get up from the bed. My legs wavered. My head throbbed. As I rose so did the dry bitterness, and I staggered into the bathroom where I crouched over the edges of the toilet waiting for the nausea to pass. I wanted to throw up but could not. My stomach turned and twisted and I rested my cheek heavily against the cold rim of the bowl, a half-year of neglect carving into my sweaty skin.

I held my breath and checked my thoughts. Helplessly. I was afraid to move, afraid that if I did, if I made the slightest of movements, if I thought the wrong thoughts, something would happen. It might be vomit; it might be something even better. But in any case it would be like nothing I had known.

And so I stayed there. Nauseus. Crouching.

Motherless.

(3)

5:07 a.m.

When I was able to stand up, I made my way to the tub, where in a dazed state I lay fragilly under a shower of hot water.

At first the water pulled my stomach from side to side. The alcohol boiled and bubbled inside me. But then, just when vomit seemed inevitable, it subsided. The nausea passed. The dry bitterness moved further down my throat to where it could be overlooked.

Outside, the city was between tomorrows. The sun had not yet risen. The night had yet to succumb. On the streets someone was scraping the winter from a sidewalk.

(4)

6:15 a.m.

An hour came and went. The scraping stopped. The sun was emerging.

Despite the lack of rest, my headache, the days spent drinking, and the news which was still somewhere very far from me, my mind seemed to take heart. To stay awake I made a schedule for the day:

1. 09:00 — Call Aeroflot/ confirm address (which metro?)
2. 10:00 — Go to institute/ pick up final pay ($450 for Jan.)
3. 12:00 — Go to Aeroflot/buy ticket (Cost:$795 — CONFIRM!; must bring passp. & visa)
4. 14:00 — Home.
   — Pack suitcase (toothbrush, jeans, etc.)
   —
5. 18:00 — Bed. (Set alarm 5:00 for dep. @ 9:15 on Aeroflot. — check-in two hours before dep.)

At about seven o'clock the effects of the shower began to wear off and I felt myself drifting away. But again I did not give in. I took another shower, this time a cold one.

(5)

9:00 a.m.

At exactly nine o'clock I tried to call Aeroflot to find out where I should pick up my tickets. But the phone was continually busy and when the call did go through no one answered. I counted the rings to one hundred. Then two hundred. At three hundred I laid the phone's receiver on the bed to pick up later.

By now the effects of the second shower were wearing off and the blood was throbbing even harder in my head. A Russian friend had once insisted that the best cure for a hangover was a shot of whatever you were drinking the night before. Back then I had smiled incredulously. Now, I filled a teacup to its brim with cranberry vodka and drank it without smiling.

When it was time to leave I stood holding the door open. Something wasn't right. There was something I was forgetting. I tried to remember what it might be. A sickening vague feeling. *What was it?* I patted my pockets. I searched my memory. Once again I double-checked my list. Everything seemed to be in order. Still, the vague feeling....

I closed the door. Trying to ignore my premonition I left for the institute where, I hoped, my last month's salary would be waiting for me.

(6)

9:50 a.m.

My salary for January was actually due to be picked up several weeks ago but after I was fired I had told Erica Martin that she could keep her money and had even suggested a safe place for it — a place, I had told her then, where only trolleybus drivers would find it.

But now my wallet contained only three hundred fifty-one dollars and two kopecks; in order to buy my ticket I would have to ask for my salary.

The trolleybus drivers! ... They were the ones that would do me in!

Of my three supervisors, Erica Martin was the most feared. At birth Erica had been loud, pink, and painfully Canadian; since then she'd tanned slightly. During three and a half years in Moscow she'd managed to learn as many Russian words and wasn't interested in associating with anyone who knew more; she hated vodka; she stubbornly refused all cigarettes, especially the filterless Soviet ones; her two favorite phrases were 'God I hate this country!' and 'Damn Russians!' and for some reason — usually on Tuesdays — she enjoyed repeating them over and over and over.

With Erica it would be hopeless. She was not the type to forget offenses, especially those concerning trolleybus drivers.

Phil was the absolute opposite of Erica; he relished the role of 'foreigner who *despite everything* loves Russia.' He was proud that he loved the country and did so conspicuously; he spoke fluent Russian, even when other people were speaking to him in English; he quoted Pushkin; smoked Primas; bragged about the Russian Soul as if it were his own; he laughed louder at Russian jokes than at English ones, and although his passport was blue, he seemed to respect poetry; *his* favorite phrase — which he had the habit of returning to on Tuesdays — was 'God I love this country!' And so, as annoying as this love was, Phil represented my best bet to get my salary.

Whereas Erica and Phil were exact opposites, Dave — my third supervisor — was the exact opposite of them both; aloof and awkward, he criticized Erica for criticizing, yet at the same time could never forgive Phil for forgiving; he studied Russian, but poorly; he drank vodka with juice; he smoked Marlboros, but only when it counted; rumor even had it he was writing a biography of Gorbachev. At work Dave was widely misunderstood, partly because he had no favorite phrases, and partly because Tuesday was his day off....

In the midst of all this, I began to spend less effort at work and more time at home with my Russian friends, my books, and my bootleg vodka. In effect I fired myself. Everyone knew it. It was only a matter of deciding which supervisor would tell me. And when that long-awaited day was at hand — Erica volunteered immediately — the only person surprised by the news was Aunt Helen.

(7)

10:03 a.m.

When I walked into the office at the institute it was a little after ten. The Russian secretary, a prissy middle-aged woman who liked me exactly as much as did her boss — who was Erica Martin — raised her eyebrows as if to say *Well, look who's here!*

Good morning, I said.

A little early for you, isn't it? she answered.

I just wanted to show you that I can be an earlybird if I want to.

Your morning students might have appreciated some of that consideration.

The secretary had been working with Erica for all three and a half years and agreed with her in everything: sometimes — usually on Tuesdays — she would utter her two favorite English phrases which were 'God I hate this country!' and 'Damn Russians!'

Look let's not get into that, okay? I need to know who I can talk to about my pay for last month.

You'll have to talk to Erica. She handles those questions.

What about Phil or Dave?

No. Only Erica. She's in her office now if you want to talk to her.

As I walked down the long corridor I remembered the very first time I met with Erica in her office. She had explained the job to me and made it all seem so exciting. She had believed then that I would be a faithful employee and a good teacher and now for the first time I felt a pang of guilt.

I knocked on her door and walked in without waiting for a response.

Well look who's here! she said.

Hello, Erica.

To what do I owe this honor?

She knew damn well 'to what'!

I just thought I'd drop by to see how *you* are, you know, shoot the breeze, reminisce about old times.

That's nice.

There was a pause, and it became clear that Erica was enjoying the moment. She was acting as if we actually would have a pleasant conversation about old times.

I looked at her. And she at me. Only one of us was smiling.

So how are you? I asked with mock interest.

I'm fine, thanks. And you?

Never been better, I said.

Good to hear it, she nodded and then: How's that friend of yours, the one that used to wait for you between the breaks... with red hair... what's his name?

The redhead? He's fine. I mean I guess he's fine. We haven't spoken for more than a year.

Is that right? What happened?

Marlboros.

Erica shook her head empathetically:

That's too bad, she said.

Yes it is....

There was a silence. I tapped my foot on her floor. She did the same.

Damn! She wasn't going to let me off the hook; she wanted me to ask for the money.

Look, Erica, I need to talk to you.

I'm all ears...

...Something came up. I need to have my pay for January.

Your what?

You know what I'm talking about — my pay for January.

Oh that! If I'm not mistaken you said you didn't want it.

Not exactly. What I actually said was...

Now it was Erica's turn to smile.

...Look it's not important. The important thing is that I need the money. I need it today.

Sorry.

What do you mean *sorry*?

It's too late. The payroll for January's already been sent back to Accounting. You'll have to wait until next month.

What are you talking about? You sent my money all the way to Accounting?

That's right. By trolleybus.

You bitch!

Erica smiled deeply:

That's not going to help you, she said.

Erica was staring at me coldly and for the first time I felt the hopelessness of the situation:

I'm sorry — I didn't mean it. It's just that I need the money. I need to buy a ticket to America. It's an emergency. I mean, you know it has to be important if I'm coming to you like this...

Can't help you. If you were still working here I could give you an advance, but since you're not...

Erica's words hit my heart like a fist.

...Since you're no longer an employee there's nothing I can do.

Wait a minute... What's an advance? I asked.

It's when you receive money ahead of time against *future* paydays. But you won't be having any more of those, will you?

Well no, but can't you give me the money as if it were an advance and then just pay it back when the next salary comes?

We don't do that.

Well, do you think that you could do it just this once.

With you it's always *just this once*. Why should you be an exception? You think that you can always do things your own way and everyone else will just bend over backwards for you! The students come on time but *you* can show up at your leisure. Like, Here I am: God's gift to teaching!

Look, I'm not asking you to bend over. I'm just asking you to give me the money you owe me for January. I earned it and you owe it to me.

Earned it? You call what you did 'earning'...? You couldn't even explain the difference between *high* and *tall*!

Dammit Erica, can't you see it's important? Look at me — I'm practically groveling at your feet?

The room was still and in the silence she let out an exasperated sigh. Her pride had been satisfied. The trolleybus had been buried:

I'd need to talk to Dave. He's the one who gives authorization for advances....

Can you do what it takes, please? I have to buy my ticket today.

She looked at me distrustfully and so I added:

...I need to buy it by four o'clock... Today's Saturday and the Aeroflot office closes early.

(8)

11:05 a.m.

After I had received the cash, I stood in the lobby putting on my coat. Both Erica and the secretary were regarding me curiously, as if they wanted me to share my emergency with them. But I didn't have that much good will. Good-bye Erica, I said and thought, *Let them share that too*. Erica told me to have a good trip and without thanking her, I left.

Outside, the February air was rigid and bitterly cold. The merciless wind stung my dry eyes. Mercifully it forced me to wake up. On the street a snow blower moved slow and menacingly, flinging old snow to the side; bystanders on the sidewalk scurried to get out of its way.

I took a deep breath of cold air. My strength was almost gone. The blood which had pumped me through my discussion with Erica had now slowed. My body was tired. My breathing had quickened to take up the slack. But at least it was almost over: one final stop at the Aeroflot office — it would be open until four o'clock — and then back to my apartment, my bed, and a short but long-overdue rest.

(9)

11:15 a.m.

How much will the ticket cost? I asked.

Exactly seven hundred ninety-five dollars, the voice answered.

(10)

It was Aunt Helen who told me that my father was dying. She had taken me to the circus and afterwards when we sat down to eat our lactose-free ice cream she broke the news. By then he lived in another state with his second wife, I hadn't seen him for years, and my memories of him were vague.

Even at that age I understood what death meant — that he

wouldn't be *here* anymore, that from now on he would be *there* — but for me there was nothing unusual about it.

I don't see why people should be sad, I told Aunt Helen who seemed surprised by my reaction.

What do you mean? she asked.

Well when someone dies people should just remember all the bad things that he did to them when he was alive and then they won't be sad anymore.

Aunt Helen smiled wistfully:

But when a person dies, she said, It's not that easy to remember only the bad things.

You can try.

It's not fair to the person, she said, Being sad is a way of saying you love the person.

I thought about her words. In time, of course, I outgrew them. But three months after we visited the circus, when my father died for good, I was already old enough to remember nothing, big enough to feel little, and far enough away to be absolutely silent.

(11)

12:07 p.m.

By the time I found the Aeroflot office, a long line had formed outside the door. At irregular intervals a burly guard would stick his head out into the cold and bark at the next person. When the person had entered, the guard would close the door behind him and lock the door from the inside.

The other people — the ones who had been locked out — tried to warm themselves by hopping from one foot to another, their gloved hands stuck straight into their pockets:

I can't believe it, someone said.

Yeah, this isn't the Russia *I* was promised!

You got that right — It's worse!

And with this the discussion turned, as it always did, to politics.

Listening to the debate I began to feel for the first time how tired I really was. My eyes were dry from the cold; my legs were stiff; and worst of all, the vodka shot hadn't relieved my headache.

Just stick with it! I told myself: *Don't quit now! You're almost at the front of the line...!*

But this line was more dynamic than it should have been. While some people waited, others would bypass the line, knock on the door, slip something green to the guard, and enter immediately. Each time this happened the rest of us grumbled bitterly. But time after time, knock by knock, the line was bypassed. *At this rate would we ever reach the line's front? If so, would we make it before the lunch break? Would we make it before they closed at four?* Once when the guard had just unlocked the door a man who had become fed up with the line tried to open it himself and to force his way through. But this man was empty-handed, and the guard, with a sharp blow to the man's chest, shoved him back outside.

Seeing this, the other people in line shook their heads disapprovingly, some at the guard, some at the man.

I shook my head as well. It was 12:35.

(12)

12:56 p.m.

Finally, the guard opened the door and grunted at me. I entered. A heavyset woman motioned for me to sit across from her and I did:

Hi, I said, I need to pay for...

Lena! We're breaking for lunch, a voice yelled from behind: You coming?

I'm on my last person, she said and turned to me: What were you saying?

But again the voice: Should we wait for you?

Just give me a minute! said Lena, I'll be right there...

Impatiently, the woman turned to me:

How can I help you? she asked.

I need to have a ticket issued, I said, My Aunt reserved it in America, but I need to pay for it.

What's the date of travel and where are you going?

I told her.

And what's your name?

I told her.

Are you from America?

Yes.

Your Russian is quite good. An accent, of course, but really very good.

I didn't thank her.

The woman looked at her watch and then typed something in the computer.

Len-a...?! her friends summoned again.

I'm almost done... just give me a minute!

I did not say anything and the woman typed some more on her keyboard.

Should I pay here? I asked and took out the eight hundred dollars from my wallet.

Yes.

Raising her eyes, the woman noticed my money:

We don't accept dollars, she said.

What do you mean?

We only accept rubles.

I was told the price was seven hundred ninety-five dollars...

Well it is, but you have to pay that amount in rubles.

Since when?

It's our policy.

But I just called a few paragraphs ago... and the girl told me the price in dollars. She didn't mention anything about rubles!

We told you the price in dollars because that's what the computer shows, but you still have to pay in rubles.

I can't believe this! I made a special point of calling to confirm the price and I asked very clearly I said 'How much does the ticket cost?' and your employee told me just as clearly that the cost is exactly seven hundred ninety-five dollars.

Yes, but in rubles.

In rubles? Seven hundred ninety-five dollars in *rubles*?

That's right.

What's right?

Seven hundred ninety-five dollars in rubles.

And if I don't have rubles?

Then you'll have to change your dollars at a currency exchange.

You're kidding me!

I looked at the woman but her expression was expressionless.

Where's the nearest exchange? I asked.

By the metro — about ten minutes walk.

What!

The woman had stopped typing on her computer and I noticed that the other people in the room were looking at us out of the corners of their eyes. I was beside myself; and the angrier I became, the more my Russian degenerated:

You mean that I have to go out in the cold and then wait in line for another hour just to get back in?

...It's not that far and I'll give you a special green pass so you won't have to stand in line again. Just slip it to the guard and he'll...

I want to talk to your supervisor! I interrupted her.

My supervisor?

Yes. I insist that your supervisor come here and personally explain to me why people tell me one thing on the phone and then something completely different... why you're telling me something completely different now.

First of all I don't have a supervisor...

The woman was turning red:

...And second of all she has nothing to do with the fact that you can't pay in dollars. All you have to do is go down the street and change your money into rubles.

I want to talk to your supervisor and I'm not leaving until I do.

The woman threw her pencil on her desk and walked away. The other people in the room were staring at me and I looked away to avoid their stares. After a few minutes a tall woman in a business skirt came up and Lena introduced me as the American who had brought dollars to pay for his ticket.

Sir you can't pay in dollars, said the supervisor, It's illegal to pay in foreign currency, We don't have the right.

Don't give me that — I pay in dollars all the time! Everybody does!

There's been some new legislation. We can't accept dollars anymore.

So why didn't you tell me this on the phone? I could have

changed my dollars on the way here so that I wouldn't be wasting my time. Or maybe you *enjoy* wasting my time?

No, I don't. All I'm saying is that we cannot accept your dollars and that you will have to exchange them for rubles.

The woman looked at me sternly.

I can't believe this! I said and grabbed my coat, Okay That's what I'll do then, That's what I'll do. Sure, no problem. But I'll tell you one thing: this place is really messed up! *Really* messed up!

Everyone in the room was looking at me, but I couldn't stop. For some reason I had to say something else, something both meaningful and loud:

But how could I express what I was feeling at this moment?

Could I find the words?

Or had these last few years been in vain...?

And then they came together:

GOD I HATE THIS COUNTRY!!!

I had screamed it and shouted it and yelled it at the same time.

With that I stormed across the room, past the guard who opened the door for me. In the silence, the others were still staring at my words, curious but unimpressed.

As I exited I slammed the door behind me and then, back outside, heard as it locked from the inside.

(13)

I don't know how many times I realized that my mother loved me differently; it's not the type of thing that comes as isolated incidents. But even now I can remember the first time: it was our last birthday together before Aunt Helen came to take me.

My mother had been out late the night before and as usual I had waited to greet her, only to lose the time and drift off. In the morning when I went into the kitchen she was standing in front of our stove peering into its glass window.

What're you doing, Mom?

It's someone's birthday today, she said yawning and coughing at the same time, and today we're having cake.

Her hair was ragged and worn and dangled in front of her face. She rarely cooked and it was funny to see her in the kitchen.

What's your favorite topping? she asked.

Vanilla!

Okay, then, that's what we'll have. For your birthday we'll have vanilla.

While she baked the cake, I sat in the livingroom watching television. A cartoon mouse hit a cartoon cat with a cartoon hammer. From the kitchen the banging of pots and pans mixed with the sharp sounds of swearing. Then a silence. On the television a cartoon cat was now torturing a cartoon dog.

When the cake was finished and my mother had spread the frosting over its surface, I sat down to eat. The cake was lopsided, the frosting uneven. The candles leaned awkwardly against themselves. Sitting down heavily, she poured herself a cup of coffee and then a tall glass of milk for me. I ate the cake but didn't touch the milk. She did not eat, and instead lit up a cigarette:

Can you tell me how old you are today? she said blowing out a ring of smoke and wiping her eyes.

Four, I answered.

That's right. And what comes after four?

I don't know, I said.

Yes you do. Now think hard... one... two......three.........four...

Five?

That's right! I think you're going to be a mathematician when you grow up. I think you're going to teach people to count. You'll make me proud, won't you?

Uh-huh!

My mother looked at me and holding the cigarette between her fingers brushed the hair out of my eyes with her palm. Her hand was cold. Her eyes were still black from the previous night:

So what comes next? she said, What comes after five?

I don't know.

Of course you do. You know just as well as anyone that there are more than just five numbers. Now try again from the very beginning: one... two......three...

...four...

Good.

...five...six...seven...

Good...

...Eight... nine...

That's right... and then?

I don't know any more... I only know to nine.

Well, think about it carefully: ...seven......eight.........nine...

...Eight!

You already said *eight*! Okay, I'll help you. Now listen: Seven... eight......nine......TEN!

Oh yeah! I forgot *ten*. I always forget *ten*.

You see? You're four now. Which means that you'll be five next year. Then you'll be six, then seven, then eight.

...Then nine!

That's right! And then ten. Eight... nine......ten.

But why?

Why *what*?

Why do I have to be nine first? Can't I be ten and then nine?

No, you can't.

Why not?

That's just the way the world works: first you're nine, then you're ten. Whether you like it or not. And whether we like it or not we can't be ten without being nine first.

But does ten always come after nine?

Yes it does. Ten always comes after nine.

Always?

Always.

I nodded.

My mother laughed and stroked my hair again:

How's the cake? she said.

I wish we could have it everyday.

You probably do, don't you?

While I ate, my mother watched me intently, gazing tenderly, smiling each time I looked up at her. When I was finished with the cake, I licked the frosting off my plate, then fingers, and started to get up from the table:

Hey...!

I stopped.

...Your milk!

I sat back down:

I don't want it, I said.

Why not?

It's gross.

It is not gross. It's good for you. It's calcium and a growing boy needs calcium....

I hate milk.

Oh you do not either, now drink.

Why?

Because I said. Go on — it won't kill you.

I sat with my chin on my chest and my palms tucked sweatily under my thighs.

I mean it, she said, You want to be big and strong like daddy, don't you?

No.

What do you mean *no*?

I don't like it.

You always drank it before.

It makes me feel sick.

I'll give you *sick*!

My mother looked at me hard and I stared down at my empty plate.

Do you hear me? she said.

I started to cry.

And knock off that crying. Only girls cry, and you're not a girl.

My crying turned to sobs.

Do you want that? Do you want for all the other boys to say *Look at him... he cries like a girl!* Is that what you want?

No.

Do you want everyone to mock you for crying all the time?

No.

So why don't you stop crying?

My shoulders were heaving with my sobbing:

I... doo o on't ... kno o oow w...

Then suddenly she reached out for me. I saw her hand and shrieked away from it. Instinctively. My eyes closed for an instant, then opened to see my mother's hand moving toward me again, this time slowly:

Oh I'm not gonna hit you... You've got frosting all over your damn mouth...

And licking her thumb, she used the taste of her cigarette to wipe my cheeks.

For a few moments we both sat silent and then she said:

You know I don't ask a lot of you, do I? Do I ask a lot of you?

No.

I work all day and when I come home all I expect of you is that you listen to me when I talk to you. Is that too much to ask?

No.

Then why don't you ever listen to me? If your father tells you to do something you don't give him any backtalk. He sees you two weeks in the damn year, but for some reason you listen to him. I'm here everyday, but if I ask you...

My mother stopped. She was shaking her head, apparently remembering something from our past:

You know you didn't used to be like this, she said, You used to be a good boy....

I had started crying again.

You used to listen... But now... Now I don't know what to do with you.

She was looking at me hard:

I shouldn't have to beg you to do things. Should I have to beg you?

...SHOULD I!

My shoulders were heaving.

Now I'm asking you for the final time... dammit stop that crying!... I'm asking you for the last time. Are you gonna drink or not?

No, I said in tears.

Fine. You made your choice. I wanted to have a nice birthday with you and all you can do is think about yourself...

And with that she left the table and went into the livingroom. I heard her snap the dial on the television, the cartoon voices became organ music and then a grating voice.

Not a sound from you until that glass is empty! she yelled from the other room, Do you understand?

The television voice became more pronounced. The organ started up. And then a choir.

...DO YOU UNDERSTAND ME?

For two hours — two child hours — I sat in front of the glass. In tears I stared at the milk until my eyes turned dim. Then dry. From time to time my mother would walk into the kitchen, look at the untouched glass, and without saying a word, without even looking at me, leave to the other room.

Each time I tried to speak to her she did not hear me.

I waited... and waited... until there was nothing else to do: I began to drink the milk. It was bland and pasty and warm like the room. Closing my eyes, I poured the liquid down my throat and felt it gurgle and bubble. As I forced the milk down — one swallow at a time — tears fell into the glass, and I drank them too. Holding my breath I drank as much as I could, felt the warm liquid churning sickeningly in my throat and then my stomach.

But the glass was so tall. The milk was so high.

At last I could drink no more. I stopped. The glass was half-full. Half-empty, but half-full. I had done the best I could.

Taking the glass of milk I walked to the kitchen sink. The sink was higher than I was and to pour the milk out I had to hold the glass over my head with both hands and stretch up on my tiptoes...

And that's when my mother came into the room. I seized up. The glass dropped from my hands and smashed on the floor. The white pieces mixed with the liquid at her feet. Even before she moved toward me I started crying:

No Mommy...! NO...!

But just as quickly she was over me, grabbing me by the wrist and yanking me. I fell to the ground but she was already pulling and as she pulled she dragged me across the kitchen floor over the broken glass.

NOOOO!!! I screamed. But seeing what had happened only made her madder:

...Now look what you did! she was screaming, *Now look...!* And she dragged me twisting and turning over the rough hallway carpet into my room....

When it was over I sat on my bed all cried out. Never again, I promised myself, would the tears get out. Never again would I make my mother mad. From now on I would be as good as God. From now on I would be as good as *she* was.

Just then the door opened. My mother was standing in the frame of light. She was holding cotton balls and tweezers.

Piece by piece she pulled out the glass from my skin, her eyes filling with tears and her hands shaking:

I'm sorry, she said, I'm so sorry....

And only then did I realize that she had something to be sorry for. Only then did I realize that I loved her too.

(14)

1:15 p.m.

Back on the streets I could not find a money exchange. There was one on every corner, but the first was closed, the second had no rubles, the third was being renovated, and the fourth wouldn't take my dollars because they weren't green enough.

At first I tried the main streets, but without luck, and soon found myself wandering among old forgotten sidestreets, through alleys and residential courtyards. What are you looking for? an old woman asked me. When I told her, her face lit up: Why didn't you say so! — Right around the corner is the best exchange in town — it's open all the time, has a good rate, and accepts any bill you give it. And, as promised, when I turned the corner I saw a sign for a twenty-four-hour exchange:

NEVER CLOSED!

But when I approached I found, instead of a line, two small crosses planted recently in the snow outside. Above the crosses a bullet had shattered the glass like a spider's web. A hand-written paper taped to the inside of the window said all it could:

CLOSED.

Without understanding, I continued on.

A few hundred meters from the bullet-rattled exchange, three policemen were standing idly and laughing at something that could

not laugh back. I walked up to them from behind. Tapping one of them on the shoulder I was about to ask — only later would I realize how naive my question would have sounded — I was just about to ask them where I could find the nearest money exchange.

But before I could even find the words, the laughter stopped suddenly and a husky voice roared in my direction:

Documents!

Was he talking to me?

Your documents! he repeated and the other two circled around me. The man who had spoken was tall and brawny with a full mustache. His eyes were windowless.

I just wanted to ask for directions...

Are you deaf or what? said another who was pulling sunflower seeds from his pocket and putting them in his mouth. One by one the sunflower seeds went into his mouth — and one by one they did not come out.

The third officer, who looked to be their adolescent son, stood silent.

I took out my passport and gave it to the man with the bushy mustache. His fingers were swollen and dirty and red from the cold. He fingered through the passport and spoke up in a rough voice:

Where's your registration?

My what?

Are you deaf? said the second man, again popping a sunflower seed into his mouth; again it did not come out.

The third younger officer looked back and forth at whoever was speaking but did not contribute.

Your visa with your registration, where is it?

Oh just a minute..., I said and opened my wallet.

This was not the first time the police had stopped me. Before it had always been enough to show them my blue passport. They would admire its color, ask a few questions about America, shake my hand, and let me go. But the times had changed: *our parents were returning home!* Now there was nothing unusual about my wallet: the yellow piece of paper was there; the filthy coin; my eight hundred dollars in cash....

But my visa was not.

The officer popped a sunflower seed into his mouth.

I again looked for the visa in the place where it should have been; but again it was not there. Watching this the officer stroked his bushy mustache in anticipation.

It couldn't be! I'd just had my visa... the last time I'd seen it was... well... actually I didn't remember when I'd seen it last. But it had to be here...

I checked places in the wallet where the visa could not have been; and so, consequently, it wasn't. The third officer followed my fingers with his eyes but kept his silence. Desperate, I emptied my wallet onto the ground, spreading the eleven yellow words onto the dirty snow around me. Seeing this, the officer popped another sunflower seed into his mouth. I put the coin on the snow in front of the officers; they winced at the sight of it.

This was absurd! This couldn't be happening!

When I laid the eight hundred dollars on the snow, all three officers stepped back: The first stopped stroking his mustache. The second, in a gust of steam-filled air, spit out a half-hour of sunflower husks onto the snow. The third officer, breaking his silence, muttered grimly: Vot eto da!

Still, the visa was not there.

I don't have it, I said dejectedly.

What do you mean you don't have it? grumbled the man with the mustache; when he spoke he looked not at me but at the dollars on the ground.

I didn't bring them.

You didn't bring your documents with you?

I couldn't help it, I said.

Why are you on the streets without your documents? Where do you think you are, home?

No. I'm far from home. Look here's my passport... It's blue.

I don't give a damn about your passport. Do you have your registration or not?

No.

The officer with the sunflower seeds had regained his composure but had seemingly lost interest in the sunflowers. The third officer, as before, was maintaining his silence.

Then let's go to the station, said the bushy-mustached man grabbing me by my elbow.

My heart was beating fast, I couldn't believe what was happening. *They were putting me in jail?*

You're making a mistake...!

Let's go!

My visa's at home. I swear on my...

What are you deaf? said the man with the sunflower seeds whose eyes flashed furious and who with a sudden violent motion grabbed my other arm.

Instinctively I yanked my arm away just as violently and had started to say something when I felt a painful blow to my side, the crook of an arm over my throat, and then the firm pressure of a knee in my back; and before I could do anything I was lying face-down on the dirty snow, my arms held tightly behind me, my cheek pressed coldly against the contents of my wallet, which were, in order of importance: the yellow piece of paper, the worthless coin, and eight hundred dollars that could not send me home without a visa.

(15)

Let's say — hypothetically, of course — let's say you live at the Yuzhnaya metrostation. It could be any metrostation on the gray line, but let's say it's Yuzhnaya. In Russian 'yuzhnaya' means *southern* and because of this unfortunate coincidence you have to travel two hours each way between your home and your work which is located to the north.

Home for you is a small apartment that you have recently privatized. The apartment actually belongs to your mother who lives in the master bedroom while you and your first wife share the smaller room with the sagging fold-out bed.

The apartment needs new tiles, and wallpaper in the kitchen, and for some reason the plumbing always breaks on Tuesdays. Your wife reminds you of all this quicker than you are able to forget. You fix what you can; but her friends have husbands who earn dollars, or lovers who are good with their hands. If you only had a decent job..., she says.

But you love your wife. And besides: she's right. Your job

does pay miserably. Inflation has made your salary laughable; it has demoted you.

Everyday at work you see foreigners with their fancy clothes and their expensive suitcases. Or worse: rich Russians with their fashionable clothes and expensive foreign suitcases. And each — foreigner and Russian — with an emergency. Each of them with a matter of utmost importance which for you is merely the same urgent matter day in and day out. It is as stale and drab as the ten-year-old wallpaper in your kitchen.

But you are lucky: you work for a stifling beaurocracy. And your signature can save people time — crucial days, hours, or minutes. After all, Time is money — even in Russia! Time is money and money is wallpaper. And new wallpaper should have matching kitchen tiles. And matching kitchen tiles aren't as cheap as they could be. And if you only had a decent job...

Then one day — it is not exactly, of course, *one* day — your signature is requested. A man is standing before you, almost in tears. An emergency, of course. You can sign or you can refuse. Sign or not sign? On the one hand it is but a flick of the wrist for you; on the other hand you already bought tiles for the kitchen. On the one hand it is late and you are tired; on the other hand your wedding anniversary is approaching.

And so you listen, fighting back a yawn, as the person tells you more about his predicament than you need to know — after all, you've heard it all before. Honestly, at that moment you couldn't care less about signing or not signing, about this man who is almost in tears, about his emergency — for you it could go either way. And so what do you do...? What do you do to help you decide...?

You look at my clothes.

(16)

1:57 p.m.

The holding cell where the officers led me did not have windows. The walls were dirty; the floor stuck to my shoes. In the back of the small cell the toilet door had been left open and a well-defined smell permeated the room. Inside the cell a herd of detainees stood shoulder to shoulder in the cramped space; in shabby clothes

they shouted back and forth, their speech harsh and strange. I stood as far away from it as possible — in the back corner — not wanting to lean against anything, not wanting to be seen, afraid to speak. As the others chided and jostled, they would look back at me and our eyes would meet; I would look quickly away, trying to look at nothing. But failing. One prisoner, a man with chafe hands and chapping lips was especially interested in me. And each time he stared at me, my eyes ran away. When he couldn't stand it any longer, he shouted in my direction:

Hey you!

I did not answer.

Hey! In the corner! I'm talking to you!

I pretended not to have heard him.

The man pushed his way through the crowd, moving toward me until his face was only a few inches from mine. As he spoke his gold tooth sparkled like a coin:

Did you hear me? he yelled.

The others in the cell had turned to watch us. But I said nothing.

Did you hear me? he repeated.

I said nothing.

Where are you from?

Again I said nothing.

What's up your ass?

I did not tell him.

Ohhh...! He doesn't wanna talk. He's *important*. He thinks that just because he has these nice imported clothes, he doesn't have to talk to us. That's what you think, isn't that right, pal?

The man slapped my shoulder so hard it unbalanced me. I tried to look for a guard, but the crowd of people served as a screen. Their shouts muffled the man's words. He continued:

What we have here is royalty. The king of England! Or even better the president of the United States!!

I gasped a third time.

The man's voice was becoming increasingly insistent:

What's your name, Mr. President?

The other people were now crowding around us to watch the scene; each of them hoping sadistically that I would not tell my name.

And so I did not.

Somebody's talking to you! he reminded me: *Somebody* asked your name!

I did not answer.

Did you hear me? Somebody asked you very politely what your name is...

I looked away.

At this offense, the man grabbed the collar of my jacket and shoved me back against the dirty wall. My ribs ripped from the pain. The man moved even closer into my face and pressed the knuckles of his clenched fist against the bottom of my jaw, tilting my chin up:

WHAT IS YOUR NAME?

Again I did not answer. It would have been impossible anyway. Instead I closed my eyes. And waited.

What was my name? Where is my name? When would my name be?

With my eyes closed I felt only the aching in my head. My head was throbbing, as if to remind me of what was to happen....

Then in the distance the words sounded. All of them. My name. Someone was shouting it.

No!

I opened my eyes in time to see the heads turn around. The man let me go. Busily he brushed my collar back into place.

It was a police officer and he was waving my blue passport over his head. He shouted my name again through the crowd and I quickly raised my hand. The others looked at me. Slowly they separated to let me pass. As I walked the gauntlet to the front of the cell I could hear the others whispering about the color of my passport. The officer opened the cell door and I exited.

Follow me, said the officer.

And with my passport in his hand he led me down a long dark corridor with peeling tiles.

(17)

At the end of the long corridor was a small office where a man in uniform sat behind an old desk that was strangely absent of papers;

the desk was black except for a palm-sized spot on its surface which had been worn gray. Judging by his uniform the man was a senior officer. He took my passport from the guard and looked at the blue cover, then turned it over to look at the back cover, which was also blue. His voice was the lowest bass:

So...!

I looked at him blankly.

So! You're from the United States of America?

His voice was slow and emphasized every syllable.

Yes sir.

What do you do?

I told him.

And how long have you been here in our country?

I told him.

So long? Are you enjoying your stay with us?

Was he joking? Was he sick?

I like your country very much, I told the man and then quickly added: sir.

The man looked at me long and deep. Then unexpectedly his face broke into a strange smile:

Ahhh... America...!

Yes.

America the beautiful!

Yes sir.

Land of milk and honey! Birthplace of freedom and democracy! Isn't that right?

I... suppose it is.

Oh, I'm sorry, I interrupted you.... You were saying how much you liked *this* country?

I was?... I mean well, yes I do like this country.

Yes yes. Please do tell me what there is to like? Just between you and me... After all we both know this place is a dump.

A dump, sir?

Yes, one big stinking dump — that's all this country is.

Well, sir, I wouldn't say that it's a dump, exactly...

Oh you wouldn't? What *would* you call it?

I don't know.

Well, trust me. It's a dump. I mean, just take a look around. What do you see? What do we have here that's worth anything?

Well actually...

...Not a damn thing! — that's what we have.

Sir, I think you're being a bit hard...

Hard? You think I'm being hard? Name one good thing about this country... just one!

A good thing about the country?... I... I don't know... There are many things.

For example?

It's difficult to say there are so many...

Pick one.

...Well, for example Russian literature.

Literature!

Yes sir. I appreciate Russian literature very much.

Like what?

Like what, sir?

Yeah, what books?

Well, sir, I just finished *Anna Karenina*.

Anna Karenina?

Yes sir.

Never read it.

You would be good to read it, sir. I recommend it highly...

The man slammed his fist against the table. I jumped back but the man continued, staring into my eyes mean and deep. When he spoke he bared his teeth like a black bear:

What do I look like to you — a black bear?! I know better than you that life is better there. *There* people really live. There they don't have the chaos we have *here*.

Maybe so, but we have problems too...

Problems? What problems could you possibly have — deciding what color toilet paper to buy? Which brand of condoms? Here we have serious problems. *Real* problems. That's why everyone is leaving. That's why they're leaving in masses: to Europe, Israel, America, Canada. Leaving by the hundreds, the thousands, the hundreds of thousands. Anything to get out of here!

Yes, I know but...

And why do you think they're leaving — why, I ask you? — because this place is a dump, that's why, because it's just one big stinking dump that everyone's trying to get out of at any cost, and that's why there are so many emigrants — not that I'm justifying it of course, I mean I myself would never leave Russia for any other country, especially America, not even for all the money in the world, and to be honest I don't understand why anyone would want to leave — the damn traitors! — because say what you want about this place but dammit it's still my homeland and I still love it and it's still the best goddamned country in the world...!!!

Here the man stopped:

...Do you agree with me?

Did I agree with him? Did he *agree?!*

Yes sir, I said, I agree with you entirely.

You do?

Yes sir. Russia is without a doubt the best dump in the world.

The man slammed his fist against the table again:

What! What did you say?

Again I jumped back:

I... uh... I said that Russia is the most goddamned country in the world...

Excuse me!

...I mean what I really wanted to say is...!

Who the hell do you think you are?

Sir?

Who do you think you are, coming *here* from *there* and calling my country a dump? Who are you to damn it?

I...?

Who are you to say it stinks?

But I never...

You know, for the last couple years we've been up to our ears in America. We listen to your music. We see your movies. We eat your hamburgers....

My hamburgers?

...In the papers all you read about is America this, America that...! But I'm going to tell you something, and I want you to listen real good. Are you listening?

Yes sir.

Are you listening real good?

Of course.

You need to remember that this isn't *there*? This is *here*. And here you're nothing. Do you understand that?

No sir I don't.

You don't?

No sir. Not yet.

The man seemed to take offense at the sincerity of my answer and bared his teeth even more:

Do you understand where you are? Do you have any idea where in the hell you are?

No sir, not a clue.

What!

I'm not sure where I am, sir.

I looked at him naively and it threw him:

Where's your visa?

It's at home, I said.

Are you sure?

Absolutely, I said.

If you're lying to me...!

The man slammed his fist against the table. But this time I did not jump back.

I wouldn't lie, sir, I promise — my visa's on my shelf next to the German dictionary and my solar calculators the size of...

The man was looking at me suspiciously.

...a credit card.

A what? What did you say? What did you say it was?

A credit card. At home I have three calculators the size of credit cards.

Impossible! he said.

No no it's true, they're the latest technology — made in Japan — lightweight and convenient and especially popular among women who are intelligent and polite...

The man slammed his fist on the table:

That's enough!

I became quiet.

Listen up...! he said.

I became even quieter.

...This isn't Japan and I don't give a damn about your solar calculators. I want to see your visa with your registration. If it's at home then you get it and bring it here. It's as simple as that. If not...

The man paused:

Do you understand? he said.

No sir, not entirely.

Just go home and get your damn visa and bring it to me.

What about my passport?

The passport stays here. You'll get it back when you show me your visa.

I started to leave. Without my passport I felt thin and insignificant. As I left the room I heard the man shout after me:

Hey...!

Yes sir, I answered not turning around.

I'm warning you — no funny business! You bring back your visa or else.

And I felt his shadow point back down the long corridor to where I had been, toward the man with the gold tooth who now knew both my name and the color of my passport.

(18)

As soon as I exited the police station I felt the need to sprint as fast and as far away as possible. But what if I were to be arrested again? *And this time without my passport!* Instead I walked calmly along the building past three cops, two of whom were talking, one of whom was not spitting out sunflower seeds. My heart beat fast. My head ached. I turned the corner.

Gathering every bit of strength, I began to run.

Slowly at first I forced my heavy legs up and forward, my irregular strides jarring my headache with each step, each contact with the icy ground a test in resilience *Would it hold me?* each forward movement awkward and uncertain, my steps then becoming shorter and more concentrated, my muscles pulling tight against themselves, at first resilient and fresh, then numbed, then aching, and finally succumbing to a sharp excruciating pain that ran all the way up my legs hindering me as I raced faster and faster weaving in and out of the heavily bundled pedestrians, each forward step both shortening and lengthening the distance between here and there, the seemingly unbridgeable gap that not even I could understand. And so I ran with all my strength, not noticing what was in my path, not stopping, past people and cars and piles of snow and money exchange after money exchange, not realizing what I was doing, not worrying about where I was coming from, not caring if people were looking back over there shoulders at me; and as I ran, my lungs now hurting from the cold air and the unfamiliar contractions, as I struggled with every step forward, I realized that I would not make it, *I would not make it!* somehow I understood that this was not the way things were done, that it was too late, that I was too slow and all my running was for nothing, my watch was moving much faster than my legs could take me and that there was no sense in hoping for anything, because despite all my powers and exertions — I did not stop running — despite everything inside me I was too late.

I was too late!

And sure enough when I had reached where I was going — exhausted and out of breath — my watch confirmed what I had suspected all along.

I doubled over in pain.

It was 4:05.

(19)

4:08 p.m.

And that's how I stayed — doubled over. I couldn't straighten my body. Nor did I have any reason to: it was too late. My ribs ached. I was doubled over and only vaguely aware of the people passing me; the ones I had sprinted by only minutes before. Like soldiers they were crunching the ground beneath them.

I straightened up.

And that's when I stopped feeling my body. Just like that. My thoughts turned in against themselves and seemed to float away from me. My legs went numb. I could not feel where my hands ended and my arms began. The pain in my head had become so constant that it could not be noticed. The world around me seemed to spin, and at that moment it seemed that there was nothing.

It seemed that there could be nothing but nothing.

How clear it all was! How pointless and beautiful!

Just then the door rattled from the inside. *But now it was leaving...!* The door rattled again and then opened itself. *Now* it *was gone!* A man in green camouflage fatigues stepped out into the cold. It was the guard at whom I had shaken my head. His face was flushed. He held an unlit cigarette in his hand. I started to speak but he interrupted me:

We're closed! he said rudely.

Isn't there anyone inside at all? I asked.

We're closed! and he held up his watch to show me how closed they were.

But my ticket. It's...

C-LOSED!!!

The man looked at me angrily. He put the unlit cigarette in his mouth which curled up around it; his eyes squinted. He shoved his hand in his pocket, feeling around for something.

Look! I began, I just ran two miles to get here, *Two miles!* and it seems that I've pulled a muscle and...

Do you understand Russian? I told you we're closed.

The man felt around in his other pocket.

I... Russian?... Do I... Russian language... for me... very difficult... very very difficult.

What?

I speak the Russian very not good. Very very bad.

Where the hell're you from anyway?

Where was I from? Where was I from?

There...!

We're closed!

Here...?

Closed.

What would make him see? Where could I go from here? How could I get to there? What was left?

Russia! I said, I'm from Russia...

But by now the man was not even paying attention to me. His

attention had been thrust somewhere into his pocket. He swore indignantly.

I turned and started to walk away. It was hopeless. Everything was as hopeless as the hard ground crunching slightly beneath my feet.

Hey! a rough voice yelled after me.

I did not turn around. The voice sounded again, but this time softer than a ruble:

Excuse me sir, said the guard's voice, You wouldn't happen to have a light, would you?

A light?

I don't smoke, I said bitterly and started to walk off.

The ground crunched just as bitterly under my feet.

But wait a minute! Last week hadn't someone asked me for a light? And hadn't I apologized profusely? And after that hadn't I made a special trip to the kiosk...? ... That's right, I had! ...which meant that in my pocket...

There it was!!!

I pulled out the cheap disposable lighter.

(20)

4:18 p.m.

After taking my lighter, the guard led me into the eerie silence that is a room full of idle computers. The lights were half-dimmed. The guard told me to wait near the entrance and walked behind the plastic wall. When he returned there was a handsome young woman with him. Help him, will you Len? he said and left to smoke his cigarette.

Lena turned on the computer and hit some keys. The computer beeped and whirred and clicked. She asked for my information and I gave it to her.

Let me see your visa, she said.

I don't have it.

Well, then let me see your passport.

I don't have it.

You don't have your visa or your passport?

No I don't.

Where are they?

Well, I seem to have temporarily misplaced my visa. And my passport... I left my passport with... I left it with a friend so that I wouldn't lose it... I seem to be losing everything lately.

You realize you can't leave the country without your visa?

I know, but I'm sure I can get a new one issued in the airport.

The woman sighed:

You can always try, she said and then: Will you be paying in cash?

In dollars.

I'm sorry but we can't...

Look I know. I was here earlier today. Can you please take my dollars? Can you do it just this once?

The woman frowned but then checked her watch:

All right, she said, I'll do it this time. But *next time...*

What 'next time'? Next time I bought tickets from her? Or next time my mother died!

Yes of course, I said, Next time everything will be different. Next time I'll do it the way it should be done.

Hey Lena! she yelled leaning over her own shoulder, Len! Come here please... he's paying in dollars, what rate should I use?

Lena came out.

It was the woman from before:

You're accepting dollars? she said.

Yes. Do you know what the rate of exchange is?

I'm not sure, Lena answered, you'd better ask Lena — I'll have her come out.

Without even looking at me, Lena went back behind the wall to get Lena. When Lena came out Lena asked her for today's rate of exchange and Lena answered without hesitation:

(1USD=1620RUR), she said.

Lena thanked her, typed some more on the computer, and handed me my ticket. I tucked it into my wallet — which now contained a mere six dollars and two kopecks — and stepped out onto the street. My body was tired but I had no time to pay attention to it. Ahead of me I had an hour-long metro ride to my forgotten apartment, where I was sure my visa could not possibly be.

(21)

5:56 p.m.

So it was not.

(22)

7:04 p.m.

And then an hour-long ride back to the police precinct where I would have to tell the officer that I had been wrong. That my visa had not been at home on the shelf next to the three dusty calculators at all. That in truth I had lied. Now at the end of my hour-long ride a man waited with chafe knuckles and chapped lips and a firm conviction that I was firmly convinced I was the president of the United States.

In the metro the stations passed by slowly and grimly. As if I were on my way to a wedding.

By the time I reached the police station it was already dark. Snow had stopped falling. The wind howled. I opened the door heavily and stepped inside.

(23)

For the first time all day I thought of my mother. Until now my mind had been logical but short-sighted: *Get the tickets!* it said, *Do whatever it takes to make it home! Don't stop until you are there...!*

But what would I tell her when I saw her? Aunt Helen would meet me in the airport and from there we would go straight to where my mother was already lying in her open casket. She would not look the same. She would not recognize me. She would not be able to hear me from the distance of her final resting place. Why was this last meeting so important to me? What would I say? There was nothing that I could say. There was, of course, nothing that she could tell me.

(24)

Where's your visa? said the guard.

I don't have it, I said

(25)

I would tell her that silence is not inevitable. That love is not conditional. I would tell her that in life there are too few things that really mean something, and that it is these things that fall away first. And she would listen to me, the most captive of audiences, and somewhere deep inside she would nod and smile and through silent lips she would say, I know, I know, I love you too.

(26)

So back I went into the dirty sticky holding cell. Into the crowd of prisoners.

But this time things were different: The American's back! they shrieked and looked at each other with childish glee. In my absence I had become the celebrity in the cell. The darling of the detainees. Now I commanded respect. I was, in a way, presidential. And in Russian oscillating between Ф and Ц, my fellow lawbreakers asked me questions about the color blue, about democracy and love, about the complex relationship between black and white Americans....

In amazed voices they asked me how I had ended up in this hellhole and I answered that I had just wanted to change money, had been turned away from several currency exchanges, had naively approached the police...

No no...! they protested, Not *this* hellhole... This *hellhole!*

What do you mean?

The country.

But it isn't a hellhole, I protested.

Yes it is, they said, Nobody comes here.

I do.

Why?

I don't know, I said.

You have to know, they said.

I don't, I said.

You do too, they said.

Okay, okay, I said and showed them the two-kopeck coin.

They did not understand:

We don't understand, they said.

I began to speak about irony. Then love. Then Love. And then about danger. When I mentioned marriage, the man with the fake tooth and chafe hands, who until this had been silent, came up to me and put his arm around my shoulders. His name was Morozov.

Boy..., he said and with his dirty arm around my shoulders shook me like a son. I shuddered, but in vain:

Boy, he said, I have some advice for you...

As he spoke I gazed at his sparkling tooth:

Are you ready for my advice?

Yes I am.

You're ready?

Yes.

Are you listening?

Yes.

Good.

Still with his arm around my shoulder, Morozov looked at me compassionately:

Give me some money, he advised.

What?

Do you have any money?

I opened my wallet and pulled out a five-dollar bill.

Is that all you got? You don't have anything else in there...?

And I gave him the very last dollar.

Morozov put the money in his pocket and turned to me seriously:

Don't do it! he said.

Don't do what? I asked.

Marriage, he said, Don't do it!

And taking me into the very same corner he had thrown me against earlier, the man calmly and sadly told me the story of his existence, how life had killed him and marriage had condemned him to solitude:

'I wasn't always like this...' he began.

(27)

Although each was vastly different, my fellow detainees did share one common trait: to a man, they hadn't done anything. Guram, for example, was being held because he had not been born in Russia; Elena because she hadn't been born in Moscow; Dima had been arrested for not bribing a police officer; and Sasha had been picked up — literally — when he did not use a chaser with a liter of vodka. Then of course there was me: guilty of all of the above, in other words, of not doing a single thing. And now as I listened to Morozov's tale of lost love and misplaced marriage, I noticed that each of the detainees must have an interesting story to tell. In their own way, each of them was eager to explain their life to someone who could not understand it. But for the moment it was Morozov who was the lucky one...

'...And I say to her, Why the hell should I if it ain't even *my* kid? And the bitch says to me...'

(28)

Morozov...!

The man stopped his story at the shout coming from the other side of the iron bars.

Kashvili...!

Guram, hearing his name also jumped forward.

Let's go you two! the guard said rudely to them and then pointed at me:

You too!

The guard opened the gate. The three of us exited the cage and followed him down the long hallway. The guard knocked on the door, then opened it, motioning for us to stand in front of the large empty desk with a single gray spot: behind the desk, as if he had not moved since I last saw him, sat the uniformed senior officer:

Boys..., he began, ...things look bad — very bad indeed.

As he spoke the man massaged his hand which was poised above the gray spot:

You two don't have your passports..., he said pointing his meaty finger first at Morozov and then at Guram.

The two men nodded.

...And *you* two don't have your visa! he continued pointing at me.

Who? Why 'we two'? Was he using the polite form of the verb with me? He wasn't using it with the other two prisoners!

All three of us nodded at his words and the officer continued:

That boys is very very *very* bad.

We nodded again.

You realize that don't you? You know what this means... Do you know what this means?

No sir, we said.

It means that you will have to stay here until we can get everything squared away. You, and you, and you two...

Morozov started to say something.

Shut up! said the officer and then motioning at Morozov and Guram ordered the guard: Take those two back to the cell! I want to have a few words with '*our American*' here.

The other two were led away and remaining alone with the officer, I felt that here in this room anything could happen — *anything!* — and I would be powerless to stop it. For the first time in my life I realized that I was nothing.

I have something I want to talk to you about, the man began.

Yes sir?

It's sort of independent of the situation at hand, but I guess you could say it's connected as well...

Sir?

Okay, I'll just come out with it...

I waited stupidly.

...You say you're an English teacher?

That's right sir.

Do you give private lessons?

Sometimes.

How much do you charge?

When I told him the man whistled:

Not cheap, he said and then: You see...

Suddenly the man was stuttering and it surprised me. I looked at him curiously. The man was wringing his hands nervously behind his desk:

...The thing is that I want my daughter... She's twelve... She takes English at school, but she can't... she's falling behind... She's slower than the others, she needs special help... I can't pay you but maybe if you need a good homecooked meal...

I don't understand, sir?

Do you have a family? he said.

No, I answered.

A wife?

Not really.

Of course you wouldn't understand then, he said and hung his head.

I felt compassion for him.

He stayed that way with his head hung. Then he looked up at me:

I want you to teach my daughter to speak, he said and then after an ungainly hesitation added: sir.

He held out his massive calloused hand over the desk and not understanding what was happening, I took it. The man wrote down my phone number and thanked me.

Then, as if remembering something, his expression changed. He walked across the room, opened the door and motioned for the guard who came into the room. The superior looked at his subordinate abruptly and ordered:

Give him his passport and let him go. I think he's learned his lesson.

Turning to the side, out of the guard's sight, he winked at me and then in a rough tone added:

But remember that although I'm letting you go now, you can be sure that you won't get off so easy *next time*!

(29)

And with that I left. As I passed the detention cell, I saw Morozov and Guram looking at me sadly from behind the bars. *How long would they be in there? In how many ways would they have to suffer just because of the color of their passport?* Guiltily, I slipped out the door without acknowledging them.

Outside I was still trying to find words for what had just happened. Then I saw it: a single word written in white on the blue door of a small car. In the light of the cold winter night, the letters looked even more sinister than ever:

Милиция, they said.

(30)

9:28 p.m.

From the police station it was straight to the airport. Having no money — I had given my last six dollars to Morozov — I snuck onto the bus, exactly the way the redhead had taught me. Now instead of money I had a ticket home; instead of busfare, a filthy two-kopeck coin; instead of my visa, nothing but a blue passport and a naive to-do list. At the next-to-last stop a man got on, flashed identification, and began checking everyone's tickets. *After everything that I had been through — money exchanges and travel agencies and police stations and Canadians — would I be kicked off now? Would it end like this? Would it end so simply? So absurdly? No...! It would be too amazing, too incredible. Even for this day! No one would believe it....*

...And so I was not.

The bus arrived at the windowless airport and I stepped out onto the cold snow that led to the departure terminal.

(31)

10:05 p.m.

By the time I got to Sheremetevo it was late at night, the scheduled flights had already left. At the information booth the woman pointed down the long departure hall to where the visa section was.

The hall was strangely quiet and as I trudged from one end to the other my wet boots squeaked loudly in the empty hall. With each step forward the airport became emptier. And quieter. No travelers in sight. No workers. Even the police had seemingly disappeared.

At the end of the hall where the visa section should have been a sheet of paper pointed to a small intercom in the wall. The intercom itself was waist-high, so that I had to hunch over to speak into it. There were two buttons and so I pressed the one on the left.

The buzzer sounded but no one answered. I pressed the button on the right. Again the buzzer sounded.

Again no answer.

Frustrated, I went back to the woman at the information booth. Nobody answered the intercom, I told her. Try it again, she said. But are you sure they're working? I asked. I don't know, she said, Try it again.

For a third time I walked the length of the airport hall.

And for a third time there was no answer.

In silence I stood pushing button after button. Left. Right. Right. Left.

Finally, I heard an answer: a woman's voice from somewhere behind the wall.

Excuse me, please, I began, I have a problem with my visa, Can you help me?

The wall was quiet.

Hello? Hello? Can you hear me?

What's your name? the wall demanded.

I told her.

What's the problem?

I lost my visa and I have to leave tomorrow.

Tomorrow?

Yes, to America...

There was silence and then: Is it a business visa?

Yes I think so.

Just a moment.

With a click the intercom went dead. I was stooped over but continued to wait for the woman's voice. After a minute or so the voice sounded again:

The person you need to talk to is on break. When he comes in I'll tell him you're waiting.

But...!

Click.

I pressed the button again:

Miss I'm sorry to bother you but can you tell me when he'll be in?

I told you: as soon as he comes in I'll tell him you're waiting.

Click.

I held my finger to the button but did not press it.

On a bench a tall African man lay stretched out, an English-language newspaper covering his face. One leg draped over the edge of the bench and touched the floor. Off to the corner a woman was sweeping the floor in slow regular strokes and in the quiet airport her wiry broom sounded like a razor passing over thick stubble.

I pressed the button again.

No answer.

The other button.

No answer.

Where are they?

I pressed again and again and then stopped suddenly.

Wait a minute...!

My skin became cold.

... Wait just one minute...!

My skin became even colder.

... Why had the wall asked my name? Why did it need to know who I was? And what had made me answer so willingly? Sure, the voice had asked, but I could've refused to comment. I could've kept it to myself. This wasn't a holding cell. There I'd had to answer when the officer held up my passport, when he shouted my name through the bars. That couldn't be helped. But here... here in this windowless airport I had given it away as eagerly as if it were a painting. And now I couldn't take it back. Now the wall knew who I was and could use my name against me.

I took my finger off the button.

It was too late to take it back. This time it was too late. But never again would it happen! Never! From now on I would protect my name from everyone. From now on my name would be mine and mine alone, and I would use anything — evasion, deceit, even silence — to guard it.

I decided to wait a few minutes before trying again.

The African was still sprawled out on the bench but had turned on his side and was now lying with his nose in the back of the chair. The lady with the broom had moved closer and was sweeping the center of the floor.

I checked my watch. Ten minutes had passed.

I pressed the button.

No answer.

Why aren't they answering?

My finger was on the button and then static and: Hello?

Hello! Miss it's me again. I'm sorry. I forgot to ask... How will I recognize the person who's supposed to come? Can you tell me his name?

Just wait there. He'll see you himself.

But if he doesn't?

Click.

I stood there. Aside from the African and the cleaning lady the airport was empty of passengers. Moscow was home to between ten and sixteen million residents... and here I was alone.

The metro would be closing in less than two hours and I still had to get there by bus which would take forty minutes. I'm not going to make it, I thought.

I'm not going to make it.

I pressed the button.

No answer.

(32)

11:12 p.m.

I pressed again. Nothing. I continued pressing. Again and again and again. *I didn't care if they knew who I was, I didn't have time for this.* Again and again and again and again and...

Hello!

Ma'am I know you're probably sick of me, but do you have any idea when your representative might show up?

He hasn't come yet?

No and I've been here the whole time...

Well, I gave him the message. He should be there any minute now.

But when?!?

I don't know. Just wait there. I gave him your message.

I took my finger off the button before it could click. There was no sense in bothering the wall. I just had to wait until the man —

whatever his name was — showed up. I could only hope that he would show up at all.

The airport was hauntingly still. Nothing was moving.

And that's when he came.

(33)

11:17 p.m.

When I saw the man my heart leapt, my soul jumped. He was young and smartly dressed and his eyes looked at me attentively when he spoke:

You called? he said.

I pulled out my passport quickly and clumsily as if I had not had time to prepare. When I spoke my voice stuttered:

I have a problem, I lost my visa and my flight leaves tomorrow.

Tomorrow!

Yes, can you give me some sort of form that will let me leave?

Let me see your documents...

The man smiled and for the first time all day I relaxed. I gave him the passport and my airline ticket. The man looked at the passport attentively, turning the pages until he found something.

I'll be right back, he said and walked to a door along the side of the wall. On the door was written 'Employees only.'

Hey wait! I called after him, Do I have time to go to the bathroom? I mean, before you get back?

The man laughed and when he did I realized how ridiculous my question must have sounded.

Sure, he said. Take your time. I just have to talk to my supervisor.

Okay, I said, Thanks!

The man laughed again and headed toward the room.

Moving away from the intercom, I felt encouraged and revived, as if this day had never even happened. At the bathroom the door was propped open, the cleaning lady was mopping the floor and so I stood outside until she finished.

It was 11:41. According to my schedule I should have been at home by now. *But who could have known that this day would turn to night the way it had? Who could have imagined?! Still, there was hope. If I could catch the last bus, then I'd be able to make it home. At least rest for a few hours! With my eyes open, of course, but rest nevertheless...*

But when I returned from the bathroom the man had not yet come out.

11:50.

11:58.

12:06.

Where was he? I only had a few minutes to make my bus.

At 12:15 I hunched over and pressed the button. But then, before the wall could even answer, the man came out of the door. He was holding my passport. He smiled kindly:

Where's your invitation? he asked.

My what?

The invitation that you received your visa with.

I... I don't have anything. I gave you everything I have.

You don't have your invitation?

No. I never did have it...

I need it to issue you a replacement visa.

Where am I supposed to get my invitation from?

You should have it.

But I don't, I never had it. I don't even know what it looks like!

I need your invitation. If I had your invitation then I could issue your visa right here, just a signature and you'd have your visa.

But I don't have anything...

The man was looking at me with concern. Everything was crumbling before me like black bread. I tried to gather myself together:

Okay, let me ask you this..., I said to the man, ...How can I get my invitation, I mean can I get another one? What do I have to do?

Well, there're two things you can do. You can either go to the agency that invited you and ask them if they have a copy of the original invitation. If they do then you can make a copy of it and bring the copy to me — make sure they put the company seal on it. With that I can issue your visa.

Back to Erica? At this hour! Buried trolleybus or no, she

wouldn't do it. And I wouldn't ask! And even if I could find Dave or Phil, there wasn't enough time...

It's no good. That could take days. And my plane leaves in less than nine hours...

It does?

Yes. What's the second option?

The other option is to go to OVIR.

OVIR?!?

Those are the only two possibilities. OVIR won't be open until Monday. You could leave Monday evening....

It's impossible! I have to be in America by Monday morning. I have to be there for... I need to be there because... well you see... it's an *emergency*!

An emergency?

Yes, Tuesday will be too late. I'll miss it.

I'm sorry.

That's it?

That's it.

There's nothing else that we can do?

Nothing.

My heart sank six feet.

Then the man spoke up:

Well, there is one thing that I can try. I can't give any guarantees....

Of course, of course!

I have to ask my supervisor. It will take a few minutes...

I'll wait here!

The man left and went behind the wall. It was 12:32; I had missed my bus. The African had left and his place had been taken over by the English-language newspaper. The woman with the mop was splashing the floor in front of the intercom and so I stepped aside, walked over to the bench, and without moving the African's newspaper sat on the words.

What was happening? All I wanted was to go home, to close my eyes, to see my mother. And I couldn't....

At 12:55 the man came out of the room. His face expressed sympathy. He spoke slowly:

I talked to my supervisor and there is one thing that we can do....

What?

All you have to do is pay a fine and then I can sign the forms so that you can leave. In fact, if you can pay now, then you'll be able to make your flight tomorrow.

The man smiled again.

How much is the fine? I asked.

Three hundred thousand.

Rubles?!

Again my question was absurd. I stopped and then continued:

My wallet's empty. I don't have any money! I would pay but I can't.

...Maybe you could borrow from someone and then pay them back after you return.

I... I don't have anyone.

I would lend you the money myself if I could but...

No, no, I understand. It's not your fault. It's not your fault at all. I shouldn't have lost my visa in the first place.

I stood there, suddenly tired and weak, as if my legs would buckle at any moment. Once again home seemed so far away.

Do you know why it's so expensive? I mean, maybe it's a mistake, maybe there isn't a fine?

If you want I can ask my supervisor...

No! No! Don't go anywhere, please! Just let me think. I need to think. I need to sit down and think and I'll come up with something. There has to be a way to get the money...

The man stood for a few moments, glanced at his watch, then at me:

I need to get back to my work. If you think of something, you can call on the intercom....

It was as if he had thrown a shovelful of dirt on my soul.

...Tell them you already spoke with me: they'll relay the message.

Yeah, sure. Thanks anyway.

The man started to walk away but I called after him:

Excuse me! What's your name? I mean so that I can ask for you when I'm talking to the wall?

It's not important. Just say you spoke with me regarding a visa, They'll know who you mean.

The man smiled a final time and then left.

I sat back down on the bench. The airport was empty. There was not a sound. It was dark. The African was still gone.

And that's when I broke down.

(34)

1:03 a.m.

At that moment I broke down completely. For the first time since I was a child I cried harder than I ever had before. Tears fell into my hands which I used to cover my face. My chest heaved with sobs. Somewhere I understood that I should have been ashamed of the scene I was making in the empty airport, somewhere my mind was telling me that this was not how emotions should be expressed. But my heart couldn't care less. My soul couldn't care less. At that moment, I didn't give a damn what people thought, what they might think; or say; or write. For me it didn't matter that others might point or snicker or condescend. At that moment I cried sincerely and thoroughly, like a widow, like a new child, like a person who is unable to say good-bye...

(35)

Don't cry..., said a voice, *Don't cry...*

When I looked up I saw the cleaning woman. She was holding her mop in one hand and extending a handkerchief with the other. Don't cry, she said, *Будет, будет.*

I wiped my eyes. Liquid ran from my nose like spilled milk and I wiped it too.

You need to come back tomorrow morning. After six o'clock. Ivan Petrovich will be on duty.

It won't do any good, I said.

You need to talk to Ivan Petrovich. That one, the one you were talking to, he's always like that! Come back in the morning after six o'clock.

My watch showed one-fourteen. I hadn't slept in thirty-six hours.

I missed my bus, I said, I have nowhere to go.

You can't go home?

I don't have money for a taxi.

How much do you have?

I don't have any.

Nothing? How were you going to pay for the bus...?

But I couldn't answer.

You wait here, said the woman and left me alone on the bench.

When she returned she motioned for me to follow her and together we slipped past the lax security guards, along employee hallways, to a backroom closet that was dimly lit by one dangling bulb. A teapot was on the table, with a small dish of jam and three slices of fresh bread.

Eat, she said, Then get some rest. You need to wake up at six. You go ahead and rest. Tomorrow morning I'll wake you up.

She left, and without drinking the tea, without eating the bread, I let my eyes close for the first time.

(36)

It fits perfectly, said Aunt Helen, Just perfectly!

(37)

6:00 a.m.

Get up! Get up! said the woman: Have some tea!

I got up. The woman had changed into street clothes and I noticed that she was wearing two dangly earrings. Her face was made up. Two naked legs jutted out from under a long winter skirt.

We need to see Ivan Petrovich! said the woman.

I nodded numbly and let her lead me back through the employee hallways.

(38)

Ivan Petrovich was a slightly graying man of forty. His clothes were poor and his face was fixed in a scowl.

Ivan Petrovich, said the lady, This young man has a problem... Maybe you can help him?

I explained the whole thing. When I mentioned OVIR Ivan Petrovich cocked his brow:

He told you to go to OVIR? he asked.

Yes, to get my invitation.

Hmph! OVIR can't help you with that. Let me see your passport...

I gave him the passport. He took it and checked the pages. When he looked up, something seemed to catch his eye:

Your jacket, he asked, Is it real leather?

My jacket?

I think so, I said.

Did you buy it here or there?

I bought it there. I mean it was a gift from my Aunt.

Ivan Petrovich nodded, and without smiling went behind the wall.

(39)

6:26 a.m.

When I told the woman why I needed to go home she looked at me tenderly:

Poor thing..., she said, And how old was she?

Fifty-three I think. Maybe more.

What? You don't even know your own mother's age?

We weren't close.

Don't say that...! It's not true. A person is always closest to his mother. That's not a distance you can choose.

Maybe, I said, But somehow we managed to do it.

The woman stopped as if considering something very important, and then said:

She was very young, your mother.

She had me early, I said.

Do you have any brothers or sisters?

No I'm an only child.

Well, that explains everything...

As we spoke, the woman told me proudly that she had two children of her own and even told me their names.

Really? I said when she had finished, I had a girlfriend by that name... she liked potatoes.

A Russian girlfriend?

Yes. It only lasted a few months though.

A few months? Shame on you!

Me?

Shame on you... did you leave her? Did you use her?

No, I just... nobody used anybody, we just sort of got to the point where we understood each other too well for a serious relationship.

It's a pity, she said and then: You know, if you treat them right Russian wives are the best in the world....

Just then Ivan Petrovich came out from behind the wall. His hands were filled with papers. He walked over to us and had started to ask something, but in mid-sentence his eyes caught my jacket again:

You say this jacket was a present from your Aunt? he asked feeling the collar with his thumb and forefinger.

Yes, I said.

Any ideas how much something like this costs?

I told him approximately.

How do you like that! he said, It's even more expensive here than there...!

Ivan Petrovich nodded and handed me my passport. A paper was tucked inside.

Okay, he said, You're ready to go.

I am?

You just need to sign this form here. Just sign right there under my signature....

And that's it? I can leave?

And you can leave.

What about a fine?

I waived your fine for you. But next time be more careful with your visa...

I didn't know what to say. I wanted to say something to the man. To the woman. But I was too dumb; I took the visa without thanking them.

Without thanking the woman I left for home.

And only later, in America, when I was standing in black with my head bent and hands clasped before me, only then would I realize what I should give the woman who had helped me. At the least likely of moments I was already planning my return to her...

(40)

7:37 a.m.

But first I had to leave. And it was almost time. My mother was waiting for me. Aunt Helen was waiting. My mind was numb. My body was also numb. I had stopped understanding, but one more thing remained: my hand held the pen thickly as I did my best to fill out the faded Customs declaration:

Name:	NEVER
Citizenship:	BLUE
Country of Destination:	MY MOTHER
Arriving from:	?!?!?
Date:	(1USD=1620RUR)
Purpose of visit:	SLEEP
Luggage:	ZERO PIECES
Currency (U.S.):	ZERO DOLLARS
Currency (USSR):	TWO KOPECKS

* * * * * * * * * *

Book 6. 'Next Stop, Voikovskaya'

(1)

To understand why Russians don't smile in public we need to experience their metro turnstiles — the ones that stay open until the last possible moment only to slam violently shut if you haven't paid your fare correctly, and, at times, even if you *have*. To understand why Muscovites are as proud as second parents we need to rejoice in the regularity of their system of underground transportation — the world's finest and most efficient. And without riding a twelve-story escalator, without falling repeatedly, how can we even begin to understand the relentless complexity of emotions that hinders decisiveness?

It has been said that it is not for the mind to comprehend the Russian Soul; its width, its breadth cannot be measured. Especially by people who smile. But if we can pass uninjured through the narrow turnstile, if the woman behind us will stop pushing on us, and if we can just make out what the mechanical voices are trying to insist, then we can, at the very least, say that we've *tried.*

Carefully, we place a metal token into the slot of the metro turnstile and listen as it falls heavily into its stomach. We walk through the open gates which this time do not close on us.

And with that our journey begins, slowly and inauspiciously, at the Zhdanovskaya metro station.

(2)

That year spring arrived on Aeroflot: late but well-received. And the birds sang. And the people forgot. And the winter melted like nylon pressed lightly against a Marlboro.

(3)

'Zhdanovskaya'

It is summer. Young women stand in flower-print dresses. Men wear starched collar shirts tucked into shrinking slacks that reveal socks tucked into worn shoes. The women's hair is long and straight. Their shoes are old but well-polished. The men's shoes are also polished, but *their* hair is parted on the wrong side. It doesn't take long for a train to come — less than two minutes — and when it does the crowd enters the metro car in one sweating surge. It is the origin station and empty seats, for now, can still be found. Of course it's easier to sit, but we prefer to stand even though it is a long way to our destination: it is a long way to Voikovskaya. Inside the car, people are taking out their reading material — Pushkin, Kharms, the novelist Lev Tolstoy — and beginning to read. And as we stand, intimidated and quiet, we feel inadequate and defenseless, our hands empty, our eyes forced to travel nervously over the length of the metro car. Although we are standing, we close our eyes, pretend to sleep — it's better that way. *Tomorrow we will buy a fat book*, any *fat book!* The doors remain open for some time, the train humming in anticipation. Then they close violently with a loud crash. We are startled by the sound, shaken yet afraid to move. A few seconds later a mechanical voice comes over the loud speaker:

'Caution — the doors are closing! Next stop, Ryazansky Prospekt...'

(4)

After I was fired from my job at the institute I decided to offer private English lessons at my small apartment. The overwhelming majority of my students were young semi-professional women named Irina.

My first group was the hardest. Despite their shared name, the three women turned out to be as different as Russian women could be. Irina, on the one hand, was intelligent; her English was stronger than that of the others, and so I did my best to overlook her. Irina, on the other hand, was polite, her answers much softer than Irina's and at times more sincere than my questions. Once, when asked to use the construction 'the problem is...,' she paused to think for a few seconds before responding wistfully:

The problem is that it's not his baby, she said.

Irina, unlike the other two, was neither intelligent nor polite; she was strictly business, writing furiously in her notebook and interrogating me on subtle grammatical points. To each of my answers she would stare distrustfully at the words before writing them down and proceeding to her next question. Dutifully, I did my best to appease her, and in fact everything went smoothly enough until one day she asked me to explain the difference between *high* and *tall*.

Well, I answered, Inflation is high but Gorbachev is tall.

I don't get it? she said.

Okay, just try to remember it like this: a building can be tall but not high; a bird can only be high.

What about a mountain?

Well a mountain is high. But it can be tall sometimes too, depending on the mountain. For example, if the mountain in question is taller than you, then it would be considered high. But if it were even higher than that, then it would most definitely be tall.

Irina had stopped writing in her notebook.

It was our last lesson.

(5)

'Ryazansky Prospekt.'

The metro car is clean, shocking for its absolute lack of advertising. The seats are arranged in lengthwise benches along the windows so that the passengers can sit in long rows elbow-to-elbow and stare blankly across the aisles at each other. And that is exactly what they do. They stare blankly. Or they read — Boy, do they ever! Sitting, standing, eating, sleeping, just give a Russian a book and you can bet she'll read it. Give a Russian a poem and he will surely take it to heart. Noticing this, we pull out *our* book. It is fat but new; the words are already faded, though not yet wet. And as we stand there, it is our protection, our disguise, and our eventual downfall all wrapped into one. At this stop — the second — seats fill up quickly and passengers desiring to sit should do it now, or they will stand until their destination. Which for us is Voikovskaya. There are oh-so-many stations between here and Voikovskaya, but we will wait patiently. We will wait patiently because it is at Voikovskaya that something truly remarkable will happen, something so predictable and natural that it will shock us. It is Voikovskaya that will give meaning to it all. At Voikovskaya we will begin to understand...

'Caution — the doors are closing! Next stop, Kuzminki...'

(6)

My self-unemployment did not last long; the next day I received a call from a woman named Irina who, along with two other young semi-professional friends, wanted to improve her English once a week. The first lesson we spoke about their names. The following week we discussed America; the week after that, slavery and oppression.

This group of students was unique in that each knew English from A to Z, and would have spoken fluently if not for articles: It is so difficult, they complained. I know, I said. Can you explain it to us? they asked. I'll try, I said. Can you try again? they pleaded. I just did, I said.

But we still don't understand!

Patiently, I tried to be patient. Understandably, they tried to understand. But it was hopeless. The mistakes continued. The three women struggled, then despaired, then eventually accepted their fate, each coming to terms with it in her own way: Irina used *the*; Irina used *a*; and Irina, the laziest of the three, simply omitted articles altogether.

And a time passed. And the English improved. And like King of Clubs I led our discussions through forests of grammar, often becoming lost, but never once dying. Our fourth lesson was devoted to the color blue; the fifth to red; the sixth to measuring the intricacies of the Russian Soul. It was Irina who started the conversation:

A Russian Soul, she explained, is a very root of our society.

That's truth, Irina agreed, It is very important concept.

Have you heard about it...? Irina then asked.

Vaguely, I answered, but I still don't understand what it is specifically.

It's a...

It's the...

It's...

I can tell you in the Russian..., said Irina.

Out of the question, I said, These are English lessons so you should speak English.

Okay, It's when the... it's when the person... no no that's not right... It's when the *Russian* person... well, that is to say... no... okay... it's like this...

She stopped:

May I use the dictionary? she asked.

No, I answered.

Russian Soul, Irina blurted out in flawless Russian, eto...

I held up my finger: English only!

Irina stuttered over some English words, looked around for support, moved to grab her dictionary, but then as if realizing that there were too many words there, simply sat helplessly:

I can't say it in an English language, she said.

You can too, I lied.

I can't.

Try.

It's hopeless.

I know what you can do! said Irina attempting to be helpful, Try to explain it using gestures!

English gestures, I reminded.

But she doesn't know gestures in the English, said Irina.

Well in that case, Irina suggested, Use gestures that don't mean anything....

And so using meaningless English gestures Irina explained the intricacies of the Russian soul. I thanked them for the information. They thanked me for the lesson, paid in dollars for my time, and left for home. See you next Tuesday, they said. See you! I said.

But when they had gone I realized that I still couldn't measure the Russian Soul. I couldn't feel it... I couldn't see it...

...I couldn't even smell it.

(7)

'Kuzminki.'

Are you getting off at the next stop? someone asks us from behind as the train grinds to a halt. With time we will grow accustomed to Russians' prying questions, but for now the words catch us off-guard and we stutter over our answer: Actually, we say, we're going to Voikovskaya because it is there that something remarkable will happen, it is there that... The crowd behind us listens to our long answer impatiently. Smiling, we ask them to tell us about themselves: And where are *you* getting off? we say. But it is too late. The doors have opened and before we know it the people have pushed rudely by us without even saying good-bye. As they exit, we watch their backs move away from us and feel slighted for some reason. It is clear that we will never see their faces again and we feel an inexplicable loss. But then the mechanical voice shocks us back to reality:

'Caution — the doors are closing! Next stop, Tekstilshchiki...'

(8)

Eventually, Aunt Helen stopped writing. Unanswered letters became answers to unanswered letters. Then in winter her letters stopped arriving. The care packages continued to not arrive, until finally they stopped not arriving as well. We still talked on the phone, but our conversations had become at once more expensive and less interesting. At length she would describe her weather; in short I would announce my rate of exchange. Neither could grasp the importance of these things for the other. Whereas before I had been curt and annoyed when speaking with her, now I spoke respectfully and without interest. My words smiled falsely even though my face no longer did. And Aunt Helen, in return, demanded less and less of me during our conversations. She stopped asking questions. She did not mention vegetables. Not once did she cry.

And then at some point I noticed a change: her voice became

weak and controlled. Her laugh subsided. During our telephone conversations, her eyes no longer sparkled. As if she had resigned herself to the situation. As if she had understood fully and correctly her new place in my life.

Silently she just sort of faded. Like a husband who loves his wife enough to accept her lover; or like a lover who knows not to expect love.

(9)

With time, I came to understand the mistakes that Russians make when speaking English and jotted them down on papers which I quickly lost. This system worked well enough and in time I was able to conduct lessons without thinking.

(10)

Wrong: At last I have begun to feel myself at home.
Right: I have begun to feel at home in Russia.

(11)

'Tekstilshchiki'

It is winter. Passengers in worn jackets continue to sit, stand, crouch; books in hand, they sway and waver to the motion of the metro car. Now, with relish, they read politically opinionated newspapers. Revisionist history. Archives. Banned books. Western detectives. They read that in the United States the average American has seventy-eight sexual partners during her lifetime. Doesn't smoke. And can't even name Alexander Sergeevich Pushkin's most famous novel. In these texts they see a new world opening up before them. Words that have been around for many many years will soon disappear. New words are rising to take their place. In these black and white texts some often-heard words will be seen for the first time. Like all words they will fall short of their purpose. Though at times some will persuade. And others will offend. And still others will change and be changed.

'Caution — the doors are closing! Next stop, Volgogradsky Prospekt...'

(12)

One day, after putting on her shoes, a student came up to me and asked in English:

I'm sorry to trouble you, she said, But can I ask a favor?

Of course, I said

If it's too much of a problem you can just tell me — I'll understand.

Ask me anything, I exaggerated, Anything at all.

Are you sure?

Absolutely, I lied.

Well you see... There's this person... Actually, it's my friend... And she has... I want to say... She is...

What's her name? I mean your friend.

Irina. Her name's Irina — like mine. You see she has a problem and you're the only person I know who might be able to help her.

Really? What's the problem?

Well you see she's young and attractive and extremely polite...

Poor thing.

Yes, but the problem is that she's unmarried, I mean she doesn't have any sort of husband...

A husband?

That's right.

Wow that really is a problem! But you see I can't help. My last name...

No no! That's not the problem. The problem is that she can't get an American visa. She wants to go to America. She's applied four times, but has been refused each time.

A visa?

Yes, do you know anything about how she can get one?

Not really, but I can probably find out.

Are you sure?

In life everything is probable.

Will you help her?

I'll try.

Can I give her your phone number?

Sure.

Can she call you?

Of course.

What time is comfortable for you?

I held up my finger without thinking, but Irina had already realized her mistake:

Convenient! she said.

And at that I laughed:

Any time, I told her, You can have her call me any time.

(13)

'Volgogradsky Prospekt'

The doors open and in barrels a broad-chested old woman. In her right hand she is holding a large bag. In her left hand she holds another large bag. Using the bite of silver teeth, her mouth is gripping a cage full of live chickens. Both hands are calloused and worn; both bags contain cheap smuggled clothes that she has bought for seven and will sell for eight. The clothes are quickly sewn and poorly made; they come complete with emblazoned texts:

GENUINE QUALITY FOR THE WHOLE WORLD

or:

AMERICAN STANDARD OF QUALITY OF THE FASHION
IN EVERY TASTE AND COMPLEXSION

or:

THIS GARMENT WAS PRODUCTED FOR YOUR COMFORT
IN DAY-TO-DAY SURROUNDINGS WITH COMPLETE FIT
AND EXTERNAL QUALITY

or simply:

HELP ME, I AM AN AMERICAN SPY

Once during a long ride a friend asks us to translate the jacket across from us. We struggle to grasp the depth of its meaning, but we are far too shallow. Luckily, we have the wherewithal to oversimplify: In English, we tell him, this combination of words means *Made in Asia*. Our friend stares at the letters blankly. As do we. In fact, we stare harder. But as we have learned, this is not Asia. It is most definitely not Asia. So why the imported jackets? Why the relentless influx of Chinese clothes, Japanese calculators, and

Indian ideology? The country, it seems, is lost in its own reforms. Nothing is being done. Even less is being made. Old women no longer pawn cheese. Taxes go uncollected. Paintings are bought from time to time, but almost never sold. Even the yellow numbers on the escalator steps have begun to chip away. The nation is at a standstill; as if everyone is too busy discussing why nothing is being done, why even less is being made. And here, in the middle of this, an old woman has taken the initiative to buy for seven and sell for eight, thereby clothing a country. It is tenuous at best. But it is all we have, and for now it works. And so despite all this the train plods on... Forward, it seems. Onward, it would seem. But then, really, who knows? After all, we are in a tunnel, in the dark, and in the synthetic light we can only assume that we are really going somewhere. A hundred feet below the ground we can only turn the pages of our book and trust that we are any closer to being *there* than we were a paragraph ago.

'Caution — the doors are closing! Next stop, Proletarskaya...'

(14)

Irina's friend called early the next morning. On the telephone her voice was flustered, her words came faster than a metro station. She was calling from Irina, she said, And thanks for helping her and had she woken me? and you see the problem was that she was not married and didn't work and had talked to a lot of people and been told that it was impossible for a young single unemployed woman to go to the U.S. because she wouldn't get a visa, but it was oh-so-important, that is to say, she just had to go, she just had to visit America because...

No, I said sleepily, You didn't wake me. I've been awake for hours.

(15)

'Proletarskaya'

Something is wrong with the mechanical voice. First it speeds up excessively, announcing the stop like a shrill cashier. Then it groans to a slow halt, becomes as low and gruff as Vladimir Vysotsky's. When it can speak no more it goes on strike. Without its guidance it seems that we may have missed our destination. We try to remember what the last stop was, what the next one should be. Naively, we look through the humming window for a signpost. But all we can see is the black that is rattling by. Black, black, and more black. We are reminded of a saying that we have recently heard: Black is black, say Russians, even in Africa. And even in Africa two kopecks equal two kopecks. Even in Africa Russia is Russia. Even in Africa. Even in *Africa*...! But this train, *our* train, is not in Africa. This train is headed north. From purple to green. From there to here. From summer to winter to summer... From Zhdanovskaya all the way to Voykovskaya....

(16)

Where should we meet? she asked.

Where are you coming from? I answered.

Aviamotornaya, she said, And you?

I live at Vykhino.

We can meet in the metro.

All right. Where exactly?

Where do our lines cross?

I don't think they do, wait, let me get a map...

They don't?

Let met see... no they don't.

Well, I'll be changing to the ring line. And you're on the purple line, which means that we can meet at... what station do they cross at — the ring line with the purple?

Taganskaya.

Okay. Let's meet at Taganskaya.

Okay. Where specifically?

We can either meet at the first car, the last car, or the middle car coming from the center.

But the ring line doesn't come from the center.

Then let's meet in the middle of the platform.

Fine.

Tomorrow at Taganskaya, ring line, middle of platform?

That's right.

Great! I'll see you then...

Wait a minute! How will I recognize you — Can you describe yourself?

Sure... I'm tall, well-dressed, good looking, I'll be wearing a short sexy skirt with nylon pantyhose and a red scarf.

What color?

Red — like a long-stemmed rose. Pantyhose and a sexy skirt. I'll be carrying two books: in one hand a collection of poems by Pushkin, and in the other hand a textbook called *English For Semi-Professional Women Named Irina*. Did you get all that?

Yes, I lied.

And what about you? What do you look like?

Me? I don't know... I'm of medium height. Medium build. My hair is medium length. I have no scars or warts.

How old are you?

I guess you could say that soon I'll be middle-aged.

Will you be smiling?

No, I said, Not any more.

Then how will I recognize you?

Easily. I'll make sure to be holding my old copy of *Anna Karenina*.

(17)

'Taganskaya. Change to the Ring Line and Marksistskaya station.'

The problem, she explained over dinner at her small apartment, was that she had been trying for over a year to receive a tourist visa. Her first application had been denied because she had never been to America; the second was declined because she had already been refused the first time; the third application was returned without explanation; and after turning her down for the fourth time, the consular officer, smiling kindly, simply shrugged his shoulders and advised her to try again at a later date.

That was a month ago.

I don't understand what I've done wrong, she said, I try not to take all this personally — I really do — but I don't know how I'm supposed to take it when all a person really wants is to travel to the U.S. for tourist purposes and in order to do that you need to have a visa, which is fine, but then when you come to the embassy with all your documents and wait and wait and wait and then when you finally get to see the counselor all he does is ask you personal questions that have nothing to do with anything at all, I mean, is it any of his business who I live with? — I would say not! — and how would *you* feel if someone that you've never met before just out-of-nowhere asks you if you're married? Can you imagine — 'Are you married?' I mean how would *you* answer that question if I asked you, not, of course, that I would ever ask you because I realize that it's none of my business and even if it were my business I still wouldn't ask because...

Actually, I told her, I'm not married. I'm not married at all.

'Caution — the doors are closing! Next stop, Ploschad Nogina. Exit right side...'

(18)

And then I noticed a strange thing: suddenly my life had become inextricably linked to my lessons. My failures became confused grammar. My betrayed hopes became forgotten articles. I lost track of where my own life ended and when the lessons were beginning. I explained grammar using incidents from my childhood: '...*But the glass was so tall. The milk was so high...!*' To show future tense I spoke of weddings; to illustrate the past I described my mother. And as for the present, I explained, condoms were *uncomfortable* whereas love was *inconvenient*. To my surprise I began to laugh sincerely. I stopped not thinking. I drank vodka to wash down the vodka; and still, even in the face of all this, I couldn't make myself throw up....

(19)

'Kitai-Gorod. Exit right side. Change to the Kaluzhsko-Rizhskaya line.'

What was that? People look at each other, confused. Is it some sort of mistake? Where are they? Where are they going? The passengers are at a loss. Some rush out the door, only to rush back in a few seconds later. Others exit never to return. The majority remain in their seats annoyed but unshaken. They grumble instinctively and return to their reading material as if to say, It doesn't matter where we are — it doesn't matter where we're going because sooner or later we'll get there anyway. This is not the first place that has been unnamed; it will not be the last. For a long awkward moment the doors stay open and then close violently, dividing those on the inside from those on the outside... Unperturbed, we look up from our fat book, which by now is dry and just starting to get interesting, and lean expectantly into the future. *But at this station the platform is on the right!* And when the train begins to move against our expectations we are caught leaning the wrong way and go running through the train — from here to then — with our fat book in hand. The train gathers speed, rattling and sputtering, but most importantly, moving, running forward at the same speed as we are, but in the opposite direction.

'Caution — the doors are closing! Next Stop, Kuznetsky Most...'

(20)

The next day I went to the U.S. Embassy to find out why Irina was having problems obtaining a visa and what could be done to help her. After showing my citizenship to the Russian guard, I entered a small waiting room where an American consular officer sat behind a window. It was off-hours — I had been admitted due only to the color of my passport — and so I walked up to his window without standing in line.

The man was cordial and answered my questions dutifully. The problem was, he explained, that the officers were responsible for weeding out possible immigrants, that is to say people who travel as tourists with the real intention of staying. This, he explained, was especially prevalent among young unmarried women with no employment and so during her interviews Irina must have come across as a possible immigrant. The best thing to do, he advised me, was to collect as much documentary evidence as possible in order to convince the counselor that she had strong enough ties to Russia, in other words, that she didn't want to stay in America. There were no set documents for this, but she would be good to bring a copy of her marriage certificate; birth certificates if she had children; proof that she owned property — a small apartment or car; a document from her place of gainful employment....

...Listening to the man my eyes began to cloud. *Was it really this difficult just to go to America?*

What if she's not married? I asked.

If she's not married.... Has she been to America before?

No.

Has she been to any other English-speaking countries?

No.

Then it's a problem.

Why? I mean, what does she have to do to receive a visa — get married?!

It would help.

What about her refusals, could they play a role in her not getting a visa?

Maybe. A lot depends on how many she's had.

Four.

Ouch. She can go ahead and try. In her situation it can't hurt.

I thanked the man and started to leave:

Oh and one more thing..., he said.

I stopped.

...Whatever you do, don't lie... if the counselor catches her lying during the interview then you can bet that she'll never get a visa..!

That night I called Irina and explained what the man had told me. Although it was not news for her, she became enraged: How dare they think that just because I'm not married and have no job and no property I need to move to their country and who do they think they are anyway with their fake smiles and their broken accents because I've lived here my entire life, and do they really think that all Russians are just dying to go to America, as if that's the only thing we can think about, as if the only thing that anybody in the world wants is the honor of immigrating to America...?

(21)

'Kuznetsky Most. Change to the Lubyanka Station.'

Changes! Changes! What's the deal with all these changes all of a sudden! Before the way was straight but simple, and now at every step there is an alternate route, at every stop a decision. Mikhail Gorbachev had disappeared from the political scene. Like an exiting passenger. Like bad literature. Like anything that has been around longer than too long.... Now the metro cars jerk and bang against each other. The passengers look around, annoyed. The driver is obviously new and his inexperience snaps their necks and throws them slightly off-balance; they stumble instinctively but hang on. With the oily overhead bar in one hand and their words in the other, they simply relax their bodies to the gentle shaking of the ride — never even seeing who is really driving — and wait for the mechanical voice and the escalator that will take them home. Then the car starts into motion, the train smoothes itself out, the passengers straighten themselves, and with a whoosh of air the windows turn black....

'Caution — the doors are closing! Next stop, Pushkinskaya...'

(22)

With time Irina and I became closer. She stopped referring to me in the plural. She bummed my cigarettes. She told me about her failed loves and successful abortions. At times, she even let me get a word in edgewise. Eventually, she began to trust my words, and only then did she admit the real reason for needing the visa so badly:

In truth she wanted to immigrate to America.

Life here, she told me, is too depressing. In times like these who needs people like me? Who needs young unemployed poets?

It's not the times, I comforted her, Strictly speaking there's not a country in the world that needs poets.

Except for America. America needs them badly. And so that's where I'm going if I get my visa.

I see.

But you know it really is a pity.

What is? About the oppression of blacks in America?

No, no, it's not that.... It's just that I've always wanted to be married.

I said nothing.

Do you know what I mean?

Again I said nothing. Irina looked at me strangely and then spoke up:

Can I ask you a personal question? she asked.

Go ahead, I said.

Why didn't you ever get married?

I don't know, I said.

Do you want to get married?

I don't know. I guess so.

So why didn't you?

I suppose because nobody ever asked.

(23)

And that's when Irina proposed to me: Marry me, she said. But I can't, I said. Marry me anyway. But I don't have any money. You can find work in America. But I don't want to live in America. You won't have to. I won't? No, I'll live there by myself. Without me? The distance will be good for us. Distance? Yes, it will help you forget....

Forget...?

Like hell! Not after all we've been through...

It's just that if I had an American husband, she explained, They would *have* to give me a visa.

But I hate weddings.

Have you ever been to one?

No.

Then how do you know you hate them?

I just know.

You shouldn't say that you'll never go to one.

Why not?

Because it's inevitable.

Nothing in life is inevitable. Everything is probable.

Marriage is inevitable. Death is inevitable. Life, in most cases, is inevitable....

Why 'in most cases'?

What about taxes? I prompted her.

Taxes? Are you kidding me? In our country only communists pay taxes. And even *they* don't pay them!

(24)

'Pushkinskaya. Change to the Tverskaya and Chekhovskaya stations...'

Are you getting off at the next stop? we ask the person in front of us and she nods. The doors open and we exit. Tripping over boxes of newly purchased televisions and home computers, we exit into the swirling mass of metrogoers. Spinning, twisting, bumping into women with bags and cages. Up the stairs. Going the wrong way against the flow. Fighting through the pushing crowd to get onto the escalator which carries us to the verge of the Tverskaya station. Past semi-musicians, past old women selling Russia, past advertisements for nylon pantyhose and lubricated condoms. Then a staircase. And back once again into the spinning, twisting surge. Down the steps. Turn to the right. Proceed to where the first car will be. *It's been exactly one minute and forty seconds since the last train. One-forty-one. One-forty-two.* And then a horn sounds. A light in the end of the tunnel. A rumbling that becomes louder and louder until its breaks are screeching by us. The train comes to a stop, the doors open, people spill out. We let them pass and then we enter. Once inside we see that the faces are different but the same. Unsmiling and severe, they no longer surprise or terrify us — we are no longer interested or interesting. And neither are they. We are as similar to them as they are to us; like them we are not as young as we used to be, and for the first time ever we think seriously about sitting. It is a milestone of sorts. Gone are the naive principles that have kept us upright. Gone is the patience that helped us to stand and withstand. And besides, after the change, everyone is a little wearied. But for the moment it is rush hour and there are no empty seats. *Don't worry!* we tell ourselves *It's not so far now. The hardest part is behind us.* And it's true. For better or for worse, the danger has passed for good. Now Voikovskaya is just a matter of reading what has been given us, it is only a matter of waiting patiently....

'Caution — the doors are closing! Next stop, Mayakovskaya...'

(25)

Let's say — thank God it's not true! — let's say you don't know a word of English. In truth, it could have been any language of the world, but let's say you chose to not learn English. Of course it's impossible not to know a single word of the most mispronounced language in the world, and so, as a result, you know words like *good*, and *shit*, and *love*, and *cowboy*. Like most humans you can enunciate the letters *o* and *k* with only a slight accent, and feel at home with phrases as diverse as *happy end, step-by-step, and it's a pity...*

Home for you is a small apartment with pipes everywhere. Pipes in the kitchen. Pipes in the bathroom. Pipes behind the television and above your bed. You've been dreaming of a renovation for as long as you can remember. Nowadays, you've heard, it's possible to hide the pipes. Zip-zap and they're a memory. Problem is that renovations cost money. And to earn money you need to work. And to work you need to find a job... and to find a job... to find a *good* job you need to know English.

And so you put off the renovation. Make a promise to study English, even borrowing your friend's old textbooks from not-so-many years ago: 'The Great October Socialist Revolution,' you read aloud to yourself, 'was great.'

Surprisingly, your English does not improve. You still cannot speak. You cannot understand. And this means you cannot find good work. Which means you cannot earn decent money. Which means you cannot depipe your apartment.

In fact your English is so bad that there are no perspectives in the job market, all of which require at least a minimal understanding of English. Without English, you can go nowhere. In fact, you can't go anywhere. And this means one thing. This means that there is only one option left to you given your dim future. There is only one place where you can go even with your poor knowledge of English:

America.

Why not? Why not immigrate? After all, there's really nothing to keep you here. Just your parents, your friends, your traditions, your culture, your language, and everything else that you have ever been taught.... But how important is all of that, really? In America, you've heard, they don't have pipes. In America, you've been told, they have to create problems for themselves. In America, you've read, the average household salary is seventy-eight thousand dollars...

...per month!

And so you fill out your application. Married? No. Employed? No. Been to America? Never. Reason for leaving? To learn English. Shrewdly, you do not apply for an immigrant visa; these, you have been warned, take years to receive. You apply for a tourist visa which, if you receive it, will enable you to leave immediately. Where will you live once you are there? What will you do? How will you feel once your decision has been rendered irreversible? How will you communicate without knowing English?

In your mind the answers are simple:

You will live *there*;

You will earn seventy-eight thousand dollars per month;

You will feel yourself *okay*

And as for communication, how hard could it be? With your salary how can you not be understood? After all, money talks. Especially in America. Loudly and eloquently. Fluently and beautifully. Money talks anytime, anywhere, and for anyone.

Money talks in any language...

...Any language, that is, but Russian.

(26)

Before going to her interview, Irina and I needed to coordinate our stories. She made a list of all the questions she had been asked in previous interviews and together we concocted fail-proof answers to them, as well as to those questions that she would likely be asked this time:

Q: What were our relations?

A: We were good friends. Our relationship had begun by mail while I was still living in America. A two-year exchange of letters. Then when I came to Moscow I called her and we met in the middle of the Taganskaya metrostation. Since that day we had dreamed of going to America together. We had become the best of friends. We had looked for mushrooms. She had read me her poetry. I had repeatedly explained the black-white problem in America. She had listened. I had explained again. And again. And again and again until just when it seemed that it would never happen... we at last found some mushrooms. In time we became closer than a climax until at last we could honestly say that we were the very best of friends.

Q: What would be the purpose of her forthcoming visit to America?

A: Now as a gesture of international goodwill I was inviting her to be my guest in America. She would be staying with me and I would be proudly showing her my home. After that I would show her the rest of the city. And then, time permitting, I would show her America. Color by color by color I would introduce her to all of it. To the country where passports are blue, and democracy, in most cases, comes easier than abortion.

Q: Why had she applied so many times for a tourist visa? Why was she applying now? Was she desperate to leave? Didn't she really want to immigrate?

A: Not really. What she was trying to do was to visit America. Nothing more. But her mistake had been not fully grasping the application process: the first time she applied she had not realized that in order to receive an American visa an applicant has to have already been to America; the second time, she had applied so that she could travel to America, which, in her understanding, would help her to satisfy this first requirement and thereby receive a visa which would mean that she could travel to America.... As for the third application, it wasn't clear why she had been denied. And after refusing her for the fourth time, hadn't the consular officer, smiling kindly, advised her to try again at a later date?

Q: Where did she work? For how long? What type of company was it? What was her position?

A: For the last two years she had worked in a friend's company as a secretary-referent. The company dealt in international trade — in other words Cuban vodka and Korean Marlboros.

Q: What was her salary?

A: This would be determined by Irina's friend, the one who had agreed to give her the fake work slip.

Q: What sort of personal ties did she have to keep her in Russia?

A: Her mother and her father and brother all lived in Moscow. Two aunts and one uncle as well as a host of cousins and friends lived nearby.

Q: Yes, but what sort of close ties did she have? In other words, was she married?

A: No. Not even a little.

Q: Where was the money coming from for the trip?

A: She was paying for the airfare out of her salary. I was responsible for everything else.

Q: Did she have any property?

A: A small one-room apartment.

Q: What documents did she have to validate everything that she had said?

A: A letter from me, the date forged three years earlier. A picture of her family. A fake work slip.

Q: Did she have an official invitation from her host?

A: Of course she did.

And so, diligently, I sat down to write it:

(27)

'Dear Irina!

I'd like to take this opportunity to invite you to the United States of America for *two weeks only*. As you know, my country is a great and proud nation which welcomes people from all over the world, regardless of their race, creed, religion, occupation, age, marital status, or other such unforeseen circumstances.

During these *two weeks* you can live with me and my Aunt Helen, who has been eager to meet you for all three of the years that you and I have known each other. I realize that you have gainful and stable employment that you would not give up for anything in the world, and that you would in no way be a burden to our society while you are here. Nevertheless, I am prepared to assume all responsibility for any and all expenses that may arise during your stay, including medical and dental.

I know that you will miss your beloved homeland during your brief stay with me, but just remember that it will only be for *two weeks*, after which you will undoubtedly return home to your spacious one-room apartment and to the many people in Moscow who love you and who would be shattered if you were to emigrate. If these loved ones should complain about missing you during your trip, just remind them that this will be a *once-in-a-lifetime* opportunity for you to practice your English, and that, rest assured, after the *two short weeks* are up you will be coming back home.

Yours truly,

(28)

I looked at the words. And then paused. Completely satisfied with their eloquence, I signed my name to the letter.

(29)

'Mayakovskaya'

The doors open and in straggles a woman wrapped in dirty cloths. Her skin is crusty and blackened; her face has been burnt by the sun. In her arms she holds a baby whose skin is even dirtier. The passengers look at the woman in amazement. For them, she is the first, but not the last and not even the only person who is asking for alms in this way — in the neighboring car a five-year-old gypsy boy is playing an accordion, and in the car next to him a legless man looks up pitifully from a wooden cart. The doors close and the train jerks into motion. Dear passengers! the woman begins in a plaintive voice, Please excuse me for turning to you like this. My husband and I have come from another city that is very far away. Our documents and our money were stolen. Now we're living at the train station and don't have enough money to pay for our way back home. Help us please! Please help us by giving within your means.... By now the train is roaring in the tunnel and the woman's last sentences are less heard than felt. The woman and her baby make their way down the aisle. The other passengers give what they can — here a hundred rubles, there a green plastic metro token, here and there a fistful of worthless coins — and the woman gathers the money with her head bent humbly. Gratefully. Slowly she drags her burden toward us, bringing with her as she goes the eyes of our fellow travelers. Watching her approach, we become mesmerized. Colors become muted. Sounds fall away. Meekly the woman approaches until she is directly in front of us. Head bent, hand outstretched, she is waiting — as are the rest of the passengers — for us to give within our means....

(30)

Irina and I agreed to meet outside the U.S. Embassy on Tuesday at exactly 6:00 a.m. No Fuzz! I said. Go to hell! she said.

(31)

'Belorusskaya. Change to the Ring line.'

I took out my wallet. It contained exactly three hundred dollars and two kopecks — three one-hundred-dollar bills and a single two-kopeck coin. *Why hadn't I broken my dollars into smaller denominations? Why hadn't I brought rubles?* The train was grinding to a halt. The other passengers were looking at me. *Three hundred dollars and two kopecks! Would I really give away one hundred hard-earned dollars just like that? Or could it be that the time had finally come to part with the coin?* The outstretched hand was waiting, the other passengers were looking at me: I had to give something. I had to. *Here* things were different. Here in this tunnel; in the synthetic light that was illuminating my Russia. Reluctantly I looked at the money in my wallet. Expectantly, the other passengers looked at me looking at the money in my wallet. *What would it be? How much should I give? How much did I have to give?* The train was grinding to a halt. It was either here or never. *How much must I give?* And then suddenly I remembered something. A scene from a fat and favorite book. A scene that had not made sense to me then, but which now made all the sense in the world. *Why had I hesitated?* I took the money from my wallet. And bending over deeply I placed the three hundred dollars in the hand of the legless man on the wooden cart....

'Caution — the doors are closing. Next stop, Dinamo...'

(32)

When I arrived at the embassy it was a little after six. The American flag hung limply under the cold drizzling rain. A few people had already begun forming a line outside. With their documents in hand, they stood waiting for the doors to open. Off to the side amateur photographers offered instant photos to applicants who had forgotten them.

Standing there, I felt a dry bitterness in my throat. But the longer I waited under the rain for Irina, the wetter my bitterness became. *Who was doing a favor for whom, anyway? And how did I always get involved in things like this? And why didn't anybody in this country want my German dictionary... ?*

After an hour, Irina showed up. She had dressed wrong. I knew it immediately. A sexy mini-skirt. Lipstick the color of a long-stemmed rose. Hair combed to a frizz. I started to say something, but she interrupted me. Her voice was accusatory:

You could've shaved! she said.

What!

You might've shaved! she repeated.

I ran my hand over my face; the whiskers bristled like a broom. *My God she was right! When was the last time I'd shaved? Judging by the stubble it must have been at least three days ago... but no more than five — in other words, the worst possible amount! But why? Granted, there was a weekend, but I always drank on weekends. Sure there was a birthday party of a friend of a friend, but when you have bottles of soon-to-be-swallowed vodka, every day is a birthday of* somebody's *friend...*

...And that wouldn't be so bad, Irina continued her rebuke, But Jeez I can smell the vodka on your breath from a meter away...!

Now I remember... there had been some sort of Russian holiday mixed into the weekend. One of the new ones without its own traditions and so everyone simply drank. That's it! That's the reason for the dry bitterness; that's why we hadn't met at the embassy yesterday; that's why today was Tuesday....

I... I was going to shave, I told her, but decided not to. Besides it won't mean anything you know. In America the most important thing is to be natural, to be yourself.

Really? she said suspiciously.

Of course, I said, Trust me: the Americans will appreciate it. They'll realize that I'm one of them and you'll be guaranteed to get your visa.

Are you sure?

Absolutely. The most important thing is to make a good impression on them. You have to demonstrate that you're one of them. You have to play on the '*us* versus *them*' mentality.

And which are you?

I'm *us*.

And what would that make me?

You, of course, would be *them*. But because you're with me you automatically become *us*! See, it's all very logical.

Whatever, she said.

Look just give me your documents.

Irina pulled out a folder with the documents that she had collected.

Did you get the work slip?

Sure, she said and handed it to me. I took the paper and unfolded it; what I read made me gasp yet again: 'This is to certify that Irina Priklonskaya has worked as a secretary-referent in this company since August, 1992. During this time her net salary has averaged three thousand dollars per month.'

I read the words again, but again they said the same thing: '*...three thousand dollars per month.*'

Are you crazy? I said to Irina, You put a monthly salary of three thousand dollars!

Yeah, so?

Do you have any idea how much that is?

Well of course by your standards it's not much, but...

Three thousand dollars?!? Per month?!? For a secretary?!? Do you realize that the average salary for a secretary right now is two hundred dollars?

Not just a secretary. A secretary-referent.

What the hell is that?

It's like a secretary, but better.

Twenty-eight hundred dollars better?

Newly disheartened, I took stock of the documents we had to work with. They were as follows:

1. Two unsmiling photos.
2. A work slip stating that her salary is three thousand dollars per month.

3. My invitation

Hey Ira, I said to her, What will you do — hypothetically, of course — if they refuse you again?

Irina stopped suddenly, as if she had not considered this possibility:

You know, she said, The first time they turned me down I cried for days. In fact I cried right up until they turned me down the second time. But you know this time I don't think I'll cry at all. I don't think I'll feel anything.

That's good, I said, It's probably better that way.

When the doors opened, we shoved our way inside, paid our non-refundable application fee, and moved to the small waiting room where the interviews were to be held.

(33)

The waiting room where the interviews were being held was small, stuffy, and without chairs. The visa applicants, standing awkwardly in the crowded room, prepared for their interviews like schoolchildren before an examination: memorizing dates, checking figures, honing their conviction, practicing their smiles, repeating answers to standard questions: *I have worked as a Commercial Director in the company which deals in food products...*; in turn they cleared their throats and shuffled through stacks of papers, making and re-making sure that each and every document was in order: *My business card! Where's my business card?* Nervously they waited for their names to be called over the loudspeaker by the American counselors:

'Will the following people please proceed to Window Number Two: VOB-lina tatee-AN-a; ee-VAN-ov a-LEX-i; POP-ova OL-ga; YASH-tchlzkntrtklkchg di-MEET-ry...'

The lucky ones, hearing their name, snapped to attention and rushed promptly to the window. The others, hearing something vaguely resembling their name, looked around at each other with baffled expressions on their faces. *What was that? What did they say? Was that my name?*

'...SMIR-noff SE-men; JOOK-ovsky BOR-is; Please report to Window Number Five...'

One by one, the people approached the windows for their interviews with the clean-shaven counselors. And as they did, the others in the room — those who had not yet heard their names — eavesdropped on them, listening nervously and answering the counselors' questions in their minds. Instinctively, they huddled together to compare notes: *Did you hear what they asked the woman at window number three? They asked her how many people worked in her company! I don't have a clue how many people work in my company and I'm the director...! Does that mean they won't give me a visa...? And what was that... at window number one they asked the girl where her husband is! And how much money he makes. And where they met. And again how much money he makes. And why he isn't planning to travel with her... and again where they met...!*

Each interview lasted between thirty seconds and ten minutes depending on the person's marital status. When the interview was over, the applicant either received a light blue slip that meant the visa had been issued, or, if the person had been refused, she received her red passport back with a stamp that said: 'Documents Rec'd.'

Those who were given visas reacted similarly: Thank you! Thank you! they said. And greedily took the blue slip that meant — for them — America.

The reactions of the rejected varied as much as human character itself: some cried; some accepted their passports in proud silence; a few argued heatedly with the counselor — *What do you mean, immigrant? I just want to visit!* — while others asked for rational explanations, to which they were hastily given photocopied form letters with a form explanation: 'Unfortunately your application for a non-immigrant visa has been rejected because you have not met one or more of the following criteria...'

These rejections did not go unnoticed by the people waiting for their interviews; with each refusal their mouths became drier, their hearts beat louder: *Sure the others were being refused, but it couldn't happen to me, could it? After all, these counselors were experts, weren't they? Surely for them thirty seconds would be enough to see that I honestly don't intend to immigrate...!*

'Would the following people please proceed to Window #6: ZELD-ner na-TAL-ya; ...'

(34)

'Dinamo.'

It is late at night. The train is virtually empty except for a drunk man sprawled out on the length of an entire bench. The train is rocking us slightly. We have been standing for years, and now our legs are tired. Our body is numbed from the ride. *Haven't we stood long enough? Is there anything more that anyone could expect from us? Haven't we earned the right to sit? After all, it's late and our train is emptier than an escalator at night...!* And so we take a seat. Our eyes close in weary resolution. Our muscles relax. Our hands, which no longer hold anything fat, also relax. Sitting there, we slip into a peaceful restfulness. Finally, we fall asleep.

'Caution has no place in an aeroport when you are flying above, quietly, softly...'

(35)

This is my first time! said a voice.

When I looked up I saw that an old woman was standing in front of me and smiling blatantly; in the tension of the room her smile seemed all the more out of place.

I'm going to see my daughter in America, she said.

Really, I said.

Yes. She lives there now. Sent me an invitation!

The old woman took out a piece of paper and waved it proudly in front of my nose:

My daughter works in a bank. Makes good money! I haven't seen her in three years but she sent me this invitation. I can't understand a word of it but she said to take it to the embassy and so that's what I'm doing.

Do you have a lot of supporting documents? I asked her.

No. Don't need them. All I need is this invitation my daughter sent me. I haven't seen her for three years. She has an American husband and a baby. I'm going to see my grandson!

How's that working out? I mean how does your daughter like being married to an American?

They have a nice house. He has a good job. She's happy. She says she doesn't even miss home. Doesn't even want to come back. That's why I'm going to see her.

Irina, who until now had been absorbed in the two books that she was now reading — *Yevgeny Onegin* and *How to Meet the Provider of Your Dreams* — closed both books and looked at the woman intently:

How did your daughter find this American husband of hers? she asked, Was it here in Moscow?

Yes..., she answered.

She's very lucky, said Irina, How did it happen?

And using Irina's invitation, the woman told us the story of how they met:

(36)

The woman's daughter, after receiving her doctorate from a physics institute, and after trying to find work in her field and failing, had been forced to work full-time in a flower stand by the Alekseevskaya metrostation. Every day at work she would see a man in a coat and tie and with a briefcase: in the morning on his way to work, and in the evening on his way home. He worked as a consultant then, teaching Russian companies how to do something. He knew Russian well enough to explain that he didn't know Russian, and at first he could only stop to look at the flowers. But luckily, the woman's daughter had a master's degree in English and with time their relationship became more complex: he soon took to buying roses, first one at a time, then in pairs, and then by the dozens. Everyday like clockwork, he would present her a dozen roses which she would accept shyly. In time he found the words to ask her out, and she found the gestures to accept; they went to a Georgian restaurant by the Park Kultury metrostation. The weekend after that they went there again. The weekend after that they did this a third time, then a fourth, until at last it had become a sort of tradition: on weekdays he would buy roses from and for her, and during the weekend they would eat Georgian food like clockwork. This continued for several months. Finally, he asked her to marry him and she refused. Undeterred, he asked again but again she refused, this time categorically. In truth she was waiting for the third proposal, which in her understanding would mean that his love was sincere. A week passed. Then another week. He began taking an alternate route to and from work, he stopped stopping at the flower stand. At about this same time, she began to stop receiving roses, and the alarm bells sounded. She called his apartment but he did not answer. She left messages at his work but he did not return them. She looked expectantly for him both morning and night but he could not be found. Desperately she left a message with his secretary: 'Please come to my apartment on Tuesday at eight o'clock.' She had not indicated whether it should be in the a.m. or p.m. but they had long been on the same emotional level and that evening at exactly five minutes to eight, like clockwork, he showed up at her apartment. She opened the door. Without speaking they stood looking passionately into each other's eyes. This lasted for several awkward minutes; outside a police siren could be heard. Then, just as silently, he pulled out from behind his back — he had been hiding it from her view, waiting for the right moment to present it to her — from behind his back he pulled out a large bag of potatoes. I can't accept them, she said and invited him inside to where she could accept them. They were married not long after. Predictably, he stopped buying roses. Just as predictably, she stopped selling them. Eventually, when his contract ended, they moved to America where to this day they live like clockwork...

It's so romantic...! said Irina holding her how-to book to her breast.

'Please proceed to Window Number Three: ku-LEAK-ova ye-LEN-a; av-DE-yev VLAD-imir...'

What was that? said the woman, What did they say?

Are you Elena Kulikova? Irina asked her.

Yes I am, she said.

You have to go to window number three, said Irina, It's over there...

No fuzz! I added.

But in her haste the woman forgot to tell me where to go.

(37)

'Aeroport.'

Hey! Get up off that seat! Hey you! You heard me! Don't pretend like you're sleeping when there's a woman twice your age standing in front of you. Do you hear me? GET UP! *What's going on? Why is this old woman in front of us poking us with her umbrella? Is it raining outside? Or is it snowing? Wasn't it summer when we left? Where are we? And when? What month will meet us when we finally reach our destination? What year?* Okay, okay! we say to the woman who has taken our seat on the crowded bench. But the woman is beside herself. Can you believe it? she says to the other passengers, I'm standing there and this grown man doesn't even offer his seat! The nerve! The lack of manners! And dead drunk to boot. In the middle of the afternoon, dead drunk. It didn't use to be like this in the old days. Back then we had order! Then people respected their elders. In those days — in the days before Kitai-Gorod became Kitai-Gorod — we had a future. Back then we could....

'Caution — the doors are closing. Next stop, Sokol.'

(38)

Irina was tall, good-looking, well-dressed. She wore panty hose year-round and was especially fond of short sexy skirts which, I learned later, she bought in expensive boutiques. Her hair was originally black but had been died blonde for some reason. Her lips were redder than a long-stemmed rose and just as moist...

How long had it been? How far had Love fallen down my list? And speaking of falling, could it be that I was... Was it possible that the time had come for me to...?

What are you looking at?
What?! I said.
Why are you looking at me like that?
I... I wasn't looking at you.
Yes you were. I could feel you staring at me.
I... I didn't mean to... it was just...
You were staring at me.
I... my eyes were just sort of... by themselves...
It's okay.
I won't do it again...
It's not a problem.
I don't know what came over me... I just...

(39)

'Sokol. Dear passengers, while exiting the car please do not forget your belongings.'

At this stop a man in uniform passes through the car scaling the empty spaces for something that will hopefully not be there; tapping, patting, checking under the seats with his nightstick, the uniform travels the entire length of the car and then exits before the doors can close on him. By now everyone is afraid to sit. They're not even sure what there is to be afraid of but stand nevertheless with their reading material in hand. *But who is really accompanying us on our long journey? Whom will we thank when we have finally understood? Who will be left to answer us? Who will say, Please?* Will it be the young boy studying his history book? Or the man across from him reading Gorbachev's memoirs? Or the woman across from both of them turning the pages of a Russian romance novel and using a thousand-ruble note as a bookmark? Or maybe the African student standing with an English-language paper, absolutely cognizant of the teenage girls who are giggling at him behind his back. Or maybe the girls themselves, one of whom is pretending to read the pages of a fashion magazine, while the other looks over her shoulder? Perhaps we owe it all to the poorly dressed old woman — the one holding a communist periodical with an ironic title. Or the young thug in sunglasses and music in both ears who is thumbing through naked women. Or maybe the frightened couple with matching copies of a Russian-language book that is both thick (*foreigners!*) and in hard-back (*Germans!*). For now we are between stations, between bottles, and completely occupied by a man who is trying in vain not to reach the Kursky train station. But when this journey is over, when we have reached our destination and he has not reached his, when we have understood that we understand, when this moment has finally come, to whom will we raise our glass? Who will be left to thank? Perhaps we should drink to each of them? Or maybe to them all? — our fellow travelers! Our would-be companions! The people who at this moment of our life make up its girth. The words that fatten us. The characters that make us turn the page...

'Caution — the doors are closing. Next Stop, Voikovskaya...'

(40)

'Please proceed to Window Number Five: gribo-YED-ev alek-SAND-er; priklon-SKA-ya eye-REE-na...'

(41)

A few paragraphs from Voikovskaya

It is late afternoon. The passengers stand in the aisles, packed tightly against each other like detainees in a cell. And like detainees they are reading their newspapers and their novels and their books of poetry, all of which are nothing but words, the exact same words but in varying orders and fonts — page after page of tension and release, conflict and resolution, exclamation and ellipsis, climax and anticlimax...

Suddenly, the train slows; the passengers lean themselves sharply against the stop. With all their effort they oppose the unexpected force. Then just as suddenly the train leaps forward out of the slow-down. The passengers are caught leaning the wrong way and find themselves hopelessly off-balanced. They are leaning and hopelessly off-balanced.

And then something amazing happens and we are witness to it.

Here we see a truly remarkable occurrence, the type of thing that others will never believe, the type of improbable incident that is too incredible for newspapers, too profound for poetry, the type of thing that can cause our book to be flung violently against a wall...

The train slows suddenly, then lurches forward and the people standing in the aisles fall to the ground. One after another. One by one until there is not a Soul left standing.

Without exception they fall.

They fall without exception.

All of them.

Every single one.

(42)

'Voikovskaya.'

(43)

Irina and I stepped up to the window.

The consular officer was a middle-aged woman in a plaid business suit and reading glasses that hung from a thin chain around her neck. Her graying hair was combed simply. She did not smile. She was not wearing make-up. When she spoke her dry lips pursed in what promised to become a scowl:

What's your name? she said at Irina.

Irina told her.

And who are *you*?

I told her.

Are you the one inviting her?

That's right.

Wait over there. I'll talk with her first. If I need you I'll call you.

I stepped back. Irina looked at me pleadingly, but there was nothing I could do. She would have to answer the questions alone. In terror she turned to face the counselor who had already begun to ask her questions....

Standing awkwardly between the American behind the glass and the Russian crowd to my rear, I suddenly felt lost. Where did *us* stop being *them*? And if *we* and *us* were the same then did that mean that *they* would not understand? And where was I? — all this time it had seemed that I was making progress, that I was moving slowly but surely from there to here. But now here I was again...! Here I was standing awkwardly in the embassy and in the embassy *here* wasn't even *here*. In this crowded room *here* was there, and *there* had suddenly become *here*. This place, I had been warned, wasn't *there*. But could it be that it wasn't *here* either...?

I took a look around at the other visa applicants: at the first window a woman in a short dress was explaining that she wasn't a prostitute; at window number two a businessman was exaggerating; at window number three the old woman, in tears, stood collecting her passport: What about my daughter...? she was sobbing, ...What about my grandson?; at the fourth window an American was carving Russian names into a microphone...; and at window number five Irina was now telling the consular officer about how she and I had met, how we had spent the last three years together, how we had gradually become the very best of friends, and how after a long period of mutual indecision we were now planning to be married...

What!!!

...That's right, she said, It was love at first sight. I knew it the minute I saw him step out of the train at Taganskaya....

What was she talking about? What about the answers that we had so carefully prepared? Was she crazy?

...And then we went looking for mushrooms, she was saying, And it was then that we made love for the first time. Right there in the forest... it was great! Right there under the open sky... it was wonderful — he's more sensitive than he looks....

The counselor raised her eyebrows to look at me; I smiled sensitively.

...it's the best place for love, right there in nature, under the vast Russian sky, it's not like anything that you can find anywhere else. In America you don't have sky like this...

What was she doing? Why was she talking incessantly? She would ruin everything!

...Yeah I love him! And he loves me. In fact, he buys me flowers every day, by the dozens, brings them to me in big boxes. Not just any flowers, long-stemmed roses, the expensive kind...! And you know what's funny? The funny thing is that at first I didn't even like him! I didn't like him at first because well, he's not much to look at... but after a while I warmed up to him. And now I love him. And he loves me...

What was she talking about? What had come over her?

...And that's why I support him the way I do... that's right... almost all of my money — did I mention I make four thousand dollars a month? — all of my salary goes to support him. After all he doesn't work, doesn't have a dime, not a penny, and I can't let him starve... what? Roses? I don't know, I guess he probably steals them.... You know he would do anything for me because he loves me more than love itself, more than Love, more even than democracy...

In the middle of Irina's words the counselor held up her hand:

That's enough! she said.

What...? That's all? But I've only been speaking for thirty seconds...

I've heard all I need, the counselor said and then pointed at me: I want to have a few words with your fianceé over there....

(44)

I stepped up to the window.

The woman took a long hard look at me but did not smile:

What's your name? she asked me.

Why are you asking? I answered.

Protocol, she said.

And so I refused to answer:

Next question, I said.

Okay, she said, Where are you from?

I told her.

How long have you been in Moscow?

I told her.

How do you like it?

It's all right, I said, And you?

I don't know. I'm new here.

Do you have a favorite phrase yet?

My favorite phrase? Well, if I had to choose one it would

probably be something like 'God I don't know whether to love or hate this country!'

It's good, I said.

Thank you.

Please.

The counselor did not laugh.

Where do you work? she said.

At home.

What do you do?

I teach people to speak.

Does it pay well?

Aha... a trick question...!

It... well actually I do mostly volunteer work... I don't charge for my lessons. I mean I sort of charge but not really... actually I have a sort of agreement whereby my students pay by barter...

Barter?

Right. That way I don't get in trouble with the tax authorities. It's a good system. For example I have a student who works in a chocolate factory and so he pays me in chocolate; another student works in a perfume store and so she pays in perfumes; I have a third student who works at a... she works at a flower stand and so she brings me red roses, you know the expensive long-stemmed kind that women like... Another student of mine is a tax inspector...

So that's where you get the roses? You get them from barter. That's how you can afford roses without having any money.

That's right.

Barter, huh?

That's right.

Hey wait a minute...

What?

What about the tax inspector?

The what?

You were saying that you had a tax inspector for a student?

I was? I mean... that's right, I do.

Well I don't understand. What can she offer? As far as the flowers and the chocolate and the perfume... well that I can understand, but the tax inspector...?

I can see that you really are new to Moscow! The tax inspector, you see, brings me all three — flowers, chocolates, and perfumes.

I don't get it....?

Hang in there. Sooner or later you will.

The counselor looked down at some notes that she had made on Irina's application:

So when's the happy day? she asked.

What?

The wedding day. Have you set a date yet?

A date...? Well we were thinking of maybe having it on the first of the month.

Which month?

Which month...? We uh... haven't decided yet. Maybe January. Or April. Then again, maybe May....

Romantic.

Thank you.

But you know I can't understand one thing. First your girlfriend said that it was love at first sight, but then she said that in the beginning she couldn't stand you...

Well actually she didn't say she couldn't *stand* me...

So which is it?

Which is what?

What's the true story on how you met?

The counselor looked at me carefully and so, using her invitation, I carefully told her the true story of how Irina and I had met:

(45)

After being fired from my job at the institute and after looking unsuccessfully for a job on a non-barter basis, I had been forced to work in a flower stand at the Taganskaya metrostation. Each day at work I saw a woman in an expensive business suit; in the morning on her way to her high-paying job — did I mention that her salary was five thousand dollars a month? — and in the evening on her way home. For me it was love at first sight, but for her it was a complex mixture of apathy and punctuality that kept her from even noticing me. Meanwhile, I knew perfectly well that she was my destiny, and every morning, every evening, I would watch wistfully as my life passed before me without buying a single flower. This continued for several months until I could stand it no more: now was the time to make my move. One morning I picked out the moistest rose, the longest and reddest, and when she walked by I yelled after her in my best Russian, Hey Miss a flower for you! But she just kept walking — she had confused my accent for that of a Georgian. The next day I again picked out the most beautiful rose, along with the second-most beautiful and held out the two flowers shouting, Two beautiful flowers for a beautiful lady! but again she ignored me — this time she had confused my accent for that of an insistent Georgian. The third day when she tried to walk by I held out a dozen long-stemmed roses — I had chosen the absolute moistest and reddest — shaking them like a ruble and screaming at the top of my lungs, Dammit I'm not Georgian! My passport's blue!! It's blue! blue!! blue!!! Hearing this, she stopped. By the time she turned around, her attitude toward me had changed completely. What color? she asked. Blue, I answered and then, ... Want some flowers? Here she nodded and smiled. From ear to ear. And what a beautiful smile it was! I invited her to dinner and she accepted. Unlike my last girlfriend, she did not like potatoes. She did not like to eat at home and I did not like the idea of taking her to the Georgian restaurant — she might get the wrong idea — and so I did the only thing that I could, that is to say I fed her pilfered chocolates. Finally she asked me to marry her and I refused. She asked again, and again I refused, this time categorically. This also lasted for some time until about five minutes ago when, apparently, I said yes....

I stopped. *What the hell had I said? Where had all of that come from? Had I really made it up? Or was it some latent wish that I was only now putting into words?*

How beautiful! said the counselor who had taken off her glasses from her nose and was wiping away the tears from her eyes, How lovely! How poetic!

The woman was tearing off a light blue card and handing it to Irina.

Congratulations!! said the woman.

Thank you, said Irina but the woman was still gushing emotion:

Congratulations to you both! May God bless you in your future life together... May you find the happiness that you both deserve... May your love last forever...!

I looked at the woman:

Thanks, I said.

Then, suddenly, as if remembering something, the woman stopped. Her expression changed. Inexplicably it became as cold as concrete:

Wait a minute..., she said.

Irina had barely taken the blue card when the Counselor took it back, literally ripping it from her fingers.

Wait a minute! said the counselor, There's something you said that just doesn't ring true!

No! Why had I mentioned the flower stand? Why had I blurted out her salary? Did they even sell roses at the Taganskaya metro? Why had I mentioned marriage...!

You know, said the woman, I haven't lived in Moscow for that long and so you probably think that you can just pull the wool over my eyes... that I'll believe anything you say...

No no..., I began to say.

...But even I've been here long enough to know that what you just told me... that it couldn't have happened. Even I know that Russians never smile!

What?

I'm afraid that I don't believe your story and so I'm going to have to refuse your application. Maybe next time you'll be more careful with the stories you tell...

But... but..., I tried to say, ...But it's true! She really does smile. She smiles all the time! She has a beautiful, I would even say... *American* smile!

I don't believe you.

It's true!

Well, then, let's see it... Let's see her smile like an American!

Irina, whose English was helpless, was tugging at my sleeve:

What's she saying? she said.

She wants to see you smile. She says she won't give you a visa unless you smile.

Hearing this, Irina's face turned downward into a deep frown and it looked like she would cry — *she had been so close, had even felt the blue card in her hands!* — but then, just as suddenly, her face transformed; unexpectedly, even for me, Irina raised her head proudly and smiled as I had never seen a Russian smile: beautifully, brilliantly, falsely.

And that was that. The counselor, with a nod of her head and a smile that was just as false, offered the blue card to Irina once again:

Welcome to America! she said simply.

(46)

After we had received the blue card, we made our way to the window to pay for the visa. Irina had only brought rubles:

Hey, do you have a calculator? she asked.

A what?

A calculator so that I can see how many rubles I need to pay.

Well yeah sure... here.

Wow! This's a nice calculator! So small and convenient!

Do you like it?

It's great.

You can have it.

I can?

It's all yours.

I couldn't.

No really. Take it. I have two more at home.

You have more at home?

That's right.

Then can I have another one?

Sure.

Irina seemed touched:

You really are special! she said and then without warning kissed my words. So long and so deep that it seemed that this time it really would last forever....

(47)

Irina never did use the visa. For three months it stayed in her passport until finally it expired helplessly and inevitably like the moisture that moistens lips, or like the red of a red rose.

(48)

Wrong: Yesterday my friends came to me.
Right: My friends came over... and they brought vodka.

(49)

(50)

'Vodnyi Stadion.'

For me, life in Moscow had gone from being a constant struggle to being simply inconvenient. The danger disappeared and disappointment began to sink in. My life had become a story without a plot, a series of unconnected events without structure, without purpose, and leading to nowhere in particular. *When would I discover something that meant something? What would make this long while worth the while? Or had I been wasting everyone's time?* I was discouraged and disoriented and now, as if to add injury to insult, women with dirty bags in both hands are rubbing their dirty bags against me. My legs are pinned and sullied between the bags. I feel suffocated and frustrated. I can't move and when I try to kick my way out, the women yell at me with all their voice. My job had stagnated. My answers to questions became curt. Nothing was changing. I had stopped moving. And despite all my efforts to the contrary the bags are being piled onto each other once again, reaching up to my thighs, dirty and filthy, muddy and dusty at the same time, until they are up to my waist, then shoulders, pinning my arms to my body. *My God! Could it be that we were going backwards?* The girls that had intrigued me yesterday seemed boring today. It was late autumn. Of course I still drank, but with each passing day it required greater and greater amounts to forget about these bags that are now up to my neck; in greater quantities I drank and drank and still I cannot breathe through the dirty bags, still I could not throw up. And worst of all, there was no one to help me. With one didactic leap, all my friends had suddenly become acquaintances; the latest love of my life was living in Munich; the dollar had dropped; literature no longer instructed me; I had lost my momentum. My Russian deteriorated. And through these damn bags that are almost up to my neck and dirty and pressing me against the wall of the metro car I can't even see the faces of the other passengers. If I could just somehow climb out! If I could just learn a few more words. If only something would happen to pull me away from all of this...

And that's when it occurred to me: *the moment had come*.

At last my time here was up. It was time to leave. There was nothing here for me anymore. *But these bags are so heavy! If I can only throw off the one that has been put on the top of my head, then maybe I can squeeze my way out!*

And so it was at that instant that I decided to leave Russia forever. There was nothing to consider. I was fed up. Irreversibly. I was tired. I was confused. I am covered in muddy, dusty bags. I would leave immediately. And that was that.

That is that.

Period.

End of story.

* * * * * * * * * *

Book 6½. Epilogue

(1)

But I didn't leave.

Even now I don't know why. It had something to do, I suppose, with words. And vodka. And a coin that was still in my wallet. Or maybe it was in answer to the questions that I could not answer: *Could it really be that I was nowhere? And would I really leave without understanding what the Russian Soul was all about? Could I abandon my journey without finding the word that changes and is changed? And besides, even if I did leave, where would I go? Who would receive me?*

But maybe the real reason I stayed was something more logical, yet more difficult to explain: Standing in the metro, the women are lifting their bags away from me. And now I can breathe easier. Easier, even, than before the bags were there. I am almost home. And, as life here has already taught me, in this world good fortune can be as inevitable as anything else.

Sooner or later, I lied to myself, I would find some meaning...

(2)

The metro had taken me to where I needed to be. From south to north. From darkness to light. From past to present tense. Countless times it has taken me from here to there and back again. And for that, despite everything, I will be forever grateful.

(3)

...I open the door.

A man is standing in front of me. He is dressed in an expensive black leather jacket; his boots are well-shined; his hair is not red. I expect that he will say something but he does not. He just stands in the doorway regarding me curiously. I wait for him to speak but once again he does not. Finally it is I who speaks up:

Can I help you? I ask, holding the door between us with my knuckles.

You don't recognize me? says the man.

A strange question!

No. I'm sorry I don't. Should I?

The man is still regarding me:

I guess not, he says and pauses. Then he continues:

But I do have a score to settle with you. May I come in?

A knot is forming in my throat. My heart begins to beat suspiciously. Against all my better instincts, I open the door to let him in. As the man walks past me I do not smell the sweet scent of swallowed vodka:

No I guess you wouldn't remember me, says the man, But for the last year your face has haunted me.

The man looks around my apartment without interest and then turns around to look at me. His words are weighty:

You see, he says, We've met before. Four years ago.

I'm sorry, I say, I don't remember you. What is your name?

When he tells me, it all sinks in and I gasp yet again.

My heart beats steadily. My mind tumbles over itself trying to understand. It's him, all right. It's the man that I met over four years ago. *But why is he here? What has he come for...?*

And that's how I met the man who would teach me to believe in gravity. That's how I re-meet Vadim.

* * * * * * * * * *

Book 7. Falling Down the Up Escalator

(1)

But first things first. After all, the metro can take you only so far. Quick and reliable as it may be, it will still leave you far from home. Underground. Half-there.

And so I stumble from the metro car. It is the farthest one from the exit and now somehow I will have to make it through the crowds of people to the other end of the platform, from the darkness to the light, from *А* to *Я*, out of the past toward my future, past Customs all the way to the wedding...

By now I have begun to understand that nothing is as easy as it would seem. That exiting can be six and a half times harder than entering. By now I understand that this is turning out to be a long ride after all...

Squinting my eyes against the synthetic light, I head for the end of the platform.

Please, God, please let this be the day. I have waited so long for it. For the last years of my life I have asked and begged and prayed for that which comes so easily to others... Please, do not forsake me... Do not refuse me in this... Whatever may be Your will, do not doom me forever to vomitlessness!

I stop in the middle of the platform and wait for the nausea to pass.

(2)

Ahead of me there is a group of schoolgirls, aged eight or nine, smartly dressed with bows in their hair and ribbons sewn onto their collars. They are holding hands and waiting at the base of the escalator. Their teacher is counting them. In all there are thirty or thirty-five. Maybe forty. They are all named Natasha and their teacher, who is trying to organize the procession, is having a terrible time. Natasha! she yells, Stop pulling Natasha's hair.... And you Natasha... is that any way to treat Natasha...? But wait a minute: ...thirty-six... thirty-seven... thirty-eight... Someone's missing! Who is it? Who isn't here? she asks and the girls answer in one joyful voice:

Natasha!!!

Where is that girl? the teacher stresses, Where's Natasha?

She was here just a minute ago, says Natasha.

I saw her when we exited, Natasha adds.

Natasha...! Natasha! they all begin to shout and cast their eyes around the metro for their missing schoolmate.

Natasha...! Natasha...!

Then from the back rows, barely audible, a fragile voice belonging to a girl who until now has been standing with her hands clasped in front of her:

Natalya Vladimirovna... Natalya Vladimirovna..., she says shyly. As she speaks she twists the braids of her hair, each of her words as soft as skin:

Natalya Vladimirovna... *I* know where Natasha is!

Where is she, Natasha? answers the teacher, relieved and worried at the same time: Tell me where Natasha is!

Natasha opens her mouth to speak...

But before she can, a horn sounds, a train roars into the station, and the girl's voice is muffled: The teacher leans in to hear her words which she is twisting into her hair. And again the train is more eloquent:

.... !!! says the girl and points with her tiny finger back over the teacher's shoulder in the direction of the long escalator.

And there, standing higher and taller than her schoolmates, is a little girl with braided hair and a ribbon pinned to the collar of her dress. She is small and smiling. Beaming and ribboned....

Her name is Natasha.

Exhausted, I move around the children, past the sleeping

attendant, and step onto the escalator. My leg skids forward and I almost fall, but somehow manage to grab on to the moving handrail in time. Standing there, I feel my body being lifted over the noise of the metro platform, over the screaming children, over the distance that I have spent so long traveling. Helplessly, I am being shuffled diagonally: up and out of the metro at a speed that is faster than fast. Faster, even, than black. The Moscow metro, we are reminded by a mechanical voice, is the best and most beautiful in the world. Its tunnels the steepest. Its escalators the most efficient. And we should be proud of it. Of course at this moment, I have swallowed far too much vodka to be proud, even though I am riding the world's fastest escalator in the world's deepest metro system. Now all I can do is hold desperately on to the moving railing which is carrying me up.

up...up...up...

As always, the mechanical voice was right: this escalator *is* fast! Relentlessly, it is ferrying me past the people on the opposite escalator who are descending in single file. A million of their faces looking at a million and one of ours. Years and years of turning heads and fleeting glances. Stories rising or falling away from me, flashing for a moment only to be lost forever. Some dressed in old summer dresses. Others in ultra-fashionable winter furs. Each of them alone. A few with friends. The newly married holding their partners and kissing ambitiously on the uneven escalator steps. *These are the people that make up my Russia!* Here they are passing by me one by one. With red umbrellas, red passports, and red flags. With unborn children. With cheap reading material that they have already taken out of their pockets and briefcases: newspapers, romance novels, English textbooks, and, cheapest of all, semi-autobiographical novels set in exotic foreign places.

up...up...up...

Struggling to hold on, my senses fill with the shrieking of coins raining down the handrail; the acrid smell of burning rubber; cool breezes from nowhere; the dry taste of bitter vodka...

And as I am being carried, I feel that I am moving relentlessly. Hopelessly. That I am being taken against my will to a place that is waiting for me and that I have been waiting. Behind me, I know, there are metro cars with their bustling passengers; there are Natashas; and Tanyas; and even Irinas; in back of me there are cigarettes without filters; pickles without compunction. But all of it is disappearing somewhere behind my shoulder. Now I am moving both quickly and slowly, up the long narrow tunnel of the deepest metro system in the world. Like vomit through its throat, I am being forced relentlessly up to the surface.

up...up...up...

Then about halfway to the top I notice something illogical: My hand is moving faster than the rest of me: it is running away. *Why? How? I release the rail — almost fall — pull my hand closer to me, but again it begins to creep up the handrail. Am I going crazy? Could it be that even my hand is leading me home? But no! ...it isn't my imagination — everybody's hands are running away from them. It's just that I'm the only one who's noticed it! The other people don't even realize that the handrail is moving faster than they are. They don't see. They are as unsuspecting and as helpless as tax inspectors...!*

up...up...up...

But will my hand stay with me long enough to reach the top? Now I'm closer to a resolution than I was a few paragraphs ago. I'm closer than I've ever been. And my hand is even closer than I am. The end is near. It is in sight. It's only a few more moments... I'm almost at the top...

But then, when there are only a few words remaining, my balance gives out. The hand has been moving too fast and to keep from falling forward I have to release my grip of the railing. I pull my hand away and lean back. But it is too much. I am too drunk and have leaned too far back. My arms flail wildly and I can feel myself falling backward. *It can't be!* I grasp desperately for something to hold on to, but even without the dry bitterness it would be useless...

Before I can do anything, I am falling backward out of control down the escalator.

down...down...down....

Head over heals I am tumbling down the escalator heavily, painfully, clumsily, hitting my back then my head then my feet, then my back then my head then my feet, then my back then my... The world is swirling around me. And I am falling heavily and helplessly...

down...down...down...

Then suddenly it hits me: first in my back then on my head then against the tops of my feet: this fall is not like the others. This fall is not like any other because I am not stopping! I am falling further and further, but as I fall the escalator pushes me back up. And the more I fall, the more the escalator pushes me back up. I am tumbling head over heals, but I am no closer to stopping than I was a paragraph ago. *How long have I been falling? How long will I fall? And why in moments like these do I always think about grammar?*

down. down... up... down. down...up...

(3)

Despite my efforts I can't understand the subtleties of perfect and imperfect verbs.

In frustration I decide to leave Russia forever...

(4)

But I don't leave.

(5)

And so I am falling. But like never before; this time I am not falling down — I'm falling up. Gravity pushing me down, the escalator pushing me back up again. And the further I fall, the further I have to fall. Like clothes in a dryer, I am hurling and flinging against myself — heels over head over heels over head — spinning helplessly between two diametrical opposites: at the bottom, logic; at the top, irony. Falling and falling, I continue to fall. Like a spoon. Like a ruble. Like a foreigner who has not yet learned to drink vodka...

(6)

The dry bitterness backs up in my throat and still I cannot make myself vomit.

In despair, I decide to leave Russia forever...

(7)

But I can't leave.

(8)

And so I continue to fall. Just as hopelessly. Just as helplessly. Just as painfully.

And hopelessly, helplessly, and painfully I try to grab on to something to break my fall. But I am falling so fast that I don't even know which side is up and whether there is even anything to grab at all. Falling and falling and falling, I feel only the rush of colors and sounds and the blows landing one by one against my back then my head then my legs, then my back then my head... *But why aren't I stopping? Shouldn't I have come to rest against something by now? What about all the people who must be riding the escalator below me? Won't their legs stop me? Or could it be that I am falling right by them, that they are avoiding me, stepping over me like a puddle, dodging me like a draught? If so, won't somebody in a uniform notice me and put a stop to it? Won't the attendant whose job it is to disapprove of such things, flick a switch or give a command, or do something to bring my fall to an end?*

I can't fall forever, can I?

Naively, I continue to fall.

(9)

A Russian friend informs me that English words look naive when written in Russian.

Insulted, I decide to leave Russia forever.

(10)

But not yet.

(11)

And so I am back to falling.

By now I am falling in turns: hopelessly, helplessly, painfully, relentlessly. What should have been a simple escalator ride has turned into a bad tumble from up to down and back again. Everything that once seemed so simple has become an awkward fall from one story to the next, from the heights of naivete to the depths of marriage, airport to airport and back again. By now I have fallen both down and up. Onto and into. In and out. For and from. I have fallen every way imaginable and for every imaginable reason; at times I have fallen for the sake of falling. But until now, I have managed to get up. And down. And off of and out of. Out and in. Despite and to. I have gotten both there and here any and every way I could. Inevitably, I have reached where I am by falling, and where I am is on the up escalator — the world's fastest escalator in the world's deepest metro system — in a city that is capital to a country that isn't. Where I really am is closer to *there* than *here*, somewhere between up and down, the fraction of an instant where *what was* meets *what will be* and goes by the name of *what is...*

Again grammar...!

(12)

Despite my persistence, I cannot understand the logic of Russian grammar.

Worse, I cannot understand the logic of English grammar.

I decide that this time I really will leave Russia forever...

(13)

...just as soon as I learn the word that changes and is changed!

(14)

But what will stop my fall this time? Will it be the leg of a stranger? Or the bag of an old woman? Or will it be the old woman herself? *In my day*, she would complain, *drunks didn't fall down escalators...!* Or maybe I will come to rest against something that is itself rest: like sleep. Can it be that there is no hope for me? Can it be that I will never be able to grab on to something to break my fall...?

And as I fall, I begin to notice a strange phenomenon: the dry bitterness has left my throat, my thoughts are beginning to clear up. *I have fallen for so long that I am now sober!* And you know what?... after all these years, I've sort of gotten used to falling; and it isn't really so bad... as long as you have a good thick leather jacket to absorb the blows, as long as you have a sense of humor and an understanding that what is happening is still better than what *will* happen, both of which cannot be avoided no matter how much you scurry out of the way...

(15)

I have given away my calculators in vain.
When there is only one left I decide that there is no reason for me to stay in Russia....

(16)

I meet Vadim.

(17)

But then it occurs to me. Whereas before I hoped to slow my fall — to decrease my speed so that the escalator would carry me to the top — now it hits me again and again that my hope lies in the absolute opposite — to let my weight carry me down to the bottom. Here I am tumbling, caught helplessly between two relentless forces: on the one hand, gravity; and on the other hand, the ingenuity of the Moscow metro whose escalators are the fastest in the world. *That's it! That's the answer! Inertia will come to my rescue! Gravity will save me!!!*

And so I relax.

My muscles cease to resist and I begin to tumble faster, even as the escalator continues to push me back up. Faster and faster, head over heals over head, I am tumbling toward the bottom of the escalator where the sleeping attendant will be waiting for me.

And as I relax, I notice that I am making progress. The steps are hitting me quicker; so rapidly that my limbs are now numb to the blows. My body is gaining momentum. I am tumbling so fast that I have forgotten that I am tumbling. My mind sighs and relaxes as well. *How lucky I am to have Aunt Helen's leather jacket to absorb the blows! How lucky I am to have someone who loves me! How lucky I am that Aunt Helen is my aunt...! But when was the last time I wrote her? When was the last time she wrote me? I can't even remember the last time I talked to her... In fact it was... it was when she called to announce that Gorbachev was running for re-election! Gorbachev is running for re-election...!*

Now I am tumbling so fast that for the first time I begin to feel hope. Between the spinning sounds and rushing colors there is a place with synthetic light that is becoming closer and closer and closer and closer...

And still I am falling and falling and falling...

It is only a matter of time before it ends. A few more seconds. A few more minutes.

A few more paragraphs.

(18)

I am sick of tumbling and tired of falling.
I decide to leave Russia forever.

(19)

But what about the wedding?

* * * * * * * * * *

Book 8. Vadim's Story

(1)

Our relationship begins precariously:

Can I offer you some tea? I ask and set a plate of cookies in front of my guest.

Got any coffee? Vadim answers.

Actually I don't. Only tea.

That's all right. I'm not that thirsty.

Vadim rummages through the plate of cookies, pulls out the largest one, and pops it into his mouth:

What was your name again? he asks while chewing.

It's not important, I say but before I can finish he has noticed it on some stray papers.

You're very observant, I say.

In my business you need to be.

Really? What's your business?

Food products.

Vadim stretches out confidently on my small couch and looks around:

Nice painting, he says.

Thanks. A friend of mine gave that to me.

I take it the wrist shackles symbolize America's complicated relations with its black population?

Something like that.

Oppression and slavery?

That's right. How'd you know?

I used to be a history student. My major was American slavery.

Do you like it?

American slavery?

No, the painting.

Sure. Why not. I mean I'm no artist or anything...

The man turns his head and looks at another wall:

What about that? he says.

The wall?

No, the rug.

Nice, isn't it...? I brought it from America. The wall looked so bare without it.

Vadim doesn't laugh. His voice becomes serious:

I wasn't sure you would still be at this address — so much time has passed.

As a matter of fact, I won't be here very long. I'm supposed to move out.

Vadim seems surprised:

Why?

When I moved in I told my landlord I didn't smoke.

You lied?

Not really. I didn't smoke then.

And now you do?

Right.

And he's kicking you out because of that?

You got it.

Vot eto da!

And Vadim throws his booted leg over his knee:

What happened to your arm? he asks pointing at my bandage.

This? It's just a sprain. I had an accident in the metro... on the escalator.

As I retell my story, Vadim listens to me intently, either nodding or shaking his head, depending on the direction I am falling. Finally, he speaks up:

Do you know why I'm here? he asks.

No, I don't.

It's about the wallet that I returned to you four years ago. Do you remember if there was any money in it?

I don't know. It was so long ago. Besides, it was my own fault that I lost it — even then I wasn't so naive as to expect to get any money back.

Well that's the thing, you see when I found the wallet there was money in it, I mean your money was still there.

It was?

I took it. And now I want to pay it back to you. That's why I came.

Don't worry about it — it was so long ago, I'd forgotten the wallet even had money. For me the most important things were the yellow piece of paper and the two-kopeck coin.

Still, I want to ease my conscience, I want to give you back the money.

It's really not necessary...

I insist...!

And without waiting for my consent Vadim takes out his wallet, peels off seven one-dollar bills and holds them out for me to take.

Seven dollars? I laugh, That's all there was?

That's all.

I laugh again, but for Vadim this is a serious moment:

You have to understand, he says, The times were difficult — it was an extreme time.

Don't worry about it, I say.

It's not like me, it's really not, but it was the times. We had to... all of us had to do things that we're not proud of... I did... Everybody did.

I understand, I say.

Vadim is still holding out the money and finally I take it. He seems relieved. We need to commemorate this occasion, he says and reaching deep into his coat pocket he pulls out two bottles — *but I thought he said he wasn't thirsty?!* — of mineral water.

(2)

'Not much is new with me,' said Aunt Helen, and then: 'The weather's nice, about eighty, not a lot of humidity which is rare for this time of year. For a while there we were having ninety-degree weather almost every day. And you know how our cooler works! But other than that not much news... Oh! I remember what I wanted to tell you: I just got a new pot for the geraniums in the kitchen, you remember how the old pots were so dirty and the cats kept going to the bathroom in them. Well, last week I decided to get some new pots and boy you should have seen me at the store trying to find just the right pot! I had to ask four salespeople before one of them could point me in the right direction. And they were way in the back of the store next to — of all things — the gardening supplies. And get this: there was a sale and I saved more than thirty percent off the original price! The geraniums look completely different from how they used to look, and most of the cats have stopped using them for a bathroom, although sometimes I still find poop half-buried in the dirt. I have a feeling it's Bopper: she always liked the geranium pot and she's the hardest to get out of the habit. I rub her nose in it like they say you're supposed to do with dogs, but I guess cats aren't dogs. She just sort of shakes her head and sneezes and looks at me — you should see how she looks at me! — and I feel bad and so I just let her do it. I talked to my friend Pierre and he told me that what she really wants to do is eat the flowers because all animals need to eat green vegetables so that they can vomit it back up... which reminds me, did you get the package I sent you yesterday...?'

(3)

With the money from my wallet, Vadim invested in his first business: using personal connections in a Russian bank, he bought seven dollars worth of fifteen-kopeck coins at face value. For hours at a time he would stand near the metro exits, reselling them to passersby. Initially business was brisk, but his inexperience showed: to increase profits he raised his selling price from sixteen kopecks to one ruble; soon he was selling them for two, then four, then seven rubles apiece. The profits were converted back into dollars which were stored at home under the planks of his wooden floor, while the remainder went toward more fifteen-kopeck coins... By the time the public phones were changed to a token system, Vadim had accumulated more than seventy dollars.

He could have stopped there...

But Vadim was persistent. Taking the dollars that he had carefully tucked away, he invested in fur hats, combing the Arbat and Izmailovsky Park looking for buyers. 'Maybe you like fur hat,' he would explain and then, 'Not expensive!' His customers were mostly foreigners desiring to look Russian. Soon the money was coming in so steadily that he could travel to other countries — first by train and then later by plane — for cheap clothes which he bought for five and sold for twenty-five.

Business was good. Life was good. He wore authentic American blue jeans. He ate fruit. He had a girlfriend with purple hair and a credit card from North-South Bank. At home he smoked Marlboro cigarettes but did not use lubricated condoms. In time he began to comb his hair on the right side.

For Vadim all of this meant a new life, a clean break from the past, from the future that could have been his for the taking. Over his parents' objections, he dropped out of the history institute where he had been studying. Fearlessly, he invested everything he had — all seven dollars, all seventy dollars, all seven hundred dollars — in words without precedents, trading classics of literature for modern economics texts. He had already given himself fully to the hope that from now on — starting with his generation — things would somehow be different, that somehow life would be better. He began to trust his government. He stopped smoking. He realized he believed in God. He even gave up vodka, drinking it only when his job required it. At times he smiled in public...

And then came currency reform. Vadim lost everything. He had been caught with his money in rubles. Even now currency exchanges were on every corner, but when he needed one more than anybody there were none to be found, and after running through the streets looking for live chickens, he was stuck with the old worthless rubles. In disgust, he threw the papers out the window.

That too could have been the end...

But Vadim was resilient. By now he had contacts who could lend him enough money to get back on his feet. Within a few months his business was restored and within a year he had paid off the loans with interest. He still believed in God, still read economics texts without smoking, still abstained from vodka except during important business meetings...

...But never again would he trust his government.

Time passed, money accrued. His next project was to buy a little kiosk where he sold Marlboro cigarettes and bootleg vodka whose alcohol content ranged from twenty-two to thirty-eight percent. Business was so good that he bought a second kiosk and then a third. In time he had ten kiosks that he consolidated into a single organization called Klamagup. Not knowing what to do with his profits, he bought an office to accommodate himself and his staff of seven office workers and a cleaning lady. Each had a partitioned cubicle and a plaque with his title:

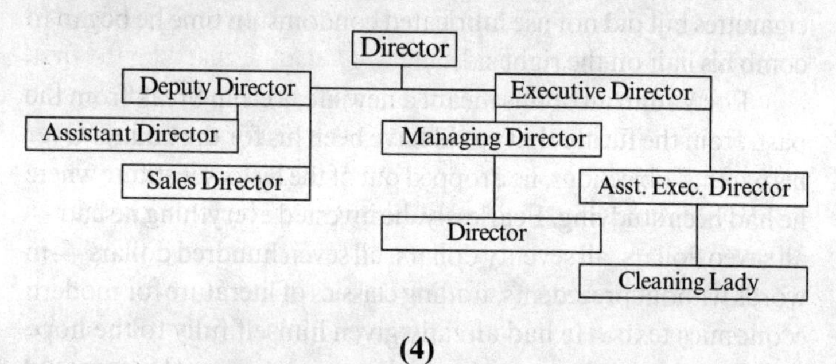

(4)

'...Well you should! I just read an article that in Russia there's a shortage of vegetables. Gorbachev has promised to import it from abroad but there's some kind of problem and they're worried that there won't be anything green by the end of the winter. You know I really don't see why those people can't get their act together. I don't understand why they can't solve their problems. But then I'm sure you're doing all right. Oh, your mother called the other day....'

(5)

For Vadim it was a prosperous time. Stores were filled with imported goods. Dollars had become commonplace. Vadim had made his fortune before I'd even turned thirty — and boy was he loving it! His business was thriving. He drove a new BMW. He ate in overpriced restaurants. He had a phone that he carried with him. Now he could afford tours around the world and in no time at all his passport was overflowing with stamps from *there*.

But most amazing of all was Vadim's apartment: it was huge! And airy. Five rooms in the center of the city. A doorman at the front entrance to inconvenience his guests. A balcony overlooking a courtyard and with a view of another balcony overlooking a courtyard....

Vadim had never been one to spare expense, and when decorating the apartment his extravagance showed: black-vinyl sofas; transparent tables; crystal chandeliers in each room; a mini-waterfall with plastic rocks; phones that beeped when you dialed them; a television that was bigger than necessary and with a smaller television sitting on top; three state-of-the-art security systems; two pure-breed dogs with American names; a large piece of endangered coral; toilets with water; matching fireplaces — guarding the first, a hundred-kilogram knight in armor; protecting the second, the skin of a sprawled-out black bear, its open jaw offering a roll of outdated rubles....

By night Vadim slept soundly. By day he avoided the tax inspectors.

Life was good.

And just when it seemed that things couldn't get any better, his father died. Vadim was left an inheritance that included a second apartment upstairs from his mother's. He used it as a library for books that he no longer read: Kharms, Pushkin, the novelist Lev Tolstoy. The apartment was small. Both rooms were dusty. Eventually, when he learned that I was being evicted, he offered to rent it to me at half its value.

But that would come later. For now his conscience was troubling him. Sitting in his spacious apartment, he began to trace everything backwards. Through Klamagup. Through the small kiosks. Back to the fur hats and fifteen-kopeck coins. Back to the seven dollars. His dubious beginning. Me. For some reason, the incident with the wallet had left its mark on him, and Vadim made it his mission to find me and return the money he had taken.

It wasn't easy. Vadim had long forgotten my address, only vaguely remembered the region where he had walked to deliver my wallet. Now in his BMW, he drove the streets searching among rows of identical buildings for my small apartment. A week passed. But the buildings were too identical, and so another week passed. Every day he drove through the neighborhoods looking for a sign that would spark his memory. After the third week, he realized it was hopeless.

He could have given up...

But Vadim was virtuous. Instead, he redoubled his efforts: He placed ads in foreign-language newspapers that I avoided. He called language schools that had fired me. He left notices at expensive supermarkets that I could not afford. He went to the U.S. embassy to inquire about me, but had forgotten that he could not remember my name. As a last resort he again returned to my neighborhood, asking neighbors if they had seen anyone smiling in the vicinity. No luck. He offered a reward for any sighting of *Anna Karenina*. Fat chance! When these attempts proved unsuccessful he put up fliers in the neighborhood that read:

NEEDED: NATIVE SPEAKERS TO TEACH ENGLISH
WILL PAY $100/ HOUR

The fliers were ripped down as quickly as they went up. Before I could even see them. Not surprisingly, his phone rang off the hook. Nevertheless, he investigated all false leads, met with more than two hundred smiling people claiming to be Americans. His English was too weak to verify their citizenship, but he was experienced enough to demand their passports which, as a rule, were far from blue. This continued for almost five months. Then, unexpectedly, somebody gave him the lead he needed — There's a Canadian guy down the block, an old woman told him, Maybe he can help you...

When Vadim showed up at my door he recognized me immediately.

(6)

'...She asked how you were and I told her that you were still working at the same job. She asked when you were coming home and I told her. She's looking forward to seeing you. She says she really misses you, and she said to ask you to call her sometime. Maybe you should. I mean, I don't think it would be a bad idea if you called her. She doesn't move around so much these days, you know. Of course you can wait until you get back, but that's months away. I know you have a lot to hold against her, but you should realize that you can't keep those things inside forever. Of course I can't insist that you call her, but I do think it would be a good thing to do. She does love you, you know. And I'd hate for you to continue to hurt her. Anyway, I won't belabor the dead horse. Not much is new here: the weatherman says that the snow should let up by the beginning of next week...'

(7)

Moving out of my apartment, the small apartment where I have spent my formative years in Russia, I feel a strange nostalgia. *No other apartment will be quite like this one, even though every other apartment will be quite like this one! This apartment where I learned six yellow words. Where I first felt the power of a whisper. Where I was explained the difference between friend and acquaintance; Love and love; living and getting by. Where I learned how to smile sincerely. And then, later, how not to smile at all...*

Cleaning my apartment for the first and last time, I find the residue of my past: a peanut butter lid; two bottles of vodka; a student's ungraded essay; a smashed calculator; discarded butts from old Prima cigarettes; a metal metro token; a plastic metro token; an expired visa; newspaper articles filled with underlined words... *Can it be that these words — the ones that I now use everyday — can it be that they were once foreign...?!*

I sigh bitterly and sweetly at the same time. My life is changing; this chapter of it, I know, is over and another one is beginning. I close the door softly and make my way for the elevator.

(8)

'...But you know how much I trust weathermen, so I'm going to take my umbrella anyway. I tried to call you yesterday about eight in the morning your time, but you weren't there, I guess you were probably at work. I just want you to know that I support your decision, even though of course I wish you would have chosen something else. Something closer. And safer. It's difficult for me because you're the only person I have, and now to think I'll have to wait *another* year for you to come home...! Another three hundred sixty-five days... it doesn't seem possible! Of course I want you to do whatever you feel is best. But I just... I just wish that...'

(9)

Spending time with Vadim, I have begun to see a side of Russia that I never saw before: the side that moves. Vadim is as active as an article. He drives fast. He lives fast. He loves money.

The funny thing, he once tells me, is that all of this is in complete contrast to how he was raised.

What do you mean? I ask him.

Vadim is driving me home in his BMW and has skipped over a curb onto a busy sidewalk; outside the window I can see pedestrians on the street scurrying to get out of his way. People curse and wave their arms at the back of our car, but Vadim has not even noticed them:

It's how my mother raised me, he says, It's how our mothers raise us.

How do you mean?

You wouldn't understand.

Try me.

Well when I was small my mother taught me habits that even now I'm trying to get out of.

For example?

Okay for example she... let's see... well for example she always told me that when I'm at someone's house and they offer me candy or cookies, I should refuse...

So...?

And if they offer again, then I should refuse again...

Okay..?

But if they offer a *third* time, then I can take it, but I should take the smallest piece. If it's meat, I should make sure to choose the piece that's burnt. If it's bread, I should eat the end piece — you know, the one that nobody wants.

Why?

So that *other* people can eat the good stuff.

But why shouldn't you be the one to eat the good piece?

I don't know!

I mean *somebody* has to eat the good piece...?

I know, I know! And you know what else? — and this is the crazy part — She drilled it into me that if *I'm* the host, I should offer my guests the very best of everything. And if they refuse, then it means that I am a bad host. How do you like that? Damned if you do, damned if they don't!

Well, I tell him, It is a bit strange for me.

That's Russia for you..., says Vadim: This is not a good place to want the bigger cookie. This is not a good place to dream about middle bread...

As if he senses something in his own words, Vadim becomes a bit somber.

Just then his favorite song comes over the car radio; his expression changes. Vadim turns up the radio, taps his thumbs on the steering wheel, presses harder against the gas...

'Yesterday... All my troubles seemed so far away...'

(10)

Can you believe our roads here? Vadim asks me as our car ruts into a hole in the asphalt. Luckily the bottom of his car is thick and hard and accepts the scrape without damage:

What a nightmare! he says and then: You know there's a book... it was written by two Russians who went to America, and they say that in America there isn't a single good road... there isn't a single *good* road because all the roads are *excellent*!

What book is it?

Vadim tells me the name of the book and even explains on which dusty shelf I can find it:

...But *Russian* roads..., he continues, ...you know we have a saying that our country is cursed by two things... have you heard this?

No.

We say that this country is cursed by two things: roads and policemen.

Policemen and roads? What about tax inspectors?

Well yeah, them too. But they're not a part of the saying.

Unfortunately, there is another silence. To break it I change the subject:

Hey you know what I heard? I say, I heard that Gorbachev's thinking about running for president again in 1996. Can you believe it?

Who told you that?

My Aunt.

Well I'm no political analyst or anything... but it's completely ridiculous. He doesn't have a chance. Everybody hates him. He's guaranteed to lose.

Maybe so, but sometimes people do things that are illogical... I mean he could run for president even knowing that he will most likely lose.

Out of the question! No way. Absolutely not. It's just not going to happen. Everybody knows that...

Here Vadim pauses. Then he continues:

...There's not a chance in hell that Gorbachev will run for president in 1996! Of course, I'm no political analyst or anything...

(11)

Wrong: Gorbachev's chances of winning the election are one in seventy-eight millions.

Right: In truth, they are only one in seventy-eight million.

(12)

Vadim is making a right turn off onto a sidestreet:

You know, he says, There's a lot of money to be made here nowadays. You just have to know where and how.

Where? I ask, How?

Have you ever thought about going into business?

Business?

Yeah. I mean just think: you've been doing the same thing since you got here, and what do you have to show for it?

Not much I guess.

That's right. If you wanted, you could find something that paid well.

I don't know what I could possibly do...

There're a lot of things. Especially for you with your expansive and thorough knowledge of...

What expansive and thorough knowledge?!

...With your knowledge of English you're guaranteed to make money.

English?

Sure. The last few years English has become a hot commodity here.

Yeah, but I don't see where the money is.

Well, it's there. You just have to look for it. The most important thing is to enjoy what you're doing. Do you enjoy teaching?

It's okay. I mean I enjoy helping people to speak.

But there's no money there.

Right.

Well then you need to find a good compromise between interesting work and work that pays well. What are some things that you like to do?

Me? I don't know... I like to read.

Reading? There's no money in reading. But you might be able to find something *connected* to reading.

For instance?

For instance have you ever thought about writing something? Maybe a book or something? I have a friend who's a publisher — if you wrote it he could print it.

A book? What kind of book?

It doesn't matter... any kind!

I'm not a good writer.

So...?

What do you mean *so*?

You don't have to be a good writer to write.

You don't?

Of course not... it just means you need to pick something that's simple to write, that's all... it doesn't have to be *War and Peace* or anything. Something simple.

Like what?

I don't know, something easy. Something like... memoirs! You know when you remember important things that happened to you and write about them. I mean I'm no expert on literature, but memoirs have to be easy enough because... because you can't be wrong about anything... If people don't like what you write then you just say, hey that's what really happened, take it or leave it!

But I...

Just think... you could write about your experiences here... about how you came to Moscow and everything was strange and scary... blah blah blah... you know, the usual bit: poor sensitive foreigner lands in Moscow expecting poetry and black bears but instead... bread lines... toilet paper shortages... people yelling and shouting... I'm telling you people would buy it up... it'd go faster than Marlboros!

First of all, you have it all backwards.

Why?

Because I came expecting toilet paper shortages... and instead discovered poetry.

Vadim stops to ponder the significance of my words.

And secondly, I've never stood in a real bread line... they were almost non-existent by the time I got here.

So what?

So... people will read and say that it's unrealistic, you know, that I couldn't actually have stood in a bread line...

Well then change it... instead of bread, make it a line for potatoes.

But I never waited in any lines for potatoes, either.

That's not the point... the important thing is that it *could've* happened. You see? And besides, if you think people will remember... well okay there will be people who nit-pick about the dates, but in general no one will remember... I mean five years from now do you think anyone will care whether something happened in this year or the next? Do you think they'll care about whether it even happened at all? Of course not! As a matter of fact that whole period has already started to blur...

Really?

Yeah. And as far as people believing you... you know I just read a statistic... it was from an American study about credibility... it showed that seventy-eight percent of all people believe everything they read.

How many?

Seventy-eight percent...

So many!

Yes. And the other people, the other seventy-eight percent, well, who cares about them! I mean, just look at me! Do you think people would believe that I could become so successful starting out with a mere seven dollars worth of fifteen-kopeck coins? Is that believable? Absolutely not. They'd say it was too unrealistic. But I did it... here I am!

But this is life, Vadim. It's not the same. In literature, everything should be logical... it should be more interesting, and at the same time, more believable than life... it should be plausible...

Vadim dismisses the idea with a wave of his arm, but I continue:

...And besides I don't think Russians would appreciate something like this.

What do you mean?

A book about Russia written by a foreigner... Russians would have a hard time accepting it.

What Russians? You'd be writing in English for other foreigners.

Nah... You see, if I did write something — even if it were in English — I'd still hope that it'd be interesting for Russians too. I know it's naive...

Vadim stops to consider my proposal. Then he pronounces significantly:

Nope. No way. It wouldn't pass. Russians are too sensitive... they'd never make it past the scene with the potatoes... in fact, we even have a special term for when foreigners write about things like that.

About potatoes?

No, about Russia. We have a term that means a foreigner is writing superficially about Russia.

You have a term to mean that specifically?

That's right.

What is it?

And he tells me the term.

Now Vadim is weaving in and out of traffic; as he passes, he curses the cars that are less expensive than his, and yields deferentially to those that are more prestigious:

Ogo! he says pointing at a large imported car: Now that's an automobile!

And Vadim lets the car cut in front of him. For some time we drive in silence until his favorite song comes over the radio. Vadim's English is vigorous but unpracticed. He's no singer, but sings loudly nevertheless to the rhythm of the music:

'Yesterday,' he sings, 'All my troubles seemed so far away...'

(13)

It is rush hour and we are stuck in bumper-to-bumper traffic. Outside, men without legs are hobbling between the cars asking for alms. Without hesitating, Vadim rolls down his window and hands a man in army fatigues a ten-thousand-ruble note:

Okay, so memoirs are out, he says rolling the window back up: Well then what about something else? What about a how-to book... for example one to help foreigners in Moscow... you know, useful advice like where to put the token in the metro turnstile, how to drink vodka effectively, the number of red roses you should never give, how best to measure the Russian Soul — you know, practical things like that...

I'm not good at giving advice... especially if it's practical.

What's so difficult? You just write: *in the slot; with your elbow parallel to the floor; twelve...*

No. No. It wouldn't work. I couldn't do it.

Why not?

I don't know. I just couldn't.

Vadim groans:

Now I see why you've stayed a teacher all this time!

What's that supposed to mean?

You can't do *anything*.

It's not that.... It's just that I would need something that suits my personality.

Suits your personality?

Yeah. You see, Vadim, writing is the purest form of self-expression and should therefore be undertaken as cautiously as if you were choosing a wife. In fact, even more so. After all, once you're married you're the only one who'll see your wife naked...

One can hope!

...But if you write something, it's like the whole world is gawking at your imperfection.

Wait a minute. I don't understand where you're going with all this nakedness? What type of imperfection *would* you want to write?

I don't know. But I do know that it would have to be something that reflected the longings of my heart, the twitchings of my soul...

Twitchings?

Yes, twitchings.

Okay, well then what about... I've got it!

What?

I know how you can express your soul!

How?

You could write a dictionary!

A dictionary?

Yeah, for example a Russian-English dictionary... or even better a Russian-English-English-Russian dictionary. Everybody needs English... you can't get a decent job without it... I'm telling you, a good dictionary... it'd sell faster than vodka.

I don't know Russian well enough.

Yeah but I do! We could do it together. You see, we just have to find an old Russian dictionary and take all the words there — I explain what they mean and you translate them into English. How hard could it be? You just start with *A* and go slowly and patiently all the way to *Я*...

It's impossible.

Why?

It's impossible to give meaning to words.

You mean in a foreign language?

No, I mean in general. You see Vadim... words are rebellious. If you try to restrict them they can be as defiant as a detainee...

Well I'm no linguist or anything, but I'm sure we could do it. For example let's take the letter *A*... let's see... what words begin with *A*...?

Vadim has stopped his car at an intersection where the traffic light is flashing yellow in both directions; but the traffic perpendicular to us has taken the upper hand, passing in front from left to right and not letting us go.

I know...! says Vadim as he swivels his neck back and forth looking for an opportunity to cross the intersection.

What? I say.

I've thought of a word that begins with *A*...

What?

...*Abort.*

What about it?

How do you translate the Russian word *abort*? How do you say it in English?

We say *abortion*.

See? See how convenient it is to translate words!

Yeah, but that was an easy one. Usually... I mean, *in most cases* it won't be so simple...

Vadim is sticking his head over his steering wheel, trying to see around a large truck that has pulled up to his left and blocked his view of the passing traffic.

Damn...! he says, I can't see anything!

He edges the car forward to improve his view; the cars are now whizzing by at irregular intervals, only a few feet from our bumper.

Like I was saying..., he says, ...it's not difficult. Well all right let's try another word that's at the beginning of the alphabet... Let's take another word that begins with *A* like... like... *avantyura*... do you know how to translate that?

Sure, it's another easy one.

See!

Yeah but you're picking words that have common roots.

I didn't mean to.

Well you are.

Okay okay, then what about... damn these cars!... what about a word like...

Vadim racks his memory for Russian words that begin with *A*:

...What about a word like... *Авось*?

Avos'?

No... *Авось!*

I don't know this word.

You've never heard it before, or you don't know what it means?

Both. What is it?

Well, it means... it's when you want to do something but... damn these cars!... It's when you make a decision that...

Vadim's foot is inching off the brake pedal, but the cars are still passing in irregular blurs before us and not letting us cross.

...well, okay, think of it this way... you're deciding whether to... well, for example, you're deciding whether to use a condom or not to use a condom... Logic would tell you to use it... but you decide not to use it despite the risk... That's Авось!

One by one the cars pass in front of us. Finally Vadim can take it no longer:

Hold on...! he says.

And without looking he slams his foot on the gas. The tires screech wildly, our car jerks forward and then goes flying out blindly into the traffic. Cars are buzzing by us like bees, horns sound all around and in all possible directions....

Flying out into the intersection, we are as vulnerable as poets. And like poets we watch through the glass of our windshields as the outside world streaks by. Within seconds we will see our publishing career end. Suddenly. Logically. Loudly.

(14)

'...But it really has been such a long time. Almost two years. And I hardly ever talk to you any more. I know you come home once a year but it's not the same. That's not a family. I'm not trying to pressure you, but I just wish that you would try to think about everything as a whole. But you have to do what you have to do... How's the weather there...?'

(15)

Let's say — don't laugh, it could happen! — let's say you sell Marlboro cigarettes. Nowadays it could be any number of imported products, but let's say they're Marlboros. Foreign cigarettes, after all, are relatively inexpensive and can be resold quickly, easily, and with a profit margin the size of a new home. The system is as true as a triangle, as proven as a percentage: buy for two, sell for five; buy for five, sell for twenty-five; buy for twenty-six, sell for fifty-one. It is, you like to say, as elementary as air; and like air, your money has come to you from nowhere, from nothing.

Home for you was a small apartment that you shared with your mother. Two small rooms with peeling brown furniture; wooden planked floors; a red-weaved carpet on the wall. This *was* home, that is to say, before you began selling Marlboros. But now, thanks to people with a habit, you have a new apartment in the center of the city. A new car that you paid for in cash. A new office with a European design and brass plaques.

And so life is good.

Every Tuesday you come to your office where your smiling employees assure you that everything is in order. The right people have been paid. The wrong people have also been paid. Confidently, your directors show you graphs and charts with numbers and percentages and words that do not speak to you. What really speaks your language is the manila envelope with a stack of unofficial dollars. This, you understand, is what really means something. This is what really matters.

But money can't buy love. Money can't buy health. Money can't buy happiness... especially in Russia. Sometimes — usually when you need it more than anything — money can't even buy *money*!

Gradually, you begin to lose touch with your company, leaving it to be managed by people who are not you: your salespeople, your directors, your two Chief Accountants — one black, one white. Let them have their chance, you think. After all, you're no economist, but what could possibly go wrong? And besides, you've paid your dues. And now it's time to reap the rewards of your hard work. Now you can relax. Now you are rich enough to search for your spiritual side, to count your money with your blessings.

Then one day your Deputy Director quits, followed soon after by your Executive Director. You call their homes but they do not answer; and nobody knows where they are. It's strange. To fill their spots you hire a Personnel Director. But it is too late: money, you are learning, really is like air; and like air, it is much easier enjoyed than managed.

With each passing Tuesday the envelope becomes smaller and smaller. Stability has retarded your growth. The company needs money to meet its debts and so you borrow against your past. First seven thousand dollars. Then seventy thousand. Luckily, you have business acquaintances who can spot you this kind of money... Luckily they give you enough to get by. Luckily, you are still able to borrow...

(16)

When we come home, Vadim sets two bottles of vodka on the table.

Today, he says, we're going to get down to the bottom of things.

What do you mean? I ask him.

Today we're going to bare our souls!

He opens one of the bottles, pours each of us a shot:

But I thought you didn't drink? I tell him.

I don't, he says and without explaining he lifts up his glass of vodka:

Make a toast! he says to me.

I can't... I don't know how.

What do you mean you don't know how?

I don't know how to make eloquent worthy toasts. In America I never drank. And besides, even when we do drink we don't really say toasts. We get by without them.

Without toasting? Drunkards!!

Vadim holds up his glass of vodka to the light:

Well, then I'll say a few words, he offers: To America!

I nod:

...And to Russia! I add.

We clink glasses and then, in two large swallows, begin to get down to the bottom of things.

You know, says Vadim — he is not wasting any time — I've come to the conclusion that in life there are only three things that can't change.

What's that?

Black. White. Gray.

Why only those three?

I don't know. That's just the way it is.

Why not blue? Why not green?

Hah! You can tell *you're* American!

(17)

After the first toast our conversation begins to take off. One by one, we discuss topics and themes that were beyond our comprehension only a few minutes, a few paragraphs, a few swallows ago. After toasting, our words heat up, the themes becoming livelier, the progressions between them as natural as nylon, as smooth as a stop. Bottle after bottle, we discuss:

fate vs. self-determinism

democracy vs. danger

Kharms vs. Tolstoy

love vs. marriage

black vs. white vs. gray

here vs. *there*

Prima vs. Marlboro

(18)

When the two bottles are finished, we buy three more. And when *they* are gone I make a trip to a kiosk, returning with six bottles of beer.

But I have forgotten one thing: Russian tradition insists that drinking beer without vodka is like throwing money at the wind. To save the day, Vadim pulls out an old bottle of vodka that he has been saving for a day like tonight. Now, he warns, we will drink *ersh*. *Uh-oh!* I think, *I know what that means!* And just as I feared our conversation turns deeply philosophical; inevitably, it turns to the discussion of language itself, or more precisely, to English vs. Russian:

You know, says Vadim, Russian is the best language in the world.

It is? I say.

That's right, he says, It is.

I look at Vadim expectantly — and seeing this, he continues:

You see, he begins, there's a well-documented case of how three linguists, a Frenchman a German and a Russian were sitting around debating whose language was the best... have you heard this? No? Good. So first the French guy stands up and says — this is a true story by the way — so the French guy says something like, You know mon amis — that's French for *respected colleagues* — In truth, he says, French is the most beautiful language in the word because we have so many words that enable us to speak about love and passion and sex....

Wait a minute... which one was this...? Who was saying this?

The Frenchman, who else...? Get it... love and passion? Anyway, after the Frenchman, the German guy stands up... the Frenchman of course is very pleased with himself, but the German stands up and says, I'll grant you that French may be good for speaking about women, but you have to admit that German is the best language in the world because it is...

...The thickest?

No.

...The hardest?

No. No. German is the best he says because it is the most logical... I guess compared to other languages German is logical.

Okay okay, let's get to the Russian. What did the Russian say?

...Okay, so then it was the Russian's turn and he listened to the others patiently and then said something to the effect of, Comrades — this is a true story, by the way — comrades, he said, I don't want to insult your fine languages but only in my language, only in Russian is it possible to write an entire story — from beginning to end — using words that begin with the same letter...!

The same letter?

The same letter.

An entire story?

That's right!

Which letter?

П.

P?

No... *П.* I saw it myself, I mean I read the story with my own eyes.

What's it about?

I don't remember, it's been a long time. Something about women.

Hmm... well you know listening to your story one thing comes to mind... of course it's a good anecdote — don't get me wrong — but there's one question that has to be asked: what about English? Where were the English and American linguists?

Unfortunately, they weren't able to attend the conference because they were preoccupied... the English linguist was writing a thank-you note, and the American was busy counting his money...

Okay, fine, then I have another question... these linguists, the Frenchman, the German, and the Russian, when they were debating these ideas... I mean, not to cast doubt on your story, but what language were they speaking? What language did they use to be mutually understood?

I don't know.

Then how do you suppose these linguists were able to communicate their ideas?

They probably spoke a language they all knew.

Which language?

I don't know... English, I guess.

See!

Yeah, but that was only because the German and Frenchman didn't know Russian. I'm sure that if they had known Russian, they would have preferred to speak in it...

Well, Vadim, I was also too busy counting my money to take part in this conference... but if I had been present I would have argued that English is the richest language in the world. And do you know why? No? Well, I'll tell you why: synonyms. That's right — synonyms. Pick any English word and I'll show you at least ten synonyms: let's take for example words that mean to 'walk without purpose.' In English we have: *wander, saunter, roam, meander, stroll, stray, rove, amble, ramble...*

Vadim stops to count on his fingers... Then his eyes light up:

That's only nine! he says.

...drift!

He stops for a second then speaks up:

Big deal! he says, Big deal... the reason you have so many synonyms in English is because all your words are made of compound words. For example in Russian we have the word *kamin*, right? It's a good word. And what is it in English? *Fireplace*. See? *Place for the fire* — two words. You need two words to express what Russian can say in one... I can give you a million examples like this: In Russian *kiosk*, in English *bookstand*; or Russian *prodavets* compared to English *salesperson*; not to mention *oboi* and *wallpaper*, *nevestka* and *daughter-in-law*, *kovboi* and *cowboy*...

By now Vadim has finished pouring the mixture, which sits on the table waiting for us to dare to drink it. Vadim's point has been well-made. But I do not back down; instead, I go straight for the jugular:

Maybe so, I say, but how can you consider Russian a complete language given that it doesn't even have... it doesn't even have any articles?

Articles? Fu! Who needs them? Who needs articles!

You may not realize this Vadim but articles are crucial to a language.

Oh yeah? How! Pushkin didn't need articles... Tolstoy didn't... Even *I've* spoken Russian for thirty years without using a single one and I've managed to live a normal healthy life thank you very much...

Here Vadim stops:

...Hey, pass me one of your cigarettes, would you...?

But I thought you didn't smoke?

I don't, he says and lights the cigarette with my lighter.

I look at him curiously and then continue:

What was I saying... oh yeah I was saying that articles are important because they add shades of meaning to your language. For example how would you translate the phrase 'a cowboy offered a salesman a Marlboro cigarette'?

Vadim translates it reluctantly.

That's right, I say, Now how would you translate '*the* cowboy offered *the* salesman *the* Marlboro cigarette'?

Vadim translates it again, this time even more reluctantly.

See! Don't you see! They're exactly the same. But in English they're different!

Yeah but...

Let me finish... now how would you translate 'cowboy offered salesman Marlboro cigarette...'?

Vadim doesn't bother to translate.

You see? That's Russian! That's what Russian sounds like...!

Okay, okay, he says, So in English you can distinguish *a* cowboy from *the* cowboy... don't get me wrong, I mean this, of course, is extremely important... but Russian has so many words that English simply doesn't have...

You think so, do you?

Of course. In English you waste all your time thinking up synonyms for the same word. But Russian has so many ideas that can't be translated into English...

Like what?

Well, for example, do you have a word for *khalyava*?

I'm sure we do....

What about *khaltura*?

There has to be something...

And what about the word *toska*?

Toska? Well... we... it's... okay okay I have to admit that we don't; we don't have a word for *toska*...

You don't have a word for *toska*...? says Vadim smiling victoriously.

No, we don't.

...A *зря* ! ! !

Well, at least my language has a word that means *girlfriend*.

Girlfriend? That's not an important word.

It is too, important!

No it's not. *Wife* is important, but *girlfriend* isn't... and besides ...and besides, we don't need it because we have words like ...like ...well, for example, like *mrak* and *uzhas* and *koshmar*...

Yeah but...!

...not to mention both *drug* and *znakomiy*...

Wait a minute! English has those too. We have them both. We say *friend* and *acquaintance*.

No you don't. When do you use the word *acquaintance*?

What? We use it all the time. We use it to mean people who are not friends, in other words, people we hate.

And another thing... Can I see your passport?

My passport? It's been years since anybody asked to see my passport. And now of all possible times!

I hand Vadim my passport.

Right..., he says holding it against the light of the window: Now, what color is it... what color is your passport?

Blue.

Good. Now what color... look through the window over there and tell me what color the sky is?

Blue.

There you go.

Where?

There's your proof that Russian is the richer language.

Why?

Because we have *siniy* and *goluboi* and English doesn't.

Yeah well in English we have *fingers* and *toes*. In Russian you just have *fingers... fingers* on your hands... *fingers* on your legs... And that's not all! You know what else you don't have...?

What?

...You Russians don't have *fun*.

I pause triumphantly, but Vadim doesn't acknowledge me:

Another unimportant word, he says.

What do you mean, 'unimportant'?

Fun is a word of course, but it's not... how should I say this... it's not a *serious* word. Now if you take Russian, then you'll see what serious words are all about.

Like what?

Well, like *mrak* and *uzhas* and *koshmar*...

You already said those! You're repeating yourself.

Fine, then let me say this: you Americans don't have *dusha*!

Dusha?

No... *dusha*.

We do, too! We have it just as much as you do. We have 'soul'!

No... I'm afraid you don't... it's not the same. You have a heart

— I'll grant you that much — but your heart is no soul, your soul is no Soul, and your Soul is no *dusha*!

But...!

And another thing...!

Here I feel that I am slowly but surely losing the debate, that Vadim has better prepared for it.

...And another thing... why is it that in English you have so few swear words?

What?

You know what they say... the measure of a language's expressiveness is in its swear words, and English has so few.

What are you talking about? We have lots. Like *fuck* and *shit*...

...And that's it! Everything with you is *fuck* and *shit*... as in *fuck fuck shit shit fuck shit fuck shit*... That's all you have. But in Russian... In *Russian*...!

And here Vadim proceeds to pronounce a list of words that I have never heard and will never hear again. Here he pronounces words, one after another, that cannot and should not be read, words that amaze me with both their beauty and their utter vulgarity:

'. . . XX XX XX
XX XX XX
XX XX
XX XX
XX XX XX XX XX XX. . .' he says.

And when he is done, Vadim stops proudly. It is clear to us both that this conversation is as finished as it will get. Now it is time for reconciliation, and so Vadim raises his glass conciliatorily:

Let's drink, he says.

Right, I say though my pride is still wounded:

To wandering without purpose! I offer.

Vadim smiles:

And to the letter *П*! he says.

We touch glasses, and Vadim grabs a pickle:

To *druz'ya*... and to *fun*! he adds.

To *girlfriends*..., I say, ...and to *toska*!

Again we touch glasses:

You know, I'm no diplomat..., Vadim offers diplomatically, ...But let's drink to English: a language that many consider to be the greatest in the world...!

I pause.

Vadim is holding his alcohol in the air, waiting for me to reciprocate. I am surprised by his diplomacy and touch my glass to his words. But my tongue is still stinging, and unlike Vadim, I am no diplomat:

And let's drink to Russian...! I say, ...a language which is rich enough to be widely regarded as the second greatest!

(19)

'Where the hell have you been...?'

(20)

But soon after I moved in, things began to change drastically. Vadim had forgotten to pay the right people. Or had remembered not to pay the wrong people. Or maybe both. Whatever the case, he was being squeezed from all sides. First he sold his car. Then his apartment. In despair he began to frequent the city's casinos, climbing further into debt. He pawned his knight. He hocked his bear. He borrowed from *B* to pay off *A*, then from *C* to cover the interest of *B*. From *D* he took money to pay off the rest of *B* and a part of *C*. With the money that *E* lent him he tried to win back his losses in the casino. When this failed he turned to *F*, who gave him a fraction of what he needed and advised him to ask *G* and *H*... By the time he got to *Z*, not a single loanshark would lend him money. No friend could help him. The alphabet was exhausted. One day his newly appointed Finance Director came to him with a stack of papers, plopping them on the desk:

It's over, said the accountant.

What is? Vadim asked naively.

Klamagup, said the accountant, The company is bankrupt.

And it was. The plaques were chiseled from the doors. The office was sold. Even the furniture was repossessed by the creditor with the biggest 'directors.'

Vadim returned to live with his mother in the apartment where he had outgrown his childhood. In his haste to the top, he had overlooked his mother's apartment, and now he had no money to redecorate it. The apartment was exactly as he had left it. With peeling brown furniture. Wooden planked floors. A red-weaved carpet on the wall.

It didn't have to be the end...

But Vadim was tired.

He still owed money left and right, but for now his creditors did not trouble him. He needed time to straighten out his affairs, they told him, and besides he was worth more to them alive than dead. And so they seemingly ignored him; not once did they come to his apartment; no one called....

(21)

...But sometimes when we are sitting in his kitchen and an unexpected noise is heard outside his door, Vadim will jump and look back over his shoulders. He knows, and I know, and the entire English alphabet knows that it's inevitable: sooner or later Vadim will be receiving a *visit*.

(22)

And so Vadim stayed at home. He lived with his mother. He stopped going out. Now he had no reason to read economics texts, and although he still believed in God, he soon rediscovered vodka. In time his ex-girlfriend became his ex-girlfriend, taking with her as she went both pure-breed dogs. His acquaintances began to shun him. His business associates avoided him like an income tax. In despair, Vadim drank even more than he had before he believed in God. What little money he had hidden under his floorboards quickly ran drier than a bitterness. While his mother worked to make the family's ends meet, the rent from my apartment became Vadim's primary source of income, and no matter how many times I tried to offer him more, my friend insisted on charging me the amount that we had agreed on at the outset, an amount that was now one-tenth of what he could have received from renting it out to someone else.

Vadim had risen high enough to fall spectacularly. He was penniless. He was kopeckless. He was BMWless.

And through it all, Vadim just seemed to take his fate in stride, resigning himself to the small room where he had left fearlessly only to return, as if everything had settled back into its rightful place, the place where everything had been and should be. He'd had his share of struggling, of striving, of wanting. For him, these last few years had been a dream, in both senses of the word, and now, having lived that dream, he was able to accept the smaller cookie gracefully and with dignity. With time he returned to literature, became increasingly philosophical about life in general and about his situation in particular, and through our discussions I at last began to make progress toward understanding my first Russian Soul.

(23)

Olga Mikhailovna is the name of the woman who reminds me to pay my rent; Vadim calls her 'Mom' and although she has become a second Aunt to me, I still refer to her as I have from the beginning of our relationship; affectionately I call her 'Landlady.'

Landlady was born sixty-four years ago in Leningrad. She is silently heroic, slightly tragic, energetic, and honest to a fault. At any given moment she will either be laughing or cleaning. Usually both. During her short lifetime she has survived war, starvation, dictatorship, communism, stagnation, Gorbachev, a putsch, rebellion, inflation, and now the uncertainty of reforms; her life has not come easy and that is why she, like other women of her generation, maintains a large collection of disposable containers and sacks.

Landlady is old but optimistic, out of date but not out of touch; it was she who taught me how to peel potatoes thinly; from her I learned not to discard bread; by her example I found the value in explaining complex ideas using generalizations. Russia's gypsies, she once informed me, are like the blacks in America: absolutely nobody likes them but for some reason they all sing in restaurants.

(24)

Wrong: There are many <u>heroes</u> in this story.
Right: There is one main character, but even he is no hero.

(25)

Sitting with Vadim in his kitchen behind a table of vodka I decide to turn our conversation toward a serious topic: I ask him about his debts, about how many people he owes money to.

Well, he tells me, the debts are consolidated into one lump sum that is owed to a certain individual. In one sense it's easier that way — less phone calls.

How much is it?

Vadim clears his throat, his words scraping against themselves. When I hear the amount I am stunned:

What are you going to do? I ask him.

I don't know, he says, They've left me alone so far but sooner or later they're bound to become more insistent.

What do you mean by *insistent*?

It's difficult to say. It could be anything. In our country we don't have laws. I don't know what they'll do....

Why don't you go to the police?

It's not an option.

Are you sure? I have a student... her father works in the police force. He's a high-ranking officer. Maybe I could talk to him...

It's out of the question.

Why?

Because this is Russia.

Well, isn't there some way that you could earn the money, start from scratch, maybe?

Not anymore. Things have changed. Back when I started, you could make money on anything. But now it's a different world. That's one of the drawbacks of stability....

Does Landlady know that you owe so much money?

Not really. She knows that I'm in debt, but she doesn't know how serious it is... Please don't tell her... I don't want her to worry...

No, of course... But aren't there any other options, anything else you can do?

In my situation there are only two possible ways out: either I can shoot myself or I can go to my creditor and say, Look I can't pay you and so I'm at your mercy. It's a risk.

Which will it be?

I don't know... I'm still deciding. I've been deciding for the last three months.

What about leaving?

What do you mean?

Leaving Russia.

Are you kidding me? Where would I go?

What difference does it make? Anywhere... for example... well for example, you could go *there*...!

Where's that?

Where's *there*? *There* is not here. *There* is there.

I know that, but where specifically?

Well America for example... Just think... you could get a new start... in no time at all you could be chasing the American dream. You could...

Out of the question. For me leaving isn't an option. I can't imagine myself anywhere else. Call it my destiny. Call it the Russian Soul... I'm not sure what it is, but I know that I can't live anywhere but here....

And here my friend becomes quiet. I raise my glass of vodka:

A toast, I say, to your Russian Soul!

And to your American Dream! he adds.

But before we can conclude the toast, Landlady has come into the kitchen with a two-liter plastic bottle:

Don't worry, she says, I'm not going to ruin your scene... I'll just rinse out this bottle and leave you two alone... .it'll only take a second.

Mom...

Landlady turns on the kitchen faucet, running the water noisily into the sink.

Mom! What are you doing, Mom, for Christ's sake?

I'm rinsing out this plastic bottle.

Why? Why are you rinsing out this bottle. It's disposable. Disposable! You don't rinse out disposable bottles... you... you dispose of them.

Landlady is holding the plastic bottle under the water. As she scrubs it, the plastic folds into itself and then snaps back with a loud pop.

There's no sense throwing away a perfectly good bottle, she answers, It's sure to come in handy some day.

Mom, this isn't the Soviet Union anymore. These are meant to be thrown away. You don't need to wash them! You don't!

Vadim walks across the kitchen and yanks open a cupboard door; the cabinet rattles in response and from within the dark shelves a half-dozen sterilized plastic bottles fall out and bounce onto the floor, then roll into the center of the small kitchen.

There! says Vadim, There are your bottles! You have enough already and still you're washing them....

(26)

'...Hi it's me. Am I interrupting something...?'

(27)

Your generation, says Landlady, just doesn't understand.... You think that everything is so simple... you'll see....

...Mom!

You think that...

Mom, do we have to go through this again? Do we?

Landlady has stopped smiling. Her voice is cracking with age:

I suppose I should just throw these bottles away? she says: I suppose I should throw away the end pieces of bread, too?

No, Mom, you shouldn't throw them away... you should give them to your guests... and if they turn them down then you should be ashamed... and if they accept, then you should be ashamed that you don't have anything better to offer them... and if they accept and like it, then you should be ashamed because it means that somewhere someone is starving and dreaming about eating this dried piece of bread and here *you* are depriving them of it....

Vadim stops. His outburst has surprised me and, I think, himself as well:

...Look I'm sorry I brought it up... let's just drop it, okay? he says.

And with that Vadim throws the sterilized plastic bottles back into the cupboard and slams it shut.

...Let's just drop it...

(28)

After Landlady leaves the room, Vadim shakes his head:

I don't know what's come over me lately, he says, It's like I'm always on edge — I guess it's the debts.

You need to get out more. You need to relax.

Where?

I don't know. Someplace quiet. Outdoors, maybe.

Yeah. You know I've been in this damn city forever.

Vadim stops to think:

Hey! he says, Let's go to the country! I have a friend who can let me use his summer cottage.

But it's not summer.

Well then I'll ask a different friend. I mean, we just have to go... now's the perfect time... before winter comes... and if we're lucky we'll even have a chance to look for mushrooms... What do you say?

Mushrooms?

Yeah, I'm no meteorologist, but I'm sure the weather will be perfect for them....

(29)

Of all my students, my favorite is also my youngest. She is the weakest and, at the same time, my most improved student. Her name is Lena. She was twelve when we began studying; she was having problems keeping up with the other students in her class and so her father asked me to help her. For the last two years we have met twice a week at my apartment. She brings me food that her mother has wrapped carefully in porcelain dishes; after each lesson she picks up the dishes from the previous time.

For two years we have studied like this.

In the beginning, Lena would sit nervously at my table. Her voice was unsure, her pronunciation terrible. For her the lessons were torturous, and as we read from her outdated school textbook, I could see why: the majority of texts were about Lenin; most of the others were about schoolchildren in western countries who admired Lenin; the remainder were about potatoes.

At some point I realized that Lena was answering my questions mechanically, without thinking, groping blindly with her answers until she stumbled onto the right one. She was so lost, so scared by the language that she couldn't even think to answer.

One day when she was reading, I interrupted her. All right Lena, I said, That's enough for today. Lena looked at me in horror, almost in tears. I'll see you next week, I said.

The next lesson, instead of her textbook, I gave her a text with English fairy tales. She was completely lost, but when I explained the words she memorized them immediately. From then on, we didn't touch her textbook, working instead with special texts that I would select for her. At school, she still lagged behind, in part because I had abandoned her textbook. But eventually, she began to show a sincere interest in English; in time she would bring her own texts to our lessons. Her pronunciation improved. She remembered words. From her parents I learned how disappointed she would become when we had to miss our lessons. Eventually her grades in school improved.

Then one day after a lesson as she was wrapping her scarf around herself and getting ready to go, she stopped suddenly:

Oh I almost forgot... I wanted to ask you one thing...

Sure, I said.

Can you explain the difference between *high* and *tall*?

NO!!!

It's... uh... getting late, Lena... We'll talk about it next time.

Okay, she said and left.

The next day I called some old acquaintances at the institute to ask them to explain the difference. But none of them could. I began to ask around among Russian friends who had studied English:

Hey what is the difference between *high* and *tall*? I would say.

You're asking *us*? they would answer.

I'm serious... I mean for me it's instinctive, but maybe somewhere you were taught the difference.

Well, our teacher in school used to tell us that Lenin was tall but coal output was high.

I don't get it, I said.

Okay, it's like this... a regular person, if he's lucky, is tall... but a beaurocrat will be higher than you in any case.

What about a mountain?

Well, if I remember correctly, a mountain is tall. But it can be high too, depending on the mountain...

And so I went to the library in search of books on the subject. To no avail. I bought countless grammar books in all imaginable languages, but there were no specialized treatments of the matter. Finally, I created a list of all possible nouns, ordered them in columns depending on the adjectives that described them. Maybe, I reasoned, I could find some sort of rule or pattern:

High	Tall	Both
wounded eagle	glass of milk	mountain
red flag	flag pole	
inflation	Gorbachev	
eighth-floor apartment	twelve-story building	
red white & blue flag	escalator	
taxes	tale	
painting	statue of Lenin	

For hours I sat with the paper before my eyes trying to make some sense of the words, trying to find some correlation. Then, strangely enough, it occurred to me one night after I had fallen asleep with the paper on my chest. In a dream I saw a man with greased hair, dressed out of fashion, with long nails and curled sideburns:

The difference between *high* and *tall*..., he began.

...is that *tall* describes things that are connected to the ground, whereas *high* describes things that are not! Do you see?

Lena shook her head. And so, for the next half-hour I explained the difference. I explained it over and over, until she had understood it several times. Until I myself understood it. Never again would I have a problem with this distinction. Never again would I feel uncertain in its usage...

...And hopefully never again will she....

(30)

The next morning, Vadim and I take several of Landlady's recycled disposable bags and go hunting for mushrooms.

(31)

It is late autumn. The leaves have fallen and camouflage the mushrooms which are scarce anyway. We walk slowly, our eyes scanning the ground. But we find nothing. Now and then Vadim bends over to examine a mushroom. After an hour our bags are almost empty. When we come to a clearing, we sit on an old rotting log. Vadim pulls out a small bottle and takes a swig. He offers it to me and I accept.

It's funny..., I say, ...the first time I ever went looking for mushrooms it was kind of like this... except it was spring. I was with my friend... my first Russian friend...

I stop.

The redhead! How long has it been since I last saw him? Where is he? What is he doing now? Is he still married to Tanya? Does he still not paint? How does he feel about the number three? Has he forgiven me since then? Has he forgotten? After all, so much time has passed...!

I notice that Vadim is waiting for me to finish the sentence: ...he's the one who gave me the painting. But it doesn't matter... there weren't any mushrooms then, either.

Vadim is wiping his mouth with his sleeve.

You know, I say after a long silence, I've been thinking lately...

Vadim is leaning back against the old log and staring up into the vast light-blue sky.

...I've been thinking lately that it might be time for me to leave.

What do you mean? says Vadim.

Leave Russia.

What! Why?

I've been here for a long time now... a lot longer than I'd planned. To be honest I'm not even sure why I stayed *this* long.

What are you talking about?

It's strange, I say, But I just seemed to have lost interest. I mean everything started so well. Everything was new and interesting. There was so much promise. And now... there's nothing new, it's as if it's the same old thing over and over, day after day, page after page. Now I'm just going through the motions.

But what about your promises... the eleven yellow words?

I've already found nine of them. There're only two more to go... and I've begun to think that it's not too bad... that maybe it's enough.

What about measuring the Russian Soul?

I give up.

What do you mean?

I've realized that I'll never be able to touch it or see it, or taste it... let alone smell it. And besides, it's not even that important for me anymore. It used to be, but now it's not.

When did this happen? You were always so determined to stick it out, not to leave until you *understand*... until you *understood*. I mean do you have any idea how many times you've used those two words!

I know, I know. Counting your last sentence... ninety-six times.

See! And now, after everything, to just up and leave... to leave just like that?

It's not *just like that*. I've been thinking about it for a while now. It's hard to explain, but the more I live here, the stronger it gets. In fact, I'm not even sure why I'm still here, what's keeping me.

I stop:

Did I tell you what happened to me last week?

No.

Well, you remember how I told you about the two-kopeck coin... about how I promised to keep the coin as long as I stayed in Russia... in other words, I wouldn't give it up until I was ready to leave...?

Yes, so?

So anyway, the other day I was having a terrible day... I mean it must have been the single worst day of my life: during the entire day no one seemed to notice that I was a foreigner; no one seemed to care; an acquaintance had complimented me on my knowledge of Russian, but didn't bother to pose any questions beginning with

'Have you read...?' On my way home the sun was shining right into my eyes...

I get the point... what happened?

Okay, so at home I'd just finished off an opened bottle of vodka and decided to get some more. When I went out for the second time the elevator was working but busy... again the sun was shining right in my eyes...

Get to the point!

I am, I am... So I finally get to the store and I'm buying a bottle of vodka and I've taken out my wallet to pay for it when suddenly I feel someone tapping me on the shoulder. When I turn around a man is standing in front of me and holding out his hand at me. Is this yours? he says. At first I don't understand what he's getting at, but then I see that in his hand he's holding the two-kopeck coin.

You'd dropped it?

That's right. Can you imagine? He picked up a filthy worthless coin from the filthy worthless floor in order to give it back to me... as if he sensed it.

As if he sensed what?

You know, that I wasn't ready to leave yet... somehow he knew that it was too early. And so he gave me back the coin, in other words he gave me a reason to stay in Russia.

I see.

Strange, isn't it?

Maybe. But there's one thing I don't understand: why don't you just leave if you feel like leaving?

I don't know. I have a lot of ties here... it's not easy to just... I mean I've been here for four and a half years, and that's an awful long time...

Vadim is looking at me sadly.

I guess I'm just waiting for an excuse, in other words, for the moment when I'll know fully and finally that the time is right...

Vadim hands me the bottle and I take it.

...I guess I'm just waiting for something to bring change... or, at the very least, the prospect for change.

(32)

Later, we hike back to the electric train which takes us to the metro station which takes us to the elevator which takes us to the light...

When I reach home I look for the redhead's number. I have forgotten it, but at last find it on an old playing card. An unfamiliar voice answers:

Hello? it says.

Hello? I answer, Tanya?

You must have the wrong number.

Excuse me... is this the Three of Diamonds?

Yes the number is right. But there's no Tanya here. They don't live here anymore. Good-bye...

Just a minute! ...Do you know how long it's been?

What?

Do you know how long ago they moved out?

I don't know. I've lived here for two years. I can't tell you when they moved out... At least two years ago.

Two years ago.

Sadly, I put the phone down:

Thanks, I say.

(33)

Some call it a dream; others a nightmare. Often their accents are flawless and their grammar impeccable. But no matter what they call it, one thing is sure: it will end as everything does, and most likely it will end — no matter how long we've been expecting it — unexpectedly.

For Erica Martin it ended under the wheels of a Russian ambulance which, after crushing her chest like a cardboard box, didn't even stop to pick her up.

It was not the first such incident.

When I heard the news I was shocked in triplicate: first, that Erica was dead; second, that she was dead because of an ambulance; and third, that it had happened — that *it* had come to its end — in Russia, that is to say, in the country that she had spent so much of her life hating. *What would she have thought of that?* I wondered in her absence: *Did she have time to curse her fate? Or had she lived here long enough to appreciate this irony?*

(34)

Do you like riddles? Vadim asks me unexpectedly one day.

Not really, I answer.

Well I heard a good one the other day. Wanna hear it?

Not really.

Okay it goes like this..., and Vadim begins to tell the riddle:

An American spy, it seems, landed in the middle of a Russian countryside, buried his parachute, and after changing into traditional peasant clothes hiked to a village where he came upon a house and an old woman sitting on its porch. The woman looked at him suspiciously, but the man approached her anyway, addressing her in flawless, accentless Russian:

Babushka, he said, Give me some water!

The old woman, listening to his request for a drink, looked at him severely and said:

I won't give you anything, you American spy!

The man's accent had been flawless, his grammar had been impeccable. So, said Vadim beaming at his riddle, How did she know that he was an American spy?

I don't know, Vadim.

Take a guess!

I don't know... he probably used the familiar verb instead of the formal.

No no! He said it perfectly...!

He probably mistook the perfective for the imperfective... you know, like I'm always doing.

No no! His grammar was perfect!

I don't know.

You don't?

No I don't

And Vadim smiles a conqueror's smile:

(35)

The spy was black.

(36)

Vadim is very pleased with his riddle. In fact he has been in particularly good spirits the whole day. I haven't seen him in such a good mood for more than half a year. Finally, when I can take it no more, I ask him:

Hey! what's the deal? Why are you in such a good mood. I mean you're smiling from ear to ear!

I am?

Yeah, you are.

Well actually there is something...

What is it?

I've met the girl of my dreams!

You have? Congratulations!

Thanks.

What's her name?

Olga.

Olga?

No... Olga.

Well of course it is. Of course her name is *Olga*!

...What?... Why? Why do you say *of course*?

It had to be Olga!

Why *had to*?

Because by now I've already met Tanya, Natasha, Lena, and Irina!

I'm in love, says Vadim, ...she's the most amazing Olga I've ever met... and *that's* saying something!

Well, tell me about her...?

You see, she's unique... she's unlike any other girl!

How so?

Well, she's beautiful, intelligent, polite...

Intelligent *and* polite?

That's right! And beautiful!

She sounds perfect.

She is!

Does she speak German?

I don't know. Why do you ask?

I'm still trying to get rid of this damn dictionary.

Vadim laughs for the first time since he started taking the metro: I'll ask her, he says, but I think she studied French....

Just then Vadim's favorite song comes over the radio, and he closes his eyes to appreciate it:

'Yesterday... All my troubles seemed so far away...'

(37)

For Vadim, Olga was a godsend; she helped him forget about his debts, about the impossible sum of money he owed to a certain individual who by now was becoming impatient with him. Vadim and Olga's relations quickly went from new to serious, and with this change, Vadim changed as well: for the first time since spring he began to leave his apartment regularly; now he had a reason to look after himself; he drank less; his state of mind improved; eventually, a friend of his found him a modest job at the history institute where he had once been a student, and every morning he would go to his unglamorous job by metro and return in the evening. He still lived with his mother in the apartment downstairs from mine; but now he spent less time with me — during the day he worked, during the evenings he stayed with Olga...

(38)

...and I am absolutely glad for him.

In fact, if you don't know about his enormous debts, you would say that Vadim is living a normal life. His salary is modest, but paid more or less regularly. He stays busy. It even seems that he has managed to put the letter Z out of his mind.

For now our conversations have become as rare as a rose, and somewhat less philosophical. But I know that this is exactly what he needs.

And besides, I still have my students; I have my vodka; I have all twelve chairs and one story of America ... or was it one chair and twelve stories...?

(39)

But according to Russian tradition it's a sin to leave an unfinished bottle of vodka. And so before moving on, Vadim and I walk dutifully back into the kitchen to finish it off.

In the other room, within my view, Landlady is trying to mend a disposable plastic sack whose handle has been ripped off by too many trips with potatoes. The bag is in full color and shows a bare-chested Russian woman with a flag wrapped around her shoulders. The flag, of course, is American, but does not cover her nipples, both of which stick out proudly — pink and red, respectively. As Landlady holds the bag, her wrinkled fingers course over the woman's breasts, bending, then folding them. Seeing this, I am reminded of a discussion that we started several weeks ago, but never finished:

Fate, I say to Vadim, does not exist.

What do you mean it doesn't exist?

It doesn't exist.

Yes it does.

No it doesn't.

Yes it does.

Does not.

Does too.

Does not.

Does too....

(40)

Aw forget it..., says Vadim, It's not important anyway...

And here he holds up his glass. By now our tongues have become heavy and our words paradoxical:

What should we drink to? he asks.

To Russia! I say.

And to America! he answers.

To Russian! I say.

And to English! he says.

To the Russian Dream! I say.

And..., he says, ...to the American Soul!

(41)

Olga is blonde now but manages to be both intelligent and polite. Her outward appearance, like that of most Russian women, is especially striking in spring. Olga has completed five years of medical school along with two years of residency and if all goes well — if there are no unforeseen cataclysms to ruin her plans — if everything goes per schedule then in approximately three weeks — nothing could happen in three weeks, could it? — in approximately three weeks she will finally become, that is to say in a little over two chapters Olga will finally become....

She will *finally* become....

(42)

'It rained today...'

* * * * * * * * * *

Book 9. Three Nines, Two Jacks, and Not a Marriage in Sight

(1)

...In less than one chapter, Olga will finally become Vadim's wife.

(2)

The two of them — Olga and Vadim — live together full-time now. The two-bedroom apartment that they share with Landlady is small, and is made even smaller by the fact that Olga and Landlady have different recipes for *borsht*. Vadim loves them both and so he eats out, usually in the cafeteria at the history institute where he works during the day. Olga is also busy with her studies, but has more free time during her afternoons. In the evenings they both come upstairs to my apartment where we sit in my kitchen eating pickles and talking about things that seem important.

Living on different floors of the same building, the three of us have become as inseparable as marriage from a wedding. Vadim has found in me a reliable drinking partner — now he drinks more than he did before falling into love, but less than he did before believing in God — whereas Olga uses my apartment as a refuge from Landlady.

It's not that Landlady doesn't like Olga. In fact, Olga tells me, relations between the two of them — soon-to-be-mother- and daughter-in-law — would be perfect if they didn't have to live in the same apartment. Or if the apartment weren't so small. Or even if it *were* small, but didn't belong entirely to Landlady...

She even criticizes how I peel potatoes! Olga complains.

Look, I say for the thousandth time. Why don't you two move into my apartment and I'll find somewhere else to live.

And for the thousandth time Vadim objects. He has given me his word that I can stay in the apartment as long as I live in Russia, and now he is stubbornly keeping it:

What about you? I protest. What about Olga?

A promise is a promise! says Vadim.

But..., I say.

But...! Olga seconds.

No way! says Vadim with a wide sweep of his arm. And that's *that*!

For the last three months, since the wedding was announced, everybody has been especially high-strung. Landlady has been running around the markets looking for the brightest and most exquisite cabbage. Olga has been trying to find a wedding dress that will still fit her on her wedding day. And Vadim, who has not been able to reach a decision about his debts, has instead been consuming pickle after pickle. Sometimes he eats so many pickles that he has to drink vodka to wash them down.

One evening while the three of us are sitting in my kitchen, Vadim suggests playing cards:

Do you know any Russian games? he asks me.

Just one, I answer, My friends and I used to play a game called *Policeman*. But it's been a long time...

Policeman? That's the most famous card game in Russia. Do you like it?

Not really. No one wins the damn game. I mean you play and play and all you end up with is a loser.

It's not my favorite either. But I know another game that's perfect for three people. I think you'll like it.

Vadim takes out his deck of cards, counts out twenty-four, and begins shuffling them:

The object of the game, he says, is...

(3)

The object of the game, as with most games, is to win. Which in theory is easy enough. But because your opponents have the same goal — they are also trying to win — your task becomes complicated.

You score points by declaring a marriage which means a king and queen of the same suit. In *this* game tens are better than jacks; clubs are better than spades, and hearts are worth as much as both of them combined. In this game, a marriage is good, but absolutely helpless unless you have an ace to protect it, in other words, with which to take a trick and declare your marriage...

...First one to reach one thousand wins.

It *is* a good game, simple enough to allow tangential discussion, but complex enough that the better players usually win. The game is called *tysacha* and as usual I usually lose:

	Vadim	Olga	Me
Hand # 1	145	55	15

(4)

Not surprisingly, Olga also eats pickles. But what is surprising is that she doesn't drink vodka. Understandably, we are all worried about her. Vadim seems the most disturbed: he stutters, he paces, he points at Olga's ankles as if it could be her fault entirely. She never says anything, but sometimes she cries. Landlady says a lot but cries too. I myself have never cried since nobody suspects me of anything. Like me, Vadim doesn't cry, even though they suspect him entirely. Instead, he paces, he stutters, he eats pickle after pickle, and asks me to proofread the translation of his favorite song. 'Vchera... Vse moi problemy...'

(5)

I don't understand what's so difficult...! says Vadim. He has gathered the cards after the first game and handed them to Olga to shuffle:

...I don't see what's so hard! You just take two fingers and slide them down the back of your throat... as far back as you can... like this...

And Vadim curls his fingers slightly and puts them halfway into his throat.

...And all your problems are solved... try it.

I can't.

What do you mean, you can't?

I don't know. I've tried, but it doesn't work.

What do you mean it doesn't work? It has to work... look you just...

I know! I know! You think I haven't thought of that myself?! You think it's never occurred to me? I mean... jeez... give me a *little* credit!

Vadim is puzzled:

It's strange, he says, You're the first person I've ever known who can't make himself throw up.

What's so strange about it?

It's strange because *everybody* can throw up... except you. What's the problem?

I'm not sure. Maybe I'm just deceiving myself... can't bring myself to commit to it and that means that I really don't want to vomit in the first place, that I prefer the alternative....

And what alternative are you so stubbornly preferring?

I don't know. But let's just say I've been in Russia long enough to know the fine line between *here* and *there*.

Olga has dealt the cards and is waiting for me to start bidding:

Your bid, she tells me.

One hundred, I say.

(6)

As the game progresses, I realize how thorough my luck isn't:

At first I receive aces but no marriages. Then I receive marriages — two and three at a time — but no aces. Then, I receive a marriage and an ace, but in different suits. Then I receive an ace and a marriage of the same suit, but it is spades — in other words, the cheapest suit — and I am outbid by Vadim....

Why are good marriages so rare? Why is it that the black cards are worth less than the others? And why... WHY doesn't anybody in this country want my German dictionary?

And then it happens: I receive the ideal hand. Ace, ten, king, queen. All of hearts. Whereas before I have had to duck out early during bidding, now it is Vadim who has passed and I who am bidding against Olga at one-sixty... one-seventy... one-eighty...

Vadim is staring at us in amazement:

Are you sure you know what you're doing? he asks.

Absolutely! I say.

...One-ninety... two hundred...

But wait a minute! Why is Olga bidding so high? What can she possibly have to match my hand?

...two-ten... two-twenty...

It's impossible! says Vadim, Two people bidding that high!

Finally, at two hundred twenty, Olga gives in. I collect my crib confidently — with this hand I can't lose — and slide my two friends a card each. But before I can even lead my ace, Olga, without even looking at the card, lays down her hand:

Four nines, she says.

Vadim looks at her cards:

Redeal, he says.

You're kidding me!

Nope. Looks like she's got four nines.

Sorry, Olga says.

I feel tricked:

Who dealt that hand, anyway? I ask.

Vadim checks his sheet:

You did! he says.

And so I pick up the cards, shuffle them, and once again deal myself an ace with no marriages.

	Vadim	Olga	Me
Hand #9	585	420	55

(7)

Without any aces, without a marriage, I can only sit and watch from the side of the table as my two friends compete against each other. Without declaring a marriage I can't score points. And without scoring points I can't expect to outscore my opponents. Sadly, my chances of victory are as slim as Gorbachev's in the upcoming elections.

Amazingly enough, Gorbachev really is going to run for president...!

For now my role is spoiler, in other words I should do everything in my power to ruin other people's games. It is not a role that is entirely interesting, but one that I have already learned to become used to.

You know, says Vadim, We have a saying in Russian... have you heard it?

I don't know.

About cards... we say that people who are unlucky in cards are lucky in love. And vice versa.

Why?

I don't know. That's just what we say. I guess if you use up all your luck in cards you won't have any left over for love.

Actually, says Olga, it's the opposite: if you use up all your luck in love then you won't have enough left over for cards.

Well, I say, judging by our game the reverse seems to be true!

I look at my score and at the dusty solar calculator on my shelf, and as if to prove my point, Olga laughs and kisses Vadim lightly on the hairy part of his ear.

(8)

Can I ask you a question? says Olga as she shuffles the cards lazily. As usual, Olga is not interested in the game as much as she is in the conversation; she takes forever to shuffle the cards, she plays attentively only when she is winning, and then only if she is close to victory. The rest of the time she plays disinterestedly, making mistakes that especially irritate Vadim, who is more passionate about cards than he should have been:

A question? I say.

Yeah, Olga says, I was just wondering... I was just wondering why it is that you never smile.

What?

Since I've known you I don't remember a single time that you've smiled.

I don't know. I mean I've never thought about it. I just smile when I want to, I mean when I have something to smile about.

Everyone has *something* to smile about. But you never do. Never.

I don't?

No, you don't. Does he Vadim?

Well now that you mention it...

See! You never smile.

I... I didn't notice. I mean I didn't realize I wasn't smiling.

Well just think... can you remember the last time you smiled? Is there a time that you can actually remember smiling?

Well, I don't know. I remember *thinking* about smiling when I was in the flooded underpass... I remember *almost* smiling when I didn't have a cigarette... I guess the last time I smiled sincerely was... I suppose the last time I smiled was...

When did I smile the last time? Was it two years ago? Was it three? No... it had to be when... That's it!

...I guess it was right before the ruble stopped falling.

(9)

	Vadim	Olga	Me
Hand # 11:	645	480	-105

(9)

In 1996 (1USD=5000RUR), while campaigning for the Russian presidency, Mikhail Gorbachev was assailed right in the face by a man who had pushed through the ranks of cordoned spectators and lunged at him as he entered a building to make a speech.

The western press revulsed in horror.

The former president was equally surprised, especially since he did not even know this man and had not done anything in the last four years to provoke such an attack.

Despite the whole messy affair, Gorbachev — who was visibly shaken — received barely two percent of the vote; this total was a bit more than one percent, but far less than the amount received by the eventual winner, a man who much to the regret of Gorbachev was not Gorbachev.

(9)

'It's really too bad. I was kind of hoping he would win. He seems like such a nice man...'

(10)

In the beginning Olga would only visit me together with Vadim. But after the incident with Gorbachev she began to come alone, at first to get away temporarily from Landlady with whom she had fallen out irreconcilably, and then, later, for other reasons.

The first time we met for these *other* reasons, I tried clumsily to give her a calculator:

It's for you! I said.

What is it?

It's a solar calculator the size of a credit card. It's my last one.

What am I supposed to do with it?

Take it.

What for?

I... I don't know... calculate with it.

It's nice of you but...

Olga looked at me politely:

...but keep it.

The strange thing about our relationship is that when we are alone together we do not say a single word until we have taken our first sip of tea. And then, as soon as the tea is gone, we become silent once again — she is not here to talk. It is actually the middle part that I prefer, but Olga has more experience in such things, and I have come to accept that it is probably more honest her way. Vadim cannot visit me during the daytime — his job does not allow it — so Olga and I spend her afternoons in slow silent minutes that gradually turn to hours; my friend does not feel any sort of jealousy about our meetings because I don't do anything with her that he himself isn't doing... and because Olga and I meet in strict secrecy.

(11)

Take it off, she says, I want to feel you.

And so I do. I take it off.

(12)

Olga drinks coffee with Vadim. With me she drinks tea. She is picky about it, and each time she comes over I take pains to make her tea exactly as she likes it, exactly how she taught me:

First, I boil water in my metal kettle until it whistles like a trolleybus driver. Then pour the water off the top — careful not to stir the dregs to the surface — into a small ceramic teapot, which I then rinse until it is as hot as the water. There are several teapots in my cupboard, but ever since Olga commented on the one with the chipped spout and pink handle, I have taken to using it exclusively. Slowly I pour the water out: now the teapot is ready for the two large spoonfuls of black-leaf tea and steaming water, which I cover with a lid. It should sit like this for no less than three minutes and while I wait, I cut a half-slice of lemon and spread it over the bottom of Olga's cup. For three anxious minutes I wait for the tea to brew, then pour it from the teapot right into the cup — just enough to submerge the lemon — and fill the cup with the boiled water from the kettle.

Olga likes her tea slightly cooled. Weaker than the color white. As sweet as silence. Three heaping teaspoons of sugar. I can't believe that anyone could stand something so sweet, but that's how Olga drinks it. Each time she comes over. In the afternoons. At least once per weekday. That's how she passes away the few minutes we spend between silences.

(13)

But of all the things I do, Olga likes one thing most. After tea when she is lying silent and flat on the pink softness of her stomach I will take her leg and bend it at the knee so that her foot points naked to the sky. Using the very tip of my fingernail I will trace patterns on the tender skin of her feet, along the heel, over the arch, and in and out of the cul-de-sacs between her toes. It is here — between the toes — where she is most tender, and as she lays there, her entire body will tense up from the sensation, her face will grimace with tortured pleasure, her lips will press together in agony in a sure sign for me to move my finger even more lightly along her skin, which I do, prolonging it all a few seconds more until her body begins to quiver. Only then do I stop, mercifully, to take the other foot. Sometimes I trace words into her: at times they are words that she has spoken, but more often they are those words that I wish she would say. When I am finished I let Olga's leg fall wearily to the bed. She will lie there for a few moments, her eyes closed, her back as straight and as smooth as a sidewalk.

When she turns over I know that she is ready.

(14)

Wrong: We are making love with you.
Right: You and I are having sex.

(15)

Let's say — you don't mind, do you? — let's say you're preparing for a wedding. Really, it could be any excuse to eat, drink, and vomit... but let's say it's a wedding. Guests will be coming over and they will expect food. And drink. And maybe even a place to sleep for the night. Everything should be festive. Everything should be loud. Each of your guests should leave having discovered something about themselves that they didn't know before they came. They should be glad they bothered to attend. They should remember this day apart from all others; after all, it is no ordinary day... it is a day for being wed!

Home for you is a small apartment that will soon become even smaller because your son was not careful. Because his Soul leans more toward *авось* than to logic. Because your future daughter-in-law has too few recipes and too much free time during her afternoons.

Who knows?

Either way it's not important. During your short lifetime you have survived war, starvation, dictatorship, communism, stagnation, Gorbachev, a putsch, rebellion, inflation, and now the side effects of reforms. Your years have taught you that in life nothing is as serious as it seems. Tragedy is transitory. Transient. Answers, you have learned, can be as painful as a puncture or as simple as a suture... it all depends on how you choose to look at it. Your life has taught you to take things simply. Without complicated ideas. Without theories. Without hope, of course, but more importantly without regret.

And so you spend your time trying to find the right cake. The greenest vegetables. The richest cheese. For years you have been saving your kopecks. For decades you have been buying the cheaper of two cabbages. The poorer of two potatoes. Money is money, you have been telling yourself, ...even in Russia. But now the time has come to let loose. Now the time has come to spend what you have managed to save. Sure, money is money...

...but *a wedding is a wedding*!

And so you spend a year's salary on salad, a month's wages on mayonnaise. With the money you earned last week you purchase bottled water. And when your savings have been reduced to useless coins, you sacrifice them without hesitation to a gypsy boy strapped to an accordion.

You do it without thinking, of course. Instinctively. Your thoughts are elsewhere. After all, the big day is approaching. Your only son is getting married. Guests are coming over. Music will play. People will eat. People will drink. People will...

...It promises to be a day unlike any other!

(16)

Once, when Olga and I have just sat down to tea, Landlady calls. We are especially nervous because Olga is awaiting the results of her tests. And so Landlady's voice penetrates like sunflower oil on black bread:

I know she's there, she says.

Vadim, I mutter, isn't here and Olga is probably...

She's there. Let me talk to her.

She's probably drinking tea, I offer.

Dammit, that girl never drinks tea!

Flustered, I call Olga to the phone. She takes the receiver and I leave the room, closing the door behind me.

I grab a cigarette and light up. Tomorrow is Saturday. Olga's weekends belong to Vadim. It is their time to be alone. I'm not sure what they do — I don't ask — but for me it means time to myself in my apartment with my vodka. And this weekend will be no different:

in fact, if the rain lets up then by Sunday evening I should be passing through Charleston, South Carolina....

When Olga comes out she is in tears. She points to the phone which is lying awkwardly on the warmth of the bed where we have just been. With my hands I ask if I'm supposed to take it, and Olga, wiping away her tears, nods. When I hold the receiver to my face, I can hear Landlady's breathing and feel her words against my ear:

What do you two talk about? she says: What could you possibly have to talk about?

(17)

It is Tuesday when Olga tells me the results of her test.

Well, I say, What are you going to do?

What am *I* going to do?

Well I mean what are we going to do? I mean what are the three of us going to do?

Olga looks at me with annoyance:

I don't know, she says, I don't know what I'm going to do.

Do you know whose... I mean is it...?

Olga puts her finger to my lips:

Shhhh..., she says, Let's not talk.

But I just asked..., I say through her fingers.

It's not important. Either way it's not important, now is it?

And taking her finger from my lips, Olga leads me from the warmth of my kitchen back to silence.

(18)

Whose deal? I ask.

Yours, says Vadim.

Again? But I just dealt.

No you didn't... I did. And since you're sitting to my left it means that now it's your deal. At least that's how the game is played *in most cases*...

	Vadim	Olga	Me
Hand # 21:	880	715	-5

(19)

And then something strange happens. I receive a call from my ex-future-ex landlord whom I have left my new address. He is calling to tell me that there is a letter from America. It is strange given that I have not lived at that address for over a year. And when he hands me the letter I am even more amazed. It was mailed more than three years ago. The letter has been traveling — who knows why — for more than three years!

The handwriting is unfamiliar. When I open it the date at the top is smaller by several months than the postmark, which itself is years smaller than the day I received it, in other words, today.

Silently I open the letter and begin reading.

(20)

But just when Vadim is on the verge of victory my luck changes. Suddenly, I get a run of good fortune. First I win a game to push me into positive figures. Then I play 'blind' thereby doubling my score. Then I get a hand that includes marriages in both hearts and diamonds. Even the one hand that I do not lead, I am still able to ruin Vadim's marriage by declaring a marriage of my own....

Game by game, he sees his score become less and less; once again his luck has abandoned him. Olga holds her ground for a while too, but then begins to slip as well. In time, our scores have evened up:

	Vadim	Olga	Me
Hand # 29	475	560	505

(21)

I think he knows, Olga says.

It is late afternoon and she is holding her tea before her lips with both hands.

Who? What?

I think Vadim knows about us.

What! Why do you say that?

I don't know. I just think he knows. He doesn't say anything, but I just have a feeling he knows.

How could that be? We're so careful.

I don't know, says Olga, All I said is that it seems like he knows.

Olga takes a sip of tea and looks at the large glass ashtray on my table. With me she is either painfully honest or equally silent. She respects Vadim enough to lie to him, but with me she can afford to be sincere. From the beginning she has not led me to believe that our relationship will in any way impose on her relations with Vadim. From the very beginning I have understood my role. And I have accepted it.

And so I take a drink of tea and light another cigarette. And Olga looks at me, moves the large glass ashtray closer to herself, and does the same.

(22)

One afternoon over tea I decide to provoke her:

What would you do, I say with a grin, if I told Vadim about us?

Olga laughs without answering.

No really... what would you do? For example what would you do if at the wedding I announced to everybody about you and me? What would you do if I objected during the ceremony, or if I stood up during the dinner and said, 'Ladies and Gentlemen I'd like to make a toast to Olga... the woman I've been having orgasms with for the last year!'

Olga has stopped laughing, but still doesn't answer. So I push further:

No really... I'm just wondering what you would do if I stood up during the dinner and made a toast like that?

You wouldn't, she says finally.

What do you mean?

You wouldn't make a toast like that.

How do you know? Maybe I would.

No, she says, you wouldn't.

Okay okay I wouldn't... but what if I *did*... what would you do?

Olga takes a drag of her cigarette:

I'd deny it, she says.

That's it? That's all you'd do?

Of course.

But what if I had proof? What if I started proving it in front of everybody?

You couldn't.

What do you mean I couldn't?

You couldn't prove anything. And if you tried, I'd deny it.

But what if I described things that only someone who knows you intimately can know...?

You don't know anything about me.

I don't?

You don't know anything about me that everybody else doesn't already know. There's nothing you could say that would surprise anyone.

I stop to think. *What do I know about her? In all this time she hasn't told me one important thing... she hasn't once born her Soul!*

...And besides, everybody would just think that you were drunk. No one would believe you.

Hah! They'd believe me all the more! You know what they say... the four people who tell the truth are children, drunks, the insane, and ... *children, drunks, the insane, and...* I forgot the fourth one...

Policemen.

...Right, policemen. Everyone would just assume that I lost control of my inhibitions and started babbling the truth. What would you do then? Huh?

You wouldn't do it. Not even you could bring yourself to do a thing like that.

What's that supposed to mean? Why 'even you'?

You understand that it would just cause problems that nobody needs. Even you understand that.

Again 'even you'!

You know if I didn't know you better, I'd think you were trying to hurt me.

You can think what you want I guess.

There is a pause as Olga crushes out her cigarette in the glass ashtray:

Look I think we've talked enough, don't you?

At that moment I feel like hitting her. But instead I look at her coldly:

Why do you even come here? I say, Why do you even bother?

Olga hasn't even stopped to consider my question, but already has a flippant answer:

I don't know, she says, Why did you come to Russia?

(23)

	Vadim	Olga	Me
Hand # 36	835	880	880

(24)

It is almost the end of the game. Both Olga and I have the chance to win if we can score the final one hundred twenty points; Vadim is not far behind. Whereas in the beginning I played passively and without purpose, now for some reason I have a terrible desire to win. For some reason, this game has taken on a whole new meaning... for me it has become as significant as snow, as important as a first paragraph.

Olga shuffles the cards and deals them out. I wait until they have all been distributed and then pick them up, unfanning them in my hands. And sure enough I receive the worst hand possible: three nines, two jacks, no aces, and to prevent me from declaring a redeal, an unprotected ten.

Across from me, Vadim is smiling and I can only imagine why. The bidding starts with me, and I immediately say one-twenty.

(25)

One-twenty, I say.

Pass, says Vadim.

Pass, says Olga.

(26)

What do you mean, *pass*?

You heard me, says Vadim.

That's right, says Olga, Pass.

But there's no way I can score one hundred twenty points with these cards...!

Well, says Vadim, It looks like you're going to have to try.

Yeah, says Olga, Good luck.

And without thinking I answer her:

Go to hell! I say.

(27)

To score one hundred twenty points you need to have an ace. But instead of an ace I have the worst hand imaginable: three nines and two jacks. An unprotected ten. And only half a marriage. I do have a lot of diamonds, but no queen to make it worth anything. Of course there's still the crib, the three cards lying face down on the table. In theory they could save me. There might be some aces there... or maybe even a marriage....

Slowly I turn over the cards, one by one:

(28)

Ace of Hearts.

(29)

Ace of Spades.

(30)

Ace of Diamonds.

(31)

I smile for the first time since the ruble stopped falling. Vadim slams his fist on the table so hard that Olga gives him a dirty look:

How do you like that! he says and then: Blind luck...!

Yeah, says Olga, If you wrote about a hand like that nobody would believe it!

I slide Vadim and Olga a nine each:

No redeals?

Olga smiles.

Vadim does not.

No redeals? I say smugly: Well then here we go...

(32)

Our hands are as follows:

Me	Vadim	Olga
A♦	10♠	A♣
10♦	Q♠	10♣
K♦	J♠	Q♣
J♦	9♠	J♣
9♦	K♣	10♥
A♥	9♣	Q♥
J♥	K♥	9♥
A♠	Q♦	K♠

(33)

In theory my task is simple: I have to take all eight tricks. It's clear that the game will come down to a fifty-fifty decision that either Vadim or Olga will have to make. And so the first six tricks go as expected. I take them without resistance, building my score to seventy-three. To win I will need to take both of the remaining tricks, in other words, this trick and the one following it:

	Me	Vadim	Olga	Total Points
1-	A♦	Q♦	9♥	14
2-	10♦	9♠	J♣	26
3-	K♦	J♠	Q♣	35
4-	J♦	K♥	K♠	45
5-	9♦	9♣	10♣	55
6-	A♥	K♣	Q♥	73
7-	A♠	Q♠	...	...

After playing his Queen of Spades, Vadim leans back from the table. Olga has stopped to consider the order in which she should discard her final two cards. And Vadim is looking at her carefully:

You realize, he says to her, that if you play the right card you can keep him from winning?

How do you know?

I've been following the game. If you make the right decision you can stop him.

Olga looks at her cards and bites her lip:

I don't know what to lead. I can't remember what's already been played.

Vadim is annoyed:

Just think carefully and make the right decision. It's fifty-fifty. Either you play the card that lets him win. Or you play the right card. Just think. You can do that much, can't you?

But it's obvious that Olga can't remember which cards have already been played, and, therefore, which card she should lead.

You know, says Vadim, If you would pay more attention to the game and less attention to whether your opponents are smiling or not...

Olga looks at Vadim spitefully:

There you go! she says and slaps her card on the table. It's clear that she couldn't care less who wins the game and has simply chosen the card at random:

There you go! she says: Are you happy?

Both Vadim and I look at the card:

10♥

Thanks, I say.

I take her ten and lead with my Jack of Hearts:

	Me	Vadim	Olga	Total Points
7-	A♠	Q♠	10♥	97
8-	J♥	10♠	A♣	120

I have my one hundred twenty points. I win.

(34)

	Vadim	Olga	Me
Hand # 37	835	880	1000

(35)

Vadim is amazed. I am gloating. For once in my life I have been purely and truly lucky. An incredible luck, a fantastic luck.

He who is lucky in cards will be unlucky in Love!

But at this moment I don't care.

(36)

After the game the three of us sit at my table. The conversation is typical, weaving in and out of itself. Then I remember something that I have been wanting to ask for a long time:

You know this is my first wedding, I say, And I wanted to ask you... how should I act... I mean is there anything that I should do or *not* do? Anything that I should keep in mind? I would hate to do something to embarrass myself...

Vadim laughs:

Just follow the flow, he says: Do what everybody else is doing and you can't go wrong.

Will there be a lot of guests?

No, we're keeping it low-key... about twenty people.

Will I know anyone?

You'll know the two of us and, of course, Landlady. Olga's parents will also be there. My best man Boris. Olga's best friend is coming — she's intelligent and polite... I think you two will hit it off. Of course a host of relatives will be there, but we'll seat you next to us... they'll be further down the table and you won't even notice them.

I nod gratefully:

Yeah, I say, You're probably right about following the flow, about doing what everyone else is doing. I can't go wrong that way. You know, it's funny: sometimes I think that I'm more nervous about your wedding than the two of you are... as if it were going to be *my* wedding!

What's there to be nervous about?

Well, I've never been to a wedding before... this will be my first.

Just think of it as practice for your own wedding, says Olga, For when you find a wife of your own and decide to marry her.

Suddenly from the other room the phone rings loudly and I leave the kitchen to answer it. Through the static I am surprised to hear a rough voice ask for Vadim.

Who, may I ask, is calling? I say.

An old friend, the voice says.

Vadim comes from the other room to take the phone and I go back into the kitchen with Olga. From the other room Vadim's voice can be heard:

'Hello?... but... but... how did you get this number... I know... I haven't forgotten... But I just can't right now... you see tomorrow's my wedding... I promise as soon as I can...'

Olga closes the door on his words. She offers me coffee and we sit drinking it in silence. Finally, I speak up:

It's time, I say.

For what?

I think it's time for me to leave... I'm thinking about leaving Russia.

You've been saying that for two years now.

This time I'm serious... I mean it.

And you've been saying *that* for almost as long.

But this time... *this time* it's forever... I'm sure of it.

What's the reason this time?

Well, I've just started thinking: I don't have anything here... no money... no future... my job's the same... my Russian's getting worse and worse... and now I'm losing you...

You Americans are all the same: money, job... your Russian is fine. And as far as losing me... as far as that's concerned, well, you can't lose me because I was never yours to begin with.

Olga stops to let the words sink in:

Just face it, she says, The real reason you want to leave is that you couldn't handle living here. Life here was too hard for you. You couldn't cope with our harsh Russian realities.

Well, actually, Olga it's quite the opposite: for me, a foreigner in Moscow, life here isn't difficult at all. In fact, if anything it's too *easy*. I've found a comfortable niche for myself, one that I can't seem to crawl out of. But now things are changing. This time I think I'm ready to do it... I mean, to crawl out forever...

9 — 1807

Olga nods indifferently.

Just then the kitchen door opens. Vadim walks in. He seems shaken.

Who was that on the phone? Olga says.

An old friend, says Vadim but his thoughts are obviously elsewhere.

Is everything all right? I ask him.

Fine... everything is just fine.

Are you sure? You don't look so good.

Everything's fine.

What does this old friend want? says Olga.

Oh nothing. He just wanted... he just wants to pay me a visit.

A visit? What kind of visit?

I'm not sure.

When's he planning to come?

I don't know, says Vadim, But I have a feeling very soon.

(37)

A few days before the wedding Olga comes over for the last time. Neither of us have talked about it, but we both sense that it can't go any further, that this will be our final meeting.

While I prepare the tea we are silent; and when it has been poured we drink slowly but without speaking. Our smiles are weak and forced, like consular officers, and for the first time our silence seems awkward. Finally, I start:

Are you nervous about the wedding? I ask.

What's that supposed to mean? she says.

I don't know, I tell her, It's just a question.

Oh, she says and takes a long drink from her cup... so long that by the time she is finished I have understood that no further questions are necessary.

Both of us are silent.

I am relieved. I am sad that it was so easy, but I am relieved. And then it occurs to me: Should she leave? Or should it happen once more for the final time? Could it be that we could still... that we would... *now*?

Why haven't I thought about this?!

I am ashamed and look away from her. I look away so that she will not see that I am thinking about this, that I do not already know.

The clink of her teacup against its saucer interrupts my thoughts. It was false, louder than it should be, and I look up. Olga's eyes are moister than I have ever seen them:

I don't love him, she says and then: He'll be a good husband... a good father someday... but I don't love him.

I take her hand and it happens. It happens for the last time. And when it is over I feel sad that this time, our final time, was no different from any other.

(38)

'...Yeah, well the weather *here* is beautiful... You know maybe you should think about coming home once in a while...'

Here Aunt Helen stops. For the first time since I can remember, her voice becomes passionate:

How long are you going to be there? she says and then: When are you coming home?

I do not answer.

...You promised that... that... It was only supposed to be for *one year*!

I can't answer.

Do you hear me?

I do not answer.

I said do you hear me?

Again I do not answer.

DAMMIT, JAMES, I'M TALKING TO YOU!

I stop.

What did she say?! What was that? It was... it was my name! How foreign it sounded. How strange...! Aunt Helen is saying my name! When was the last time I heard it? When was the last time I cared? Why haven't I noticed it until now.

Silently, it hangs in the air. Her word. My word. And in this word, I can hear a voice as timeless as vanilla, though more silent than sleep; in this single word I hear the voice not of my Aunt, but of her sister:

James..., it is saying, ...tell mommy you love her.

(39)

#863. In a daze I raise my head painfully to see a circle of faces looking down at me. I am lying at the base of the escalator and people are crowding around and offering me their words. Did you see that? they are saying in amazed voices, Did you see how he fell? Have you ever seen anything like that? The poor thing, falling all that way...! But then as I continue to lie without moving their concern subsides, giving way first to confusion, then to suspicion, then to utter derision when they realize that I am not drunk. *He's not drunk!* Then what's the matter with him? someone asks and from the crowd another person answers, I don't know but he's not even drunk! And so they disband and I am left to dust myself off, test my limbs and joints one by one. *Here I am*, I think, *I'm finally here!* Tomorrow is the wedding and everything is set: my gift is ready; my coin is in my wallet next to my last solar calculator; and for the first time ever — for the first time since I can remember — I have a name. *James, tell mommy you love her...* At last I have gone as far as I can with the eleven yellow words: only one remains. One word. One solar calculator. One German Dictionary. One old coin that is as common as a twelve-story building, as worthless as a word.

(40)

'Dear James,

I hope you get this letter. I'm going to put it in the mail a bit early so that it will beat the holiday rush at the post office and hopefully it will get to you by New Year's. In fact, I'll mail it out tomorrow.

Not much is new with me. I'm not working now because I've been sick a lot lately. I'm not sure what it is, but the doctors say that I need to stay home and rest. I have an appointment next week to do some tests and they're supposed to tell me what the problem is. The doctor says that it's not likely that it's anything serious but that we should still do some tests just in case. And so after the holidays I have my appointment.

You know, I'm writing this — you have no idea how difficult it is for me to write letters! — although I'm not even sure you'll get it. I talked to Helen last week and she says she's always sending you letters and packages that you never get. She seems really upset about it. And worried. I know it's hard for her with you being so far away. Of course it's hard for all of us, but it's especially hard for her because you're the only person she has. And I guess that's why I'm writing you.

You see I can understand why you're treating me the way you are... you don't write, don't call, and when I call... when I call you won't talk to me. I know that I've made some mistakes, and that you probably feel that you are right in this. And to be honest I can't blame you. Of course I wish you didn't feel this way, but I can't blame you.

But what makes me sick is what you're doing to Helen. You can't understand how worried she is about you. She says sometimes she can't sleep at night because she's thinking about where you are and what you're doing. It was especially bad in the beginning, but even now she still worries. I don't know what she tells you on the phone, but it's hurting her. I'm sure she doesn't admit it, but it is. I wish you could see it and do something about it. Call her more. Come home more. At the very least write her. It really is the least you could do.

You know I've never asked you for anything. I've always felt that I wasn't in the position to do it. But now I'm asking you to be better to her. She loves you more than anything, and you should have noticed that a long time ago. I don't know what's kept you over there for these last two years, but now I'm pleading... if I mean anything to you at all, if *she* means anything, try to be more considerate of her. Don't do it for me... do it for her.

I guess that's what I really wanted to say. I hope you won't take my words the wrong way. I just want what's best for you and for Helen. I'm just trying to help.

I'm enclosing a picture that I found the other day when I was going through my old papers. Your father took it of us when you were about three and a half. Can you believe I was ever that young?! It's amazing how time flies, how things come and go, how people can change and be changed without really seeing it in themselves...

Anyway, I guess I should go. If you get a chance drop me a line. You can write to the address on the envelope. It should get to me... I don't move around so much these days. In any case, I look forward to seeing you when you get back home. There's so many things that I want to tell you, but I can't say them in a letter....

Love,

Mom

* * * * * * * * * *

Book 10. The Wedding

'...I never bothered about happiness, I was able to get by without it. And now I need it for two....'

— Alexander Sergeevich Pushkin
My Lot is Cast... I'm Getting Married

(1)

The wedding begins on a cold December morning. A Tuesday. On the streets the snow has been piled up in graying banks of ice. Cars have frozen. Plans have been changed. Even the ground is too hard to crunch... as if the air has decided to make its presence felt.

A call from Vadim rattles me from my sleep:

Put on your clothes and meet me downstairs, he says.

Do you know what time it is?!? I curse into the phone.

It's nine o'clock. Come on, let's go.

Nine o'clock? Are you crazy?!

I need your help.

Why? What's the matter?

Vadim pauses for a second then speaks up:

It's Olga... she's been kidnapped.

(2)

Let's say — this shouldn't be hard — let's say you have a client whose name begins with the letter Z. It's a matter of chance of course — you could be working for any letter of the English alphabet — but let's say his name is Z. As any schoolgirl can tell you, Z follows Y alphabetically, and since Y is the penultimate letter of the English alphabet, that means that Z is the ultimate. Z is the very last letter of the English alphabet and *that* means that someone owes your client a large amount of money.

But your client is soft. Instead of calling you, he's tried to do things himself: reminding, requesting, then relenting. He's persisted only to pardon. And when that didn't work he demanded, then damned. Only to acquiesce. He has been overly reasonable. He is half-hearted. He is too sympathetic to the answers he receives: 'I can't right now... I'm working on it... I need time... if you'll just wait a little longer...'

Time is money, you know. And money talks. And when it comes down to it, talks take time....

And so, for the past year you've been chomping at the bit. Just give the word, you've been saying, and you'll collect. After all, you are a professional. You are an expert in your field. One talk with you and your subjects will do anything to pay up. One question and answer session and your subjects will beg you to take their money. In dollars. In prestigious automobiles. Those who are lucky in second apartments. The less fortunate in *first* apartments!

Home for you is a small apartment that you earned a few years back at a 'discount' from a drunk man whose hand could barely hold the pen as he signed the apartment over to you. It was a difficult night of work; as if to commemorate the deal, the man coughed up chunks of pickles all over the finished agreement, the notary's seal, the small packet of money that you had promised him in his stupor. A minor — if pungent! — inconvenience. Unpleasant, of course, but now the apartment can be resold for its real value at a handsome profit. And besides: money doesn't smell... even in Russia.

And then one day you get the call. The moment has come. Now your client is being squeezed by someone else's clients and has given you the nod, the go-ahead, and even the green light. Collect, he has told you, at any cost. Ask the questions that need to be asked. Get the answers that please.

But how?

That, you smile to yourself, is where your expertise comes in. Asking the difficult questions is your job, getting answers is your specialty. You have worked hard to get where you are, and now you have a reputation to maintain. You have a career to protect. You have a family to feed and a future to foster.

You also have a set of brass knuckles in the event that somebody disagrees with you. A false passport should someone question your identity. Six hundred dollars of cash just in case you need six hundred dollars in cash. You have four scarred colleagues to take your commands. You have the address of the twelve-story building where you will make your appearance as soon as you get the call.

And now the time has come. Now you will finally have the chance to ask some serious questions. Now you are sure to get the answers that please. Today is Monday and so you go to bed early.

Tomorrow is the day you've been waiting for. The day of questioning and atonement. The day for long-awaited answers.

(3)

Sitting with me in the backseat of the taxi, Vadim seems to be in the best of spirits. He is tapping his thumbs on his thighs to the rhythm of his favorite song. He is bantering with the taxi driver about the cold snap that has paralyzed the city. And when we pass a four-car pileup on a slick patch of ice, Vadim simply laughs and shakes his head.

How can he be so calm? His bride has been kidnapped before she can even become his bride!

Shouldn't we call the police? I say to him.

For the pile-up?

No, for Olga.

Vadim looks at me with an amused expression:

Sure, he says, that's all we need. Haven't you learned anything from your six and a half years here?

What do you mean?

Have your six and a half years been entirely lost on you?

I hope not.

Well then what police could you possibly be talking about?

Maybe you're right.

Of course I'm right!

Still, there's just one thing... I mean... what do you need *me* for? Don't get me wrong... I'm willing to help and all, but I just don't see what I'm supposed to do.

You're going to be my voice. You're going to answer their questions.

ME!

Yes. Otherwise they won't let me see Olga. You'll have to speak on my behalf.

Why me...?!

You see, these people — the ones asking the questions — are ruthless and mean. Their goal is to squeeze money from me. As much as possible. And they'll stop at nothing to do it: they'll yell, they'll shout, they'll lie, they'll try to trick you, to make you stumble on your answers. It won't be easy...

...Get to the part about me... what've I got to do with anything?

That's the beautiful part. Since you're a foreigner they'll go easy on you. I'm sure of it. They'll go easy on you and that means that you'll save me money. That's important because I don't have a lot of patience for things like this.

Things like this?!

Why do you think they'll go easy on me just because I'm a foreigner?

It's a natural. Russians have a strange respect for foreigners... they treat them differently for some reason, as if they were better... you know that!

Maybe so, but...

...Of course you foreigners like to dramatize things — about how difficult it is for you to live here in Russia... but we both know how convenient it *really* is.

Well yeah, but how am I supposed to answer their questions if I don't even know what they're asking me about?

That's the difficult part. They could ask anything. The important thing is to stay calm and to answer as best you can.

Why don't *you* talk to them? It's your fiancée.

Russian tradition doesn't allow it. It's better if someone does it for me...

Traditions? Russia has traditions about kidnapping?

...That's right. Besides, the whole thing will be over before you know it... just do your best to answer their questions and everything will be fine.

Our taxi stops in front of a twelve-story building that is exactly like our twelve-story building. The elevator takes us to the tenth floor. Without hesitating, Vadim makes his way to an apartment, rings the bell, and waits, looking at his watch and fighting back a yawn. Inside, there is a pause then the clicking and snapping of metal locks. The door opens.

Vadim walks into the apartment. A young woman is standing in the hallway and he kisses her on the cheek:

Take me to my bride! Vadim demands and peers over her shoulder. But the woman blocks his path:

Oh no you don't! she says: Business first!

Vadim sighs and begins to take off his shoes. He motions for me to do the same:

This is James, he says, He'll be doing the talking.

Olya..., she says to me and extends her dainty palm in my direction.

I am nervous and distracted, and don't immediately realize why she is extending her palm at me. Finally, I hand her my boot.

Oh! she says.

And so I hand her the other boot as well. Olya stands for a few moments with the dripping footwear and then sets them down in front of me:

You two want some tea? she asks.

You know very well that I hate tea! Vadim says and moves into the living room where he plops himself heavily onto a couch.

I wasn't asking *you*... I was asking James.

That'll be fine, I say and look at Vadim.

Where is everyone? he asks and Olya answers from the kitchen:

They had some car trouble. They're trying to find a taxi. This weather...!

When Olya comes into the room she is carrying a tray with tea and biscuits. She pours out two cups and adds steaming water to them. She offers Vadim a can of instant coffee and he stirs a spoonful into his cup:

So you're James! Olya says as she hands me my tea.

That's right.

Olga's told me all about you...

Everything?

...Well maybe not *everything*, but at least the most important things...

And which most important things did she tell you?

She says that you teach English... that you're a very good friend of Vadim's.

That I am....

That's all. Those are the things that I know.

Well those are the most important things all right.

It must be rewarding helping people to speak?

What?

It must be nice knowing something well enough to teach it... I mean... being a teacher?

Well now that you mention it... yes, it does have its moments.

You know..., Vadim says proudly, ...James here doesn't just speak English like you and me Olya... he speaks it *fluently*!

You don't say, she says.

...That's right, he can speak without accent...!

I'm very impressed.

...Without even thinking!

That's quite an accomplishment.

In fact, Vadim says, he speaks English almost without mistakes!

Oh it's nothing..., I blush.

But Olya continues:

You should be very proud. Your Russian is good too. You know when Olga told me how well you speak Russian I didn't believe her... and now I see that she was right.

Thanks.

No really. I'm not trying to flatter you... your Russian is excellent. In fact, I wish my English were that good.

You study English?

Well yes... I mean not exactly... I mean I'm embarrassed to admit it...

She knows it about like I do, Vadim explains, In other words she can read but can't listen or speak.

Yeah, but for me it's especially embarrassing given the fact that... that I had the chance to learn it firsthand.

What do you mean? I ask.

Olya used to live in America, Vadim explains.

You did?

Yeah, I moved to the United States a few years ago... you know when things were unsettled here. I was young and stupid then. I thought I was leaving forever... but returned after a year.

Why'd you come back?

I don't know...

You didn't like it?

It's not that... it's just that it wasn't what I'd expected.

What were you expecting?

I don't know... I guess... well let's just say America has pipes, too.

I nod wistfully and take a sip of my tea.

So that's why my English is so poor. I've forgotten everything. Perhaps if I'd stuck it out, I'd be fluent by now.

Of course it's difficult to learn a language without the help of native speakers, I say.

You know maybe if you have some free time I'll become a student of yours...

Yeah..., I lie, ...maybe.

Just then the doorbell rings, Olya jumps up and points at Vadim:

Into the kitchen! she screams, Quick!

Olya pulls Vadim from the couch and ushers him into the kitchen. You too, James! she says and closes the door after us:

And don't you dare come out until I tell you!

Vadim laughs:

Is this your idea of hospitality? he yells from the kitchen but Olya doesn't answer.

In the other room we can hear a group of women being let into the apartment. The sounds of lips kissing zippers. Laughter. Dripping boots being removed. Someone's loud voice complaining about the cold....

That's them..., Vadim says, Your interrogators have arrived.

But they're women!

Don't let that fool you... they may be women but they're as cruel as Customs officials.

Vadim puts a kettle on the stove to boil, then sits to wait for it. Olya's kitchen has been renovated and Vadim can see that I am admiring it:

Nice isn't it? he says, Olya's done well for herself since she came back from America. She has a good job. She remodeled the whole apartment. You should have seen the place before... there were pipes *everywhere*.

What does she do for a living?

Vadim is rummaging around in a cupboard — he obviously feels at home here — and pulls out an unopened can of instant coffee:

She's some professional type.

A director?

No, she's not a director. She works in a western company.

It's strange... her apartment — I mean the layout — is exactly like yours Vadim, just backwards.

Yeah, these twelve-story buildings are all the same... they're as common as a Russian comma.

When the water is boiled Vadim pours each of us a cup of coffee and lights a cigarette. We talk about nothing in particular... first superficially, then in great detail. After a few minutes Olya opens the door:

Okay guys, she says, You can come into the other room now.

Is everything ready?

Almost. Your future wife is getting dressed. But there is a certain matter of business that needs to be taken care of if you want to see her...!

Olya smiles.

I know I know, Vadim says and looks at me seriously: It's time James.

For what?

He laughs at my words:

For the worst...!

Without finishing our coffee we leave the kitchen. In the other room three women are sitting on a couch and Olya introduces each of them to me:

This is Olga...

...and Olga...

...and Olga.

The girls nod and smile at me. And Vadim introduces my name:

And this is James, he says, He'll be my *spokesman*.

I nod, and the women look at me politely. For some minutes we look back and forth at each other but say nothing. Finally, to break the ice they ask me some questions about America's black-white problem and I launch into my standard explanation.

Okay, says Olya appraising the situation, Let's get started...!

She has interrupted me in mid-explanation and I am grateful to her. When Olya speaks her manner is theatrical and emphatic:

...Here are the rules. Hey... is everybody listening?!

Olya pauses to wait for the room to quiet and then begins again:

Vadim, as you know, your bride has been captured and hidden away. Your bride has been stolen before she can even become your bride. Her captors are ruthless and mean, but, at the same time, they are intelligent and polite, and so they are willing to give you a chance to win her back. You have chosen James to speak on your behalf and that means that you, James, will have to answer our questions... you will have to answer one question from each of us: from me, from Olga, from Olga, from Olga, and lastly from Olga, your groom's prospective bride who is waiting, as we speak, to be unhidden....

Get on with it! Olga yells from the other room, I don't plan on being in here all day!

...Each of us has written down a question, and I will be reading them to you. If you answer the question right, then we move on to the next one. If you answer wrong, then the groom will have to pay a fine of...

One hundred rubles! Vadim jokes.

No..., says Olya, ...your ransom will be fifty thousand rubles for each incorrect answer.

What! Are you trying to bankrupt me?

No... but those are the rules. That is, if you want to see your bride again....

Racketeers!

Olya laughs.

Racketeers, all of you!

Olya laughs again:

When you have answered all of the questions successfully, James, then the bride and the groom can be reunited....

So that's what this is all about...! Why did I think...?

...So James are you ready to answer our riddles?

What?

Are you ready for our five riddles?

I suppose so.

Do your best to answer them correctly. Remember that the future of our soon-to-be newlyweds depends on your answers.

Olga pauses importantly:

Your first riddle is from Olga — so listen carefully.

Olya clears her throat dramatically, and reads in a low exaggerated drawl:

'A man was put in a windowless prison for twenty years,' she begins, 'Every day he ate nothing but dried bread. Not once did he leave the cell during his incarceration. But when they finally took him out of his cell they found a sack of bones under his bed. So the obvious question is... where did the bones come from?'

Wait, I say, You spoke so quickly... could you repeat the question just to make sure I got it all?

Sure, she says and once again reads her riddle — this time just as fast... but louder:

'A man was put in prison for twenty years. Every day he ate nothing but dried bread. When they finally took him out of his cell they found a sack of bones. Where did the bones come from?'

I stop to think. *If a man eats nothing but dried bread for twenty years... first of all, that's impossible... but assuming that it were possible, then it would mean that the bones had to come from something other than his food because there are, of course, no bones in dried bread... now if the bones weren't already there when the man was put into the cell then that would mean that... but what if they were already there... in other words, the bones didn't actually appear during the twenty years that the man was incarcerated...*

Were the bones already in the cell before the man was put there?

No, Olya says, The cell was empty. They fed him nothing but dried bread... and after twenty years there was a sack of bones that had appeared from somewhere.

Okay... so the bones weren't already there. That means that the bones had to come from somewhere outside the cell, in other words, from something that could get into the cell from the outside world... but what?

Did the bones belong to some rats?

No.

Mice?

No.

Cockroaches?

Not likely.

Then maybe they were the bones of the man? In other words, he himself was a *sack of bones*?

No.

I don't know then.

You give up?

Yes, I give up.

Vadim slaps his thigh:

You can't give up! he says.

Do you know the answer? I ask him.

Sure, he says and shakes his head, It's a children's riddle.

Olya laughs:

Well, before you two give up, I'll give you a clue. The answer is in the question. Now listen carefully... I'll read it to you again:

'A man was put in prison for twenty years. Every day he ate nothing but *dried bread*. When they finally took him out of his cell they found a sack of bones. Where did the bones come from?'

Olya smiles deviously. All the Olgas are looking at me and waiting for my words. In my mind I try to imagine an answer. But can't. Logic has failed me again:

I don't know, I say, I've thought of everything: the bones weren't already there... they didn't belong to any animals that might have crept into the cell... and he didn't eat anything but dried bread which, of course, doesn't have any bones... I don't know what to say.

You don't?

No, I say, I don't.

Then in that case that'll be fifty thousand rubles!

The girls cheer.

Racketeers! Vadim moans.

The girls cheer again.

Racketeers!

So what's the answer? I ask, Where did the bones come from?

The answer, Olya says, is that the bones came from the fish soup that he had been eating.

What fish soup?

The fish soup that he ate every day.

But you said he only ate dried bread!

No I didn't.

Yes you did.

No I didn't. Here I'll repeat it... listen carefully:

'A man was put in prison for twenty years. Every day he ate nothing but fish soup and bread....'

See? Olya smiles.

The Olgas laugh.

So that's how far I've come? Six and a half years of studying Russian, and I can't even answer a children's riddle?

You should be ashamed of yourselves! Vadim says to Olya.

Why?

Taking advantage of James like that.

How am I taking advantage of him? He knows Russian. And besides, it's a children's riddle, and he is, after all, no child.

No? Then what would you say he was?

He's our age... I mean he's an adult just like you and me.

Adult? He's no adult!

He's not?

No he's not.

I'm not?

No, James, you're not... you're a foreigner!

Olya stops:

A foreigner? she says.

Yes, says Vadim, A foreigner.

Maybe Vadim's right, says one of the Olgas sheepishly.

Yeah, says another, Maybe James's knowledge of Russian isn't as good as he thought it was.

Olya puts her index finger against her lips to think. Finally, she pronounces her verdict:

All right all right, she says, If you insist... in deference to our foreign guest, we won't count that question...

And Vadim smiles and winks in my direction.

...But don't expect any more breaks!

Olya stares at me seriously:

Are you ready? she asks.

For what? I answer.

Your second riddle. Are you ready for it?

I guess.

Okay, this one is Olga's:

'It is a well-known fact,' Olya reads from her paper, 'that Russia is not in the West. So the question to you, James, is this: if Russia is not in the West, then where is it?'

In the East! I say instinctively.

As soon as the words come out, I realize that I have spoken too quickly. That I should have taken more time to consider the question. *But haven't I had the last six and a half years to consider this question?*

Wrong! says Olya.

How can it be wrong?

It's wrong... Russia is not the East!

Then where is it? You yourself admitted that it wasn't in the West...!

That's right it's not in the West... but it's not in the East either!

I turn to look at Vadim, but he just shrugs his shoulders.

Pay up! Olya says.

How much?

I already told you: fifty thousand rubles!

What if I give you twenty-five thousand instead?

You know Vadim bargaining at this point is inappropriate.

Okay... thirty.

Vadim... I'm disappointed in you! Just remember how beautiful your bride is... how intelligent, how polite.... Do you really want to say that she's not worth a measly fifty thousand rubles?

Olga's voice can be heard laughing from the other room.

Well... of course she is. She's worth all the money in the world.... All right, thirty-five!

Fifty!

Forty...?

Fifty!

Forty-five... and that's my last offer.

Vadim, do you want your future bride to see that you are so cheap as to bargain over five thousand rubles? Is that what you want?

Forty-five....

Fifty.

Fifty?

Fifty.

Vadim takes out a fifty-thousand-ruble note and hands it to a smiling Olya:

Racketeers! he says.

Olya pretends not to have heard him:

Do you see how this works James? she says.

Yes. Unfortunately I do.

Good.

Olya clears her throat once again:

And now for *my* riddle, she says and taking out the next piece of paper begins to read her riddle:

'This scene takes place in the Moscow metro...'

Where? I interrupt her.

'The metro... where else? As usual, it's rush hour. The metro car is packed. There are people sitting, standing, leaning, crouching. But something is terribly wrong, in other words, something is not right: one of the passengers is an American spy! That's right... an American spy! Right there in the midst of a carful of unsmiling metrogoers. But which one is it? How can we pick him out? None of the passengers is dressed conspicuously. Each of them speaks Russian perfectly, without accent. But at the next stop, a KGB officer enters the car, walks right up to the American spy and says, "Next stop Lubyanka." The man hadn't even said anything, he was dressed like a Russian — no brighter no worse — so how did the KGB officer know that he was the spy?'

I smile to myself at the riddle. I look at Vadim knowingly and he nods back. Still, I am careful to pretend that I have not heard it before, pause for a long time, as if weighing all options. Finally, I speak up in a voice that is falsely uncertain:

Maybe it's because... let me think... could it be that... that the spy was black?

Vadim smiles at my answer.

Olya claps her hands:

Wrong! she says.

What do you mean *wrong*?

You're answer is wrong. The spy wasn't black... he was whiter than winter!

No he wasn't! Vadim says, He was black!

How do you know? Olya says, Were you there?

No but...!

Don't try to get out of it, says one of the Olgas.

Yeah, says another, Pay up the fifty thousand rubles!

But...!

A crash of female voices drowns him out. Hopelessly, Vadim takes out a fifty-thousand-ruble note.

But wait a minute..., I say, ...What's the right answer ...How did they know ...what gave the spy away?

Olya smiles broadly:

The KGB officer understood that the spy was not Russian because he was reading *Anna Karenina*!

What! That's not how the riddle goes... you changed it! You tricked me!

You're answer is wrong! Next question....

Wow, these women really are ruthless. They really are mean! In fact, they're even meaner than...

Olya's voice snaps me out of my contemplation:

Whose question haven't I read... ah yes... Olga's. It's a good question because it is simple. You're probably ready for a simple question about now, aren't you?

You can say that again!

Good, then all you have to do is tell me where the sixth calculator went.

What?

Remember, you came to Moscow with six solar calculators. You gave three of them away. . You threw one against a wall. That leaves two. In theory you should have two calculators left. But if you look in your wallet right now you'll see that you have...

One!

...That's right. So your question is this:

'Where did your sixth calculator go?'

Sixth calculator? I'd forgotten I even had a sixth calculator!

I don't know, I say, I don't even remember having it, let alone losing it.

You don't know?

No I don't?

Jeez! says Vadim, How can you not know? Why did you bother bringing six calculators if you don't even know what you did with them... Most normal people would have settled for five... but not *you*... noooo... five isn't enough for you... you had to bring *six*. And now you can't even say where they all went!

Look, Vadim, you don't really expect me to spend my time keeping track of calculators, do you? With all the important things that are happening in my life I've got better things to do than to waste my precious time, energy, and attention on...

Do you two know the answer or not? Olya interrupts us.

What answer?

Do you know where your sixth calculator went?

No. I don't.

Okay, says Olya, Then pay up...!

Vadim looks at me in mock annoyance. Without protesting he takes out another fifty-thousand-ruble note:

You women are severe! he says and shakes his head.

Love ain't cheap! says Olga.

And neither is *Love*! Olga says.

I know... I know... but this ain't love... this isn't even Love: this is *marriage*!

The girls laugh at Vadim's joke.

All right everybody! Olya says, It's time for Olga's riddle.

Olya pauses and waits for the room to become quiet.

I am still confused, trying to remember where my sixth calculator went, but before I can remember, Olya turns to me:

And now, she says dramatically, you will hear the final riddle which has been chosen by the bride-to-be herself. It is the fifth of five questions, and honestly speaking you haven't had too much success with the first ones....

The girls laugh. Olya's face is in a big smile. She is apparently delighted by the question that Olga has written:

Quiet everyone! Quiet!! I'm going to read the fifth and final question to James. It's a complicated one... easy but complicated. Are you ready?

Yes, I say.

Okay, then here goes. Listen carefully:

'Olga — our beloved bride-to-be — is driving a trolleybus...'

Olya stops:

Are you listening carefully? she says.

Of course, I say.

Good..., she says and continues her riddle:

'...Olga is driving a trolleybus. It's a cold winter day and so at the first stop seven people board the bus. Three of them are wearing fur hats. The trolleybus moves on and at the second stop one of the hatless passengers gets off and four people get on. They are foreigners so all of them are wearing fur hats...'

Olya is speaking quickly and my mind rushes to keep count.

'...At the third stop two hatted passengers get on along with two passengers without hats; five people get off, but none of them are wearing fur hats...'

I tally them. Olya pauses and then continues:

'...At the fourth stop three people get on and four people get off... Then at the fifth stop...'

Wait a minute!

What?

Wait just one minute!

Why?

You didn't mention the hats.

What hats?

How many passengers were wearing fur hats at the fourth stop?

Hats? Oh yes, hats... it doesn't matter. Now where was I...

'...At the seventh stop three people get on and three people get off...'

It doesn't matter?

'...And, at the eighth, ten people get off and four people get on...'

Wait a minute...!

'...But then at the next stop nobody gets on and six people get off. The bus moves on and at the next stop...'

Wait another minute... she must have made a mistake!

'...at the next stop everyone gets off!'

Olga smiles broadly:

'Everyone gets off and seven people get on. The doors begin to close, but at the last moment they open... and up steps former president Mikhail Gorbachev with two bodyguards...'

Hey! says Vadim, Former presidents don't ride trolleybuses...!

Gorbachev does, Olya replies.

And they don't need bodyguards...

Gorbachev does!

Vadim laughs.

Stop interrupting! says one of the Olgas.

Yeah, says another, You'll ruin Olya's train of thought!

Yeah..., says the third.

Okay okay... sorreee...!

And Olya continues:

'...Anyway, the trolleybus is lighter now but plods on just in case... At the next stop one person gets on and two people get off... Then one person gets on but changes her mind, only to change her mind again and then once again...'

How many times did she change her mind...?

'The doors close violently before she can change her mind a fifth time. At the next stop, nobody gets off and seventy-eight people get on, most of whom are wearing fur hats...

Fur hats?!

'...So seventy-eight people get on, but right before the doors can close *another* seventy-eight people try to get on, cramming themselves desperately into the doors. It's too crowded in the bus, a fight breaks out and as a result former president Mikhail Gorbachev is punted out of the trolleybus, along with one of his bodyguards... *'How many people boarded the bus? How many bodyguards did Gorbachev have? Where were the ticket collectors when you really needed them? Were they wearing hats? And where... WHERE could I find someone to take my German dictionary?!*

But here Olya stops. A smile lights her face:

Have you been listening carefully? she says.

I tried, I say.

Have you been keeping track of the passengers?

As best I could.

Good... here's your question... Are you ready...?

Olya pauses dramatically, her voice becomes softer, almost a whisper:

Your question, she says, is as follows:

(4)

'...How does the bus driver like her tea?'

(5)

What?!

Olya laughs:

How does the trolleybus driver like her tea? she says again.

Twenty-four! I blurt out.

No no... listen to the question: how does she like her tea... how does *the trolleybus driver* drink her tea?

Sixteen! I say desperately.

No no, says Olya, The question is *how does Olga — our bride-to-be — like her tea?*

I gasp once again.

Wait a minute! Vadim jumps in: Olga doesn't even drink tea... she drinks coffee. How is James supposed to know how she likes her tea if she never even drinks tea... I mean, *I* don't even know how she likes her tea!

It just so happens that your future wife *loves* tea... that is to say when it's made a special way, that is to say when it's made to please her...!

Vadim moves to speak, but Olya interrupts him:

...*And*, she says, if James can tell us how she likes her tea, then you, Vadim, can see your bride... for free!

Vadim turns to me helplessly, his face pinching against itself. But this time I have the decency to lie:

I can't say for sure, I say, but most likely she likes it burning hot... As dark as darkness... Stronger than sex.

Olya laughs loudly:

Are you sure?

Absolutely, I lie.

Wrong! she says.

It can't be... it can't be...

Wrong!

But I'm sure that she likes her tea hot and dark and bitter...!

Wrong!

Again a burst of female voices fills the room and covers us in excited words. Everyone is yelling and shouting. Olya is shaking her collected ransom at Vadim and screaming something about sugar. Vadim, in response, is shaking his finger at Olya, and swearing something about coffee. The Olgas are laughing and coercing at Vadim to pay up.

And then we stop.

Suddenly, as if a breeze has swept over us, the room falls silent. We all turn our heads to see that Olga, in her wedding gown, is standing in the doorway: she is dressed whiter than late autumn. Layers and layers of lace and silk flowing from the top of her head to the floor. Her face is slightly adorned, more beautiful than I have ever seen it. Her smile is radiant.

In the quiet room I am not the only person to gasp.

Olga stands for a few seconds in the silence that she has created:

I like my tea cool and sweet, she says, As cool as a salted cucumber. As sweet as a suture.

I nod.

Therefore your answer to my question is wrong.

I nod again.

The three women laugh. Vadim swears and peels off another fifty thousand rubles. Olya looks at Olga and smiles.

Triumphantly, Olga walks over to Vadim and kisses him on his wrinkled forehead. They embrace.

Everyone is happy.

(6)

After Vadim has paid the two hundred thousand rubles, he grabs his coat:

Now I'll leave you girls alone to do your girl thing, he says, We men have an appointment of our own...!

He motions for me to put on my coat and I do. For several minutes he stands in Olya's hall making detailed arrangements for the girls to meet us later at the registration hall where the ceremony will be held.

When that is done the two of us leave for home.

Back in my apartment I choose my whitest shirt, my least-wrinkled pants, and do my best to arrange a tie around my neck. I take the stairs down to his apartment — *when will they ever fix the elevator?* — where Landlady, in her soiled apron, lets me in. She is preparing the food for tonight's dinner banquet, and looks both exhausted and blissfully needed.

How did the ransoming go? she asks.

Two hundred thousand, I answer and am amazed to see that without a calculator she has quickly and correctly converted that amount into kilograms of butter.

Vadim! she yells through the apartment, James is here!

I'll be right out!

I take off my shoes and walk into their living room where several tables have already been set up for tonight's dinner. Chairs have been pulled from every room of the house, from the small kitchens of kind neighbors, from the larger kitchens of unkind neighbors, even a pair of old wooden stools from my apartment...

I take one and sit down.

In the other room Landlady is banging pots and pans in the sink. There is the hissing of running water. The opening then closing of an oven door.

While I wait I try clumsily to straighten my tie which has been knotted too tight around my neck.

I pull and twist and finally decide to take it off and tie it once more from the very beginning.

Suddenly, a doorbell sounds. Landlady, wiping her hands on her apron, hurries from the kitchen to open the heavy metal door which Vadim had installed somewhere between *V* and *W*. Without looking through the peephole, she twists and turns the locks until the door is openable. When she opens it I see a short stocky man in an old trenchcoat.

Boris! she says, Come on in!

The man walks in with a toothless smile and a handful of flowers, both of which he gives to Landlady:

These are for you, he says.

Landlady thanks him and leads him into the livingroom where I'm already sitting with my tie in my hand:

Have a seat, she tells him, Vadim's getting dressed... Do you know James?

No, he says, Although I've heard a lot about him...

James, I say and extend my hand.

Boris, he says, I'll be Vadim's best man.

Nice to meet you, I lie.

Likewise, he exaggerates.

Pick a chair Boris! Landlady says, Vadim'll be out in a few minutes.

Landlady returns to her kitchen preparations. Boris picks one of the wobbly stools from my kitchen. For a few moments the two of us are left to sit in squeaking silence and then finally he speaks up:

I really have heard a lot about you, James.... Vadim's told me that you live in his Dad's old apartment... that you are extremely lucky in cards...

That's right.

He says you have a blue passport.

I do.

That must be nice, huh...?

Having a blue passport?

No. I mean being lucky in cards.

It's okay... it saves on lubricated condoms.

Yeah.

Not to mention solar calculators.

Yeah I suppose it has a lot of advantages...

Boris pulls out a cigarette:

You smoke? he says.

Sure, I say and we light up.

As we talk, I notice that although Boris is short and stocky his voice is low and strong and for some reason commands respect:

You know James, he says from behind his cigarette, Vadim and I go way back... I've known him forever...

Is that so?

Yeah, since the days when he believed in our government.

That long?

Yeah... in fact I remember him when he couldn't even give an opinion.

It can't be.

That's right, we go way back. But nowadays we don't get the chance to see much of each other. It's a shame: both of us have jobs and a family, you know, commitments...

Boris pauses thoughtfully.

That's too bad, I say.

Yeah, he says, Time's a strange thing...

We become respectfully silent. Then as if remembering something, Boris smiles:

I hear you answered riddles for Vadim, he says.

I tried.

How'd you do?

I got them all wrong.

All of them?!

Yeah, all of them. Especially the one about the busdriver.

And how much did they take you for?

Two hundred thousand.

Racketeers! Racketeers, plain and simple. Especially given Vadim's financial situation. Oh well I guess it doesn't matter. You only get married once, right?

I guess.

And besides, it's not like the money'll go to waste: I'm sure the girls will use it to buy vodka for the dinner tonight.

I'm sure.

Did they ask you the question about potatoes? You know, which is heavier: a kilogram of potatoes or a kilogram of potatoes purchased from an old woman on the street?

No, they didn't.

They didn't? That's strange... they usually ask that question.

You seem like you know a lot about this whole process... I mean the wedding process.

I should: I've been to enough of them.

Really, how many?

Well, let's see... this will be my one... two... three... four... *fifth*!

You've been to five weddings?

That's right. And that's not including two of my own.

Seven weddings! You're like a specialist or something!

You could say that.

It's my first. I've never actually been to a wedding...

You mean in Russia?

No, period.

So how do you like it so far?

The wedding?

Yeah. How do you like it?

It hasn't begun yet.

Sure it has... this is all part of the process. Everything that happens today can be considered crucial to this wedding. You see in Russia a wedding isn't just the ceremony... for us it's a state of mind. It's an important and festive occasion in the life of everybody connected with the marrying couple. The important thing is that the day be different from all others. And that's why on this day anything can happen... and usually does.

You mean to say that it's magical, or something?

Well yeah, magical.

Boris stops:

See this...? he says and points at a large gap where a tooth normally is.

Yes.

...Well, there used to be a tooth there many years ago. I lost it during my first wedding celebration. My best man knocked it out.

He did?! Why?

Aw... you know how it goes... too much revelry... But he didn't mean anything by it...

Boris smiles a toothless smile:

In America do you celebrate weddings like this, too?

You mean by fighting?

Well no... I mean *unconditionally*?

I doubt it. But then again I don't know... like I told you I've never been to a wedding.

You seem concerned about it.

Well, you know, for a long time now I've had this strange premonition that I would embarrass myself if I ever went to a wedding... I'm not sure why, but something tells me I'll make a series of wrong decisions and become the laughingstock of the party... Something tells me that that's what's going to happen today.

Why?

I don't know.

Then don't think about it. Put it out of your mind. And if you're worried you might accidentally do something egregious, then just remember this simple advice: watch what everybody else is doing and follow their lead. You can't go wrong that way...!

That's the same advice Vadim gave me last chapter.

Well, there you have it!

Do what everybody else is doing? How simple that is! How logical!

Yeah, I say, You're probably right.

Of course I'm right!

I should just watch what everyone else is doing and follow their lead.

Absolutely!

I nod happily:

So, I say, what types of things are going to happen... specifically, that is?

You mean today?

Yeah, what can I expect from this whole wedding process?

Well the agenda basically looks like this... first, we need to mark the passing of Vadim's independence. As we speak, the girls, for their part, are mourning what will soon be the loss of the bride's virginity — ha-ha! — and we men need to do the same thing for Vadim. The three of us will wash down his ugly past... that is if he ever comes out of that room...

Boris checks his watch and yells toward Vadim's room:

Hey in there... hurry up! We don't want to be late, now do we?!

I'm almost done! Vadim answers.

...So anyway, after we wash down his past we'll go to the actual ceremony....

What will that involve?

Ah ...it's nothing too spectacular. First you wait around with some other wedding parties, then you go into an adjoining room, an orchestra strikes up, the ceremony happens for about ten to fifteen minutes, the orchestra strikes up again, and the wedding party leaves with the bride and groom who are now — for the most part — married.

Sounds magical!

It is.

So then what?

So anyway, after the ceremony we'll go for a ride... we haven't decided where yet. Probably the Kremlin. Maybe Vorobyovye Gory. And after that it's back home for the dinner banquet.

You mean food and drink?

Yeah, that's the most important part. That's where we actually celebrate the wedding. We'll talk and talk and talk... ! It should be lots of fun... in fact Vadim says they've got all the makings for an unforgettable celebration: twenty bottles of vodka, eight bottles of champagne, ten bottles of red wine, ten bottles of white wine... not to mention all the food... plates and plates of it... I hear Vadim's mom is even making her special dish...

Boris stops in the middle of his thought:

Have you ever tried Olga Mikhailovna's special dish?

No, I haven't.

Wow! You don't know what you're missing! She promised to make it tonight in honor of the occasion. The last time I had it was twelve years ago... and I still remember the taste.

Boris pauses to remember the taste of Landlady's special recipe:

Yeah, he says, This day should be a day unlike any other...!

A day unlike any other? A day unlike any other... A day unlike any other!

When Vadim comes out I am surprised to see that he is not dressed formally, but is wearing a sweatsuit and old house slippers instead.

Let's get started! Boris says, We're already behind schedule because of you!

Vadim tightens the string around his sweatpants:

Let's do it! he says.

Wait a minute! I say, You're going to your wedding dressed like that?

Of course not, Vadim says.

Boris laughs at my words:

Remember James... before we go to the wedding we need to wash down his ugly past...

My past, Vadim protests, wasn't *that* ugly!

It was ugly enough.

Vadim laughs.

...And that means that there's one more thing that we need to do before the actual wedding ceremony can begin...

I look at them blankly and so they both answer in one voice:

Vodka!!

(7)

While the three of us are sitting in her livingroom, Landlady continues to prepare for the dinner banquet. She actually started months ago with her shopping, then a week ago with the last-minute preparations, and then two days ago with the finishing touches. She has already made her purchases, and now she is in her element. Like an author struggling painfully toward a conclusion, her time has come at last. And like an author she is cutting, and trimming, and adding, and mixing, and salting, and sighing, and discarding...

(8)

There you go! Vadim says pouring our vodka into plastic cups that Landlady has recently recycled.

10 — 1807

Oh no you don't! Boris objects, I'm driving!

Oh you can have a little bit..., Vadim pours.

A little bit? Even a little bit can cost me my license!

You won't lose your license from one shot of vodka.

How do you know?

Experience.

Experience? This from the man who totaled a brand new BMW!

I was sober then... thank you very much.

That's right, I say, He was as sober as a scientist.

Boris grunts.

Actually, I say, Scientifically speaking there's no reason why you can't have a drink. In fact, I just read an article about alcohol tolerance... it said that there's a certain amount of pure alcohol that your organism can absorb without it affecting your coordination at all.

How much?

Well for my weight it's seventy-eight grams.

See! Vadim says, So for you, Boris, it's probably twice that much!

Well all right all right... I'll drink... but only symbolically!

Vadim nods deeply and pours him one hundred fifty-six symbolic grams.

Holding our cups, we sit in silence:

Ah...! Boris says finally, This is the life!

You got that right! Vadim says.

Aren't you going to miss it?

What do you mean? Vadim says.

Well you do realize that after you're married you won't be able to spend time the way you spent it before... you realize that everything will change.

Ah, that's rubbish!

No it's not... take it from me my friend: your bear hunting days are over.

Vadim laughs and holds up his cup of vodka:

I'm no bear hunter, he says, But I can say without a doubt that my future will be no different from my past, no worse than my present.

He stops importantly:

So let us drink to the future! he says.

And to your ugly past! Boris adds.

The three of us drink aggressively, chasing the vodka down with pickles that Vadim has brought from the kitchen. After we have downed our first shot, the process of male bonding begins: our conversation becomes livelier.

You know, Vadim says, I've always wondered who it was that thought to think up vodka?

Vodka?

Yeah, who ever invented it?

Russians of course!

Well yeah, but who specifically?

I don't know.

Actually, I lie, It's a proven fact that Americans invented vodka...

Americans?!

No really it's true... I read that Americans were the first to actually...

But before I can even finish my sentence I am drowned out in an uproar of objections:

Americans?! says Vadim.

Vodka?! adds Boris.

They both are looking at me fiercely:

Invented?! Vadim says again.

Vodka...?! Boris adds.

Okay okay, I concede, It was a joke... it was just a joke!

Not funny, Vadim says.

Yeah, says Boris, There are some things in this world that you just don't joke about!

That's right, says Vadim, Just think how you'd feel if we told you that Russians invented peanut butter.

I see your point.

Or, says Boris, if we said that American democracy was conceived in Russia.

But actually, I say trying to save the situation, vodka was invented by an American who had moved from Russia.

From Russia?

Yeah... an immigrant to America.

Immigrant?

Yeah.

In other words, a Russian?

Well, an American from Russia.

Ah... well, that's a different story altogether...!

I laugh and take another pickle.

...You should have said that to begin with.

And with that the conversation turns — as it always does — to politics.

At some point Boris looks at his watch:

It's almost time to go, he says, The girls will be waiting.

Lazily, Vadim gets up from his chair to change once again, this time into his wedding clothes. Landlady has not stopped preparing for the dinner banquet, even though she has exchanged her apron for formal wedding attire; as she chops beets, her dangling earrings jangle back and forth from her ears.

While waiting for Vadim, Boris helps me to re-tie my tie. And when Vadim is dressed in a black coat and tie of his own, and Landlady has washed most of the purple from her hands, Boris pulls out the keys to his car and looks at us seriously:

Are we ready? he says in a voice splashed with vodka.

I am, Landlady says.

So am I, I second.

Let's get this over with! Vadim says.

And with that the four of us set out in Boris's Zhiguli for the local ZAGS — the others will be waiting for us there — where the ceremony is due to take place.

(9)

Arriving at the registration hall, the four of us pile out of Boris's small car. Another Zhiguli of acquaintances has just arrived and is waiting for us inside. When Olga smells the alcohol in Vadim's words, she isn't even surprised, doesn't even ask how he has spent his last few hours: she simply reaches up and kisses him lightly above his bushy eyebrows where his hairline used to be.

We move inside.

The government building is dark with cold corridors and peeling floor tiles. Not noticing the small signs on the walls, our wedding party — led by Boris, Vadim, and Olga in her billowing white wedding gown and veil — makes its way through the dark halls, boisterously, laughing and joking, loud and joyous and celebrating the moment...

...Gaily and loudly we barge into a room that we have taken to be the wedding room. But as soon as we enter, we realize our mistake: a room full of divorce petitioners looks up in surprise from the documents they are signing. For an awkward moment we stare across the room at each other: they at us nostalgically; we at them naively.

Oops! Boris says, Wrong room!

Wrong room! Vadim repeats.

Yeah..., I add, ...This isn't France!

You need the last door on the right..., says one of the people in the room and goes back to filling out his form.

Vadim grabs Boris playfully and pulls him out of the room. And we again make our way — more carefully this time — back down the hall to the last door on the right.

(11)

Behind the last door on the right we enter a waiting room where everyone is dressed like us. Approximately five couples and their entourages are standing around in the small room waiting to be summoned to the 'wedding chamber,' in other words, the small adjoining room next to the large wallmap of the Soviet Union. Laughter can be heard from all sides and the gaiety is so infectious, so pervasive, that it isn't even dampened by the fight that almost breaks out between two brides, each of whom has worn the other's gown. The festive mood is not even tempered by the old woman who is running around from couple to couple, asking them, telling them, at times yelling things that are important now but that will be forgotten in just a few short years.

In the small room the wedding parties do not mix. Grooms do not congratulate grooms. Best men do not compare their statures. In fact, only the brides bother to notice their fellow brides-to-be.

Couple by couple the process gets closer. And closer. One by one the people ahead of us are swept into matrimony. Now it is happening to a thin groom and his thinner bride: happily, the couple and their entourage enter the adjoining room where an orchestra strikes up; after a long pause of about ten or fifteen minutes the orchestra strikes up again, the doors burst open, and the entourage exits behind the bride and groom who are now — more than ever before — married.

I gasp.

In the small room the anticipation builds. The minutes pass slowly. Everyone is bursting with expectation: Vadim is telling jokes that everybody has heard and although he is no comedian, everyone laughs anyway; Landlady is engaged in a conversation with her friend Olga Ivanovna — heatedly, they are comparing cures for the common cold. Olga, her future daughter-in-law, is not laughing but looks beautiful anyway, and as she stands in a corner talking to Olya the three Olgas gaze at her with pride, admiration, and envy, respectively.

I smile.

With his video camera in hand, Boris is moving from person to person, entreating each of us to record our wishes for the soon-to-be-newlyweds. Word by word he films our congratulations until the only people left are the three Olgas and I:

Hey you guys! Boris says, Say something for the bride and groom!

Boris points the camera at the Olgas:

May you enjoy all the best in life..., says the first Olga.

...May you love each other forever..., says the second.

...And may your family be happy..., says the third.

Boris aims the camera at me:

Your turn James! he says and I look reluctantly into the camera:

Give me please four kilograms potatoes, I say.

Boris looks at me strangely.

I shrug my shoulders.

But before he can say anything a man from a competing entourage taps me on my shrug. I turn around to see a sweating hysterical groom:

Excuse me, he says, Have you seen my bride? She was supposed to meet me hours ago, but she didn't show up... I thought she might come here, but I don't see her.

I don't know, I say, What's she look like?

The man tells me.

And what's she wearing?

The man tells me.

Well, actually, I say, I did see someone fitting that description... Is that her?

No, the man says, That's not her.

What about that girl over there... the one dressed in white... is that her?

No, he says, that's not her either.

The man looks as if he's going to cry.

I don't know, I say, She might have had some problems with the roads. This weather...

But the man, not waiting for my consolation, has already moved on to ask other people if they have seen his missing bride-to-be.

Just then another person, apparently noticing my explaining to the unfortunate groom, taps me on the shoulder and asks if the orchestra takes requests.

I don't know, I explain, This is my first wedding. Ask that woman over there.

And when he does, the old woman explains from the very beginning:

'First,' she says, 'you and your entourage will enter that adjoining room over there. An orchestra will strike up. The ceremony will last about ten or fifteen minutes, after which the orchestra will strike up again and you will walk *slowly* and *calmly* — no bursting! — out the doors followed by your bride and groom who will now be married.'

Is that it? he asks.

That's it... if you have any other questions just watch what everybody else is doing and repeat after them. If you follow everyone else's lead you can't go wrong.

Thanks, says the man.

No problem, the woman sighs.

(12)

Standing in the small waiting room Vadim seems to be especially upbeat. I walk up to him:

Hey Vadim, I say patting him on the back, Are you nervous?

Naw, he says.

Honestly?

Of course, what's there to be nervous about?

In about thirty minutes you're going to be a married man!

So?

So aren't you afraid that things will change after this?

Change? What can possibly change?

Well your relationship with Olga, for one — just remember what Boris said this morning. Not to mention your life in general.

Vadim laughs at my words:

Look, he says, Do you see Olga over there?

Of course.

What color is she wearing?

White.

That's right. Now take a look at me... what color am I wearing?

Black.

Right.

So?

So...!

I don't get it.

Not even a little bit?

No, unfortunately not.

And here Vadim smiles:

I'm no fortune-teller, he says, but I can say with certainty that nothing will change... that this day will be no different from any other.

No different from any other?!

But Vadim, I protest, Everyone knows that a wedding stands for... that it represents change... or at least the prospect of change. Otherwise, why would anyone bother?

Vadim smiles at me and shakes his head like a father:

You my friend are as naive as the letter *Q*!

Just then Olga, who has been mingling with her friends, walks up and puts her arm around her soon-to-be-husband:

What are you two talking about? she says.

About change, Vadim says.

About the color gray, I lie.

Really? says Olga, That's my favorite color...

But once again a voice interrupts our conversation:

Excuse me? it says, Have you seen my bride? She was supposed to meet me here, but I don't see her...

I don't know, Vadim answers, Ask that woman over there...

But the man, not listening to Vadim's answer, moves to ask another wedding couple

What's the deal with that? Vadim says.

The old woman told us that he's a regular here, Olga says.

A *regular?*

Apparently, a few years ago his bride stood him up at the altar... left him waiting with his wedding party, his family, their friends... and since then he's been coming here to look for her. Every Tuesday he dresses up in his faded suit and tie and comes here just to ask wedding party after wedding party if they've seen her...

Strange.

Yeah. Oh...! I almost forgot to tell you Boris needs your help with something... he asked you to help him over there...

What for? Vadim asks.

I don't know. He said something about a signature...

Vadim leaves to help his friend and Olga and I are left to talk alone. When we are out of everyone's earshot, she addresses me:

How'd you like my question this morning? she smiles.

Nice touch.

I thought you'd appreciate it.

Very much so.

Oh don't worry... No one suspected anything. I was just testing you... you know to see how you'd answer.

That's not very nice.

I know. But now I can be sure that you won't open your big mouth during the ceremony.

My big mouth?

Yeah. Now I know you won't make any silly toasts during the dinner tonight.

Are you so sure?

Of course.

You know just because I covered for you this morning that doesn't mean that I won't — as you put it — *open my big mouth* during the ceremony. Maybe I'll decide to object after all...

You won't.

Or even better — maybe I'll make a toast during the dinner... 'Let's drink to Olga,' I'll say, 'the girl that I've been having orgasms on!'

You won't do it.

Are you sure?

Of course... you're not strong enough. You're too mild to make a toast like that.

Well I guess we'll just see about that, won't we?

...James you're too weak to make any bold decisions... In fact, *that's* why you're still here... that's why you're still in Russia...

What? What did she say?!

Hey everybody...! Boris's voice interrupts her.

I start to say something to Olga but Boris's voice again interrupts:

...Hey everybody... it's our turn!

Without looking back at me Olga goes to where Boris and Vadim are standing. The rest of our party gathers excitedly around them.

What did she mean that's *why I'm still in Russia?* That's *why I'm still here?*

It's time! Boris says.

Olga tucks her arm into Vadim's and together they head for the adjoining room, followed by the rest of the wedding party.

And with that, the ceremony begins:

(13)

We enter the adjoining room, an orchestra strikes up, there is a long speech of about ten or fifteen minutes, the orchestra strikes up again, and our entourage exits — bursting wildly through the doors

—followed by Vadim and Olga who are now—was there ever any doubt?—married.

(14)

After the wedding ceremony we pile into three cars and set out, for some reason, for Red Square. The four of us—Olga, Vadim, Olya, and I—have squeezed into Boris's car. Olya is sitting in the passenger seat next to Boris and the two of them are laughing about all the strange and interesting things that happened during the ceremony. In the backseat Olga is sitting next to me on her husband's lap and kissing him romantically—as if for the first time, as if for the last—and I am sitting tangled in their love, wading in the white lace of her flowing wedding gown. Along the way Boris pulls over to buy some cigarettes, Olya goes with him, and the three of us—Vadim, Olga, and I—are left in the backseat.

But they are so involved in their kissing that they do not notice that I have not exited, that I am helplessly lost in Olga's wedding dress. By the time the front doors open, the three of us are so intertwined that it is not clear who is kissing whom. And who is not.

Knock off the affection! Boris says to us, You'll have the rest of the week for that!

Olya giggles slightly. Vadim straightens his tie and asks me to take my fingers out of his ear, which, of course, I do:

Sorry, I say.

After starting the car, Boris opens a pack of cigarettes and offers it around. The newlyweds refuse. I refuse. Olya accepts and pulls out her lighter.

Boris throws the car into motion and our excursion begins.

From the backseat I can hear Boris and Olya trading their impressions about the unusual wedding ceremony. Next to me, Olga is whispering sweet nothings into the hair of Vadim's ear; and each time she does, I try not to listen—but fail.

So that's what she thinks in moments like these! So that's what she hasn't been saying to me all this time. Oh, how much difference an "s" can make... how different nothing *is from* nothings...!

Being driven through the city, I see the landscape flashing by my window like each of my six and a half years. So much has changed. Even the drab lifeless buildings that formed my first impressions have been miraculously transformed by the neon signs that now spread from them like suspended cranberries. Colored billboards line the road. Expensive foreign cars weave in and out of traffic quicker than a drunken conversation.

Hey James..., Boris says to Olya as he lights another cigarette, ...I wanted to ask you...

He cracks his window and blows a large stream of smoke into the cold.

...your passport's blue, right?

That's right.

...And that means that you're from America, right?

Right...

So how's life there?

Life?

Yeah, life. How's life in the United States of America?

What do you mean?

In general... how do people live there?

Fine, I suppose. I suppose they live fine.

Not like here, huh?

Well...

I'm sure you don't have all the problems we've got in our country!

Well, actually we have most of them...

Nonsense!

No, really... there are many issues that the U.S. has yet to resolve...

You mean to say you have problems, too?

That's right.

You have problems that are serious but unaddressed?

That's right.

Boris pauses to consider my words:

Maybe so, he says, But we've got *more*!

I don't know about that...

It's true.

I'd beg to differ...

But here Boris looks at me with a pronounced expression of superiority:

There's not a country in this world, he boasts, that is as hopeless as Russia!

To the side of the road a traffic policeman is flagging down passing motorists.

Boris slows his car to the speed limit, and approaches the policeman. But luckily the policeman pulls over the car immediately behind us.

Whew! Boris sighs, That was close!

After a few minutes, he resumes his conversation:

You know, James, this may sound like a strange question... but I was wondering... maybe you know... just out of curiosity, how much wallpaper costs in America?

Wallpaper?

Yeah. You see, my second wife and I are redecorating our first kitchen...

That's nice.

Yeah, and that's why the question is relevant for me.

I don't know, I say.

You don't have any idea how much a meter of wallpaper costs?

No. I don't.

Actually, Olya says, it depends....

What does?

In America the price of wallpaper depends on several factors.

How do you know?

I lived there.

There?

That's right. For a year. You see, in America everything depends on something....

In great detail Olya elaborates on this dependence, and as he listens Boris either shakes his head or nods, depending on what is depending on what. Outside our window the scenery is changing: we are getting closer to the center of the city — in other words the neon signs on the drab buildings are becoming bigger and brighter. Colorful billboards proclaim proudly:

NORTH-SOUTH BANK:
SERVING YOU FOR <u>FIVE</u> LONG YEARS!!!

To the side of me, as before, Vadim and Olga are wrapped violently in each others' arms, rolling over the backseat of the car, covered in layers of lace, completely enthralled in their kissing. It is impossible to make out their bodies in the pile of white. Without noticing, they have pinned my leg under them, and as I try to take part in the conversation, I am working to free it.

Hey James! Boris says, How much do cigarettes cost over there?

Cigarettes?

Yeah, in America how much do Marlboros cost?

I don't know... it's difficult to say because I haven't been back for a while now, in fact, since I started smoking...

You didn't smoke when you lived in America?

No. I started here.

So you don't know how much your cigarettes cost?

No.

It's funny..., Olya says, When I first got there and saw the price of cigarettes I thought I'd drop dead! But then after a while I sort of got used to it... in other words, I quit smoking....

And she explains in great detail about the cost of cigarettes in America.

Hearing this, Boris is amazed:

Poor people! he says, How can they live like that?

They have higher salaries, Olya explains.

How much higher... I mean what's an average salary?

It depends on the occupation, Olya says.

Well, for example, let's take my profession... let's say a person working as a Customs official in an airport located north of the city... how much would I be able to get... what would my *official* salary be?

She tells him.

And what about my *unofficial* salary?

They don't have unofficial salaries.

They don't?

No. It's considered illegal.

Poor things....

Boris seems lost in reflection and sympathy:

Hey James... did you hear that! You don't even have the possibility to earn 'on the side'?!

Strange, isn't it? I say.

Boris shakes his head:

And they say America's the land of opportunity...!

But before I can agree, a Mercedes goes screaming by us. It is loud and Boris is barely able to swerve his Zhiguli out of the way to avoid a collision. The three of us — Boris, Olya, and I — lunge heavily to one side.

Vadim and Olga are too busy to lunge — they are now completely consumed by their display of affection and are sprawled out over the backseat.

After the Mercedes has passed Boris cusses and then, in retaliation, cuts in front of a beat-up Zaparozhets:

Outta the way! he swears.

Olya smiles.

What was I saying... oh yeah... I was asking you about America...

You were? I ask.

Yes, he says, I was....

And so, one after another, Boris eagerly asks me questions about America — How much do cars cost? How much do small apartments cost? How much do policemen cost? — and just as eagerly, and in the exact same order... Olya answers them.

Finally, when we are near the Kremlin, Boris parks his car and he and Olya exit from the front doors. In the back Vadim and Olga are now so heatedly entwined — and I with them — that none of us exits. They have not noticed that the car is stopped, and although I have, I am still helplessly caught in the white lace. For some time Boris and Olya stand outside the car waiting for the three of us to exit.

Hey...! they finally say.

Hearing them, I try to raise my head, try to push away a heavy weight that is grinding into my shoulder. But it is too heavy. I am hopelessly swamped in white.

Listen up... all three of you...!

I can hear Boris's voice, but am helpless to do anything.

Hey..., Boris finally says exasperated, ...Are you guys coming or not?

There is a long pause that lasts for several seconds. Finally it is broken by Olga's emphatic answer, half-scream, half-whimper:

ДА!!! she says.

(15)

Wrong: In America everything depends <u>from</u> something.
Right: In America everything depends on something.

(16)

Meanwhile, Landlady has returned home to continue preparations for tonight's dinner banquet. Olga's mother is helping her and together they are chopping vegetables. Boiling potatoes. Baking chickens. Carefully, they are slicing coldcuts to be folded and neatly overlapped. Proudly, Landlady is making her special dish, a dish that is so special it is served only on days like this, a dish so delicious that no one can refuse....

Like a gypsy in a restaurant, Landlady is singing gaily as she chops and slices and folds and bakes and fries and rinses and...

(17)

When we have exited the car, the five of us, accompanied by a second carful of Olgas, proceed through Red Square toward the eternal flame. Olga, whose own jacket cannot fit over her padded shoulders, has been given a large *telogreika* to put over her wedding gown. As she walks, Olga does her best to lift up her dress slightly above the ground. But it is no use: by the time we reach Lenin's tomb, the bottom of her white dress is grayer than a shattered ashtray.

As we stroll through the cold square our wedding party laughs and jokes. Vadim and Olga are walking hand in gloved hand and Boris is ahead of them, shuffling backwards and filming them with his video camera:

Say something! he yells at the newlyweds.

Vadim smiles and waves at the camera.

Olga looks admiringly at her husband and gives him a kiss on his mustache.

Behind the newlyweds, at a respectful distance, I am walking with Olya who is telling me about her job.

Say something to the camera! Boris yells at us.

Like what?

Some sort of wish for the newlyweds.

Olya looks into the camera:

Well, she says, I'd just like to wish the newlyweds all the best.

That's perfect! he says and still shuffling backwards aims the camera at me:

Hey James!

Yeah?

How much do video cameras cost in America?

I don't know.

You don't?

No I don't.

And so Olya tells him.

Boris shakes his head at the price and runs ahead to film the whole procession in wide angle. When he has left, Olya returns to her conversation:

...Where was I...? Oh yeah... I was telling you about the company where I work. So anyway, above me is my boss, who is from Australia. He's a nice enough guy, but he swears all the time. He's having a *liaison* with my friend Tanya even though it's officially against company policy and both of them could be fired for it...

As Olya tells me about her job I notice that in almost every sentence she is using one of my eleven yellow words. And as she says it over and over again, I try my best to ignore it.

Without success.

...I mean Tanya always says that the real reason is that foreigners, I mean even Australians, are way more respectful of women than Russian guys. I told her that's not necessarily true... I mean for example Russian guys will bring you flowers and help you put your coat on, but the guys from America don't. I mean it's like they've never even seen it done it before! Can you imagine... I mean...

(18)

...and splits and dices and sets the table. Carefully she is arranging plates and silverware and chairs around the long table in the livingroom. Wiping the bottles of wine. Wiping the bottles of champagne. Wiping the bottles of vodka. Placing each of them at arm-length intervals on the table. Excitedly, she is waiting for the wedding party to return.... Happily, she is peeling and grating, re-tasting and re-testing, salting and sugaring, dipping and sprinkling...

(19)

In theory значит means it means, which means it means both *it means* as well as *значит*. But that is in theory. In practice *значит* not only means *it means*, but also *doesn't* mean *it means*. In fact, *значит* doesn't mean *it means* as much as it doesn't mean *it means*; and this means that although it means *it means*, *значит* doesn't really mean anything at all. In fact it means nothing.

Although it's as frequent as *finally*, it is, at the same time, as meaningless as *I mean*.

Значит...

(20)

We move on.

Surprisingly, ours is the only wedding party in Red Square. But because Olya and I are now walking apart from our married couple, we are hounded by vendors peddling photos, fur hats, and excursions around the city.

No thanks! we say.

Not expensive! they insist.

No thanks! we say again and hurry to catch up to the rest of the wedding party.

Can you imagine going on an excursion of the city... *now*? I laugh.

Have you ever seen the city on an excursion? Olya asks me, It's really quite beautiful.

Actually, you know it's funny... I haven't. Although I did have to give an excursion once.

You gave an excursion?

That's right.

You were a guide?

That's right. A very good friend of mine came to visit me and I showed him around the city for a while.

Your very good friend?

Well, actually now that I think of it, he was more of a good friend.

And you showed him around?

That's right... he was a friend of mine and I promised to show him my Russia and so he came to visit me...

(21)

'And this...,' I said pointing with all my arm, 'is St. Basil's Cathedral. Do you recognize it? No? Well, I'm sure you've heard about it... No? Well, anyway, it's famous. And over here we have Red Square... that's right the world-renowned Red Square... what... no, it's always been that small... I mean it's never been any bigger... well, it's just that on television it looks bigger because there're usually tanks going through it or something. You know I have to tell you that this is one of my favorite places in Moscow... I love Red Square because here you can feel the culture of Russia, the history, the... what... I'm not sure, I think it's over there by the hill... no, no... no problem... I'll wait...'

When my friend came back I continued my excursion:

'And around the corner here...,' I said proudly, '...we have the Eternal Flame in memorial to all the cities that suffered during World War II. Poignant, isn't it? What... I don't know, I don't think so... I mean I guess it's possible if it rained real hard...'

A week later I was happy to escort my acquaintance to the airport.

(22)

After paying our respects to the Eternal Flame, we get back in the car and set out for Vadim's apartment where the celebratory dinner is waiting.

(23)

But Boris has forgotten not to drink. And along the way a traffic policeman standing to the side of the road randomly waves a nightstick at him to pull over. Boris starts to open the door to exit, but Vadim stops him:

Don't get out, he says.

What?

Don't get out.

Why?

Just trust me — stay in the car.

Boris settles into his seat:

Shit shit shit shit shit! he mutters as he sits in the car waiting for the policeman to approach. When he does, the officer bends down to take a look into the car, introduces himself with a limp salute and asks for Boris's documents.

Boris hands them to the officer. For several minutes the officer examines the documents then walks back to his car. When he has left Boris looks back at Vadim:

How much for speeding? he asks.

At least a hundred thousand...

What about alcohol?

You're looking at between two hundred and two fifty... it depends.

On what? I ask.

On when his wife's birthday is.

Boris takes out his wallet and prepares the money just in case, hiding it under his thigh. After a few moments the police officer returns and again looks into the car:

A wedding? he says.

That's right, officer! Boris answers, We were on our way to the marriage hall and didn't want to be late.

U-hmm...

Did we do anything wrong?

I guess not. But *next time* be more careful.

What?

You didn't do anything wrong... but next time be more careful...

Sir?

...My wife just had her birthday, but who knows about the next guy who pulls you over...!

And the officer hands Boris his documents, salutes again, and without taking any money, goes back to the side of the road.

(24)

...and serving and greeting and seating...

(25)

When we finally arrive Landlady is washing and drying:

What took you so long? she asks Vadim as he comes into the apartment, Have you forgotten that the most important part is still to come?

Behind him the rest of us are waiting to take off our shoes and jackets. Some friends and relatives have already been seated at the table.

Traffic! Vadim says and makes his way to the table where he accepts everyone's congratulations with a proud smile. After him, the rest of us take off our jackets and move into the small livingroom with the long table.

Expertly, Landlady shows us where to sit. It is not an easy task given the twenty-odd guests, but she does it masterfully:

Olga! she says, You sit over here next to Olga. And you Olga across from Olga over there. Now as for Olga... let's have you sit at the fourth seat from the front between Olga Ivanovna and...!

After about ten minutes, we are seated as follows:

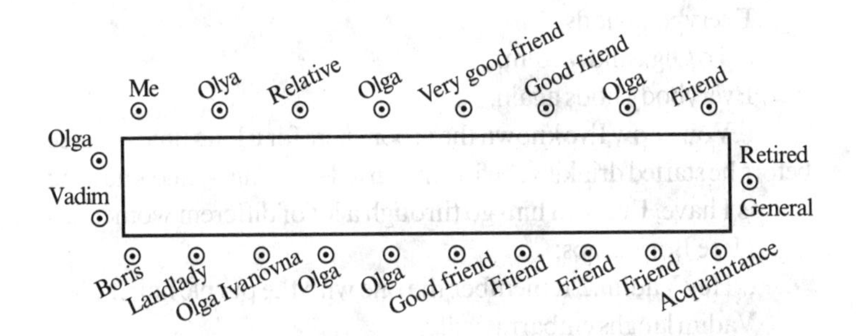

The arrangement is amazingly effective: Vadim is the man of the hour and so he is sitting at the head of the table to the right of Olga, who is now his wife. Boris — who will be expected to be the life of the party — is within an extended arms reach away from him. Landlady has positioned herself nearest the kitchen — this way she can more easily serve the guests — next to her longtime friend Olga Ivanovna.

Because I am from *there* I am also seated near the front of the table between Olga — who is now married — and Olya who is just as unmarried as I am.

But will I be able to tell them apart during this dinner? Olga, the bride, on my right; Olya, the non-bride, on my left... Olga Mikhailovna — Landlady's real name — across from me, and Olga Ivanovna, her friend, next to her... Sure it's easy now, but what about when I've had too much to drink?

Finally, everybody is seated. The food is ready. The drink is ready. The guests are seated and ready to begin the dinner celebration. Shyly they are sitting with their hands below the table waiting for someone to take the first piece of *seledka*.

(26)

As if understanding this, Boris grabs his glass of champagne and stands up:

I'd like to make the first toast! he says in his deep commanding voice.

Dutifully, the room becomes quiet.

...I'd like to make the first toast to our married couple!

Everybody nods.

...To Olga and Vadim!

Everybody nods again.

...You know I've known the groom here for a long time — since before he started drinking, before he started smoking — and knowing him as I have, I've seen him go through a lot of different women...

Here Boris stops:

...Hey Vadim... remember the one with the purple hair?!

Vadim laughs embarrassedly.

...Anyway, I've seen Vadim here with many different women and so I can tell you honestly that of all the women he's been with, Olga is by far the best!

The wedding guests murmur their agreement.

...And I'll tell you why: It's no secret to anyone that our bride is beautiful... that goes without saying. But what you may not notice from a distance — it comes when you know her more closely — is how intelligent she is. How intelligent and how polite...

The wedding guests smile their agreement.

...So I'd like to drink to her beauty, her intelligence, her politeness. Vadim, I know you're smart enough to realize what you have in Olga. May the two of you have the best of everything... May your family be joyous and happy... May you live and love as long as you see fit... May you have as many friends as you need... As many children as you can manage... And as much money as you choose to deserve. And most importantly: May everything in your life happen when it should... no sooner, no later!

Boris raises his glass:

To Vadim and Olga! he says.

For the next few seconds the sound of toasting fills the room as the guests touch their glasses to as many other glasses as they can reach. Happily, they swallow their champagne.

Boris also swallows his champagne happily.

But then, suddenly, Boris makes a distorted face as if he has consumed something toxic. Looking suspiciously at his emptied glass he yells out:

It's bitter!

Yeah! somebody else yells, Bitter!

Soon everybody is chanting in unison: Bit-ter! Bit-ter! Bit-ter!

Taking his cue, Vadim grabs Olga and kisses her long and passionately:

One...! the crowd chants, Two......! Three ......!

Vadim and Olga remain embraced, kissing heatedly.

...Four......! Five......! Six......!

I look at my watch and shake my head:

Here we go again! I think.

...Twenty-two......! Twenty-three......!

(27)

Seventy... Seventy-one... Seventy-two...

By now everyone is a bit weary of this tradition, but continues to count anyway.

Finally, at one hundred twenty-two the newlyweds come up for air, and each and every guest — even those who have lost count — suddenly shouts and cheers approval.

Olga sits down at the head of the table, and Vadim, who has remained standing, holds up his hand until the room is quiet:

You know, he says, I'd like to thank everyone for coming... Everyone! And since we have a lot of guests tonight and not everyone is acquainted with each other, I'd like to introduce you all...

And here Vadim begins to introduce the guests one by one. In turn they either stand or wave their hands to acknowledge the introduction. When it is my turn he presents me as follows:

...And this is James... he likes vodka.

The other guests applaud.

When everyone has been introduced, Vadim sits down. But then, as if remembering something, he stands back up:

Oh I almost forgot! There's something that I've been saving for a long long time... for a special occasion... And now, I would say, the occasion has arrived...!

Vadim leaves the room to the surprised murmurs of his guests:

What could it be? says one.

I don't know, says another, but it must be important if he stood back up like that!

And sure enough, when he returns Vadim is holding something behind his back out of view of his guests:

I've been waiting so long for the chance to enjoy this..., he says.

And slowly and dramatically he pulls his arm from behind his back:

There it is! he says and with a loud clink sets a dusty bottle of French cognac on the table.

(28)

And with that the dinner banquet begins.

(29)

At first the conversation is sluggish and self-conscious, like a foreigner offering a bribe. But in no time at all the guests relax, words come faster and freer, and the temperature in the small room begins to rise.

For me this party will consist of those people within a word's distance away, in other words the ones that I can talk to, in other words, the following six people:

> Vadim, the groom;
> Olga, his wife;
> Boris, the life of the party;
> Olya, my possible downfall;
> Landlady, the hostess;
> Olga Ivanovna, just in case.

So these are the people that will be my companions this night? So these are the six people that will help me meet this most remarkable of days? Here we all are! After so many years, after so much time, after so many pages we have finally been brought together unto one place...!

Hey James...! Vadim's voice interrupts my thoughts. Strangely, he has put his forefinger to his mouth. He looks around to see if anyone is watching and then leans over across Olga and whispers in my ear. I strain to understand.

Do you see that elderly woman over there? he asks me.

Which one?

The one sitting across and to the left of you... with the veins in her neck... do you see her?

Landlady's friend... Olga Ivanovna?

Shhhh!!!!! She's not deaf, you know!

Who's not deaf?

Olga Ivanovna.

I didn't say she was deaf...!

I didn't say you said she was deaf.

Vadim, I say, What was your question?

Do you see that woman over there with the veins in her neck... the veins like purple worms?

Of course I see her.

Well, I need to tell you something about her.

All right.

Are you listening?

Yes.

Are you listening real good?

Geez Vadim what are you getting at?

You see she's an old friend of the family...

Okay...?

She's an expert in Russian literature...

That's fine.

...She reads voraciously... sitting, standing, sleeping... you can ask her about any book ever written and she'll tell you everything you could ever want to know about it. If not *more*!

All right...

You can talk to her if you like, but there's one word that you must never say in her presence.

Why?

It doesn't matter. Just promise me you won't mention the word.

Sure. What's the word?

Do you promise me you won't mention it?

I said I promise. What is it?

Here Vadim leans even closer to my ear and his voice becomes even softer.

When I hear the word I laugh:

That's it? I say, *That's* the word?

Don't you dare say it!

But why?

Look we all have our idiosynchracies.

I know but...

Shhhh!!!! Just don't say the word and we won't have any problems, okay? If it were *your* wedding I wouldn't say anything to *your* guests.

(30)

Of the people sitting around me — that is to say, the six people that I can have a conversation with — the only one that I have not met before is Landlady's friend, Olga Ivanovna, the woman Vadim has just warned me about. *How bad could she be, really? How important could a single word be to her? Surely he was exaggerating?*

Careful not to say the forbidden word, I decide to introduce myself:

My name is James, I explain, I'm a friend of Vadim's... and of Olga's.

James, huh? I've heard a lot about you.

You have?

Olga Mikhailovna says you're renting the apartment upstairs for one twentieth its real value... that you have a lot of free time during your afternoons...

That's right.

She says you discard bread...

Well, yes, it's happened. But nowadays I try to be more conscientious.

I'm sure.

Olga Ivanovna pauses and then continues:

Where are you from again? she asks.

America.

North or South?

North.

And you came *here*? From *there*? Weren't getting enough excitement in your *own* country?

Well...

Thought you'd have a little fun at our expense?

Well I...

I take it you're planning to write a book?

What?

You're probably going to write about your life here — the usual bit, I'm sure: poor rich foreigner comes to Russia with dreams of finding a Russian wife, but instead leaves with one.

Actually, I never...

Of course you're going to write a book like that! All foreigners want to tell the world about their *experiences*, as if they have something pertinent to say!

But...

Olga Ivanovna! Vadim rescues me, Olga Ivanovna how are you today?

Hearing Vadim's voice, Olga Ivanovna turns to him without enthusiasm:

I feel like hell, she says.

That's fine, Olga Ivanovna. Just fine.

But what was she talking about? Books? Wives? Experiences? Why was she so certain that I cared enough to become a writer? That I was that indulgent? How did she know to insult me like that?

Vadim stops, as if trying to think of something to say:

So how are Seriozha and Tanyusha? he says and then to me: Those are Olga Ivanovna's two children, James.

Same as always, she answers, Curious and devoted.

Why didn't you bring them? We were hoping they'd come with you tonight.

They weren't interested.

Why not?

The age. When you were sixteen and twenty-one did *you* want to spend time with your mother?

Sixteen and twenty-one! Wow, I haven't seen them since they were... well since Seriozha's fourteenth birthday party.

That's right. You spilled juice all over my table cloth.

I ...uh... well yeah I did...

After you left I spent two days getting the red out.

Vadim blushes. Watching the conversation between Vadim and Olga Ivanovna, I am surprised to see Vadim flustered by Olga Ivanovna's brisk tone.

It was an accident... I was just reaching out for a piece of cake...

The largest one, probably. You always take the largest piece of cake.

Just then Landlady comes into the room from the kitchen and whispers something into Olga Ivanovna's ear and they exit together.

When she has gone Vadim smiles and looks at me:

What did I tell you? he says.

I see what you mean!

You know she really is a nice lady. Did I mention she has a thorough education in Russian literature? I did? Well, she does. In fact if it hadn't been for all the changes here, she probably would have become a lecturer or a critic... for the longest time she had dreams of becoming a literature professor... but her dreams were shattered...

She doesn't work as a professor of Russian literature?

No, unfortunately not.

Why? What does she do?

It's a sad story... you see, Fate has been unkind to her and so she's been forced to earn a living in an unrelated field... for the last ten years she's been working as...

...As a cashier selling potatoes?!

Worse... as a school teacher. She teaches Russian poetry to eleven-year-olds.

Vadim shakes his head. I nod sympathetically:

Poor thing, I say.

(31)

Gradually, the conversation becomes warmer. Olga, who is sitting to my left, and Olya, who is sitting to my right are talking to each other about love and fidelity, and as they speak their words go right through me. Vadim is listening to them and nodding naively. Boris who is sitting across from me, is still fascinated by my citizenship, and as I fill my plate with appetizers — potato salad, vinaigrette, coldcuts — he is once again asking me questions about America:

...What about wine? he says, How much does a good white wine cost in America?

I'm not sure.

...What about red wine? How much does that cost?

I don't know.

Well then what about vodka... you have to know how much vodka costs!

I'm not sure... let me ask Olya...

When Boris hears the price he smiles and shakes his head:

That much? he asks.

That much, Olya answers and goes back to her conversation.

Boris shakes his head again and then turns to me:

You know, he says, it's funny... Just a short while back it used to be a real occasion to meet a foreigner. A few years ago it was something special.

And now?

Well now things have changed. Nowadays in Moscow there are more foreigners than cockroaches.

I laugh.

No offense or anything... I mean I have nothing against cockroaches... In fact we have a lot of them where I work. They're disgusting when they gather to form crowds, but in small numbers they can be quite tolerable.

You mean *cockroaches*, of course?

Well now that you mention it, I suppose the same can be said for cockroaches...

Boris stops to consider the coincidence.

Have you known many foreigners? I ask him.

Are you kidding me? I've known them by the wagonful! In fact I even had an American friend from New York. He was a great guy... spoke Russian perfectly. Alex was his name. Alex Podkolesin.

Does he live in Moscow?

Not anymore. He was killed.

What?

An ambulance ran him over while he was trying to cross the street. Crushed his chest like a cardboard box.

I gasp.

...That's right and here's the real kicker: the son-of-a-bitch didn't even stop to pick him up!

I gasp again:

You know, I say, It's strange—I also had a friend who was run over by an ambulance.

A friend?

Well yeah, a friend.

While crossing the street?

That's right.

What about his chest?

Crushed it like a cardboard box.

Boris becomes somber. But then he shakes his head:

Hey enough talk about cardboard... this is a wedding, not a funeral!

I nod.

Boris pulls some appetizers onto his plate and looks at me:

So, what's it like being from *there*? he asks.

Sorry?

What's it like being an American?

I don't know... I've never thought of it... myself... in those terms.

Never thought of it?

That's right.

Let me get this straight... You were born in America, right?

Right.

You lived there your entire life, right?

Right.

And you've *never* thought about what it means to be American?

Well, actually it's not that important to me. And besides, I've only been an American for six and a half years.

What are you talking about? How can it not be important! It's your culture... your traditions... your language.

I know but...

Do you smile in public?

Yes...

Do you respect peanutbutter?

Well, yes...

And you speak English without thinking, don't you?

I do...

There you go!

Where?

That's what it means to be American!

Boris stops to shove a spoonful of food into his mouth. As he chews, he seems to be thinking about something that is at once pleasant and unpleasant. Finally, he speaks up:

Yeah I studied English in school, he says, I used to know it pretty good, but now I've forgotten it all. No practice.

That's too bad.

You can say that again, all that effort... But you know how it goes... other things come up that are more important and the next thing you know it five years have gone by, then six...

Then six and a half...

...Yeah, and you look up one day to see that all this time has passed and what do you have to show for it? Nothing. As if you never had anything in the first place.

I know what you mean.

Hey can I ask you to do something...?

Why not.

You speak English, right?

I try.

I'm just wondering... Can you say something for me?

In English?

Yeah, just so I can hear how it sounds from the lips of a native speaker.

Like what?

It doesn't matter... anything.

I don't know...

Just the first thing that comes into your head.

Well, I'll do my best....

Boris looks at me excitedly, but I remain silent:

Go ahead! he says, Say something!

I don't know what to say. I can't think of anything.

Just say the first thing that comes into your head.

That's no good... it should be something more significant.

Okay then say the first significant thing that comes into your head.

That'll take too long. I need you to give me some sort of topic...

A topic?

Yeah a theme of some kind...

Well okay... what about... what about reciting a piece of poetry... you know a piece of English verse?

I don't know any poetry in English.

You don't read poetry?

Not in English I don't.

Oh... that's too bad. Well then what about something like...?

Boris stops to think:

...What about some words of wisdom... a piece of advice, an English saying, you know... something that will help us better understand the world we live in?

Huh?

Give us some words that will amaze us with their depth and profundity... something that will provide a unique insight into the intricate labyrinth that is the human soul!

I'd rather not.

What?

I mean, I can't.

Why not?

Because to offer someone words of wisdom you yourself have to be wise... to provide insights you have to be insightful... and as far as helping others to understand the world... well, in order to help *others* understand... you have to understand something yourself.

I don't understand.

And I don't either... that's the point. How can I help others find meaning when I myself don't even know where my sixth calculator went?!

I see.

You do?

Yes, I think I do.

You have to keep in mind that I'm not an omniscient narrator, and therefore it would be silly to expect any sort of meaning out of me...!

So I guess insights into the human soul... I guess they're beyond you, as well?

I'm afraid so.

That's strange. You don't know any poetry in your own language. You don't have anything to tell the world. Well then what about something like... let me think... for example, do you have a favorite phrase?

What?

Most foreigners in Moscow have a favorite phrase that they like to repeat over and over. You probably have one, too?

Well actually now that you mention it... I have *two* of them...

There you go!

Boris stands up at the head of the table:

Hey everybody! he announces, James is going to say something in English!

At this, the entire table becomes attentive:

That's right! he says, It's Tuesday and so for those of us who've sort of studied English he's going to say his two favorite phrases...!

The other guests turn to look at me in anticipation and so I clear my throat.

Well, go ahead! Boris says.

Nervously, I clear my throat again and then, switching to English, I say the first of my two favorite phrases:

'God I love this country,' I say, 'but damn I hate it, too!'

Boris looks at me blankly:

One more time! he says, Say it one more time!

And so I repeat the phrase:

'God I love this country... but damn I hate it, too!'

Everybody looks at me blankly. Both Vadim and Boris have a confused expression on their faces. Olga and Olya are smiling dumbly. After a respectful silence, it is Boris who finally breaks it:

What did he say? he asks.

I don't know! Vadim answers, I can't understand him when he speaks fast like that... When he speaks slow I have a chance... but when he speaks fast I can't make out a single word!

Yeah, says Olya, me either... you know, that's how all Americans talk... it's like they have peanut butter in their mouths or something.

Let's hear the other phrase! Boris says, That one was too hard... so let's hear the second one. Maybe we'll have more luck with it.

Again everybody becomes quiet, as if awaiting an elusive riddle. And in the silence I pronounce my other favorite phrase, this time so slowly and so distinctly that I myself understand it's full meaning for the first time:

'Damn I hate this country...,' I say, '...but God I love it, too!'

(32)

But again nobody can understand me.

Wow! says Vadim, That's depressing... you study English for

years and years and then when you need it... POOF! you can't understand a damn thing!

Yeah, says Olya, It makes me wish that I'd studied harder...

It makes me wish I'd studied *English*, Olga says.

You didn't?

I studied French, remember? And what did it get me? Nothing! No one needs it.

What do you mean, no one needs it? Of course I agree with you that it has no practical value... but French is a beautiful language, nevertheless. Just think of all the expressive words it's conceced to other languages: *nostalgia*, *liaison*, *cognac*...

Yeah, Olga says, maybe you're right...

Maybe, says Vadim, But that's nothing compared to all the words that have come into Russian from his language, I mean from English... words like *business* and *drink* and *racket*...

...Not to mention *okay*..., Olya adds.

...And *boyfriend*..., Olga reminds.

...And don't forget *Marlboros*! Boris brags.

I nod.

Hey James..., Boris says, What about in English? Do you have any words adapted from Russian? Are there any of our words that Americans use without thinking?

Well we have a few... like *vodka*... and *kiosk*... and...

I rack my brain to think of another one. *Vodka... kiosk*... Finally it comes to me, and before I can stop it the word slides off my tongue:

...And *perestroika*...

Hearing the word, the other guests let out a collective groan. Vadim looks at me with a pained expression.

What was that? says Olga Ivanovna who until now has been merely watching our discussion with vague interest.

Nothing! I lie.

What did you say?

I...uh... I didn't say anything.

Yes you did. You said something about *perestroika*!

No I didn't! No I didn't... I said something else entirely...!

But it is too late: she is already speaking...

I have said the forbidden word.

(33)

And so for the next forty minutes Olga Ivanovna told the wedding guests the truth about *perestroika*.

And for each of these forty minutes the rest of us sat helpless, like Aeroflot passengers, unable to change the subject.

On and on she went. And just when it seemed that she had exhausted her knowledge of the subject... she would begin again. About the perils of western democracy. About Jewish anti-Semitism. About black American spies infiltrating the Moscow metro...

'They're so insidious they disguise themselves as white people...!'

On and on and on and on... until finally we felt — each of us felt — that we would be sick if we heard the word *on* one more time.

And still she continued. Again and again. And again and again she continued... stopping only to continue once again.

On and on and *on*...

Finally when I'd saved up enough courage I interrupted her:

But Olga Ivanovna! I said, Look at me... *I'm* American... and *I'm* not black!

That's what *you* say, she says, But can we really be sure?

What!

Can we really be so sure that you're not black?

Well yeah, we can... I mean just look at me... my skin isn't black so... well, that means I'm not black!

Hah! she says and then: Hah!

What do you mean?

That doesn't prove anything!

What?

Just because your skin's not black... that doesn't mean that you yourself aren't black!

It doesn't?

No, it doesn't!

And so for the next thirty-nine minutes I tried to convince Olga Ivanovna that I wasn't now — nor had I ever been — black. But each time without success. Look at my hands! I would say, Look at my ears! But no matter which body part I offered as proof, Olga Ivanovna remained unconvinced.

Everything you've just said, she explained, each of your body parts just demonstrates that you've been brainwashed by *them*!

What?

That's just part of *their* plan... that's exactly what *they* want us to think.

And before I could ask who *they* were, she had already begun to explain:

They, she said, were old democrats, new communists, leftists, rightists, bankers, prostitutes, journalists, intellectuals, beaurocrats, immigrants, emigrants, trolleybus drivers, Mafia...

(34)

Eventually, when our patience has run out, we leave Olga Ivanovna to her monologue and return to a discussion of our own:

Speaking of Mafia..., Boris says, Did you hear they killed another banker yesterday?

Another one? Vadim asks.

Yeah. It's the third one this month. Shot him when he was entering the stairwell of his apartment building. How do you like that?

What for? I ask.

What do you mean *what for*? In this country you don't need a *what for*!

There had to be a reason... I mean you don't just kill someone for nothing...

He owed the wrong people money.

And so they killed him?

And so they killed him.

How much money was it?

Boris tells me.

And they killed him for that amount?

That's right.

But it's so little... I mean that's less than the amount that Vadim owes...

Suddenly, I realize where this conversation is leading. But before I can change the subject, Boris has already unchanged it:

That's right. Nowadays you can make a few calls and order a hit on somebody. It's very simple... and not that expensive...

So that's how much a human life is worth?

That's right.

Boris stops to reflect on what has been said. His voice becomes serious:

Hey James, he says, How much does human life cost in America?

But before I can even not answer him Olya has interrupted our conversation:

Hey look! she says, James is sitting between me and Olga!

What? I say.

That's right! says Olga, I didn't even notice.

Notice what?

Today's your lucky day James.

Why?

You're sitting right in the middle of the two of us.

So?

You see, in Russia we have a belief that if you're seated between two people with the same name, then you can make a wish and it'll come true. And look, you're sitting between Olya and me!

Hey James, Boris says, I bet you don't have these kinds of beliefs in America!

No, I say, In America we have a lot of names for women.

So make a wish! Olya says.

A wish? A wish! What could I possibly wish for? What am I lacking? What do I need?

It's funny, I say, but there's honestly nothing that I can think to wish for.

There has to be something? You don't mean to tell us that you're absolutely happy, do you?

Well, no but...

Then make a wish!

But...!

Go on... make it while you still can!

Olga is waiting to the right of me. Olya is waiting to the left. Boris and Vadim are also looking at me:

A wish? I say, All right, I guess I can make a wish...

But what should I wish for? What do I want at this point in my life? What do I need more than anything? Is there anything in this world left for me to want...?

And then it comes to me.

That's it! That's what I want more than anything! That's what I need...

Closing my eyes, I make my wish.

(35)

Wrong: From the one side, this day seems like any other...

(36)

When I open my eyes, Olya is looking at me with a big smile:

Well...? she says.

Well what? I answer.

Well, what did you wish for?

I can't tell you.

Why not?

Otherwise it won't come true. Everybody knows that.

Well well, Vadim says, Look who's turned superstitious all of a sudden! For the last two years you've been telling me about how a person can determine his own life... and now here you are making wishes on silly superstitions!

Well of course I know my wish won't come true, but...

Then why did you make it?

For the same reason you believe in God, Vadim ...just in case.

Yeah but you're the one with the I-can-do-anything mentality... you're the one who believes in self-determinism as opposed to non-self-determinism.

What does he believe in? Boris asks.

Oh James here has this simplistic theory that a person can do anything he wants... that each person is the master of his own destiny...

Vadim let's not get into that again...!

Not get into what? Boris asks.

You see, Vadim explains, James here has a theory that a person can control his future — in other words he is in direct control of everything. In his opinion everything is determined by individual choice... and therefore fate doesn't exist.

That's right, I say, And therefore fate doesn't exist.

But it *does* exist! Vadim says.

No it doesn't, I argue.

It does too.

Does not.

Does too....

(37)

...No it doesn't Vadim.

Yes James it does. And tonight I'm finally going to prove it to you.

Oh yeah? How? How can you prove that fate exists?

Well let's take something that everybody accepts... something that is a given...

For example?

Well, for example there are things that everybody knows... no one will argue that ten comes after nine... that the Russian alphabet begins with *A* and doesn't end until it reaches *Я*... that death is impossible without life...

First of all, I say, Ten doesn't *always* come after nine... secondly, not everyone knows that *A* leads to *Я*.

Vadim stops to think:

But you have to agree, he says, that death is impossible without life...?

Not necessarily! *In most cases* it is, but not in all of them...

Okay then what about this: if I throw something in the air... what will happen? It will fall back to the ground, right? It's gravity. Logic and science have proven that it will fall. You can't choose for it not to fall!

Maybe it will, and maybe it won't. Science can prove gravity a million times, but it can't actually predict that it will always hold true.

What?

You can't be certain that this time it won't stay suspended just because every other time it has fallen.

Yes you can.

No you can't.

Yes you can.

No you can't

Yes you can....

(38)

No Vadim, you can't.

Landlady, who has come into the room from the kitchen, places a bowl of salad next to us:

Are you two arguing about gravity again?

But Vadim doesn't pay attention to her:

So let me get this right..., he says, You're telling me that if I throw this spoon in the air you actually believe that it won't come crashing down?

Vadim has grabbed a heavy soupspoon from the side of his plate....

That's not what I'm saying. I'm only saying that it's possible that it *might* not fall down. There's a chance that it could stay in the air.

Are you sure?

Absolutely... I mean I'm absolutely sure that it's *possible* it might not fall down.

Are you positive?

Well, in a way, yes.

Then let's make a bet on it!

A bet?

Yeah! If you're so sure that it won't fall...

Well... I...

I say that if I throw this spoon into the air it will fall back to the floor.

Of course it's possible but... you know there're times when things don't fall... there exist certain conditions under which things don't fall the way they're supposed to... the way we're used to them falling.

Oh yeah? Like when?

For example, you could throw that same spoon on the moon and it wouldn't drop.

Maybe so. But this isn't the moon. This is Russia. And in Russia the spoon falls.

Vadim is holding the spoon and thumping it heavily against the palm of his hand:

So what about a bet? he says.

A bet?

Yeah. We should bet on whether the spoon will stay up in the air or whether it will fall down.

I don't want to bet... I'm not the betting type.

Well I'm no gambler, either...

But here Vadim is interrupted by a cackle of voices:

You? says Boris, You'll bet on the weather!

Yeah, says Olya, There's not a casino in Moscow that hasn't taken your money!

All right all right..., says Vadim, That's not the point... the point is that I say the spoon will fall while James here maintains that it will stay in the air...

You're all missing the point..., I try to explain but am interrupted by Boris:

Hey! he says, I know what the bet should be!

What? says Vadim.

The bet should be as follows: if Vadim wins the bet, in other words if the spoon doesn't stay in the air, then James should have to do a dance of some sort... do you like to dance James?

I hate dancing... I don't know how...

Perfect! So the bet should be as follows: if James loses, in other words, if the spoon doesn't stay in the air, in other words it actually falls, then he has to do a dance in front of everybody... yeah... I like that...!

Here? Olga objects.

Of course. Why not?

Well, because there's not enough floor space with all the guests in the room.

We can just clear off a place on the table.

But what should we do for music? Vadim asks.

Do you have a guitar?

Sure.

Well there you go... we'll just pick a song and I'll play it on the guitar and James will dance to it right there on the table!

Wait a minute! Vadim says, Who'll choose the song?

You of course... any song you want.

Any song I want?

Yeah Vadim... your favorite song.

His favorite song?

Oooohhh no you don't! I say, If you think I'm going to get up in front of everybody and dance to Vadim singing 'Yesterday' then I'll just remind you that you have another think coming...!

Let's not forget one thing..., says Olya who until now has been watching our discussion silently.

What's that?

You're forgetting that Vadim may just as well lose the bet... you haven't even mentioned what he should do if he throws the spoon up and it doesn't fall!

Yeah...! I say.

I mean you guys are acting as if it's a foregone conclusion that the spoon will fall... but that's not an equal bet, now is it! Here's what I propose for the case if the spoon stays in the air, I mean, if the spoon doesn't fall... I mean, if Vadim loses...

What what? I say eagerly.

...If Vadim loses the bet, in other words, if the spoon stays in the air, then Vadim you will have to give up drinking for the remainder of this party... in other words, while the rest of us are drinking and celebrating you won't be allowed to consume anything with alcohol in it!

No wine?

No.

No champagne?

None.

What about vodka?!

Out of the question.

You mean to tell me that if I lose, in other words, if I throw this spoon up and it stays hanging in the air, then I'll have to abstain from all alcohol during my own wedding party?

That's right! Olya says and winks at me.

Vadim stops. It is clear that he didn't expect this turn of events. Gravely, he weighs the options, first to himself and then aloud:

Okay, he says, On the one hand I know that the spoon will fall and so there's no way that I can lose the bet... it's a sure thing. But, *on the other hand*, if I *do* lose the bet... if I lose the bet then I'll have to spend my entire wedding night sober...!

Vadim looks to Boris for help, but he just shrugs his shoulders:

It's your wedding... your call, he says.

Come on come on! Olya pressures him, Are you in or not?

Vadim holds the heavy spoon up to the light, as if examining it for clues. Finally, he looks at Olya:

No, he says.

What?

It's too risky. I mean of course I know the spoon will fall... but if it doesn't it'll ruin my entire wedding...

Olya is smiling.

...And I can't chance it. The bet's off.

I sigh fully.

Olya beams.

Olga, who has been watching this whole scene, laughs at her husband and kisses him lightly on the large mole on his cheek.

Hey, says Boris trying to save the situation, There's no reason why we can't throw the spoon up anyway... you know without a bet. We can throw it up anyway just to see who would have lost the bet... in other words whether James would have had to dance, or whether Vadim would have had to stay sober.

Vadim is still holding the heavy spoon between his fingers and flicking it in his hand:

So you think this spoon won't fall? he says to me.

Honestly Vadim I don't know.

You don't?

No, I say, I don't.

Well I do...

And with that Vadim tosses the spoon into the air.

(39)

Like a bald eagle, the spoon sails higher and higher over the table, end over end, sailing toward the ceiling until it can go no higher. Like a miracle it stays suspended in the air, hanging over the table of wedding guests, who are staring at it as if at an apparition.

(40)

And then it falls. Straight down onto the table landing with a crash against my plate and catapulting my knife, which has been resting unsuspectingly on the side of my plate, over my shoulder onto the ground.

I am amazed.

Landlady is less amazed and simply holds out her hand for me to give her the dirty knife. For an instant she looks at Vadim reproachfully... but then, as if remembering that this is his day, she stops.

Realizing that his hypothesis has come true, Vadim looks at me sadly:

See, he says, In Russia *everything* falls.

(41)

After Landlady has taken the fallen knife to the kitchen, the conversation recedes, and I can begin to enjoy the food on my plate. The pork is good, the fish is good, the salads are green and good....

You know James, Vadim finally says, When you write your book about Russia...

What?

...When you do get around to writing your book about your experiences here...

What's he talking about? What book? Why does everyone think that I'm just itching to write a book about Russia?! Why are they so sure that I haven't got anything better to do... ?!

When that finally happens, have you thought about how your book is going to portray all of us?

Vadim... I have absolutely no intention of writing anything...

Have you given any thought to how you're going to show Russians?

Absolutely not...

Well you should start thinking about it right now. Before it's too late! You see, it seems to me that if you're not careful you may give people the wrong impression.

Of Russians?

That's right. You should be very conscientious... otherwise people may not understand you correctly. I mean, I know you... I know that you have nothing interesting to say, so I'll give you the benefit of the doubt. But strangers, people who haven't met you, won't be so forgiving. Especially Russians... they'll think you're just another ignorant foreigner. Or even worse: that you actually do know something!

Vadim I don't want...

Don't take this the wrong way!

Of course not.

I'm just trying to help you...

Of course.

It's just that people trust words they can see and touch more than those that they can't. Like it or not, people believe what they read.

Well that's *their* problem...!

And therefore you should avoid the cliches about Russia... you know the obligatory observations that all we do is drink... that we never smile... that we only have five names for our women... I mean, you should avoid the cheap and convenient themes like those.

Well I...

I mean there are some themes that are so obvious, so common, that it's best to leave them alone. Just think — you'd never think about writing something as hackneyed as... as... well, you'd never write about something as cliche as a love triangle, now would you? Of course not... because it's already been done a thousand times!

Well actually...

And besides... it's not true... you know, about us drinking, not smiling, and having only five names for women! It's not true at all! We smile *sometimes*!

I never said you didn't...

You've *implied* it.

No I haven't!

Okay then you've *insinuated* it.

If I did it's because I didn't mean to. Honestly! In fact, I find that Russians smile quite often. It's just that for some reason it tends to be in vain. Truthfully, I'd say that Russians don't smile any less than Americans... that we smile about the same!

Well I wouldn't go *that* far...

It's true! And as far as Russia only having five names for women... well...

Hey! says Olya, What's this about us having only five names?

Yeah! says Olga, We have a lot of names...

That's right, Vadim says, don't forget that we have Katya, Svetlana, and Marina!

I know but...

And Anya!

Yeah but...

And Nadya and Alla!

But Vadim... I'm not interested in... I mean you're missing the point. Even if I were to write something... I wouldn't be interested in making conclusions about Russians. Or Russia. It may look that way, but that's the last thing on my mind. For me the most important thing is...

Wait a minute! Are you trying to tell me that everything you've been telling us all this time... that everything you've been leading us to believe is nonsense? That all of it is... that it's all... *arbitrary*?

Well... yeah. And frivolous. You see, Vadim, for me the most important thing isn't the meaning. For me the most important thing is...

Hold on! Are you saying that all this time you've been misleading us?

I'm hardly the first...

You've been deceiving us?

Sort of. You see, for me the most important thing is...

I expect to be interrupted, but am not; gratefully, I finish my sentence:

...At this point in my life the most important thing is *irony*!

Vadim nods.

Olga nods.

Olya smiles and nods.

When Landlady comes back into the room she is holding a clean knife for me and two large bowls filled with white:

Could it be?! Boris says excitedly and then: It is!!!

Landlady puts one of the bowls on the table next to my new knife.

There it is James! Boris says to me, There's the dish I was telling you about!

Landlady nudges the pot closer to me:

It's my special recipe, she says proudly.

I've heard a lot about it, I say.

Try it... I'm sure you'll like it.

Looks good. What is it?

It's simple: garlic, mayonnaise, cheese...

Cheese?!

That's right... finely grated cheese, mashed with garlic and mayonnaise. It's everyone's favorite... no one can refuse!

Mom! Vadim says, James can't eat cheese... I've told you that a million times!

Oh a little bit won't hurt him...

No really I can't..., but Landlady has already put a heaping serving on my plate:

There you go..., she says, I'm sure you can try a little bit!

But I...!

I stop. Landlady is looking at me with the absolute best of intentions, and I cannot bring myself to offend her.

Disgusted, I look at the sickening mound of lactose on my plate:

Thanks, I lie

(42)

As everyone eats and drinks, our conversations twist and divide, weaving in and out like a drunk driver:

Boris and Vadim are talking about driving drunk. Landlady is explaining once again to Olga how she should peel potatoes. Olga Ivanovna is still railing against *them* — *they*, of course, being:

...Centrists and tax inspectors and rich foreigners in blue jeans and non-Muscovites with dark accents...

Here, Olya says, Let me help you...

What?

Let me take that off your plate...

And taking her fork she scrapes the pile of cheese onto her own plate.

Thanks, I say.

It's nothing... I love cheese.

And thanks for helping me get out of the bet... I owe you one.

No problem. Vadim and Boris are nice guys but sometimes they don't know the limits of their impulsiveness.

Olya sets my empty plate back in front of me and begins to pick at the cheese on her plate:

Try the *seledka*, she says, It's excellent.

I pick up a piece of dripping fish and place it on my plate:

Hey Olya? I say.

Yes?

I was just wondering...

About what?

About you.

Can you be more specific?

You know I was just wondering why you made the decision to leave America? This morning when I asked you, you just sort of mentioned pipes... but I know that there must have been more serious reasons.

Why do you ask?

It's a personal thing, really. You see, lately I've sort of been considering leaving Russia.

For a change of pace?

No, forever. You see, I've been here for almost six and a half years, and now I've begun to think that the time has come to leave.

Why?

I don't know. I guess I've changed. I'm a different person from the one that came here six and a half years ago.

You are?

Yes. Russia has changed me.

How so?

It's small things, inconsequential things: I gasp more than I ever did in America. I smile less. I've learned the difference between *high* and *tall*....

You have?

Yes, I say proudly, I have.

Can you explain it to me?

Of course... you see, something is *tall* if it's connected to the ground. If it's not, then it's *high*.

What about a mountain?

Well you see a mountain can be both... if you're talking about the whole mountain then it's *tall*. But if you're talking about just the top part...

...Then it's *high*!

I nod.

It's so simple!

That's right.

Here Olga takes a forkful of cheese and places it in her mouth:

How else have you changed? she says.

I don't know... in the beginning I was full of optimism, but now I've sort of lost hope.

In what?

In everything... Before I actually believed that I could measure the Russian Soul... I was convinced that I could find someone to love my last solar calculator... I even believed naively that there might be at least one person in this country — *one person!* — who would actually want my German dictionary...

Sounds like you really are ready to leave.

That's what I keep telling myself... but no matter how many times I decide to leave, I can't bring myself to do it. I'm still here.

You lack decisiveness, that's all. When the time is right, you'll leave. The fact that you haven't just means that there's still something you're looking for... it means that something deeper is keeping you.

Did you know when the time had come to leave America?

Of course. I knew it from the very beginning. As soon as I stepped off the plane.

What do you mean?

It's a long story.

I'd be interested in hearing it.

Well, I wouldn't want to get into it.

Why not?

I just wouldn't?

Was it something personal?

No.

Then why don't you want to tell me?

It wouldn't be polite.

What?

It wouldn't be in good taste for me to complain about a country that was gracious enough to welcome me, to host me for a year.

But...

It wouldn't be right for me to start listing all the things that I didn't like about it.

Why not?

It's impolite and unintelligent. I mean there's nothing worse than a person who goes to a foreign country, lives there, then comes back and dissects it.

But I'm asking you... I'm truly interested. You're the first Russian I've met who's lived in America and I'd be interested to hear what you have to say, what made you leave.

I don't want to talk about it.

Why?

Because I don't want to.

Why not? What's the big deal?

Well obviously for you it's not a big deal... but for me it is.

What is? I don't understand.

You see I hate those kinds of people who feel that they... the kind that write about cultures they themselves don't belong to. It's disgusting. There's nothing worse than a person who tries to explain something... as if he himself understands it. There's nothing worse than that!

Well, yeah but...!

Listening to Olya, I am overcome with respect and affection for her. And despite her objections, this respect and affection only strengthens my desire to hear her speak of America. Finally I resort to a different approach:

Olya..., I say.

Yes?

There's something I need to tell you...

What's that?

Olya...?

Yes?

I'm homesick, Olya.

What?

I miss my country.

I don't understand.

Please tell me why you didn't like the United States. At this point in my life it's something I need to hear.

But Olya is too polite:

No way, she says.

And so I try a different approach:

You see Olya, I lie, It's just that I can't understand why you would want to leave America to come back here?!

What do you mean?

Why would you possibly prefer Russia over America?

Well...

I mean given that this place is just one big dump.

Well it's not a dump, exactly...!

It's not?

No, it's not... And besides, you have problems, too...!

Problems? What problems?! In America we don't have problems...!

You don't... you don't have problems? I could spend an hour talking about all the problems in America...

Will you?

...Is that what you really want...?

It is!

You want me to tell you what I didn't like about America...?

That's right.

Are you sure you want to hear?

Absolutely.

Okay then I'll tell you...

Olya pauses to collect her thoughts:

...But afterward don't say I didn't first try to be intelligent and polite...

No no... of course not! You are intelligent and polite in any case!

And with that, Olya begins intelligently and politely to share her impressions. Intelligently and politely, she explains why she didn't like America:

(43)

First of all, she says, I should start by explaining what I was expecting when I left...

Okay.

You see for many many years we were constantly told about each of the problems in America... about the economic problems... about the political instability... and of course about all the social injustices and meteorological mishaps... I mean, we didn't put much stock in any of it... but nevertheless, that was the official version...

Okay...

Right. And then, suddenly, the iron curtain came up and we were flooded with a backlash of information saying the exact opposite: about how great everything was in America; how peaceful; how prosperous; how freely everybody could live... I mean, it was like the other side of absurd. Of course that wave also passed eventually and nowadays we understand that it's just as overstated... but for a few years *that* became the official line. Unofficially. And you see, in my case it was a question of timing; because just when all of this new propaganda was appearing... just when it seemed that a new truth had emerged... that America really was heaven on earth... at that exact instant...

Something happened?

Yeah. My pipe broke. In the middle of winter. And for me that was the last straw. I decided to leave. I applied for a tourist visa, by some act of God received it, and after borrowing a large sum of money from a relative, I bought a ticket to America.

It was brave of you.

Well of course I hadn't really thought the whole thing out... but how could I go wrong, right? I would be in America, and America was, after all, the best country on earth...!

I laugh.

A month later I was on the plane to the United States. During the flight I was ecstatic... no that's not the right word... I was *elated*! Here I was on a plane to happiness... here I was flying through the clouds to a new life... here I was eating as many free peanuts as my heart could stomach...!

You thought you were leaving forever?

I thought it was forever.

So then what happened?

So anyway I step off the plane and what do you think I see?

I don't know.

The first thing I see when I step off the plane is a smiling Customs officer. In uniform and just smiling away as if he's known me for thirty years... as if he's my very best friend and lifetime companion: Where are you going? he says. To America, I answer. What for? Tourist purposes only. Not to work? No, to study English. Can I ask you a question? Of course... I mean, you already are. Why aren't you smiling? *What*? Why aren't you smiling... this is America, and in America everyone smiles — whether they want to or not...!

Olya shivers from the recollection:

Can you imagine? He wouldn't let me into the country until I smiled!

It's strange.

Yeah, and what do you think I saw when I stepped outside the airport? Ten smiling porters. So I choose one and he smiles all the way to the hotel... all the way to reception... all the way to my room with my heavy luggage... and then he stops. He's panting like a dog and smiling at me. I'm looking at him: Thank you, I say but he doesn't leave. I think maybe I've said something wrong: Thank you, I say again but again he just stands there smiling like a jackass....

He wanted a tip.

Now I know that... but back then I didn't... back then I was...

well let's just say that when he finally left my room he wasn't smiling!

I laugh.

...Yeah, and so I get to my room and I think, At last! Now I'll have a drink and a smoke... and what do you think? That's right... I'm in a non-smoking room! Okay, I think, no problem... I'll just go downstairs. But when I go to the hotel bar it's closed. I go to another one and the bartender there asks for my identification... which I've left in my room and by the time I come back the same guy tells me they're closed now, that hotel rules forbid them to serve alcohol after one o'clock and that now it is exactly one-oh-two, and I say you've gotta be kidding... and he says no, there are cameras, and he would if he could... but he could lose his job... and so I go to another bar which is open and which doesn't mind if I buy a glass of vodka, but there the waitress can't make heads or tails of my passport, then can't understand when I try to order — nobody there speaks Russian, of course — and then to top it all off after serving me a few rounds she has the nerve to tell me that I've had enough to drink... that she could lose her job if she serves me any more, that the bar could lose its license...

As Olya is telling me this, I notice that she is losing all traces of her previous intelligence and politeness.

...For me it was like a slap in the face. I mean in Russia you can always reach some sort of agreement... you know... slip the bartender a few bills so that he'll serve you liquor, or to the policeman so that he'll let you off the hook, or to the Customs official so that he'll issue you a replacement visa... In Russia you have a chance to beat the system. But there you can't do that... If the bar closes at one o'clock it means it closes at one... and that's that. Our system is more humane.

More humane?... I've never thought of it that way!

...So those were my first impressions... But I was still optimistic... Just have a good night's sleep, I told myself, and everything will be better tomorrow... So the next morning I go to a park — you know, just to take a look at the people — and I'm horrified!

Why?

I'd always thought that Americans were a healthy and fit nation, but sitting there in the park I couldn't believe how many fat people I saw. I mean, really fat. Sickeningly fat. Grotesquely fat. Not to mention old people and handicapped. And all of them walking around the streets in broad daylight without being ashamed of it... without even trying to hide it...

Daylight? Hide it? Why would they be ashamed?

And the women! Fu! In your movies American women are always attractive — but the women I saw were plainer than prose! They're nothing compared to Russian women!

Olya stops as if remembering herself:

Should I continue? she says.

Please do...

Olya has taken a forkful of cheese from her plate and raised it to her lips. But just as she is about to put it into her mouth, she remembers something else that she didn't like about America, specifically, that...

...Americans are such big patriots!

I am?

Yeah, you are. For you everything is democracy this, democracy that... as if America is the only birthplace of democracy! As if America really is the best country in the world. You are too proud of yourselves. You love your country too much. You are too patriotic...!

Patriotic? Americans? Doesn't she realize that Russians are... that they're the ones... I mean I've never seen people trying so hard to be patriotic...!

...And this despite the fact that Americans don't read anything!

We don't?

No. I mean just go to any American's house and what will you see: a few detective novels, a bible, some how-to books if you're lucky... I don't think I saw a single piece of literature the whole time I was there that could challenge an eighth-grader in one of our schools.

Well, actually we read, but...

And another thing...

Why was I so insistent about her telling me all this? What was I thinking?

...Americans are so insulated... they don't have any clue about what's happening in other places of the world. Ask them to name five French actors... or ten British poets... Yeah right! Most of them can't even name their own poets...

Well, just because we don't read them, doesn't mean we can't *name* them...

...And you know what surprised me? Americans have absolutely no clue about Russia. None. I mean you can ask any schoolboy in Moscow and he'll tell you that today's rate of exchange is fifty-nine twenty (1USD=5920RUR)... any schoolgirl can tell you the price of Marlboros... But in America nobody knows anything about Russia... I mean they still think that bears run loose around the streets of Moscow!

Actually...!

...And what really starts getting to you after a while is all the questions... you know when they find out that you're from Russia they start asking you questions. Which wouldn't be so bad if it weren't the same question over and over and over and over again... I mean no matter who you talk to they always ask about the same thing... after a while you just feel like puking!

What do they ask about?

Take a guess... what do you think they ask about?

I don't know.

Go on, take a guess!

I really don't know.

You don't?

No I don't have any idea.

Gorbachev!

What?

That's right! No matter who you talk to they always ask about Gorbachev! *What ever happened to Gorbachev?* or *How about that Gorbachev?* or *Why don't you Russians like Gorbachev?* or *Is Gorbachev really as good as everybody says he is?...* you know, stupid questions like that...!

Really?

Yeah... after a year I got nauseous just hearing the word!

Olya stops as if remembering herself:

Should I continue? she asks.

By all means, I lie.

Olya moves to eat the forkful of cheese in front of her mouth, but again forgets:

But you know what was probably the most difficult thing about living there?

What?

Strangely enough, the little things, the things you can't explain.

Like what?

I don't know... people are people no matter where you go, I guess... but they think differently nevertheless... they have different norms for socializing...

I've noticed that too.

...They eat differently.

I agree.

...They drink differently.

You can say that again!

...They have different senses of humor...

Senses of humor?

I don't know Olya... I mean I'd agree with you that Russians and Americans eat and drink differently... that they have different norms for socializing... But as far as humor, I'd have to object!

It's true.

I'm not so sure. I think Russian and American humor is actually rather similar... I mean I can appreciate Russian humor.

But that's because you've lived here.

Not only.

Well all I know is that I lived in America for one year... eventually I learned to smile... but not once did I laugh!

Do you really think Russian humor is all that different from American?

Of course... In America your humor is — how should I put this? — stupid.

Stupid?

Well yeah... it's not witty like Russian humor... it's slapstick.

What do you mean *slapstick*?

You know... base, simplified humor.

Can you give me an example?

Well off the top of my head...

Something from an American movie or book?

Let me think...

Slapstick? Stupid?! How can she say that Russian humor is better? Doesn't she realize that American humor is the best in the world...?!

...I've got it, Olya says.

What?

I've thought of a good example.

Okay...?

Well for example, remember this morning at my apartment...

Of course.

Well remember how I offered my palm daintily and you didn't know what it meant and so you handed me your boot? Well, I didn't want to say anything at the time — I'd just met you — but *that's* a perfect example of stupid American humor.

I start to argue but can't; and so instead I offer a series of improbable excuses:

It was early in the morning... I was confused... I was worried... I needed to show the alienation of the situation...

But it is too late. Olga has made her point splendidly:

So, she says, after a year of people smiling at me, and asking me about Gorbachev, and when I began to miss Russian humor, when all of this finally got to me... I knew that America wasn't for me. And that's when I decided to leave.

Olya stops.

Did I answer your question? she asks.

Yes, I say, you did.

Good.

Olga smiles politely and puts the forkful of cheese into her mouth.

(44)

'...and policemen, and teenagers, and drug addicts...!'

(45)

Hey! Vadim says suddenly breaking into our conversation, Are you two talking about humor?

He has apparently become tired of his own conversation, and decided for some reason to join ours.

That's right, says Olya, I was just telling James here that every country has its own humor, that American jokes and Russian jokes are different.

Well that goes without saying, Vadim says, Everyone knows that the best jokes in the world are Russian!

You can't say that Vadim... American humor is every bit as intelligent... our jokes are just as funny as your anecdotes!

You're crazy! Vadim says.

No I'm not... In fact they're better!

They are not.

Are to... And I can prove it!

How can you prove that American humor is better than Russian?

Well, I mean I can't *prove* it exactly... but we can do an experiment...

What do you mean?

We'll do an experiment. I'll tell some American jokes and you can tell me some Russian ones. We'll go back and forth and see whose humor is more humorous.

It's a good idea.

Thanks.

But wait a minute... who'll be the judge, you know, who'll decide which jokes are funnier?

Well, I guess it's up to each person to decide for himself... that's why you should pick the very best joke that you know... your very favorite.

But there are so many!

Yes, but pick the best. The very best Russian joke... the most representative... and I'll do the same with an American joke.

You're on! Who should go first?

It's up to you Vadim... you're the groom!

Okay then I'll go first... I'll tell you my clever Russian joke... and then you can tell me your stupid American one!

Hah! We'll see whose joke is funnier...!

By now Boris and Olga have stopped their conversations and joined Olya to listen to Vadim and me being humorous.

Here goes! says Vadim, Is everyone ready?

Of course! we say.

Vadim clears his throat and begins to tell his favorite Russian joke:

(46)

'Okay,' Vadim says, 'Three friends — a Georgian, an impotent rabbit, and Ivan Susanin's mother-in-law — get drunk and are trying to find their way out of the woods... when suddenly they are run over by a Mercedes and taken to a doctor whose wife is having an affair with a golden fish...'

Vadim stops:

Have you heard this one? he says.

Of course, I say.

You have?

Of course. Many times.

Oh, well in that case we won't count it. I'll tell you my second-favorite....

Wait!!! everyone else screams, *We* haven't heard it...

You haven't?

No, we haven't.

And so Vadim tells them the joke. Everyone laughs.

After he is finished, he looks at me:

Your turn, he says.

All right, I say, here is a typical American joke...

Vadim moves closer to me to hear better.

I start my joke:

'How many electricians does it take to change a lightbulb?' I ask.

Vadim looks at me:

I don't know, he says, How many?

'One!' I laugh, 'Just one!'

But the others look at me blankly.

'Just one!' I repeat.

Olya chuckles politely:

Vadim clears his throat.

I stop:

Well, in America it's funny...

Hey Vadim! Boris prompts, Let's hear another Russian joke.

Okay!

Vadim looks at me:

Are you ready for another anecdote? he asks.

Sure, I say.

All right then, here goes...!

Vadim pauses seriously and then begins his second-favorite Russian joke:

'Once upon a time there lived a farmer, his wife, and two children. This farmer was an honest and hard-working man and every day he toiled from sunup to sundown to feed his family and provide a roof over their heads. The farmer had always dreamed about having a large brick house and so one day he started to build it, working at night under the light of the moon. Piece by piece he built his sturdy brick house: first the sturdy brick foundation, then the sturdy brick walls, then the sturdy brick roof. Story by story, he worked to build the house until one day — ten years after he had started — it was finally built. All the neighbors came to look at his house and admire it. And the man was *proud* that he had built such a sturdy brick house. But then, not long after the house was completed, an earthquake shook it down, killing his wife and leaving him to raise his two children by himself. The man was devastated but not deterred. He worked especially hard to sell his crops, scrimped and saved to buy new materials for a wood house. By the light of the moon the man began to build his wood house. Every night he worked. Piece by piece he built his reliable wood house: first the reliable wood foundation, then the reliable wood walls, then the reliable wood roof. For fifteen years he worked to build the house and then one day it was finally built. All the neighbors came to look at his house and to approve of it, and the man himself was *happy* that he had built such a reliable wood house. But then, not long after it was completed, a fire ravaged the house, burning it to the ground, and taking one of his two children. By now the man was older, his strength had been expended on better days. But still, the man was not discouraged. Ardently, he began to build a modest straw hut. Working by the light of the moon, he built his modest straw hut: first the modest straw foundation, then the modest straw walls, then the modest straw roof. For twenty years he built and built until one day it was finally finished. By now the man was too frail to move. Still, looking at his modest hut, he was *satisfied*. But then, not long after it was completed, a strong wind came along and blew the hut to the ground, killing his last surviving child. By now the man was too old to move, too blind to see, and there were no children or relatives to take care of him. And so the man went out to an open field, lay down in the grass and died under the open sky.'

Here Vadim stops.

There is a hush in the room. Finally, it is Boris who breaks the silence:

I know an even funnier one! he says.

But it is too late — the room has exploded with laughter. Olga is laughing. Landlady is laughing. Boris is laughing. Even Olga Ivanovna is smiling at Vadim's joke. Vadim, seeing that his joke has been appreciated, is laughing so hard that tears are rolling down his eyes:

Ohh... that's funny! he says.

Wait a minute! I say, Wait a damn minute here... That's it? That's the joke?

You don't get it?

Get what? Where's the punchline?

That's it! That's the punchline... You see, after everything, after all his efforts the farmer dies!

It's not funny Vadim.

What do you mean *not funny*?

It's not funny... it's tragic... look Olya, explain to him... tell him it's not funny!

But Olya is too gripped by laughter to listen to me.

Vadim...! You of all people should understand how unfunny that joke is!

James, do you really mean to say that you don't get the joke?

No I don't!

Well that just goes to show that you haven't lived in Russia long enough to understand the things that Russians can laugh at!

But I...!

When the laughter has subsided Boris begins to tell his joke:

'Two Jews are buying *salo* from an Azerbaijani...!'

But I'm not listening to him. I'm still trying to see the humor in Vadim's joke.

After struggling and striving his entire life, the farmer loses three houses, his wife, and his two children... and then, after all of that, he dies! In Russia that's funny*?*

A burst of laughter tells me that Boris has finished his joke. I look at Vadim:

I don't like your joke, I say. Tell me another one. Tell me one that *I'll* think is funny.

Okay... let me think... well, I heard one the other day...!

Vadim clears his throat again and begins to tell another Russian joke:

'Okay,' he says, 'Four men are flying in an airplane — a German, a Frenchman, an American, and, of course, a Russian...'

Vadim stops:

Have you heard this one? he asks.

Not so far....

Good....

'So anyway. Four men are flying in an airplane. Here are their reactions to the following situations:

1) A beautiful stewardess comes walking down the aisle:

The German:	"Excuse me miss... did you know that I'm *unhappily* married?"
The American:	"Wanna be my seventy-*ninth*?"
The Frenchman:	"Let us go, my love, to the aft lavatory..."
The Russian:	"Hey you, got any more of those free peanuts?"

2) Ordering drinks:

Frenchman: “I’ll have your most expensive cognac.”
German: “I’ll have your thickest beer.”
American: “Money.”
Russian: “Yes, thank you.”

3) The plane begins to fall:

American: “My business...! Who’ll take care of my business when I’m gone?!”
German: “I knew I should have bought *economy* class...!”
Frenchman: “Where’d that stewardess go...?”
Russian: “*Oi, blya...*”

4) In heaven:

German (to American): “With a little tidying up this place could be quite nice...”
American (to Russian): “Yeah, with the right foreign investment, it could really be something...”
Russian (to Frenchman): “Maybe so... But *I’d* never immigrate here!”

Frenchman: (to himself): “This isn’t heaven... all the women are American!”

5) In heaven (back-up variant):

German again (to American): “With a little tidying up this place could be quite nice...!”
Russian (interrupting): “Don’t look at *me*, you son-of-a-bitch!”

American (to Russian): “See! I *told* you I had a soul!” ’

12 — 1807

Here Vadim stops:

So how do you like it?

It's cute... I mean no one doubts that Russians have a unique ability to laugh at themselves... and others.

That's right.

But you didn't finish the joke... I mean what about the Frenchman? What did the Frenchman say in heaven?

I don't remember...

You forgot?

Yeah... but I'm sure it was something funny.

I nod.

So do you think you can do better than my jokes?

Vadim... I will tell you an American joke that is so funny you will fall down to the floor from laughter!

It's that funny?

It's that funny.

Funnier than the joke about the farmer?

Well... yes, funnier. It's my favorite joke... And I think it sums up the American approach to humor. Are you ready for it?

Do you think we'll like it?

I'll be surprised if you don't.

Well then we're ready!

Okay here goes...

I start to speak and then remember something:

...Oh, and pay special attention to the end — that's the funniest part!

Everybody nods. And when I see that they are listening attentively I begin my favorite American joke:

(47)

'A busdriver is driving his bus down the street when a drunk man staggers on, fumbles with his fare, and sits right behind him. The busdriver doesn't pay any attention to him and drives on. But after a while he hears the drunk mumbling to himself: "You know what the problem is nowadays?" the drunk is mumbling, "The problem is that nobody has a sense of humor! That's right: everybody's so serious all the time... nobody can appreciate humor anymore...!" The busdriver listens to the drunk go on about this for a while and being in a good frame of mind himself, decides to engage him in his conversation: "You know," says the busdriver, "You're not exactly right about that. After all there are a lot of people who can find humor in any situation. In fact, I'll show you..." The drunk, of course, is very interested. "Just watch," the busdriver says, "what I say to the next beautiful woman who boards the bus..." The bus moves on and at the next stop a woman gets on. She is paying her fare. The busdriver looks at her. The woman looks back. The busdriver smiles. "Tickle your ass with a feather?" he asks. The woman can't believe what she's heard. "What did you say?" she says, "What did you say?" But without missing a beat the busdriver looks at her again and says, "Particularly nice weather?" "Oh," says the woman, "Yes it is... the weather today is just fine!" When the woman has walked past them, the busdriver looks back at the drunk: "So how'd you like my joke?" "It's great!" says the drunk, "Tickle your ass with a feather... Particularly nice weather! It's great!" The busdriver smiles: "So you see... you shouldn't say that nobody has a sense of humor. You're wrong assuming that people have forgotten how to laugh." The drunk thinks for a minute and then says "Let me try it! Let me try it! I want to do it too!" But here the busdriver turns serious, "Don't even think of it," he says, "You're too drunk... you'll say the wrong thing." But the drunk is adamant: "No I won't... I can do it too... Tickle your ass with a feather... Particularly nice weather... Let me try!" The busdriver tries to argue with the drunk but then finally relents. "All right," he says, "I'll let you try... but first I'll show you one more time. Now pay close attention to what I say so that you don't screw it up." And at the next stop, when an even more beautiful woman boards the bus, the busdriver asks her the same question: "Tickle your ass with a feather?" and when in outrage she asks him to repeat himself he follows with, "Particularly nice weather?" And again the drunk is beside himself with glee. "My turn! My turn!" he says, but the busdriver looks at him seriously. "Repeat after me... Tickle your ass with a feather... Particularly nice weather... Tickle your ass with a feather... Particularly nice weather... Got it?" The drunk is bursting with excitement. "Sure

I've got it: Tickle your ass with a feather... Particularly nice weather... Tickle your ass with a feather... Particularly nice weather... I'm ready!" The busdriver looks at him cautiously: "You sure you won't mix it up?" "Not a chance!" says the drunk, "Tickle your ass with a feather... Particularly nice weather... I've got it!" The busdriver looks at the drunk seriously: "All right then," he says, "the next woman is yours..." '

The sound of a doorbell interrupts me.

What's that?

Someone's at the door.

Are you expecting anyone?

No.

Me either.

Dutifully, Landlady gets up from her seat and goes to open the door, snapping the locks on the heavy door.

Well...! says Vadim turning back to me, Don't leave us in suspense... how does the joke end?

And so I continue:

'All right so anyway the busdriver pulls up to the next stop and a beautiful woman gets on. She's extremely beautiful... and sophisticated. She's standing and counting out her change. The drunk, meanwhile, has sort of stood up and is staggering in the aisle waiting for the woman to board. But he is stone drunk and can barely stand up by himself. The woman steps up into the bus and is paying her fare when suddenly she notices that the drunk man is staring at her. She tries to look away but feels that the man is watching her. Trying to ignore him, she pays her fare and steps forward... but the drunk man blocks her way. The woman moves to the right to step by him, but the drunk slumps that way too. For a few awkward moments the two of them — the woman and the drunk — stand there looking at each other in silence. But then, finally, when it seems that he has forgotten what to say, the drunk man opens his mouth to speak. At first his words evade him, but then finally they come out all at once. As the woman looks at him in surprise, the drunk man says...'

Vadim!

What?

Vadim, says Landlady, Some friends are here to see you...

Friends? I'm not expecting any friends.

So what did he say... what did the drunk man say?

Vadim!

When we look up, we can see that Landlady is standing by the entrance to the room next to five large men. They are wearing dark coats. Their heads are closely shaved.

What the hell! Vadim says.

Silently the five men walk into the room. The first of them has a scar on his cheek. The second on his forehead. The third on his neck. The fourth is scarless, but with a mashed nose and boxed ears. The four men walk into the room and stand around the table above the wedding guests. Each of them is husky and dense. But it is the fifth man who does the speaking:

Remember us? he says.

Who the hell...?

But Vadim's protests are in vain: it is Tuesday; the knife has already fallen; the moment has come for atonement...

In other words: you have arrived.

(48)

Remember us? you say to Vadim, Or have you forgotten your friends?

Vadim doesn't answer.

Vadim, you say, I asked you a question...

Hey guys...! Boris says and moves to stand up... but before he can, you swing violently at him. With a loud crunch your fist crushes the side of his face and sends his body falling to the floor next to the table. Like a sack of potatoes it crumples heavily onto a shriek of women's voices.

You think we're joking around here? you say to the rest of the guests, Is that what you all think?

No one dares to speak.

Do you think this is a big joke?!

Boris is lying on the floor, groaning and holding his head in his arms. Seeing him, Landlady moves to help him. But before she can, one of your men grabs her by the shoulder... and she slaps him.

Amazed, he stands motionless for a second and then, with the full force of his open hand, slaps her across the face, sending her — all sixty-six years of her — to the ground.

Again the women shriek.

Sit down! you scream at Vadim who has stood up, Sit down!

He sits.

That's enough! you yell at the wedding guests, That'll be enough!

The room becomes silent. Only Boris can be heard convulsing on the ground. Landlady has half-raised herself onto one knee, and is groping blindly for her chair.

Help her up! you tell your men and one of them walks over to Landlady and pulls her onto the chair. Her wrinkled cheek is red where she has just been struck. Dazed, she is looking blankly at the wall across from her.

Now listen up, everybody... We're just paying a friendly visit to the groom here. We're just here to ask a few questions, that's all. All we want is to get a few answers...

Look, Vadim says timidly, maybe we can go into the other room...

Shut up! you yell, You just sit your ass right where you are and shut the hell up!

Vadim looks down to the ground.

Is that clear? you say bending down into Vadim's face.

He nods.

Is that clear? you say to everyone else.

They answer with silence.

Now Vadim... there are some questions that it's time you answer... Look at me, dammit, when I'm talking to you!

Vadim looks up into your eyes and when he does you can see how frightened he really is:

Now Vadim I'm going to ask you some questions and you are going to answer them... do you understand?

Vadim nods.

I said DO YOU UNDERSTAND?!

I understand... I understand... I just... I just don't know what you want from me...

What we want? What do you think we want Vadim?

I don't know.

Well, think... think real hard... what could it possibly be that we might want?

I don't have it... I'm doing my best but I can't get it to you now... You have to believe me!

No Vadim I can't believe you... That's not my job, to believe people... There are people in this world who are paid to believe people... I have a different job.

Vadim is looking up at you and you slide your heavy palm over the back of his head, stroking it tenderly:

No Vadim, you say, I'm going to ask you some questions and I want you to give me some straight answers, understand?

Yes.

Now are you going to answer my questions like a good boy or are you going to give me the same answers you've been giving my client for the last two years?

I don't know.

You don't know?

I can only say the truth...!

Well that's a good start...

Vadim is sitting nervously in his chair and as you speak you look down at him:

...So tell me the truth Vadim: Did you take the money?

I...

Vadim the question is very simple: Did you take the money?

It's not that simple...

Did you take the money Vadim?

I borrowed some money, yes that's right.

Vadim you're not listening to my question. The question was: Did you take the money?

Here you stop stroking the back of Vadim's head:

Well... yes, I mean... yes I took the money.

You took the money?

Yes, I did.

Good. Now we're getting somewhere... Now my second question is as follows... Are you ready?

Yes.

Are you ready for the second question?

Yes.

You took the money, right?

Well... I...

Vadim did you take the money?!

Yes... I took the money...

Are you sure you took the money? It seems to me like you're not real sure... that there's some doubt in your mind... Think real hard... Did you take the money or not?

I took the money.

You took the money?

Yes.

So when are you going to give it back?

As soon as I can... I promise.

No no no no no... That's not an answer. Listen to the question again: When are you going to give back the money that you took.

As soon as...

NO! you scream and slam your heavy fist against the table; the wedding guests jump in their seats. Vadim is looking up at you, scared, and you tilt his chin with your hand:

That's not an answer... Now let's start from the very beginning... Vadim did you take the money?

Yes.

You took the money?

Yes.

When are you going to give it back?

I'm doing everything I can! I've tried to do everything I can...!

Whoa whoa whoa... Vadim... you're getting away from the issue... I asked you a simple question:

I know, but...

Now did I ask you a question or didn't I?

You did?

That's right. And do you remember what question I asked you?

You asked me when I'm going to give the money back.

That's right Vadim when are you going to give the money back?

I can't tell you... I'm trying!

You can't tell me when you're going to give back the money?

No I can't.

You can't tell me when you're going to give the money back?

No.

Then why did you take the money in the first place?

What?

Why Vadim did you take the money if you can't tell me when you're going to give it back?

I don't know... I don't know...

Okay, then let's start once again from the very beginning...

Here you stroke the top of Vadim's head like a loved one:

Vadim, you say, Did you take the money?

(49)

By now you are standing so close to Vadim's face that his eyes cross to look at you.

Yes I took the money... I took the money and I promise that I'll do everything I can to give it back.

When?

I can't tell you when.

Then how can you promise?

I do. I promise. I just need time... I just need some time to get the money...

No Vadim. You've had enough time. Time is money. And so my question to you is very simple: When are you going to give the money back?

I don't know!

You don't know?

No, I don't know... I'm trying to be honest with you... I'm not lying to you!

Vadim you've been lying for the last two years... And that's why I'm here. You see, you've been taking advantage of my client's kind heart... You've been using the generosity of his soul... And that's why he's come to me... you see, I'm not quite as nice.

Vadim says nothing.

Do you understand me?

Yes.

What did you say?

I said I understand.

Good. Now where were we? Oh yes, you were telling me when you're going to give back the money...?

(50)

I was?

You weren't?

I don't know.

You don't know?

No... I don't...!

Vadim looks like he is about to cry.

Then why did you take the money? Why Vadim did you take the damn money in the first place if you can't tell me when you're going to give it back?

I don't know...!

What *do* you know?!

Hey! says one of your men — he is right on cue — Our boy here doesn't seem to be too cooperative!

Yeah, says another, He's not answering the questions.

But I...!

Let's take the son-of-a-bitch outside...

No! Olga screams.

But Vadim puts his hand on hers:

It's all right, he says.

What did you say! one of your men yells at Vadim, You think everything's all right? Did you hear what he said? He said everything is all right! To me that means he has no intention of giving the money back... why should he give the money back if everything is *all right*?

Let's take the son-of-a-bitch outside!

Damn, your men are well-trained! Now their professionalism is showing... the timing... the teamwork... the use of repetition for dramatic effect...!

But here you object:

Now don't be so brash boys, you lie, I'm sure that Vadim here is just a bit confused... he's not a bad guy, are you Vadim?

No.

That's right... he just needs to think a little bit about the situation and then he'll be more cooperative.

Vadim says nothing.

He's not a bad guy, but he just needs to do some thinking in order to best understand the situation at hand.

Vadim says nothing.

Isn't that right, Vadim?

Yes.

What?

I said yes.

Good.

The room is silent.

Hey Vadim? you say.

Yes?

Are you thinking...?

(51)

Eventually, your attention begins to wander. Words flow over you, but at this point they have ceased to interest you. Vadim is straining to justify himself, and as he does you nod without listening.

How long has it been? Twenty minutes... twenty-five...? By now it's been a good thirty minutes and this character — what's his name... Vadim? — hasn't said one worthwhile thing! Over the last thirty-five minutes he hasn't lied. Hasn't promised the impossible. In fact, he hasn't done anything at all to incite you or to hold your attention...

I know I know, Vadim says, But I can't...!

...To be honest you expected much more from this encounter... you thought it would be a challenge... that maybe it would be different from all the others you've been witness to... as if it might provide you with a new perspective, something unlike anything else you've seen... You thought that it would be unique... or even better: convincing...!

I told you... I'm trying... I just need time... Give me another chance...!

...What a let down!...

Please...!

How much longer will this last? Hasn't it already been forty minutes? Hasn't it been forty-five? ...And besides, maybe he's had enough? Maybe fifty minutes really is enough to get the point across? Maybe this would be a convenient time to leave? Maybe this is the lull you've been waiting for? Maybe now's the excuse you've needed to bring this whole thing to an end?...

But I...!

Yeah, he's gotten the message... time to wrap this up... time to call it a day. Time to conclude this scene with your standard ending... the one that you have become infamous for.

And so, fighting back a yawn, you interrupt him in mid-word:

(52)

Look Vadim..., you say , I hope you don't take all of this personally. I have a job to do just like anyone... I mean just imagine that you were in my place. What would you do? Can you answer me that? What would you do if you were wearing my shoes?

I don't know...

How would you feel if I owed *you* money? Would you like it if I'd been leading you around by the nose for two years? Would you respect me if that were the case? Would you?

No.

That's right... so I'm just asking you to try and be a little more understanding... You're not the only person in this world who has problems... I think you need to try and put yourself into the position of other people more often....

Here you stop. You have spoken these words so often that they have been inscribed into your mind like an inscription. And so, once again, you start in:

Let's speak hypothetically, you begin, Of course I realize it's difficult for us to crawl out of our narrow points of view... but let's try...

Vadim is staring up at you, and as he does you drive your point home with a voice that is teeming with certainty:

Let's speak hypothetically — Vadim are you with me on this? you are? Good! — Let's speak hypothetically. In other words, let's say...

(53)

Let's say your name is Olga. That's right — let's say your name is Olga. Of course it could have been any one of the five names that Russians give their daughters, but as long as we've come this far let's say it's *Olga*.

Home for you is a small apartment with one bedroom where you and your new husband will sleep. It is not a big bedroom, but it's the only one aside from the one where your mother-in-law lives and which you avoid like a serious conversation. There is a livingroom of course but it is cramped, especially when the table is brought out for special occasions. Especially when it is cluttered with chairs from other rooms, other apartments, other floors of your twelve-story building.

You actually have another apartment, but it is being rented out for one-thirtieth — *or was it one-sixtieth?* — its real value. The money, though small, comes in handy. Still, it cannot make the small rooms any larger...

And then one day you have guests over. Special people on a special day. And on this special day one of the special people gets so drunk that he passes out on your floor. Of course he can't go home in his condition — he can barely stand to be rolled over, let alone carried past the broken elevator up four flights of stairs. And it is decided that he should stay the night. Here. In your small apartment.

But where? Where should you put him? Where should he be put?

The livingroom is full. Your bedroom has only one bed. The kitchen is cold with roaches. Even the bathroom — the last resort — is currently and constantly occupied by the rest of your special guests, those who are still able to celebrate. Of course there's your mother-in-law's room, but unfortunately it is being used by your mother-in-law who has gone to bed long ago.

And so the question is as follows: Where do you put this special guest who has passed out on your floor?

Where will you put him?

What can you suggest?

What would *you* do in this situation?

(54)

I don't know what I would do, Vadim says.

You don't? you ask.

No... but I promise I'll try to be more understanding of the situation.

You will?

Yes I will.

That's good Vadim. That's all we want... You know I'm happy that we had a chance to talk like this. I feel like I know you better. I feel like we understand each other. What do you think?

I understand you, Vadim says.

You do?

Yes. I understand completely.

That's good.

You stroke the back of Vadim's head once more and then take your hand away.

Vadim lets out a relieved sigh.

Boris, meanwhile, has risen to a sitting position on the floor and is holding his jaw:

Look buddy, you say to him and offer your wieldy hand.

Boris winces away from it.

Look, you repeat, I'm sorry about that... but you have to understand how it must have looked when I came in and you started getting up at me... I hope there're no hard feelings?

Boris grunts.

Good. That's good that you won't remember us badly. And as far as grandma over there... well, she sort of asked for it, now didn't she?

Bastards! Boris mutters.

But you don't have time for niceties:

Let's go! you say and your men rush to the door ahead of you. Olga fumbles with the locks and finally after some difficulty, opens it.

One by one, your men leave the apartment. Quickly, you follow them. The stairwell is cold and from the outside you listen with a satisfied grin as the apartment door is locked from the inside.

(55)

As soon as the door is closed, Vadim rushes over to Landlady:

Are you okay? he says and holds his mother's face in his hands.

I'm fine, she says, I'm fine... I've lived through worse things than those thugs... and I'll live through *them*, too!

Almost in tears, Vadim embraces her:

I'm so sorry, he is saying, I'm so sorry!

Hey! says Olga, Bring me a cold rag!

She is leaning over Boris and pressing his bleeding cut together. When the rag has been handed to her, she pours some alcohol on it and begins to dab at the wound lightly:

How do you feel? she says.

Aside from my bloated scrotum I think I'm okay.

Olga nods and again dabs at his wound, this time firmly.

TSSSSSS!!!!! Boris hisses.

Trust me, Olga says, I'm almost a doctor.

Boris looks at her strangely:

Almost a doctor? he says — his lips curling up in a painful grin.

Olga laughs.

Seeing Boris grin, the entire wedding party lets out one collective sigh of relief.

Landlady is okay. Boris is okay. The metal door is tightly locked and everybody is okay!

There is a moment of grateful silence, and then the room explodes:

(56)

Quick! Somebody call the police before they get away... somebody call the police... We all saw what they looked like... the first one had a scar on his cheek... the second had a scar on his forehead... or was it the other way around? And which one of them was the leader? Probably the one who did all the talking... the one with the angelic face and brass knuckles! But what if they're waiting outside? No, of course we shouldn't call the police. We shouldn't call the police because this is Russia. But can you believe they almost took Vadim outside? And did you see the punch that Boris faced? And can you believe... can you believe they had the nerve to slap Olga Mikhailovna? At her age! Can you imagine? But wait a minute... how did they know that today was the wedding... or was it a coincidence? How did they get the address of this twelve-story building? Who gave it to them? And how did they get into the apartment in the first place? Who let them through the heavy metal door? It must have been Olga Mikhailovna. That's right... but why did she let them in? She must have thought that they really were Vadim's friends. But does Vadim have friends like that? He must if Olga Mikhailovna let them into her own apartment...!

For the next half hour the apartment is abuzz with people running from room to room. Some phoning their relatives with the details. Some standing and gesticulating wildly and trading exclamations with other people who are standing and gesticulating wildly. Some guests approaching Boris to ask how he feels. Some approaching Landlady.

In fact, in the ensuing chaos, there is only one person sitting apart from the rest, as if the others are afraid of him: Vadim.

Seeing this, I walk up to him:

Are you all right?

You and your stupid American questions! Do I look all right?

I don't know how to take this and so Vadim helps me:

It was a joke... I'm fine.

Were you expecting this? I ask him.

In general yes... but not tonight.

I nod.

...No way was I expecting this to happen tonight.

And so what now? I ask.

What do you mean?

What do we do now?

You sit down... that's what. You sit down and finish your *seledka*.

Is he crazy? After the scene we just had... he expects me to eat seledka? After all of that he wants to continue the wedding? Doesn't he realize that everyone's mood has been thrown out of balance? Their concentration has been betrayed. Doesn't he understand that nobody will be able to focus on the scene at hand... that it will require at least ten pages to get the party re-started?

Maybe we should call off the celebration? I say, Maybe we should leave you alone?

Not a chance... I'm not going to let those thugs spoil my wedding... I'm not going to let them ruin the second-most important day of my life!

Well yeah, but maybe we can come back another time... you know when the atmosphere is more conducive...

James! Vadim says.

I stop.

Sit down! This celebration will end... over my dead body!

(57)

And so once again Boris stands up:

Everybody! Attention everybody!!! Can I ask you to return to your seats, please!!

The wedding guests are still talking wildly.

ATTENTION!!! Boris says, PLEASE TAKE YOUR SEATS... THIS WEDDING ISN'T OVER YET...!!!

Gradually, the people return to their seats, at first continuing to speak as before, but eventually becoming quiet enough to hear Vadim's voice, which is still trembling slightly:

My friends..., he begins, I know that we've just been witness to an unexpected, unjustified, and extremely unpleasant scene...

The guests mumble in agreement.

...I realize that the atmosphere we worked so hard to create... has been rudely violated by what took place here minutes ago...

The guests mumble again.

...I realize that many of you are considering leaving...

Everybody is silent.

...But now I'm turning to you with a humble request... now I'm asking you to forget about everything you just saw... What happened tonight *had* to happen... it was inevitable. I expected it. James expected it. The entire English alphabet expected it. But now it is over and so I ask you to please put it out of your mind. My wedding party is now in your hands... either you can forgive me for the scene that happened and we can move on...

Vadim stops importantly:

...Or we can call an end to the whole thing and go home.

The guests are silent.

The choice is yours, Vadim says, Either you can give up now... I won't hold it against you... or we can continue all the way to *Я*....

(58)

After a moment of hesitation our decision is made:

(59)

I don't know about the rest of you..., says one guest, but *I'm* staying!

Me too! says another.

As if on cue, Boris grabs a bottle of vodka from the table:

Hey, he says, There's one thing I can't figure out: Are we drinking or aren't we?!?

The guests cheer and begin to fill their glasses with vodka.

You're damn right we're drinking! says one.

Yeah, says another, We're not Americans!!

Yeah! I say.

But what about a toast? somebody says, Who's going to say the toast?

Let's have James say the toast!

Why me...?

Yeah! somebody says, Say a toast James!

I can't... Vadim, you know I don't know how to say toasts!

What! says Boris, What do you mean you don't know how? Have your six and a half years been completely lost on you?

No, but...

Have you spent the last six and a half years in vain?

...Well no...

Then make a toast!

But...!

The other guests are looking at me. Encouragingly. Sympathetically. Meticulously.

But how can I make this toast? Any other toast, maybe... but this one... this particular toast will be one of the most important so far. This toast is crucial because it has to serve as a transition. After the unpleasant scene with Vadim's friends, this toast will have to re-establish the mood! It will have to persuade everyone to forget... !

I'll make a toast! a woman's voice says and each of us looks around to see who it is.

Who could be brave enough to make a toast at this critical point?

I'll make the toast, says Olga Ivanovna, since our American over here doesn't seem to know how...

Olga Ivanovna? Vadim says, Yes yes... please do make a toast! What are you drinking?

I'll have what you're having!

Vadim pours Olga Ivanovna's cup half-full with vodka. But she looks at him severely:

I *said* I'll have what *you're* having!

Vadim blushes and fills her glass to the rim.

Olga Ivanovna waits for the liquid to settle in her glass, then speaks up confidently:

'I don't know what kind of toast you're expecting from me... but if you're expecting me to praise the newlyweds... if you're expecting my toast to be some sort of convenient transition, then you're sorely mistaken! I have no intention of toasting these two... I want to make a toast to the groom's mother... Olga Mikhailovna!'

Landlady, who has just come in from the kitchen, smiles modestly at the mention of her name:

Me? she says, Why me?

I'll tell you why..., Olga Ivanovna says, I'll tell you exactly why:

'You see *you* Olga Mikhailovna are a true hero!'

Landlady waves off the suggestion, but Olga Ivanovna continues:

'I've known this woman here for thirty years and she is a true hero. It's no secret that during her short lifetime she has survived war, starvation, dictatorship, communism, stagnation, *perestroika*, a putsch, rebellion, inflation, the failure of reforms, and *now* deep into her sixty-sixth year, she can say that she has suffered through what would have broken a lesser person... on this night, she has managed to survive *gravity*!'

Everybody nods.

'But that's not why I want to drink to her. What is most remarkable about her is that no matter what happens she is always there for *other* people. When my husband left me it was she who let me cry on her shoulder; and when he died it was she who came over to console me just in case. And during the most difficult time — when my daughter was sick... when she was incurably ill...'

The room is silent.

'...And when my daughter died it was Olga Mikhailovna who helped me get through it. And all this despite the fact that she herself has suffered through so much. All this despite the fact that her life has been far from easy. But no matter what she has been through, she is always there to help other people. And so I want to tell you two newlyweds... you Vadim should give thanks everyday that you have such a mother... and you Olga should do your best to be a worthy daughter-in-law because she deserves nothing less!'

The two nod.

The other guests wait for Olga Ivanovna to continue, but she does not. Instead she sits back heavily in her chair.

To Olga Mikhailovna! Boris says.

To my favorite mother-in-law! Olga seconds.

To Landlady, I say, My second aunt!

Vadim is sitting with his glass of vodka in his hand. It looks as if tears are forming in his eyes once again. Finally he speaks up:

To the woman, he says, who despite the disposable containers... is still my mother!

(60)

After Olga Ivanovna's toast, the party slowly gets back on track. The conversation revives itself. The scene with the five unexpected guests comes up less and less until eventually the issue stops being an issue at all.

Landlady, after acknowledging the toast in her honor, has gone back to serving the guests, and now she is shuffling back and forth between the livingroom and the kitchen with plates and bowls:

So how was it? she says looking at my empty plate.

How was what? I say.

My special dish? How'd you like it?

I didn't actually... I mean well, yes... Thank you... I enjoyed it tremendously... it was the most delicious lactose I've ever eaten.

I knew you'd like it... here have some more...

And Landlady slops another heaping portion of cheese on my plate:

But...!

I knew you couldn't refuse my special recipe.

But I can't... it's delicious, really!... but I already ate so much the first time!

You can make room for another portion... after all, this is a wedding!

Again Landlady is looking at me, and again I thank her:

Thank you, I say.

Sitting at the table I look back and forth at the conversations enveloping me: Boris and Olya are talking about gauze. Vadim and Olga Ivanovna are discussing the number eleven. And in the center of it all, as silent as soup, sits Olga, who is now — *at last it's beginning to sink in!* — hopelessly married.

What can she be thinking at this moment? About her husband? About me? Or can it be that she's already married enough to have forgotten? Can it be that I was wrong in thinking that her silence means more than it really does?

But Olga's face seems peaceful. Her expression looks no different than if we were celebrating my wedding. Even now she seems as if she knew that everything would end up right here, right now, exactly like this. *Could it be that she never really doubted it? Could it be that she never once thought that we... that she and I... that the two of us...?*

Hey..., I say, ... Why so quiet?

Olga seems to barely notice my question, lazily turns her head to look at me:

What am I supposed to do, she answers, Cry all night?

I don't understand.

You don't?

No.

Well, it's not important.

Vadim is already involved in a heated explanation concerning the color yellow, and after looking at him, Olya turns back to me with a devious smile and a hushed tone:

So why didn't you say a toast while you had the chance?

What?

You know you've been 'promising' to say a toast... but when you were given the chance you refused.

Yeah well the timing wasn't right. After the unpleasant scene and all... you know it wouldn't have been a good transition.

You're such a liar.

What?!

I'm not sure if you lie more to yourself or to others.

I don't lie, I say.

Yes James you do.

Well that doesn't prove anything.

It doesn't prove anything... but it means the world. You're not going to make any toast tonight... and you know it!

Oh yeah...?

But before I can finish my sentence Vadim has interrupted me:

What's that I see?

Where?

On your plate... cheese!

What? Oh, this! Landlady offered me seconds.

Here, he says, Give it to me.

And looking around to see that Landlady isn't watching he quickly shovels the cheese from my plate onto his own.

Thanks, I say.

No problem.

Vadim takes a big bite of the cheese and then looks at me:

You know, he says, Olga Ivanovna and I were just talking and I was telling her about your search for the eleven yellow words... about how you've been trying to find them.

Actually I haven't been trying to find them... I've been waiting for them to find me.

How's that? Olga Ivanovna asks, How do you *wait* for words?

Well, I just sort of live. I mean that's all I do, I live. And while I do that, they sort of come by themselves.

That's right, Vadim says, And now he just has the eleventh word left. But it's the hardest to find, isn't it James?

That's right. It's the hardest.

What's the hardest? Boris says.

I was just telling James that I was telling Olga Ivanovna that for the last six and a half years he's been trying to find eleven Russian words. He's found all of them except one.

All of them?

All except one.

Except one *what*? Olya jumps in.

Except one of the eleven words.

What eleven words?

Well, Vadim repeats, like I was saying I was just mentioning to Boris that I was telling James that I was explaining to Olga Ivanovna about how he — James, that is — has been trying to find eleven Russian words.

And he's found all of them but one?

That's right.

What's right? Landlady asks.

But thankfully Vadim doesn't hear her:

And so James has been actively not seeking these words. Instead he has spent the majority of his time living. In other words, he has been waiting for the words to come themselves.

Everybody nods.

But why am I telling this story? Let's have James tell us in his own words... you know, about what the German man told him during the flight over.

Yeah James... tell us what the German said to you!

I tell them.

Wow! they say, And where was he going?

I tell them.

...And how would you characterize his forearms?

I tell them.

...And tell us again how he described the eleventh word!

I clear my throat:

'...But it is the eleventh word that is most elusive because you already know it. Unlike the others, it will change and be changed until it will seem to be hopelessly beyond your grasp...'

What?

What does that mean *change and be changed*?

Nobody knows. That's all he told James. He said the word would change and be changed.

Like the weather? Boris says.

No Boris, Vadim says, Not like the weather. That's not tricky. You see it should be something beautiful and surprising... that's why it's the most difficult.

Maybe we can help him find the word! Olya says.

Yeah, says Boris, Maybe as a group we'll come up with something..!

What did the German man say again? What were his exact words?

Once again I repeat myself:

'...But it is the eleventh word that is most elusive because you already know it. Unlike the others, it will change and be changed until it will seem to be hopelessly beyond your grasp...'

And that's all he said?

Yes that's all.

Damn Germans!

Well let's think... what could it be?

Do you have any ideas, James?

No.

None?

Honestly, I try not to think about it... you see, if I think about it I won't be able to find it. I just need to wait... I just need to read carefully and patiently, in other words, I have to force myself to live long enough to...

I know what we should do! says Vadim, We should take the German man's clue, examine it piece by piece, and see if we can help James find the eleventh word...

Now you're talking! the crowd answers.

...Let's look at his clue carefully...

Yeah! the crowd seconds, *Carefully*!

...The German man said that the eleventh yellow word is *the most elusive*.

That's right! the crowd cheers.

...So what is elusive? What are some things that can be considered elusive?

Well for one, Boris says, democracy is elusive....

That's right, says Olya, as is Love....

...And danger!

...And don't forget about logic!

The crowd cheers again.

That's all fine and well, Vadim says, but the German man said that the eleventh yellow word is the most elusive because *he already knew it*... So maybe we should look at those words that James already knew when he came to Russia. In other words maybe the eleventh word isn't one that was waiting for him here... maybe it was one that he already knew?

Now you're on to something!

So James... what other words did you know before you came to Russia?

What?

What Russian words did you know before arriving into the windowless airport?

Well that's the thing: I didn't know any.

You had to know some?

Not really... although now that you mention it... Well yeah, I guess I did know a few... I mean I knew the three that had already come into English from Russian. The ones I told you about earlier. You know, like all Americans I knew words such as *vodka*, and *kiosk*, and, of course the most important Russian word ever to enter the English language...

Olga Ivanovna is looking at me with interest.

What? the crowd prompts, What is the most important word to enter the English language? What Russian words did you know?

Nothing, I say, Just those two: *vodka* and *kiosk*.

Vodka and *kiosk*?

That's right.

Vodka and *kiosk*!

Right.

You only knew two Russian words before coming here?

Well yes.

Those are no good. Vodka doesn't change! Vodka is vodka!

That's right. And kiosks aren't beyond your grasp — there's one on every corner.

So the word has to be something else.

You know, says Olya, Maybe we've got this all wrong... I mean maybe we're going at this whole question from the wrong angle. Maybe the important thing is that the eleventh word is *unlike all the others.*

So...? the crowd reacts.

So... if we know what the other yellow words are, then by deductive reasoning we can arrive at the word that is *unlike* them. In other words, we should try to find a word that is different in some way from all the others that you've already found.

Yeah! says the crowd, Tell us the words you've found James! Which ten yellow words do you already know?

One by one I list them. As I do, my fellow wedding guests do not laugh; nor do their ears bleed; in turn, their hearts do not burn, and their eyes are not caused to moisten. Passionately they listen, soothingly they nod, but even when I have finished saying absolutely nothing, my words are still in vain:

Have I been wrong all these years? Could it be that these ten words mean nothing to other people? Could it be that they have value for me alone?

So those are the ten words?

That's right.

It's strange....

Why?

I was expecting something a bit more... how should I say this... universal!

But no! These are *the ten yellow words! No matter what other people say! These are* my *ten yellow words!*

Sorry, I lie.

It's not important... it's not important... the important thing is that those are the ten words that James found... and so those are the words we have to work with.

Well what do they have in common?

Nothing.

Yeah, unfortunately they're absolutely different.

I know! says Boris, I know what they have in common!

What?

They're all Russian! I mean, all the words he listed were Russian. So maybe that means that the eleventh yellow word isn't Russian at all... maybe it's a foreign word.

Good thinking! the crowd agrees.

Way to go! someone else seconds.

Yeah, says Vadim, I'm no linguist or anything... but I'm sure that each of those ten words were Russian!

So, Olya says, maybe the word he needs is from another language?

Yeah, but which one? the crowd answers.

Hey James which foreign words do you know? Which non-Russian words do you like?

There are so many...

What's your favorite?

My favorite non-Russian word?

Yes... there has to be a foreign word that you rely on constantly, like a crutch?

Well, I like the word *naive*. I use it an awful lot. It's French.

No no no! says Vadim, It can't be! James didn't come to Russia to learn French words!

He didn't?

No, he didn't.

Well okay then what about English?

He didn't come to Russia to learn English, either!

Actually, I say, I've learned a lot about English from being in Russia...

See! So which *English* words do you know?

There are so many...!

Try to pick one!

Well I can't just... I mean off the top of my head...!

Just list the first English words that occur to you!

Yeah... just tell us the words that mean the most to you!

But it's so difficult... well, all right... for example there's *finally*, *hopeless*, *inevitable*...

Good...

...*Dutifully, instead*...

Okay...!

...I tend to *make my way* alot...

You sure do!

...Then of course there's *understand, besides, after all, wistful*...

´Atta Boy!

...*eventually, which, silence, really, beaming, flustered, but, violently, desperately, reluctant, disapprovingly*...

Whoa! says Vadim, Not so fast... keep in mind that we can't understand you when you speak fast like that!

Yeah, says Boris, Just because you're familiar with those words doesn't mean that we are!

Sorry.

It's okay... please continue...

...*relentless*...

Wait a minute! says Olya.

I stop.

Wait a minute...! We have it all wrong again. The eleventh yellow word can't be an English word!

Why?

Because that wouldn't be *beyond his grasp*. Remember? How can it be beyond his grasp if he knows it without thinking!

She's right.

Yeah, it can't be an English word...

So what does that leave us?

Yeah, what do we have left?

German!

German?!?

And so over the next couple minutes I list every German word I know. Then Italian. Then Spanish:

...and *tequila*, and...

But wait a minute... this isn't Spain!

Finally, Olya interrupts me:

Hey! she says, I have an idea of what the word might be!

You do? everyone says and turns to her.

I'm not sure, but... it seems to me that the most important part of the clue is that the word *changes and is changed...*

Okay...?

Well, let's remember back to when James arrived. The year was 1991. It was before the putsch. Before Gorbachev became ex-president. Before currency reforms and advertisements for pantyhose. I mean let's not forget that he arrived long before people started using lubricated condoms or combing their hair on the right side...

We remember... we remember! the crowd shudders.

So that's it!

That's what?

That's the word that *changes and is changed*!

What is?

The word is *Russia*! I mean, just think... since James has been here Russia has changed greatly. The last six years have brought one change after another.

That's right... and then it brought even more change.

That's right... but these changes are for the worst!

Maybe so... that's a different question entirely. But from a purely linguistic standpoint we can say without a doubt that Russia has changed tremendously during the last six and a half years.

Okay, granted it *changed*. What about it *being changed*? What does that mean?

I don't know... maybe it means that the country has on the one hand changed *by itself*. And on the other hand it has been changed because of *outside influences*.

Like it has changed actively and passively? Internally and from without? Deliberately and against its will?

Something like that!

What do you think, James?

I don't know. Anything's possible.

Possible?!

Yes, possible.

Why is it only possible?

I don't know... it's just possible, that's all.

But you yourself say that in this world everything is *probable*!

Yeah James! Why do you think *Russia* isn't the eleventh yellow word?

Well because...

Hey! says Vadim, You know what else just occurred to me? You know what else it might be... I mean if we're talking about things changing and being changed?

Vadim has interrupted me before I can answer:

What? everyone asks.

Vadim looks around the table at each of the faces surrounding him:

The *ruble*! he says.

What!

The *ruble*.

The ruble?

No, the *ruble*. Just think: it changes... in other words its form has changed from old to new notes... remember 1993?

How can we forget!

...And soon it will change again... you know when they drop the zeros from the banknotes!

They're dropping the zeros?

You haven't heard? Inflation has been banished for good. And so by the beginning of next month prices will be in *rubles*... instead of *thousands*.

Everyone smiles at the news.

...So, says Vadim, Maybe that's the word? Maybe the word is *ruble*?

It's possible..., I say.

But what about it *being changed*? the crowd demands.

That's simple. Like any currency it is changed in money exchanges! You know, for dollars!

Hey that's good! everyone says.

That's real good! someone else says, What do you think James? Do you think the eleventh yellow word is *ruble*?

I don't know. Maybe.

Maybe?! they ask.

Yeah, I answer, Maybe.

The crowd roars:

We did it!

We helped James find the eleventh yellow word!

Uraah!!! The eleventh yellow word is *Russia* and *ruble*!

Uraah!!!

But..., I say.

Uraah!!! Uraah!!!

But there's one small problem....

Slowly the cheering subsides.

You've all forgotten one thing... those two words can't be the eleventh... for one simple reason.

What do you mean?

There's one obvious reason why these two words can't be the word I've been looking for all this time.

Why not? Both words are *beyond your grasp*... they both *change and are changed*... and you had to have *already known them* before you talked to the German man!

That's true... but you all are forgetting one important fact.

What's that?

Assuming that you are right... that the eleventh yellow word really is *Russia* and *ruble*, then why is it that they are written... why are these words written using English letters...?

The guests look at me in silence.

...Why, I say, aren't these words written in Russian?

(61)

If you want my opinion, Olga Ivanovna says, *all* of your answers are wrong!

What?

If you ask me, it's obvious what the eleventh yellow word is...

Everybody waits expectantly.

...The eleventh yellow word, she says, is *dusha*!

Dusha?

That's right. It changes... it is changed... and it is hopelessly beyond your reach...!

Hold on..., says Boris, Why do you say it's beyond his reach?

It's beyond his reach because ever since he's been here he's been trying to measure the Russian Soul... and has failed miserably.

He's been miserably measuring the Russian Soul?

That's right.

That's crazy... everyone knows that it's not for the mind to understand Russia! Everyone knows that the Russian Soul can't be measured!

You're not exactly right, says Olga Ivanovna. The Russian Soul can be measured... if you take time to learn the *soul of Russia*.

What do you mean Olga Ivanovna?

I'll explain...

Olga Ivanovna stops to look at me:

James, she asks, What have you read?

Excuse me? I answer.

What do you read? she asks again.

In general or specifically? I answer.

Both, she asks.

I don't know..., I answer.

You have to read something...?

Well yes... different authors.

Like what?

Well like Kharms.

Okay, and what else?

And Tolstoy...

Tolstoy! Olya interrupts, Fu!!!

What do you mean *fu*?

Olya looks at me as if I have offered her something bad to eat:

I hate Tolstoy! He's a terrible writer!

Olga Ivanovna tries to continue her questioning, but I interrupt her:

Wait a minute, I turn to Olya, You mean to say that the novelist Lev Tolstoy is a terrible writer?

That's right.

Why?

Because he was mean to his wife.

What?

He was mean to his wife and so he was a terrible writer.

Have you read his works?

I read *War and Peace*. We had to read it in school. It was long.

Did you read *Anna Karenina*?

No.

Why not?

Because he was mean to his wife.

Well look Olya... You're not being fair to *Anna Karenina*... You're not being fair to Tolstoy as a writer...

Why should I be fair to him when he didn't even treat his wife fairly?

Olya you shouldn't confuse Tolstoy the author with Tolstoy the person... in other words, the life of the author with his works. You have to keep them separate. A piece of literature is self-contained. You shouldn't judge it by the life its *author* leads.

Why not?

Because they're unrelated.

They're the same. You can't write about that which you don't know. Authors don't live in a vacuum, you know!

No, unfortunately they don't. It would be better, of course, if they could. Nevertheless, a character in a story is just a character. The author is a person. Just like you... Just like me...

Here I expect that somebody will object, but nobody does. Enheartened by this, I continue:

You know let's take an example...

An example? Olya says, Haven't we had enough examples for one night?

Yes yes... but let's look at one more just in case.

Olya sighs.

I continue:

Let's say, I admit, that I decide to write a story about Russia — the usual bit, you know, about a delicate foreigner who comes to Russia to find the Russian Soul and instead learns to drink vodka — let's say I were to write a story like that...

But you're not a good writer! Olga says.

I know I know... this is just to make my point! Anyway, let's say I write my little story about Russia and finish it...

Okay?

...Right. So I finish my book, take it to the publishers, and on my way back home — trying to cross the street in front of the metro — right there in broad daylight... I'm run over by an ambulance. Boom! I'm dead. My book gets published with a posthumous note about my life in Russia... people feel sorry for me, buy my book quicker than a condom, and in no time at all it becomes a bestseller!

A bestseller?

This is all hypothetical, of course...

Okay okay. Your book is a bestseller. You're dead. What about the ambulance?

What ambulance! The ambulance crushes my chest like a cardboard box and doesn't even stop to pick me up. The end.

I don't get where you're going...?

Right. Now let's imagine a different scenario! Let's say I publish the book and then, instead of getting run over by an ambulance, I leave for America where I open a quaint flower shop specializing in roses....

Roses?

Yes, roses. So in this case my book is published, but I'm still alive. I'm still breathing. I'm still walking around.

In other words you're alive?

Exactly! And that's bad enough... but the worst part is that I've left Russia for America. And in the book there is a pre-posthumous note that says that the author of this book has left Russia and is currently selling flowers in America. In *this* case nobody will take my book seriously because number one I'm selling flowers, number two I'm in America, and number three...

I get it! I see! I think what you're trying to say is that...

...What I'm saying is that I don't want to be run over by an ambulance, and so I'll be damned if I write any books about Russia!

(62)

I stop triumphantly. But my triumph does not last long:

...And number *three*..., Olga Ivanovna says, ...Your conversation reminds me of eleven-year-olds trying to discuss poetry. I mean are you two listening to yourselves? Neither of you is making a bit of sense!

We stop.

Two toasts and already *ambulances... roses... bestsellers...*!

Olya looks at me embarrassedly and I do my best to reassure her:

Don't worry, I whisper, When I write my book I'll make sure to leave that last scene out!

Olya nods gratefully.

Olga Ivanovna clears her throat:

As I was saying, she says, before that digression into publishers and ambulances... In order to understand the power of Russian words you have to read Russian literature. This isn't America, you know. Here we have a proud literary tradition.

What do you mean?

Well in America what's the most important thing? What's the thing that Americans treasure more than anything else?

Toilet paper, I say.

No.

Marlboros, Vadim offers.

No.

Marriage? Olga suggests.

Close... All right I'll tell you... In America the most important thing is Democracy. That's all you hear about... democracy this... democracy that! Well in Russia we've never had democracy... and so we have literature instead!

I don't understand?

You know what they say... when in Rome do as the Romans do. In other words, when you are in doubt you should look to see what everyone else is doing and follow their lead. You should look to see what everyone else is doing and do as they do.

But Olga Ivanovna... this isn't Rome!

That's right, it isn't. This is Russia... and in Russia we *read*.

I don't get it?

If you can't understand the Russian Soul it's because you

haven't understood the soul of Russia... in other words, you haven't done justice to our literature.

Olga Ivanovna! Vadim objects, James reads a lot. He's read all the classic Russian authors.

Oh yeah... like what?

Well, I say, Like Kharms and Tolstoy and...

Kharms isn't a classic. And Tolstoy was mean to his wife!

But...!

What about Pushkin?

Pushkin?

Yeah, Alexander Sergeivich Pushkin. The greatest Russian poet ever...

I know who Pushkin is!

I'm sure you do. But what have you read by him?

I'm sure James has read many things by Pushkin! Vadim says.

You know it's funny...

James...! Vadim says, You have read Pushkin, haven't you?!

Well, I repeat, It's funny...

AHA!!! Olga Ivanovna yells, You've never read Pushkin!

Well no I haven't. I've been meaning to, but...

You've never read Pushkin!

Well I've wanted to for some time but I've never...!

You've read Kharms and Tolstoy but you've never read Pushkin?!

Well no...

What do you mean you've never read Pushkin? Vadim says, What about the citation about getting married... you know about needing happiness for two people? Where'd that come from if you haven't read anything of his?

I saw it in the metro.

In the metro?

Yes, next to one of those new anti-abortion posters. I thought it might come in handy so I jotted it down... But I've never actually bothered to read an entire work of Pushkin's.

Olga Ivanovna points at me significantly:

See! she says, That's my point exactly: you, James, don't read Pushkin. And because you don't read Pushkin, you can't understand our literature. And because you can't understand Russian literature, you can't understand the Russian Soul. And because you can't understand the Russian Soul, it remains beyond your grasp. And because the Russian Soul is beyond your grasp, I suggest that it is the eleventh yellow word.

I stare at her blankly.

In other words, she says, the eleventh word is *dusha* because it is beyond your grasp because you don't read Pushkin.

Hey! Boris says, Are you guys talking about Tolstoy?

Tolstoy?

Until now Boris has been watching our discussion of literature without interest, and now he is eagerly grabbing his chance to say something literary:

You know, he says, I heard something funny about Tolstoy — of course I'm talking about the *novelist* Lev Tolstoy. I read somewhere that Tolstoy was Russian *on his mother's side*!

Yeah, says Olga Ivanovna, A lot of people have been saying that lately.

Really? I say, You mean to tell me that the great novelist Lev Tolstoy was Russian only on his mother's side?

You've never heard that? Olga Ivanovna asks in amazement.

No, I say, I've never heard that!

No one ever told you that Tolstoy was Russian on his mother's side?

Never.

How long have you been in Russia?

I remind her.

Six and a half years? And you've never once heard it said that Tolstoy was Russian on his mother's side?!?

Well, yeah... I mean maybe I heard it somewhere...

It can't be that a person living in Russia for six and a half years didn't once hear that...!

Well I guess... I mean I probably have heard it, but I just didn't pay attention... you know...

You didn't know that Tolstoy was Russian on his mother's side?

I can't say that I didn't know... I mean I always suspected...!

NONSENSE!!!

What?

It's all nonsense, says Olga Ivanovna, Tolstoy was Russian on his father's side too!

I say nothing.

All those people who maintain that Tolstoy was Russian on his mother's side... they're only giving half of the story...

But you said...?

Hey! says Boris, You wanna know something else I read about Tolstoy?

Wait a minute... I must have missed something... Was Tolstoy Russian on his mother's side? Or on his father's side? Or was it both? Or neither?

That's right, says Boris, I read something else interesting about Tolstoy!

The rest of us wait for him to continue and so he does:

We're all familiar with *Anna Karenina*, right?

The guests are silent.

All of us sitting here *are* familiar with *Anna Karenina*, aren't we?

Actually, Olga admits, To be honest, I've never read it...

Well yeah yeah... me either. But nevertheless we're *familiar* with it...

Everybody nods.

Well anyway, the other day I was reading an article... you know about Tolstoy, and it said that while Tolstoy was still alive he had a practice of writing letters to his friends — it was some sort of hobby, I guess — and in one of his letters he wrote something about a book that he was then working on. He said something to the effect of 'Now I'm going back to work on my boring and mediocre book *Anna Karenina*. All I want to do is get it out of the way so that I can move on to something else.'

Boris stops.

Can you imagine?! he says, While he was in the middle of writing *Anna Karenina* he was already looking ahead? In the middle of his story he was so sick of it that he just wanted for it to be over as soon as possible... Can you imagine that?!

Can I imagine? Can I imagine?! At this point in my life I can imagine nothing better!!!

(63)

And so Vadim stands up:

Enough of this discussion about literature! he says.

I breathe a sigh of relief. The other guests grumble their agreement. And with that our discussion of Russian literature ends.

Vadim continues:

Let's not forget that we're drinking...!

Vadim stops to wait for the cheers to die down:

...This will be our third toast. Thank you Boris for making the first toast... and you Olga Ivanovna for making the second...

Everyone begins to fill their glasses with alcohol.

...And now I'd like to take my turn. And for this third toast I'd like to pronounce one of my favorites... It's a toast that I heard a long long time ago — in fact, right after I'd finally given up on our government — and once I heard the toast I swore that I would remember it for the rest of my life!

Vadim takes his wife's hand in his own as he pronounces the toast:

'Once upon a time there lived a farmer...'

No!!! I scream, We've already heard this one... everybody dies. Everybody dies. *Everybody* dies!

Relax James, Vadim says, This is a different farmer.

I sit back down.

The other guests are looking at me sympathetically.

Sorry, I say.

And so Vadim continues his toast:

'Once upon a time there lived a farmer who had four young daughters. The first one was intelligent, but not very polite. The second was polite but not very intelligent. The third was neither intelligent nor polite... but as beautiful as freshly baked bread...'

Vadim stops to kiss his bride on her forehead:

'But it was the fourth daughter that the farmer loved most: she was neither intelligent nor polite... but, at the same time, as ugly as an uninvited guest...'

Vadim stops to make sure that everyone is following his story. Of course each of the guests has heard this particular toast several times, but listens with rapture anyway:

'So anyway, the farmer had four daughters. And it was time to marry them off. The eldest daughter, because she was intelligent, was wed to a tax inspector and together they had five children — only one of which was declared officially — a handsome summer cottage outside Moscow, and of course a small apartment. The second daughter was polite but not intelligent and so she was given away to a trolleybus driver and together *they* had three children — all daughters — whom they named Olga, Olga, and Olga, respectively. The third daughter, though neither intelligent nor polite, was beautiful and so she married a foreigner and together they lived like clockwork, although they never did have children — largely because the husband insisted on using condoms — until one day while trying to cross the Garden Ring against the light he was run over by an ambulance.'

Vadim laughs.

Hey Vadim! Boris yells out, Did the ambulance stop to pick *him* up?

I don't know... but I doubt it.

Boris laughs.

And Vadim continues:

'...So anyway each of the daughters was married off except for the fourth one who was unintelligent, impolite, and far from beautiful. The farmer searched for a long time for someone to marry his daughter. But no matter how hard he tried, he couldn't find anyone to take her. Then finally, it occurred to him. *It would be ideal!* he thought. *It would be a match made in the heavens!* And to his delight, when he offered his daughter to the prospective groom, his offer was immediately accepted...'

Vadim pauses:

'...and to this day Mr. and Mrs. Gorbachev live in blissful matrimony!'

The guests laugh.

Vadim laughs even louder:

'And so,' he says dramatically, 'for this toast — our third —

I'd like to raise our glasses... *To Women!*'

The men grunt their approval.

'To all of the women at this table... each of you are special in your own way. And so I'd like for us to raise our glasses to your uniqueness, your individuality, and your intricate and complex personalities!'

The men sitting around the table raise their glasses.

To women! Vadim repeats.

To women!! we confirm.

Happily, we touch our glasses and down our vodka.

(64)

After Vadim's toast, the conversation takes off like an unstranded Aeroflot flight. Vadim is doing some explaining about the color purple. Olga is listening intently. Olga Ivanovna has finally explained that by *we* — not to be confused with *they* — she means everyone seated at this table. Boris, using his newfound authority, is making claims to have successfully measured the Russian Soul:

The Russian Soul, he has read, measures exactly seventy-eight cubic inches.

Olya tells us how much a soul of that size would cost in America.

I thank them both.

Landlady, who has not stopped for a minute to enjoy the atmosphere, comes into the room periodically to place cheese on my plate...

...And just as periodically, I spoon it off.

(65)

But by now the emphasis has shifted. Whereas before our conversation was interspersed with toasts, now our toasts are interspersed with conversation.

Shot after shot, we swallow the occasion. Slowly, my reactions slow. The vodka takes hold, and my mind relaxes.

As the night progresses, we learn each other's opinions of the Gorbachevs. We compare literary tastes. Eventually, we learn that none of my fellow guests has read *Anna Karenina*. But that each of them has known at least one foreigner who was maimed by an ambulance.

With time our discussion becomes softer and less defined, like a piece of black bread in vodka. The room warms. The light dulls. Things that are square seem rounded. Things that are rounded seem round.

Then Olya stands up:

I want to make a toast! she says.

Olya is holding a half-glass of champagne that she hasn't finished from the last toast.

Easy for her to say! She's drinking champagne... and she's not even drinking that... she's half-drinking it!

I'd like to make a toast, Olya says.

The other guests fill their glasses.

And when she has made her toast we drink it down.

Then Boris makes another toast... and we drink it down too.

We have barely swallowed our vodka when Landlady walks into the room with a pan of food:

Is it my turn to make a toast? she asks.

Of course! we lie.

Okay then, she says and makes a toast.

And we drink it down....

(66)

By now, the toasts are coming faster and faster:

> 'To the future of the newlyweds!'
> (vodka)
> 'To the bride's mother!'
> (vodka)
> 'To the irrigation of Uzbekistan!'
> (vodka)
> 'To Russian humor!'
> (French cognac)
> 'To American humor!'
> (Russian vodka)

'To our health!'
(red wine)

'To us!'

'To *them*!'

'To whom it may concern!'

'To be or not to be!'

'To my mind!'

'To understand why Russians don't smile!'

'To be continued...!'

(67)

With each toast, the party livens. One after another we down the alcohol to consummate the idea expressed.

And as I drink I feel the alcohol backing up in my throat as it has thousands of times before. But by now I am experienced: I have made sure to layer my insides with oil. I have made sure to flush the vodka with water. I have made sure to eat pickles with each swallowed dose.

Once, when I am in mid-swallow, Boris looks at me, amazed:

You drink like a Russian! he says.

Thanks, I gasp.

No really... I'm not just saying that... You really know how to drink!

Thanks, I say.

Boris takes my glass to pour me another shot.

Hey! says Olya, What are you doing?

I'm offering James some more vodka.

What for?

What do you mean *what for*? So he can celebrate Vadim's wedding like everyone else.

But he's not *everyone else*!

He's not?

No he's not.

I'm not?

No James, you're not... remember!

Oh knock it off! Boris says, James here can hold his liquor! Isn't that right, James?

I nod.

See?

No I don't see! All I see is that for the last hour James has been matching you shot for shot.

So?

So... you're Russian.

So...?!

So, aren't you afraid that he's just drinking in deference to you... that he really doesn't like vodka?

Of course not. All normal people like vodka!

But he's not normal.

He's not?

No he's not... he's a...

I know I know... I'm a foreigner!

That's right! says Olya, And foreigners don't know how to drink... no offense, James...

None taken.

But here Boris objects:

You're no foreigner, he says.

I'm not?

No you're not.

He's not?

No he's not... he speaks Russian... he reads poetry... he likes vodka... any way you look at it, he's '*ours*.'

I blush from the compliment.

...But if you still have some doubts, Olya, about whether his drinking is sincere then why don't we ask him?

Okay, says Olya, Let's ask him.

Okay, says Boris, Let's ask him!

Okay...

Olya turns to me:

Hey James, she says, You don't like vodka, do you?

But before I can answer Boris objects again:

What kind of a question is that?! he scolds Olya, You're phrasing it all wrong. Here let me try...!

Boris turns to me:

Hey James, he says, You *do* like vodka, *don't* you?

(68)

When I was younger I had a friend who would give his dog beer. The dog would lap wildly at the foam and the rest of us would laugh and laugh because it's funny to see a dog drinking beer.

(69)

Of course, I say.

Boris smiles broadly and pours me another shot of vodka.

By now each person has pronounced at least one toast — many have already said their second. And each time a toast comes up, the others implore me to contribute. With each shot of vodka, I feel my body relaxing, becoming weaker. Like it or not, my defenses are coming down. I have forgotten my fears. I can ignore my inhibitions.

Hey! I yell out suddenly.

The other guests look at me, surprised.

I just remembered... I just remembered a piece of English poetry! I just remembered a poem that I like a lot... some people wouldn't consider it serious poetry, I suppose, but I like it anyway...!

And when the other guests are listening attentively, I recite it with feeling:

Fuzzy Wuzzy was a bear..., I say.

But Boris interrupts me:

Not so fast... not so fast... I want to see if I can understand it myself!

And so once again I begin to recite my poem — this time just as fast... but louder:

Fuzzy Wuzzy was a bear.
Fuzzy Wuzzy had no hair.
Fuzzy Wuzzy wasn't fuzzy, was he?

But again nobody can understand.

Do you have any idea what he said? Boris says.

Not a clue, says Vadim, When he speaks fast like that I don't understand a thing...

Yeah me either... but it sounds beautiful.

It is! I say and translate the poem for them:

You see, I explain, Fuzzy Wuzzy used to be a bear... but because he doesn't have any hair we can't really continue to call him *fuzzy*, now can we!

There is an awkward silence. Then, suddenly, my fellow wedding guests bristle, as if I have insulted them:

Maybe so, Boris says, Maybe so... but you just wait and see... one of these days Russia will rise up... one of these days Russia will be a superpower again!

(70)

And with that the conversation turns — as it always does — to politics.

But even when someone suggests drinking to Mikhail Gorbachev, I refuse to make a toast.

C'mon James, someone says, Make a toast for us!

Yeah, says someone else, You're in Russia now and now you have to play by our rules!

But I refuse.

Go on James, says Olga, Make a toast! We're all interested in what you have to tell us!

But again I refuse.

Why is she baiting me? Could it be that she really wants me to make a toast? Or is she just trying to prove something? Can it be that she knows me that well? I myself don't even know whether I'll make a toast or not! But for some reason she seems to know...!

And each time I refuse, someone else assumes the toast for me.

At some point Vadim comes out with a guitar:

Here! he says to Boris, Play us something.

Boris grabs the guitar and twists the strings until they are more or less in tune. Instinctively, he fingers an A-minor chord:

What should I play? he says.
Something about women, Vadim answers.
And so Boris starts into his favorite song about women:

How many women fair,
How many tender names!
But only one of them can touch you,
Disturbing even rest and sleep,
When you're standing in love so deep....

As he sings, the rest of the guests sing along in drunken voices that sound even better than they would have had they been sober. Those who have forgotten the words hum along to the melody. Those who have forgotten the melody mouth the words. Those who know neither — in other words, me — sit and smile happily at the makeshift chorus:

I love you, Russia,
Our Dear Russia,
Unspent power,
Unseen sadness.

Sweepingly boundless,
Without end,
For centuries beyond the reach,
Of foreigners with yardsticks.

Many times *they* tested you,
For Russia to be or not to be,
Many times they tried and tried,
To kill the Russian Soul in you.

But you can't, I know,
Be broken or intimidated,
You are dear to me, my homeland,
For your unconditional nature....

(71)

One after another, Boris plays traditional Russian folk songs and the other guests sing along drunkenly, until the room is louder than lactose. In fact I am the only one sitting quietly. And when Boris notices this he pokes over at me:

Why so quiet James?

Oh no reason... I just don't know the songs you're singing.

What songs *do* you know?

Well, can you play anything by Vysotsky?

Can I...? Can I play anything by Vysotsky?! Who do you think you're talking to?!

And Boris squeezes the guitar a little harder and slams his fist against the strings. The guitar hollers out in pain:

> If your friend suddenly turns out to be,
> Neither a friend nor an acquaintance,
> If you can't make out whether he,
> Is 'good' or 'very good' then take him at once to...

Here, I join in singing with all my voice words that I memorized years before:

> ...My neighbor's wedding banquet...

Vadim, who has been sitting relatively quiet, suddenly joins in in a voice that would be horrifying if it weren't a Vysotsky song:

> ...My neighbor drank another liter,
> Then sat with glazed eyes
> And wanted me to sing.
> *Did I think the drinks were free, or something?!*

In time, all of us are doing our best to sing Vysotsky:

> ...And then came the fish soup and dried bread,
> And then someone grabbed the groom,

Boris strums the guitar a final time as we sing the very last words of our song:

It isn't night yet... *It isn't night yet.*

(72)

After we have finished singing Vysotsky, Boris plays his favorite Russian folk songs one after another:

My Wound will Never Heal

Snow, Snow, and Even More Snow!

For Some Reason I'm in Love with a Gypsy Girl

Moscow City Lights (Burn Brighter in Moscow)

Your Naive Jewish Eyes

And one after another we do our best to accompany him with words.

And when his Russian has been exhausted, Boris turns to songs he knows in English. Specifically, the wedding party — in four-part solidarity — begins to sing Negro spirituals:

We Shall Overcome

Swing Low, Sweet Chariot

Sometimes I Feel Like a Motherless Child
(A Long Way from Home)

Go Down, Moses (Let My People Go!)

Hey! says Vadim finally, Play my favorite song!
But Boris acts like he doesn't know what Vadim is talking about:
Which favorite song? he says.
'ou know which favorite song! Vadim says.
ll right all right... I'll play your favorite song!
~ room becomes quiet.

And thrashed him thoroughly.
The guests danced in the small room,
And beat each other without malice...

All of us are singing at different times, as if we are singing different songs entirely:

...For what is a wedding without roses!
Just a drinking binge, that's all!...

As we sing, I can feel my heart losing all sense of control. My voice becomes louder. My eyes close so that I can scream out the words:

...But why is it that things aren't the way they should be?
Everything, it would seem, is as always:
The same sky — light blue once again...

With each line I feel my soul being released. The words come faster and louder until I am screaming them from the very depths of my lungs:

...I'm gone. I've left Russia forever!...

I'm singing without thinking. I'm feeling without wor
living without trying:

...And I'm laughing, I'm dying of laughter:
How could they believe all the madness that th
Don't worry — I haven't left!
And don't get your hopes up... I won't!...
...For it isn't night yet. It isn't night yet....

Vadim, who has had his share of vodka,
loud, belting out the words as if they were a ru
singing just as loud, it is Vadim's harsh voic
the others:

It isn't night yet... he sings, It is

Boris steadies his fingers and gently picks out the first few chords of Vadim's favorite song. The rest of the guests listen to the music silently. Vadim closes his eyes. When the introduction is finished, he begins to sing softly to Boris's accompaniment:

> Yesterday, all my troubles seemed so far away.
> Now it looks as though they're here to stay.
> Oh I believe in yesterday....

Suddenly, I stand up. Scooting back in my chair, I make my way to an open space in the crowded livingroom. And just in time for the next verse, I begin to dance to the music. Twisting and turning... stepping and swaying... I do my best to dance to the song.

It isn't easy.

> I'm not half the man I used to be.
> There's a shadow hanging over me.
> Oh yesterday came suddenly.

Awkwardly, I try to find an appropriate step to the music. Right foot... left foot... right foot... again right foot... left foot... again left foot... left foot... left foot... again left foot... left foot... left foot...

Right foot, James! someone yells.

But it is too late. My feet — both of them — are pointing in different directions. I have lost track of which foot is which and which direction it should go.

But it doesn't matter. Boris is playing guitar. Vadim is singing. I am drunk and dancing. It is a moment that is difficult to describe. It is a bond that goes beyond words.

Finally, the music stops playing.

Then Vadim stops singing.

And then I stop dancing. Proudly I return to my seat where I am congratulated on my performance.

Nice job, they say.

Thanks, I say, Believe it or not that's the first time I've ever danced in public.

They nod.

In fact, that's the first time I've ever *danced*!

They nod again.

I smile proudly and look at the table in front of me: like clouds on the horizon soon to collide, there is a glass of vodka and a mound of uneaten cheese.

(73)

'To err is human!'

(74)

But something about this night really is different from all others: the vodka. On this night it tastes even more bitter than normal. On this night it is even drier. And no matter how many pickles I eat, I can't reconcile the taste...

For six and a half years I've been able to swallow the taste of vodka. But now for some reason, it has begun to taste foreign. Now, at the worst possible time, it's bitterness has lost its charm...

I down my shot of vodka.

But why? Why am I losing my taste for vodka? For six and a half years I've drunk with both vigor and determination, with both vinegar and determinists... for the best years of my life I've drunk it with salted pickles and seledka... with anyone and everyone who asked me to. But now... now something is different.

But what? Is it the taste of the vodka? Or am I the one who has changed? And if I really have changed, then maybe that's why I can no longer savor the dry bitterness of vodka? Maybe I really have changed? Maybe I've changed more than even I realized...?

I down another shot.

But how? And when? And for what reason? Where was I when it all happened? Was I here*? Was I* there*? Not so long ago everything was fine... everything could be swallowed in easily measured doses... everything was as predictable as prose... everything was as it always was... it was, as it always was, that is, until now.*

I choke down my glass of vodka

Until now it was all so simple. It was natural and beautiful. Until now I could drink and be confident that I was drinking not just for the sake of drinking... but for other more noble reasons. Until this day I was able to savor the taste of vodka as if it were my own. Until today I truly and honestly believed that it was mine. That it could be mine. That it would be mine.

Until today.

I raise my glass to my lips but do not drink:

But what are you worrying about?! This day is just like any other. So just drink and be thankful that you are drinking... just hold your glass up to the window over there... just hold it right up to the light blue sky... to where the sun is still struggling to shine on this cold December day! Just look out the window at its warm rays... just let them warm you...!

I hold my glass up to the window.

But it's too late: it is already night.

(75)

Hey wait a minute! In the midst of all the drinking I almost forgot... I almost forgot to give my friends their wedding present! It's still sitting upstairs in my apartment... it's still propped against the wall! In all the revelry I forgot to bring it down. Should I get it now or should I leave it for later? But no... I've already swallowed too much vodka... if I wait for later it's quite possible that there won't be *a later! I won't be able to get it... I can still make it... If I leave now I can still get it....*

Carefully, I stand up from the table.

Where you going James? someone shouts at me.

I... what... my wedding present... it's in my apartment... it's in my apartment so that's where I'm going....

Now?!

I nod.

In your condition?!

I nod:

It's upstairs in my apartment... I'll just... I need to get it now... while I can still walk....

As I stand I feel my knees buckling and I have to grasp on to the edge of the table to keep from falling. But luckily nobody is paying attention to me. Diligently, I push the chair behind me and squeeze my way out. The vodka is backing up in my throat and I can feel it surging to the top of my throat... *Just a few more steps...*

past the guests... along the wall... into the dark corridor... okay, there's the metallic door... just a few more steps...!

James!

What?

Hey James... where are you going with that? Landlady asks me.

My hand is already turning the handle of the door:

Where am I going with *what*? I say.

With that shot glass! Why are you going to the bathroom with your shot glass?

Bathroom?! What bathroom?! I'm going upstairs to get my gift...

No James... you're going to the bathroom...

Bathroom?!?

Yes, bathroom. Where did you *think* you were going with your shot glass?

I thought it was the heavy metallic door. I thought I was taking the shot glass out into the cold stairwell.

No James... it's the bathroom. It's the bathroom and you are holding a shot glass. In other words, you are holding the plastic doorknob of the bathroom in one hand and a shot glass in the other. In other words, James, you are very drunk.

Yes I am... it's clear... it's clear to everyone... but could you... could you just open the metallic door for me so that I can go up to my apartment... just open the door for me...?

In your condition?

Could you please open the door?

Are you sure you can make it?

I need to get my painting... it's upstairs....

You don't look so good.

I'm fine... could you just open the locks on the heavy metallic door for me?

Whatever you say... but put on your jacket... it's cold.

Landlady takes my empty glass while I twist and struggle with the jacket.

The sleeves... somewhere behind me there should be two sleeves... but for some reason there's only one... where's the other?...

the other sleeve has to be there too... but it's not... oops!... missed again!... okay one more time...!

Luckily, the arm slips into the sleeve.

Landlady fastens the buttons on my coat:

Here..., she says and hands me the shot glass.

Quickly, she unsnaps the locks on the large metallic door, and as I exit I listen in despair as it closes from the inside.

(76)

The stairwell is cold and dark. Silent and still. Through the heavy metal door I can hear the low hum of voices and then a burst of laughter. But that is on the other side. That is there. And I am here. I am alone and drunk and still holding my empty shot glass. Slowly, struggling to move my feet in front of me, I begin to approach the elevator. Step by step. One after the other I coax myself to the elevator. *Okay... it's up ahead on your left... just a few more steps... just a few more steps.*

I push the button and wait.

But nothing happens.

I push again. But again nothing happens.

How long have I been waiting here next to the elevator? How long will it take to reach me?

I push and push. And wait and wait.

How long will I have to stand here between floors? How long will I have to stand here in the middle of these twelve cold stories?

I push again. And again. And again and again...

But the elevator never comes.

The elevator works eleven months of the year... but when you need it more than anything...!

I give up and set out along the stairs.

One step at a time I try to find my apartment:

up............. up...........up..........up..........

Slowly I climb the stairs:

up.....................up..............................up......

One after another I climb and climb and climb:

up..up...

(77)

But these stairs are unlike any other: one after another they come and go... and as soon as one has gone... another comes to take its place. I climb and climb, but the more I climb the more I have to climb. Like a drunk on an escalator, I am stepping and stuttering — left foot then right foot then left foot — straining helplessly between two diametrical opposites: below me, marriage; above me, love. Climbing and climbing, I continue to climb. Like a spoon. Like a price. Like a foreigner who has not yet learned to give up....

(78)

The dry bitterness backs up in my throat.
But I can't stop.

(79)

...And so I continue to climb. Just as hopelessly. Just as helplessly. Just as painfully. And hopelessly, helplessly and painfully, I try to see something that reminds me of where I am going. But I am climbing so slow that all I can see are the shadows shifting reluctantly under my feet. Climbing and climbing and climbing, I feel only the flickering buzz of the dim lights above me. *But why aren't I stopping? Shouldn't I have reached something by now? Shouldn't I have found what I am looking for? Shouldn't I be where I am trying to go...?*

Naively, I continue to climb.

(80)

But how many steps have I conquered? How many more are there to go? It's always easier when you can see the end in sight... but now I can't see anything. I can't feel anything. I can't hear anything but the sounds of my shoes on the cold concrete steps:

......up..

How many steps? How many steps are left? How many? And who are those unknown people going into my neighbor's apartment... Who are these teenagers with joints... why are they closing Olga Alexandrovna's door behind them? Why are they looking at me so strangely? And who is that man I just saw stumbling past me up the stairs... why was he holding his throat?

Finally, I reach my door.

I take out my key and put it into the lock but it doesn't turn this time either. I try again, but again it doesn't turn. I try again and again. And then again. And again.

But the lock doesn't turn.

Almost in tears, I bang on my door.

Open, damn you! Open!

Somewhere in the distance something crashes against the hard concrete.

But the lock doesn't open.

Defeated, I slump with my back against the door and fall onto the floor.

The hall is so cold. And so dark. The concrete below me is so cold. And so dark.

Is this all there is?

I am sitting on the cold cement, both hands palm down on the ground, my chin resting heavily against my chest.

Tired and confused, I sit there.

(81)

'To no avail!'

(82)

And then I close my eyes.

(83)

(84)

When I wake up Vadim is standing over me. Olya is next to him.

There you are! she says.

I don't answer.

James! Vadim says, What are you doing *here*?

My key... my key doesn't work.

What key?

The key to my apartment... it doesn't work.

Vadim and Olya trade glances:

James what floor do you live on?

The twelfth.

Right. And what floor are we on right now?

The twelfth.

Are you sure?

Of course.

We're on the tenth floor James. You've been gone for forty-five minutes and now you are sitting in the dark on the *tenth* floor of our twelve-story building.

What tenth floor? What are they talking about? Do they really think I can't recognize my own floor? My own door? Do they really think that I've never sat slumped against this very wall a hundred times before? It's just the key... the damn key is failing me again... and the lock... these treacherous Russian locks...!

Vadim leans over to pull me up.

There you go...! he grunts.

I grab on to his shoulder.

What should we do with him? Olya says.

I'll take him up to his apartment... he's in no condition to join the party...

What? My apartment? They can't! My apartment's empty... it's dark and there's no one there! There's nobody to drink with! In my apartment there're no songs... no food... in my apartment there's no wedding!

Vadim, I mumble, I want to go back to your apartment.

James if you could see yourself you wouldn't be saying that.

I'm fine. Really.

You can't even stand up.

I'm fine Vadim.

You can't even speak clearly.

Trust me... I'll be okay.

Vadim is looking at me skeptically:

Are you sure?

I'm sure.

Vadim throws my arm over his shoulder and with his hip torques my weight onto himself.

Step by step Vadim and I head back down the cold dark stairwell:

down.............. down............ down..................down

(85)

'To and fro!'

(86)

When we enter the apartment Boris smiles widely:

Wow! he says, We thought you'd been hit by an ambulance!

I'm fine, I say.

You don't look fine!

Boris gets up to help Vadim carry me to my seat.

You don't look fine at all!

I'm fine I say.

Are you sure?

Boris, I lie, I'm fine.

(87)

When I am finally seated, I look in front of me. A new shot glass has been placed in front of me. And next to it, as warm as the room, my plate of cheese.

The conversation dulls. Boris and Olga are talking about themselves... but neither of them is listening. Vadim is retelling a joke about three men and a Frenchman.

But what about this cheese on my plate? What should I do

with it? Who will take it off my plate this time? Everyone is talking around me. Everyone is busy with their own problems. For now my cheese is not important to them...!

I push the plate away from me.

But wait a minute! What am I worrying about? Why am I struggling against the flow? Why am I tying to separate myself from the others. After all, when in doubt a person should do what everyone else is doing... you can't go wrong that way! You can't go wrong if you watch what everyone else is doing and then follow their lead... and everyone else is enjoying the party to its fullest... everyone else is drinking beyond their limit... everyone else is eating cheese...!

I pull the plate back to me.

Everyone else is eating cheese!

The cheese is as warm as the room. As white as early spring. With my fork I scoop a large mound and hold it before my eyes. My hand is shaking and by the time I put it into my mouth most of it has fallen back to my plate. When I have swallowed the first bite, I take another one. And then another. And then another and another until my plate is as clean as a carpet.

And then I wait.

It really is delicious! It really is as good as everyone has been saying!

I wait.

How long has it been since I ate cheese? What was I so afraid of? What was I worried about? Since I was five I've turned down anything that smelled like milk, anything that resembled lactose... and now, after all this time it turns out that all my fears were unjustified! Now, it turns out that I was wrong all this time. But how many times did I deny myself? How many times did I convince myself that it was in my best interest. But no more! From now on I will eat every piece of cheese that is forced upon me! From now on I will eat every glass of milk that is set before my eyes...!

So what did you wish for?

What?

Olga's voice has woken me from my contemplation.

Have you forgotten... you made a wish earlier this evening.

What wish?

Remember... you said you made a wish because you were sitting between Olya and me.

I don't remember.

You can't remember what you wished for?

No I can't... it must not have been important.

Do you believe it will come true?

I don't know... but I want to believe.

What?

I want to believe. And maybe that's the most important thing. Maybe I've been making a mistake all this time... maybe I've been trying too hard. For six and a half years I've been trying so hard to measure the Russian Soul. For just as long I've been trying so hard not to try to find the eleven yellow words...

What are you talking about?

It's not important. It's not important. Hey Olga... will you be honest with me?

I don't know.

Olga please tell me the truth... Are you married or aren't you?

Yes, James, I'm married.

Irreversibly?

And irrevocably.

Irretrievably?

And hopelessly.

Olga...?

Yes?

Congratulations.

(88)

'To love, honor, and obey!'

(89)

Olga is silent.

No really... I'm... I'm happy for you.

But she says nothing.

Olga... hey Olga... can I ask you to... can I ask you a favor?

What?

Can you just... can you just say something to me?

What?

I've had too much to drink and it just occurred to me: I don't even know you... I feel like you haven't let me know you....

What are you talking about?

Can you just tell me about yourself, something that nobody else knows... can you please do that for me?

James! You're acting ridiculous.

Please Olga...!

But she has already stopped listening to me.

Olga...?

She is not listening.

Olga...?

And that's when I understand how married she really is.

(90)

'To little too late!'

(91)

And so I hold up my glass to consummate the toast. Rocking slightly in my seat I hold my glass up:

Clink! it says, Clink! Clink! Clink!

Four times.

But there are five people within arm's reach... and that means that someone has snubbed me... that means that one of them has not noticed my glass.

Olga!

I offer my glass to Olga. Leaning over the table, I hold my glass in her direction. But she is not looking at me. She is kissing her husband on the curly part of his dense beard.

But why? Why is she moving away from me? Why does it have to end like this? I've known my role. I'm not demanding anything more from her than she can give! Surely she sees that I haven't touched her glass? Surely she knows that I have been left toastless?

Say a toast James!!! someone is yelling.

I can't, I say.

Why not?

I don't remember why... but for some reason I just can't...

What do you mean you can't? Have your six and a half years been lost on you?

But again Olya steps in to make a toast.

And when she is finished we drink.

And when we have drunk she turns to me:

You know James, she says, You really don't have to drink every time... you can take a break if you want...

I'm fine...

You're drinking as if you're trying to prove something. As if it means more for you than simply being drunk.

I'm fine...

James...?

Olya has put the flat part of her hand on my upper arm, and for the first time since I can remember I feel a flutter in my heart.

Do you feel all right?

What do you mean?

You seem sullen and despondent... You haven't smiled since you danced to Vadim's favorite song... as if you're afraid of something.

I'm not afraid of anything.

Are you sure?

I'm just doing my best not to make a fool of myself... that's all I want. All I want is to get through this wedding... all I want is to last long enough to make it through Customs with dignity...

You know, Olya says, You shouldn't worry what other people will think... you should just be yourself.

Who?

Yourself. Don't try to follow other people's example.

But...!

You shouldn't worry about what other people are doing... you should do what *you* think is right.

Olya strokes my arm again and then lets go.

What did she say? What is it supposed to mean? And why did my heart flutter when she touched my arm? When was the last time that happened?

I smile at Olya.

It was... it was when she was telling me about why she disliked America... it was when she had cast aside all remnants of politeness and intelligence and was insulting me with the truth... that's the last time my soul jumped from joy... that's the last time my heart moved!

She smiles back.

Wow! I knew it! I knew I could find someone like her! Someone who is intelligent enough not to be intelligent. Someone honest enough to be impolite. She's beautiful, of course, but it doesn't matter... we all have our faults. The most important thing is that she is neither intelligent nor polite!

I smile again. She does the same.

She's perfect!!! That's right... she is neither intelligent nor polite... and so she's perfect! Could it be that she...? Could it be that she and I...?

Hey Olya...? I say.

Yes.

I was wrong about you.

What?

I thought you were like all the others... but you're not.

What are you talking about?

You're not polite at all.

Excuse me?

And you're not intelligent either!

What?!

You know, you're beautiful — no offense, of course! — you're beautiful but you're neither intelligent nor polite... do you know what I'm saying?

No.

You don't understand? I just said that you're neither intelligent nor polite!

James you're drunk.

No I'm not. I've never been more sober.

That's what I've heard...

Olya... I want to give you something...

What?

You see Olya there's something I want you to have... I should probably tell you the story behind it... but no... I won't! It's self-explanatory.

What are you talking about?

Olya, I want to give you something, but you have to promise me that you'll take it!

What is it?

Olya, do you promise me that you'll take it?

I don't know...

Promise me, Olya.

I don't know...I mean, I guess I promise.

Thank you! Thank you, Olya!

I reach into my pocket for my wallet:

Olya, I say, I want you to have this...!

With heavy fingers I separate the wallet.

...Just a minute... I can't... it's too thin... I just need to...

James! What are you doing?

...I just need to pull it out... but it's the size of...

Olya is looking at me fighting with the wallet:

There! I say, There it is... Please take it! Please take it... don't refuse me...!

Olga is holding out the palm of her hand.

There it is! I say and place the two-kopeck coin in her hand.

(92)

What is it?!

It's a two-kopeck coin... from me to you!

But...

Olya I want you to have it!

But...

I want you to have it as a souvenir.

A souvenir?

Yes... something to remember me by.

But it's filthy... and sticky!

Olya tries to give the coin back, but I push away her hand. Again she tries to offer me the coin and again I push away her hand. Again she offers, again I push.

Then she offers enthusiastically. And just as enthusiastically I

14 — 1807

push her arm away... the coin falls out of her hand and with a plop lands in my glass of vodka.

I watch the coin settle lazily to the bottom. *There it is. Even now gravity has won out! Even now it is night.*

Through clouded eyes I look at Olga who is sitting next to me: but she is not looking back. She has not taken her eyes off her husband since the last time she talked to me. She will never again look back. She will never again look at me.

...But should I say a toast, or not? On the one hand everyone is begging me to say a toast... they are pleading with me. On this same hand, it's Russian tradition... after all I would hate to think that my six and a half years in Russia really have been lost on me! But on the other hand... on the other hand... wait a minute... what was the other hand?! There was some reason that I'd decided not to make a toast... something that I'd been afraid of? But what was it? And why am I not afraid now? That must mean that it wasn't anything important...! It must mean that it isn't all that important after all....

(93)

I stand up:

A toast! I say.

(94)

Sit down James, Olga says.

Olga!

Look... he's absolutely drunk... he can barely stand up. Boris why don't you make a toast instead...?

Olga! Vadim says, What's come over you?

Look at him...

Olga! I for one want to hear what James has to say.

Yeah, says Boris, So do I....

As I stand swaying, my glass of kopeck vodka in hand, I hear the voices brushing by me.

He's too drunk! Olga says.

Oh let him give a toast! Vadim says.

But...!

After all, James is a person too... so let's hear what he has to say... let's give him a chance to express what's on his mind!

Olga looks as though she is going to cry:

But he's not a person... he's not...! No matter how well he knows Russian... no matter how much he likes our literature... no matter how many glasses of vodka he can drink... he'll never be Russian... he'll never be one of us... no matter what, he'll always be...

Vadim holds up his hand:

That's enough Olga, he says, Now dammit... James *is* a person.

But...!

Vadim turns to me:

Okay James, he says, Go ahead with your toast...!

And so I do:

(95)

'My toast?' I say, 'Oh yes... my toast... I guess that's what I stood up for. I stood up because I wanted to make a toast and so that's what I guess I'll do. I'll make a toast because I'm standing up and I've got my glass in my hand. I'll make a toast because everybody is expecting it from me. So my toast goes like this... I mean, I should start at the very beginning and for me the beginning began at the beginning... in other words at the windowless airport... that's right... but then some other things happened — in some order or another — and the next thing you know it... here I am! That's right... here I am. After six and a half years here I am standing in front of you. Believe me it wasn't easy... you have no idea how many toasts I've consummated, how much vodka I've swallowed over the last few hours... over the last few years. But nevertheless, here I am standing before you. And since I'm here, and as long as I'm still standing, I guess I might as well make a toast of some kind...'

(96)

'...But what should I say? What can I tell you? You know when I came here six and a half years ago I was... can you believe it?!... six and a half years younger. I was naive then. I didn't understand Russian. I didn't understand Russians. I couldn't even have told you whether Russia was even Russia. Or whether it wasn't. Back then I didn't know your beliefs or traditions, I couldn't understand your customs or your Customs, and to be honest I hadn't even heard of Mr. Pushkin. But that was six and a half years ago. And a lot has changed since then. Now, at the very least, I've *heard* of Pushkin. Now, fortunately, I am familiar with your customs... and, unfortunately, with your Customs. Now, I understand where to put the new metallic strips in the metro turnstiles, and how to peel a potato so that it sparkles, and why it is that Russians smile so rarely. Now I know that the Russian Soul is too Russian to be measured... that mushrooms are more plentiful in the fall... and that BMW's are neither as hard nor as thick as an oncoming trolleybus. Now I know that the novelist Lev Tolstoy most likely had some sort of familial ties to Russia. I've learned all this. I've been lucky enough to be able to learn. Luckily, I have been taught. And I have taught...'

(97)

'...But you know during all this time I never once stopped to let people know how grateful I was. Not once did I stop to tell the redhead that it was he who taught me Russia. Not once did I thank Vadim for being my best friend. Not once did I let them know what they really meant to me. The people who make up my Russia. All of them: friends and acquaintances and students and co-workers and policemen and lovers and trolleybus drivers and cashiers and poets and politicians... and everyone in between. There're so many people I never had time to thank. So many people I had time to thank, but never did. So many people who have helped me during the last six and a half years. And all of them are worthy of a toast. You, Landlady, for showing me how to suffer, and how to generalize, and how to eat bread; you, Boris, for being my best friend's best friend; you, Olga Ivanovna, for making the second toast; you, Olya, for touching me on the upper part of my arm when I needed it more than anything. For six and a half years I have lived with all of you... and yet I never once told you what I really feel about you....'

(98)

'...And so, now, I'd like to thank you all. Now I'd like to drink to all of you. Vadim, Boris, Olya, Landlady, Olga Ivanovna... Now

I'd like to drink to you all. To all of you. And to all the other people who have comprised my life for the last six and a half years. All the people who have helped me out of the kindness of their hearts... who have opened their souls to me... who have passed me on the opposite elevator, and in the crowded metro, and with whom I have scurried to get out of the way! Now I want to drink to all of you! To each and every person who helped me find a building... or conjugate a verb... or understand the meaning of a word. To all of you I owe more than I can ever say. Words are poor substitute for ideas. But nevertheless, I want to try. Nevertheless, I want to raise my glass to Tanya... but then again, no... I *don't* want to drink to Tanya; actually, I want to drink to Tanyas, to *all* of them! And to all the Lenas! And to every single Natasha that has ever lived... In fact, what the hell... let's even drink to Irina! Let's drink to all of them at once... to all of you because you are all so beautiful... all of you, every single one! Tanya, Natasha, Irina, Lena... and Kirill and Evdokia... You are all so beautiful... As beautiful as... as beautiful as... as a new born baby... as pure as a soul. As a Russian Soul...'

(99)

'...And so let's not forget to drink to the Russian Soul and while we're at it, to the American Dream — they're the same thing, aren't they? — and to all the Russian immigrants who invented America and the American inventors who invented the Russian Soul. And to smokers and trolleybus drivers who don't invent anything at all; and to non-smokers and non-trolleybus drivers who most likely don't invent anything at all... and to black bears and white snow... to yellow words and red flags and light blue skies, to snow and vodka and both blacks and whites and the number three, and eleven, and six and a half and to the letter *П* and the letter *Ф* and to all the other letters from *А* to *Я*. (Except, of course, for *Х*.) But on second thought... no!... *including Х*! But no, that's not right either... *especially Х*!!! After all, the expressivity of a language is measured by the amount of words that begin with *Х*... and so let's drink to the Russian language, the most logical, the most romantic, the most expressive and beautiful... To Russian! To Russian!! To Russian*s*!!! All of them! And to all the Russians who invented Russian, in other words to Alexander Sergeevich Pushkin! And to Kharms for teaching me that Pushkin is fallible... and to the engineers of the Moscow metro for teaching me how to fall! Of course I have to drink to Lev Tolstoy for showing me how to read Russian... and to a very special married... I mean separated... I mean dead woman who taught me how to love... and to each of my Russian girlfriends — all three of you — with your accents and your whispering voices and your calculators and red painted lips and nyloned legs and cold cold hands... Even I understand that it's over... even I can see that it is all coming to an end: my friendships, my loves, my story in Russia... all of it is coming to an inglorious end. But not before I make a toast: not before I make a toast to this country... that's right! For six and a half years I lived without saying thanks and now it's time to make a toast to this country that is... that was... I don't know what she *is*, or what it *was*... all I know is that she is not Canada and I want to drink despite it. All I know is that it was not America and I want to drink because of it. All I want to do at this moment is drink to this country which is neither East nor West... neither Europe nor Asia... neither *it* nor *she*...'

What the hell am I saying?

'...My dear friends, let's drink to this country, to this beautiful beautiful country... a place which for six and a half years I called home; a place that you call many things but that I will forever call mine; let's raise our glasses to the land which, for lack of a better word, we call Russia!'

(100)

I sit down.

(101)

And then I stand up.

That is to say, I continue my toast:

(102)

'But I almost forgot... I almost forgot about Olga! I almost forgot about the most beautiful woman in this room... in this world! There's a lot that I could say about her: About her mellifluous voice...

about her virtue... about... well there are a lot of things I could say about her. But what I really want to say is as simple as a suture, as lonely as luck. What I really like about her I can express in one simple word. That's right... one word! And that one word is... *toes*. Let's drink to Olga's beautiful glorious toes! Yeah, I know what you're thinking... you're thinking that I'm going to say something like, "Hey everybody let's drink to Olga — the girl that for the best part of my life I have been having orgasms in..." You're probably thinking that I'm going to say that in front of all of you... but I'm not! I just want to drink to Olga's toes! Nothing more. Even *I* understand that it's over. Even I understand that my relationship with Olga is finished... even I know when to give up...'

(103)

I stop. Everyone is looking at me. My toast is finished. I have said everything I wanted. Everything I needed. But no... there is something else I should say. I need to say something profound so that they will remember me after I have left. I need for them to understand me when I am gone. Now is my chance to cleanse my soul so that they will forgive me...

But I can't. Instead I lift my glass up weakly and mutter the following words:

'That's it...' I mumble, 'That's my toast.'

I look at them helplessly.

But nobody responds.

Why is everyone so silent? Why is everyone looking at me so strangely? Don't they speak Russian? Don't they realize that my toast is over and that we should be drinking? Haven't they understood my words? If so, then why is everyone looking at me as if I am speaking in a foreign language? Why aren't my fellow guests drinking my toast in their glasses? Could it be that I said something wrong? Could it be that I used the wrong words? Why the strange, blank faces? Why isn't anyone drinking? And how was I able to translate the word 'girlfriend'? And 'fun'? And 'toes'? Where did I find these Russian words? Or could it be that I... Could it be that these words were... Could it be that...

I sit down.

(104)

Here Boris raises his glass to me:

What the hell did he say?

I don't know, says Vadim, When he talks slow I have a chance, but when he talks fast like that...

Yeah, me either! says Olya, The only word I understood was *okay*.

It seemed like he wanted to tell us something!

I've never seen him so animated!

It must have been important...

Is he finished?

I'm not sure.

Me either... but let's drink anyway...!

And they do.

(105)

The last time I saw Aunt Helen she was looking out of the curtains of our house, watching me get into the taxi. She'd had enough of the airport ordeal, she'd told me, and so we agreed that this time I'd take a cab.

It was three years ago.

Even then her hair had begun to turn gray. Wrinkles were appearing in places where they hadn't been before. Her smile was becoming thin and brittle. Even then she was learning to give up.

Since that time I have only seen her words. Rarer and rarer. Less and less demanding. Since then I have been busy with things that seemed important. For the last three years I have been getting by without her. For the last three years I have been living here. For the last three years I was living here.

For six and a half years I lived *there*.

(106)

After my toast the conversation degenerates even further. By now everyone is speaking without understanding, and the conversation floating around me mixes together like a mixed drink:

the men are talking about politics... while the women are telling me about their unwanted pregnancies:

Of course it's not an easy decision, they say, It never is... but then why should we have to carry the burden for nine months...? For the rest of our lives? Why should we have to pay for the mistakes of a handful of Communist leaders? But we're still paying! You can see it in the tax system... you can see it in the stifling beaurocracy... You can see it in the organized crime. But do you know what this country needs? Do you? I'll tell you... What this country needs is a good suction cup... I mean just take a look around... what do you see: cockroaches running over the examining table... old women in dirty medical gowns... a flickering lamp above our heads... and standing there in surgical gloves and a mask over his face... Mikhail Gorbachev! Can you imagine that? I mean I'm no anesthesiologist or anything, but how can you expect a country to function when its doctors go unpaid and its nurses have to be bribed to pay any attention at all to the ailing economy? Yeah sure you can take the zeros off the ruble, but is that going to ease the sick feeling in your stomach? Sure you can drink prescription medicine by the flask, but what about the *next* elections? Do you see what we mean, James? James can you see what we're trying to tell you?

Do I see? Do I see? I can barely see my hand in front of my face... and they're asking me if I see?!

But in fact six and a half years have not been lost on me. In other words, my six and a half years have not been spent in vain; in other words, I can speak Russian while drunk:

I see, I say, I see.

(107)

But what about this dry bitterness building up in my throat? And what time is it? How long will this wedding last? How long should it take? How will I know when it really is over? Will it be clear to me... ?

Hey! says Boris, What are you thinking about?

Me? Nothing.

Yeah me too.

Boris stops:

James...?

Yes?

Are you drunk?

No.

You're not?

No. Are you?

No.

You're not?

No.

Me either.

Good.

Boris stops again:

James... hey James... I have a question for you.

All right.

Can I ask you a question?

All right.

Now James I want you to answer honestly...

I'll try.

Are you listening?

Yes.

Are you listening to my question?

I am.

James, tell me the truth... do you respect me?

Boris I respect you tremendously.

That's good. I respect you too.

I'm glad.

But there's only one thing that I can't understand... there's only one question that I'd like to ask you.

Go ahead.

It's something that I've been wanting to ask you all evening... but haven't.

Okay...?

It's something that's always interested me.

I'm all ears.

I'm not sure if anybody's ever asked you...

What?

I doubt if anyone's ever asked you this before... but I was just curious...

Boris looks at me:

James... what's the deal with the blacks in America?

(108)

#795 And that's when it happens. At that moment my wish comes true: Before he can finish his sentence, I am vomiting.

* * * * * * * * * *

Book 11. How I Made the Decision to Leave Russia Forever

(109)

In this world there are things that should never happen and therefore don't, and things that should happen but do anyway. The former we call hopeless. The latter we call inevitable.

Or maybe it's like this: there are things that shouldn't happen but do, and things that have to happen and therefore do. The first, we call danger. Or luck. The second we call fate. All three of which, if you get right down to it, are irreversible, and beautiful, and, when you have swallowed something that doesn't agree with you, intricately unconditional.

Or maybe it's...

...But no. It's too late. Any way you look at it, it's night. It's night and over the last six and a half hours I have drunk far too much vodka.

(110)

And so it begins deep in my stomach... in my soul... so deep that I can feel it with all my heart... For six and a half years my vodka has been going down one way. For six and a half years I was able to drink without regret. For six and a half years I have been extremely extremely lucky.

But not tonight. Tonight I can feel something deep in my stomach that I have never felt before. The dry bitterness that has been balancing in my throat for the last six and a half years is finally bubbling to the surface. The sickening feeling that rested so stubbornly between here and there is finally coming up.

up.........up.........up.........

Hours and hours of swallowed vodka is now coming up my throat like an escalator. Like the fastest escalator in the world it is rising higher and higher. Along the trails of my insides. Over the back of my throat and past my teeth. And when I open my mouth it explodes out in one mass of regurgitated orange, pink and yellow. Like a water cannon it is shooting out of my mouth: vodka and cheese and beets and mushrooms... chunks and scraps of my past are spurting out of my mouth onto the table, onto my plate, onto the surprised guests...

Hopelessly, I am vomiting. Relentlessly I am throwing up. And relentlessly, hopelessly, and violently I am feeling things come out of my mouth that I've never seen before: black bread and butter... red salads and sauces... liquid pork. Bits of garlic. Pickles. For the first time ever the dry bitterness has pushed its way out and now it is exploding past the back of my throat with a vengeance.

out......out......out......

With a vengeance it is coming out, first in gritty chunks, then in chewed bits, then finally in waves of hot bilious fluid. Spurting and coughing I choke it all out. Bits and pieces. Chunks and slivers. Articles and gerunds and prepositions. Gagging and lunging I cough out words that have been resting sickeningly between my stomach and my throat. Underlined phrases that have been swallowed only to be forgotten. Consumed only to be ignored. Digested only to be finally and painfully undigested.

By now I am puking hopelessly and naively. Relentlessly and sincerely. Finally and unconditionally. I am vomiting and vomiting and vomiting... and when I press my hands to my mouth to stop the liquid streaming from my mouth, it only comes out even faster, forcing its way through my fingers in a concerted spray that is showering the table, my plate, the screaming guests...

(111)

'...Jeeeezus Christ!...'

(112)

...And then, finally, the floor.

Hopelessly, I am coughing up years and years of rhyme and reason. Verse and vodka. Vanilla, lactose, and tequila. Now I am on my hands and knees coughing up nouns and adjectives and both perfective and imperfective verbs....

(113)

'...Do something with him...!'

(114)

And as I hover over the floor, my mouth open, I can feel a stream of food pouring out onto the carpet. From my mouth oozes a cascade of stereotypes, a river of misunderstandings. Percentages and prices. Visas and metro tokens. Fish soup. Poetry. Kopeck coins. Marlboro cigarettes. Chunks of oily *seledka* mixed with bits and pieces of unheeded advice.

Like a puddle of mud it collects and mixes with the chunks, forming a pool of my past. *There it is! There's everything that seemed so beautiful just minutes ago... everything that has kept me! There it is on the floor in front of me... here it is before the tip of my nose! There it all is in the fibers of the carpet! But can this be it? Surely there must be something else to keep me? Surely there has to be something more, right?*

...Right?!

(115)

Wrong: ...<u>From the other side</u>, this night is *not* like any other!

(?)

And so I am throwing up. And out. And from. And onto. I am throwing up and up and up....

(??)

'...Is he finished...?'

(???)

And then it stops.

(???)

'Here... grab his arm! No... not like that... like this... hold his head... okay, okay I got him... Ready, now on three... one... two... THREE! All right... good! This way... right in here... that's right... now move the pillow... right... don't drop him!... okay... that's good... easy does it... set him down... right there... all right... on three... one... two... three... OPA!'

(??)

(?)

(1)

When I wake up it's early morning. And I smell pickles. There is a woman lying next to me in my bed. Her back is to me. This is not unusual. But what is unusual is that there are hands and elbows sticking out of her back. They look like men's hands. They *are* men's hands. It's Olga's back, but not her hands. *Why does Olga have men's hands growing out of her back? Unless they are... they are Vadim's hands. It's Olga's back and Vadim's hands, which is natural enough because yesterday was their wedding... yesterday was their wedding and that means that last night was... it was...*

NO!

NO

NO

NO

NO

NO!!!!!!!!!!!!!!!!!!!!!!!!!!!!!!!!!!!!!

(2)

Okay. Calm down! It's not so bad. They put me here. I certainly wouldn't have insisted on it. Not in my condition. They put me here first. They did it. And the fact that they're sleeping here with me just means that... it just means that... I don't know what it means! But I know that I was here first. And that I need to sleep because I'm very very sick. Just stay still and try to go back to sleep. Sleep, and when you wake up it will all be over.

It will all be over when you wake up.

When you wake up everything will be finished.

But that will be then... for now, just close your eyes and sleep....

(3)

* * * * * * * * * *

Book 12. Тоска

(A)

Sheremetievo-2 airport was designed by people who lived in small apartments. Its ceilings are low. Its lighting is even lower. There are round metallic things on the ceiling. And although there really *are* windows, if you ask anyone who has been there, they will insist with both arms that the airport is as windowless as a Soul.

That's where I am now. My flight leaves in just a few hours. I have come early so as not to miss my flight. I have checked both my passport and my visa which are tucked safely into my wallet. I have made sure to make sure to be sure.

And so that's where I am. Sheremetievo-2 Airport. Here I am waiting for the plane that will take me home. Waiting for these hours to pass as quickly as have the last six and a half years of my life.

Here I am waiting...

(Б)

...But before I can be here, I need to be there... back on the twelfth floor of my apartment building. Back in the place that was home. Back in the past tense. Before I could leave for the airport I had to gather my things, to clean my ex-apartment, to give back the keys.

But most important I needed to go back because I had to say good-bye; after six and a half years I couldn't leave just like that, now could I?

(B)

'Hi, it's me... James... look I'm calling because... I mean I know

I should be telling you this in person, but... well, you see, it all happened so suddenly... I mean I've been thinking about it for a long time now, but now that the time has come it's all happening so quickly... you see, Lena, I'm leaving... I'm leaving next week, I've already bought my ticket... no, I won't... this time I won't be coming back... I know, I know, we were supposed to read O. Henry after the holidays... but you know, Lena, you've made a lot of progress over the last four years... I'm amazed at how well you can read and speak and listen... Lena, you're my best student... and you know, I just want to say that after I leave... after next week, you have to promise me that you'll stick with your studies... you have to promise me that you'll continue with English. You can continue on your own, I'm sure of it. It's important. Trust me... you'll be surprised at how fast the time can pass... five years, then six years, then six and a half... and I wouldn't want you to... I mean I wouldn't want for you to give up... do you see what I mean? Do you promise me you'll stick to English when I'm gone... huh, Lena, do you promise? You do? You promise! Okay. That's a good girl. I knew you wouldn't let me down... I knew I could count on you, Lenochka...'

(Г)

And so I stood in my apartment. Cleaning it for the last time, I felt a cold sense of loss. *No other apartment would ever be like this one. This apartment where I'd learned four yellow words. Where I'd been explained the difference between coffee and tea; silence and marriage; loving and getting by. Where I'd learned to play tysacha. And then, later, how to play it and be lucky...*

Cleaning my apartment for the last time, I collected the remnants of my past: a Three of Diamonds; a dusty calculator; my fur hat; the tattered copy of *Anna Karenina*; my mother's letter; the German dictionary...

Now it was time to leave. Now there was nothing to keep me here. Now I could leave without contrition:

I had given away the two-kopeck coin.

I had given up on the eleventh yellow word.

And saddest of all, ever since the wedding my Russian had dissolved. Like an antacid tablet it had fizzled and popped until there was nothing left of it. Now I was misusing words that for many years I'd spoken without thinking. Now I was confusing grammar in ways that I never had before. As if I were already saying good-bye. As if I had already begun to forget.

Carefully, I placed my six and a half years into my suitcase.

(Д)

My doorbell rang loudly, echoing through my apartment. When I opened the door I saw Vadim:

Hi, he said, are you all packed?

Almost....

Well everyone's waiting downstairs.

I'm almost ready.

Here let me take your suitcases... the elevator's broken again.... just these two?

That's right. Just two.

Well, give me that big one over there...

Vadim picked up the larger suitcase and disappeared out the door.

A few minutes later he returned for the small one.

For a few moments I stood without leaving. *Again it seemed that I was overlooking something. But what? What could it be? But no... I'd checked everything. I had everything that I needed to leave Russia forever. It was all right there in my wallet.*

I sighed sweetly and bitterly at the same time. My life in Russia was ending; this chapter of it, I knew, was over, and after it there would be no more.

I closed the door tightly and made my way for the stairwell.

(E)

It is New Year's Day.

It is the beginning of a new cold year.

But it is raining. Instead of a thick white snow, the city is covered in rain. And nobody is surprised. Nobody is surprised, and nobody is surprised that nobody is surprised. But why? Why isn't anybody surprised at the rain? Perhaps because we have come to accept the weather as an inevitable yet unpredictable part of our lives? Perhaps because rain is as unavoidable as change? As inevitable as fate? Perhaps because it rained the day before?

But no! It's nothing like that. Surely, it has something to do with the last six and a half years... surely, it has something to do with the years that I have spent here. Surely, it means something more significant.

(Ë)

Landlady let me in.

Vadim had already left my suitcases to clutter their hall. Carefully, I took off my shoes and put on my pair of slippers. When I walked into the kitchen Vadim and Olga were waiting for me.

Hi James, Olga said, We missed you last night.

Last night?

At the new year's dinner. Everyone was here.

I was... well, you know, with my flight today and all I didn't think that I should risk it.

Olga waves off my words:

It's not important, she said, It's just that Olya was here... she asked about you....

I cringed.

...She said to tell you hi.

That was nice of her, I said and took my seat at the table.

As we sat together for the final time, each of us could feel that this conversation really was our last; and each tried to ignore it: we discussed the weather; and politics; and the problem of blacks in America.

As we sat I learned from Olga that today's rain was really tears being shed at my departure. And that Vadim had finally managed to pay off his debts... by borrowing once again. And that it was highly unlikely that America would solve its black-white problem in the near future.

At some point Landlady came into the room with a recycled plastic sack for me to take back to America: inside were the collected works of Alexander Sergcivich Pushkin — Olga Ivanovna had left it for me — and a large jar of black currant jam.

For an instant we all sat silently.

Finally, Vadim turned to me:

So what now? he said.

What do you mean? I answered.

What are you going to do when you get back to America?

Oh that. I'm not sure... I haven't decided. My aunt's been looking for a job for me... she says she already has an offer to work in a flower shop.

A flower shop?

Yes, selling roses. I have an interview after I get back.

What about your book?

What book?

The book you're going to write about your experiences in Russia. Have you started it?

No... I haven't. I mean, I'm not planning on writing any books.

Well, in any case, when you finish it, make sure to send us a copy.

Yeah, said Olga, With an autograph!

But...!

I stopped:

Okay, I said, I'll send you a copy.

And James...?

Yes?

When you write your book... remember what I told you... don't forget Katya, and Sveta, and Marina...!

(Ж)

Of course, I said.

Vadim smiled but then, as if remembering something, his expression changed:

Oh... I almost forgot! Olya asked me to give you this.

Vadim reached deep into his pocket and fumbled around for something:

She didn't want you to leave without it...

Clumsily, Vadim rummaged in his pocket and pulled out my two-kopeck coin:

Here! he said, She wanted you to have it... she knows how much it means to you.

I smiled and took the coin.

(З)

And when our conversation could go no further, the four of us got up from the table. Back in their hallway, I put on my winter hat. Then my boots. Slowly, I buttoned my jacket.

For a moment we stood there.

Let's sit, Vadim said.

And the four of us squatted on whatever was available: Vadim on my large suitcase. Olga next to him. Landlady on my small suitcase. And I next to her.

In silence we sat in the cramped hallway next to the heavy metal door.

For a minute of silence we sat looking at each other. Vadim. Olga. Landlady. For a silent minute they were all right there in front of me. They were close enough to touch... or to thank.

And then Vadim stood up:

All right, James! he said, It's time to show everybody what you've learned!

(И)

And so I stood up:

Thanks for everything, I said in Russian.

Everyone nodded.

Expertly, I unsnapped the locks on the large metal door. Grabbing my suitcases and the recycled packet I turned and walked into the cold stairwell.

One last time I turned around to look at my friends: Vadim, Olga, Landlady. And having looked at them a final time I turned back toward the cold stairwell.

Hey James! Vadim's voice called after me.

I looked over my shoulder to see his words.

Hey James! he said, Be careful on that escalator!

(Й)

I walked down the flight of stairs and out into the cold air. Purposefully, I found the bus stop where I caught the bus to my metrostation. Inside the metro, I handed the uniformed attendant three plastic metro tokens and along with my two suitcases passed through her turnstile unscathed.

The platform was not crowded. And when the train had screeched fully into the station, and the passengers had exited, I entered.

No, I explained, I'm not getting off at the next stop.

And kicking my suitcases up against the far-side doors I cleared a path for the exiting passengers.

Across from me an old woman stood squinting at a metro map:

Can you tell me how to get to *Taganskaya*? she asked me.

And I told her.

(К)

One by one the stations flew by. For the last time the metro was taking me from there to here. From *К* to *Л*. From past to present tense. For the last time I was looking at the people who had made up my life in Russia. My fellow travelers. My friends.

One by one the stations flew by until there was only one left.

And as we approached my destination, I stood waiting. I stood waiting for the final words that I would ever hear the mechanical voice say to me, the final words that I would ever hear in the past tense. And sure enough, the words came loudly:

'Rechnoi Vokzal. Terminal Station.'

(Л)

I exit the car.

I set out along the platform for the short escalator.

I go from bottom to top without injury.

I exit onto the street.

In front of me people are hustling and bustling and so I walk to where bus number 517 will take me to the airport.

On the streets people are slushing through the falling rain. Banners announce the coming year. Billboards congratulate passersby on yet another year of prosperity:

HAPPY NEW YEAR!
FROM NORTH-SOUTH BANK

Under these billboards old women are selling bottles of vodka from wooden crates. A plaque in an exchange window announces today's rate of exchange:

(1USD=6RUR).

Stupidly, I stand in front of the sign. Blinking and confused, I try to understand it.

(M)

And that's where it could have ended — that's where my story could have come to its untimely end:

From my blind side an ambulance hops over the median and cruises along the sidewalk. Bystanders on the street scurry to get out of its path. But I have been caught looking for the zeros, and do not see it.

Could this be the end! Could it be that my story will end right now... right here in the middle of a crowded sidewalk? In the middle of the Russian alphabet! Truthfully, the end is only inches away. Just a few more centimeters and my story will end prematurely... before it even begins!

Without even noticing me the ambulance comes screaming in my direction... but just in the nick of time I step back, the ambulance goes blaring by... leaving a dirty streak of mud on my clothes.

I gasp for the final time.

(H)

Breathing heavily, I stand there.

Thankfully, I have been spared.

My bus comes. The people enter. And I with them.

(O)

I stamp my tickets and wait.

When the ticket controller approaches me, I show him my tickets. And he walks by.

But the man next to me hasn't paid his fare and when the controller asks him for his ticket the man justifies himself as follows:

I didn't buy a ticket, he says, because I'm only going one stop.

Well then, the ticket taker points out, if you're only going one stop then there's no reason why you can't walk that one stop!

But the man doesn't lose heart:

Sure, he says, I can walk... of course I can walk... but why should I walk when I can ride for free?!

The ticket taker stops to think this over. And then moves on.

One by one he checks tickets until he reaches two teenage boys who haven't stamped their tickets.

And here, I am witness to an ugly scene:

(T)

Tickets! the ticket taker tells the two teenagers.

Tickets? they tremble, Tickets?

Tickets! Tickets! the ticket taker tells them.

Truthfully the two teenagers thought that this time... *this time...* they'd trick the ticket taker; truthfully, they thought that this ticket taker took the trolleybus toward town, that they'd therefore travel trouble-free.

The... the tickets... they're...

Tensely, the teens try to trick the ticket taker.

Tell the truth..., the ticket taker tempts them, Tell the truth...

The truth?

The truth! The truth!

They try to think this through.

The truth? That they tried to travel ticketless? That they thought they'd trick the ticket taker?

Truants! the ticket taker thunders, Teenage truants...!

Together they try to turn the tables:

There! the taller teen tries to talk, There're the tickets!

The ticket taker takes the teens' two tattered tickets, tears them to ticker tape, then throws them toward the teens.

Terrified, they turn tearful.

The ticket taker terrorizes them:

Take that! the ticket taker tells them, Take that!

That'll teach them! the tyrant thinks, That'll teach those two to try to travel ticketless! That'll teach them to try to trick this *ticket taker...!*

(Р)

Wow! says one of the people standing next to me after the ticket taker has exited with the two teens:

That sure was unpleasant! says another.

Yeah, I agree, even *I* thought that scene would never end.

The things some people won't do to make a point! the first person says.

I hope we'll never have to suffer through anything like *that* again..., says the second.

We won't, I say, We've already passed *П*... in fact, the next stop, if I'm not mistaken, is...

(С)

Standing in the bus, I watch the Russian countryside pass me. *How many times have I seen that same countryside without noticing it? How many times has it skidded by? And now that I'm leaving, I see it for the first time. Isn't that the way of it... isn't that how we live our lives... not realizing what we've left behind until we've passed irretrievably through Customs. Isn't that how it always is? Doesn't the fallen snow seem infinitely more beautiful from an airplane window than from the naked viewpoint on the street? Aren't people more exotic and beautiful when they no longer exist for you?*

(Т)

Mile after mile I pass open fields of green flaked with white. Wooden shacks. A tall building with a ninety-foot Marlboro man. Mile after mile I watch the countryside turn from city to suburb to pasture. Stop after stop the bus carries me toward my destination.

(У)

But is this really forever? Can it really be that I will never return to this place that has been my home for so long? Why is it that this final bus ride seems so final? Why does it seem so permanent? Somehow I expected the ending to be more glamorous, more significant. I guess right until the very end I expected more conclusions to be made. More meaning to be given.

At the next stop the bus grinds to a halt. The doors open.

(Ф)

The doors open and a woman steps up into the bus. She is sophisticated. She is taking out her ticket and looking for a place to stamp it. Suddenly, a man approaches her. He is wavering — he has obviously swallowed too much vodka — and staggering with each step forward, he approaches her. The drunk's eyes are fluttering and he is opening his mouth as if he wants to say something. The woman, cautious, hesitates by the doors. It is clear the man has something he wants to tell her, or maybe ask her. The man slumps up to the woman. The woman tries to look away but feels that the man is watching her. Trying to ignore him, she punches her ticket and steps forward... but the drunk man blocks her way. The woman moves to the right to step by him, but the drunk slumps that way too. For a few awkward moments the two of them — the woman and the drunk — stand there looking at each other in silence. Then, finally, when it seems that he has forgotten what to say, the drunk man opens his mouth to speak. At first his words evade him... they will not come. And then in one instant they arrive... As the woman looks at him in surprise, the drunk man screams into her face...

(X)

F U C K Y O U!!!

(Ц)

The woman steps back. But the man is not finished. He stops for a moment to think, and turning his eyes to the sky, then adds: Can you believe this rain?

(Ч)

After the man has been thrown out the doors onto the street the bus arrives at the terminal.

I exit.

I walk the short path to the airport.

The doors open and I enter.

(Ш)

Two hours ago I arrive into the second Sheremetievo Airport with two suitcases, a disposable sack, and a German-English dictionary that nobody in this country seems to want.

The larger suitcase is filled with junk: pens and papers, clothes and hats. The smaller suitcase contains each of my six and a half years — in other words, *Anna Karenina* and a solar calculator the size of a credit card.

The disposable sack, a present from the woman who was my second Aunt, contains a book of Pushkin and a large jar of black-currant jam.

In my pocket, filthy and sticky, is my two-kopeck coin — a coin that is as worthless as a word...

...and just as priceless.

(Щ)

I walk to the tables where the Customs declarations are lying scattered. But there are none in English. There are none in Russian. There is only French and German.

Without thinking I open my suitcase and take out my German-English dictionary. It is as thick as my tongue. Harder than a hard sign. In time I have translated the form and filled out my declaration as follows:

(Ъ)

<u>ZOLLDEKLARATION</u>

NAME AND VORNAME:	JAMES
STAATSANGEHORIGKEIT:	AMERICAN
ABREISELAND:	RUSSIA
BESTIMMUNGSLAND:	USA
SOWJETISCHE RUBEL:	TWO KOPECKS
ZWECK DER REISE:	OTHER

After I have finished with my Customs declaration, I start to put the German dictionary back into my suitcase. But stop. Instead I leave it on the tables next to the scattered forms.

And from there I head toward Customs.

(Ы)

At Customs the uniformed officer looks at my suitcases. But he does not rummage. He does not ask me questions. He does not even scrutinize my Customs declaration. Without smiling he simply hands me back my passport and motions for me to pass.

And I do.

(Ь)

And so here I am. Nowhere once again. In the departure section. Too soon to be *there*, but too *there* to be here. My passport has been stamped. My ticket has been checked. My luggage has been checked and re-checked.

Here I am between Customs and the flight that will take me home. Sitting next to me are twenty or twenty-five foreigners. Three of them are working on rough drafts of their books about Russia; the rest are polishing up the final versions.

I wrinkle my nose in disgust and look away.

But before I can, an announcement comes over the loud speaker: our flight is being delayed. Aeroflot is having technical problems and that means that our flight will take off later than expected.

I have some time to kill.

(Э)

But what should I do with these extra minutes? How should I spend these last few hours between *here* and *there*? What should I do until I leave?

And then it occurs to me: I'll write something!

Nothing too serious or meaningful, of course. Just the usual bit: naive foreigner goes to Russia, lives there for six and a half years, then leaves forever.

Even I can write something like that!

But how should I start it? The beginning is the most important part. The beginning is the part that will set the tone. Lay the foundation. Attract or repel!

This morning, in his apartment, Vadim said that I should show everybody what I learned. That's it!

After all, my six and a half years in Russia haven't been lost on me... and so I should tell the world what I have learned!

But what have I learned? What do I now know? What can I possibly say about this large country that for the last six and a half years has been my home?

I take out my pen and begin to write. Furiously and carefully. After a half-hour I have a page that looks as follows:

~~Finally...~~
(No good... By now I've already overused the word finally*)*

~~Now I know that Russia is Russia.~~
(Too logical)

~~Now I know that Russia isn't anything else but Russia. She doesn't smile.~~
(An unsubstantiated generalization...)

~~Now I can say that Russia is neither East nor West, but...~~
(Confusing and misleading!)

~~Now I can say that Russia is neither here nor there, but...~~
(Too obvious!)

~~Now I can say that Russia is neither here nor there, but less hopeless than inevitable...~~
(Terrible, of course. Pretentious and contrived. Blunt and stilted. But if I want to finish this sentence sometime before my flight leaves, I'd better leave it! Besides, I can always change it later...)

At some point I look at my watch. I have been sitting for over an hour. I have been writing for more than sixty minutes.

How much longer will I have to wait for my flight? How much time will I have to write my story? How far will I get into it before my plane takes me away forever? Don't think about it! Just write and write until you are no longer here! Write until your plane has come to take you there!

'At last I can say that Russia is neither here nor there, but less hopeless than inevitable. Her people are...'

(Ю)

But still I haven't found the eleventh yellow word. The word that changes and is changed. The word that is unlike all the others. The word that is neither *Russia* nor *ruble*. The word that has been, and still is, hopelessly beyond my grasp.

Still, I haven't found the word that will dot the *i*. That word that will allow me to place the final period on my story. Still it has remained beyond my grasp.

But maybe, just maybe, it's better that way? Maybe there's something to be said for wanting and dreaming? And for having something to elude you? Maybe I am happier for not having found it. Richer for not diminishing its beauty by claiming to understand. Perhaps it really is better to hope than to seek. To live than to love. To fall than to be elected.

Maybe there is something to be said for these six and a half years of silence punctuated by words. Or words accentuated by silence. Or both silence and words overwhelmed by fifty grams of clarity.

Well, yeah. It's probably like that.

(Я).

* * * * * * * * * *